Shadows and Light

by

Tanya Cimone

Copyright Notice
This is a work of fiction. Names, characters, places, and incidents are either the product of the author's imagination or are used fictitiously, and any resemblance to actual persons living or dead, business establishments, events, or locales, is entirely coincidental.

Shadows and Light

COPYRIGHT © 2024 by Tanya Cimone

All rights reserved. No part of this book may be used or reproduced in any manner whatsoever without written permission of the author or The Wild Rose Press, Inc. except in the case of brief quotations embodied in critical articles or reviews.
Contact Information: info@thewildrosepress.com

Cover Art by *Lea Schizas*

The Wild Rose Press, Inc.
PO Box 708
Adams Basin, NY 14410-0708
Visit us at www.thewildrosepress.com

Publishing History
First Edition, 2024
Trade Paperback ISBN 978-1-5092-5742-3
Digital ISBN 978-1-5092-5743-0

Published in the United States of America

Dedication

To my beloved family, your unwavering belief in me fuels every word on these pages. To my better half, your constant effort to provide the time I needed has been my greatest support. To my sister, your faith made the impossible, possible. And to the incredible authors I've had the privilege to meet along this journey, thank you for not only sharing your wisdom but for reading my work. This book is a testament to the collective encouragement from each of you.

Prologue

In the shadows of the alley, the sound of steps echoed. The small city of Eden had been separated in two. The people lived on one side, along with a trading market, the port, and most businesses.

The other side of the city remained vacant. Although it wasn't forbidden, most people didn't dare to set foot there. True evil had claimed it. No one in their right mind would even glance in that direction for too long. Even the damned with little left to lose didn't venture that far.

Given the choice, they avoided it.

All of them.

That night, the moonlight hid shyly behind dark clouds. A man—brave enough or crazy enough—walked alone on the cursed side.

The chill of the night breeze didn't faze him. As he pressed forward into the darkness, the wind relentlessly tugged at his thin cotton pants and whipped against his bare chest.

A man of focus. Someone with a precise goal.

He suddenly halted his progression into the murky space, his gaze roaming the filthy alley as if he could see anything beyond the shadows.

A thick and lingering scent enveloped the whole side of the river. An earthy type of sour aroma. Few people could tolerate it for more than a couple of minutes. Yet, he didn't seem to notice it.

"You know why I'm here," he fearlessly called out into the void. His voice was calm. It had a confidence you'd never expect from a young man who looked barely eighteen.

Silence answered.

It didn't faze him. A moment passed, and he continued, "I was told you were the only one powerful enough to help me."

The ground trembled. The pebbles around the man's feet jumped into the air. A thick, gray fog rose from the cracks in the earth. The mist crawled like a magnet toward the man.

"You are not ready for the cost." The voice was dark and scratchy, barely above a whisper, but the warning resonated through the empty space.

Weaker men had fallen to their knees at the sound of the voice. Yet, the young man didn't flinch. "If I'm here, I'm ready to pay any price."

"That's your first mistake," the voice mocked. "You just revealed your weakness."

The man tilted his head, but his eyes stayed fixed on the darkness. "Shall we not pretend you weren't aware of this? That you don't know anyone's wicked intentions?" he questioned.

Silence. The man waited.

"Yes, I wanted to test what your essence was made of," it said after a few beats. "I must say, it did not disappoint. I wonder if you're also aware that this will change everything? That there are consequences for your selfishness?"

For the first time that evening, the man's mask cracked, and he hesitated. With his shoulders slumped and a heavy sigh, he responded, "Yes. This is the only way."

"For what you seek, it is."

The young man knew more than most about the first evil. About the rules.

Real evil didn't hide its intentions.

Real evil didn't tempt innocents with empty promises.

Real evil spoke the truth and recruited souls with the potential to become just as evil.

No secrets. No maybes. No lies.

"So be it," the man answered.

The fog, which had been steadily floating above the ground merely a second before, encircled the man. It danced around him until his figure was completely engulfed by the black clouds.

"This will be biblical, my son."

Chapter 1

My struggles got lost among the lively ambiance of chatter, slamming lockers, and hurried footsteps down the University of London halls. With an unladylike grunt, I yanked my coat from a cramped locker barely spacious enough to hold my textbooks.

In moments like this, I wish I was part of the elite circle, where my peers had the privilege of storerooms four times the size of mine. Considering my unwelcomed acceptance into a prestigious program, I guessed I was lucky to even get a locker at all.

I put on my sandy beige trench coat and closed the buttons up to my neck. I'd never get used to England's humid cold. It's exactly as gloomy as it sounds.

Wet. A place of forever rain. My own personal nightmare.

Not that my feelings on the matter made a difference. We'd moved from New York half a year ago, despite my complaints.

I exchanged the book in my bag for the ten-pound brick I needed to complete my essay for Professor Vero's class.

Adjusting the strap of my heavy bag on my shoulder, I shut my locker to find Isabelle reclining behind the door, her arms crossed over her chest, one foot propped on the metal surface.

"Why do you even put up with this?" she asked,

her nose wrinkling as she glanced around. "Buy one close to me or, better yet, put your things in mine. There's enough space for three of me. Come on, Nyssa, don't be stubborn about it."

It was a weekly debate. I didn't want to take advantage of the circle I wasn't even part of. My last name complicated things enough.

"I know." She couldn't understand. "This is fine, Isabelle."

She pushed off the locker with a "Whatever."

"You have class?"

She lifted a shoulder. "I'm ditching."

"Isabelle." I scowled. The darling daughter of Professor Jones never had to worry about her education, or anything, really. As an only child, her wealthy parents catered to her whims. Isabelle had always been a free spirit.

My total opposite.

"What? Me and the babes have a wicked night planned. You coming?" She arched her perfectly manicured auburn brow, with a naughty smile tugging the corner of her full, red lips.

We both knew my answer. I didn't do *out*.

Especially not with her party partner, Caroline, who barely tolerated me. I wasn't her type of girl. Not fun enough. At least not by her standards. I didn't party hop, get wasted, smoke weed, or sleep around with strangers.

Caroline cataloged me as boring. I called it self-respecting, but what do I know?

I had a hard time understanding what Isabelle even saw in her. But who was I to judge? I had no other friends.

To each their own, I guessed.

"I have to close the shop today, and I have an essay to finish." The usual excuse.

She rolled her flawless coffee eyes, painted up as if a professional makeup artist had worked on her all morning. "Nyssa, live a little. You're not even twenty and you do nothing but stick your head in books. Look at yourself." She mimed an hourglass shape with her hands. "You're faffing about with studies. For what? You could snatch up any lad you fancy. Go for a rich bloke and stuff the degree. No need to work then, aye?"

Yeah, not my thing. I had no interest in a man or partying. I had one goal.

Get this diploma. Prove my worth to my family.

"Another time, okay?"

Her brow arched. "Sure." Before moving on, she added, "Anyways, I've got to go get ready. Hit me up if you change your mind. I'll come get you." I glanced at her. Isabelle was already dressed to impress in black leather pants with a V-neck shirt that left little to the imagination. Her effortless red curls hung loose, brushing her hips. What more could she possibly need to do?

"Sounds good."

"You headed to the shop now?" she asked.

"Yeah, why?"

Isabelle slipped her arm around my waist. "I'll give you a ride."

Perfect. I'd stay dry. "Thanks."

As we walked the hallways toward the exit, we crossed a bunch of guys from my program. The "cool" ones I avoided at all costs.

Isabelle nudged my side. "Mike is gawking at

you." She could hardly contain her excitement.

Dear Lord, have mercy on my soul.

I didn't need Isabelle to start playing matchmaker. My nose wrinkled. "He's probably staring at you." Especially with that outfit. "He can't stand me." A sideways glance confirmed the whole group had their eyes on us. "Actually, he *hates* me."

They all did.

Whether it was because they thought I'd gotten in on clout rather than earning my place in the program or simply because I was an American, or it possibly had to do with my gender, in any case, I had no interest in solving the true source of their hatred. I simply felt its existence.

"Trust me. He doesn't hate you, Nys. No one could hate you. Believe me, I've tried," she joked. "Mike's buggered he can't get your attention. He's not used to it."

"Whatever." I had no expertise in the brain functions of the opposite sex. I intended to keep it that way until I achieved my goal. Or until I found someone worth my attention, which might be close to never.

We walked by them without incident. As soon as we stepped outside, the chill breeze assaulted me. Caroline's figure stood out in the parking lot, wearing a short, flashy red dress. Did she not feel the cold?

She leaned on Isabelle's black sedan, her fingers busy tapping on her phone screen at expert speeds. She tossed her blond hair, tied back in a high tail. When we got close enough, she lifted her dark eyes and smirked.

"Oh, you brought the fun police with you?"

Caroline's obnoxious voice rattled me. The sides of my temples throbbed, signaling a headache coming on.

Isabelle gave her a fearsome look. She might lecture me in private, but she considered that to be her duty and hers alone. She never let anyone speak a judgmental word to me, even if we both knew she shared the opinion.

"Watch your mouth or you'll be catching the bus home. Got it?"

Caroline peeked at me from the corner of her brown eyes. "She knows I didn't mean it as an insult. Right, Nyssa?"

Yeah, she totally did. Not that I cared.

"Hop in the back, Care," Isabelle told her.

"Why? She's getting off first!"

Another signature Isabelle stare did the job. I took shotgun. Isabelle put on her sunglasses, although there wasn't one ray of sunshine in the gray sky. With a scream of her tires, we took off, music blasting.

My father's shop was only a ten-minute walk from school. The car jolted to a stop in front of the antiquated building. Father had acquired it for its prime location, but you couldn't even tell we were in business. The old red bricks covering the facade gave nothing away, and we didn't expose wares through the large windows. It wasn't that type of store. The white sign, written Glory in gold, seemed to be the only indication needed.

The top floor had two windows and a small balcony. It was rented by a single mom, Maria, and her daughter, Krista. Father had let them stay after he bought the building.

"Thanks, Isabelle."

She leaned over the console and kissed my cheek.

"Always. Call me if you change your mind."

"Will do. You girls have fun." I didn't bother

turning to Caroline. "Be good, Isabelle," I told her softly.

She winked at me. I shook my head lightly as I slid out, my caramel waves dancing in front of my eyes. Being good didn't pair with fun. At least not for them. Hanging around them, I often felt like an outsider from a different planet or time.

I unlocked our family shop—closed in the middle of the afternoon. Yet despite our irregular hours, we lived in luxury. A conundrum for many of my dissenters, I was sure.

We only opened whenever my brother or I could be there because God forbid Father trust anyone else with the shop. It still amazed me he even entrusted *me* with his one and only real baby.

Furthermore, it baffled me he let Krista and her mom keep the apartment. Although, I was glad he did; they didn't have much, and London's cost of living was astronomical.

My phone vibrated as I stalked between the two shelves of artisanal trinkets on display. I reached into my bag and saw Micah's name flash on the screen.

"Tell me you're making time for me today," I said as soon as I pressed the green button.

"Always, Nyssa Bear. You at Glory?"

"Yep. You'd better have my seashells." Micah had returned from his trip to Jordan in the dead of night, and I hadn't had time to see him yet.

"As if you'd ever let me hear the end of it if I didn't." I heard the smile in his tone.

I beamed while heading to sit at the bureau to man the registry. "Might even stop talking to you."

He laughed. I had missed this. So much. Aside

from Isabelle, I really only had him. "Don't mention it. I'll try stopping by later, before you close."

"I'll be waiting."

I dropped the phone on the wooden desk and retrieved my book, determined to make some headway and get my course work done. The midterms were near, and I needed to be ready. Favors wouldn't be granted.

Not for me, anyways.

I fidgeted my pen between each finger, unable to concentrate. My head wasn't in it. Anxiety crept up on me without cause. The sign I needed to go see *them*.

I pushed the thought away. I had tried to stay... normal.

That should've proved easy. Boredom and ennui kept me company for ninety percent of my life. But for the leftover ten percent, I had my Shadows.

Thank the Lord. The problem—aside from sounding crazy—they became my addiction. Whenever they stayed away too long, nervousness engulfed me. Loneliness soon followed. The episodes had worsened with the years, but they showed to help through the rough times.

My fingers tapped the wooden counter in time with the echoing ticks of the antique standing clock. I glanced at the ornate hands for the zillionth time.

Four o'clock.

Could the minutes pass any slower? Where was Micah? Maybe Father had requested his assistance. Wouldn't be the first time.

My antsy feet guided me to the one spot I was forbidden access to. The one section of the store that truly interested me. The door hiding behind the bureau. To casual shoppers, it resembled an inner office door.

But it was my own personal temptation.

My hands grazed the soft design carved in the thick, hand-cut wood—a dense slab with no handle in sight. I'd imagined the objects on the other side of that door many times. It held the most precious treasures my father discovered. Priceless items from around the world. Rows of books that hid secrets people would kill to discover.

Myself included.

I'd tried everything to jimmy it open. Pushing. Sliding. Knocking. It never bulged. Not in the slightest. I still tried.

Every. Single. Time.

Again, it didn't work.

I went back to sit at my usual seat, bored. Very bored.

My eyes lazily trailed around the nearest dark-stained shelf, assessing the newest pieces to join our collection beneath the glass covers.

It was my job to clean, polish, and restore them to their original beauty. Father curated anything, from necklaces to mirrors, to pottery and sculptures, so long as they had a valuable aspect.

Not every piece sat on that shelf, of course. The valuable items stayed in the private collection alongside the books I longed to access.

Strangers had the opportunity to come and admire them, but never had the pleasure of touching. Then again, those coveted invitations were few and far between.

And an invitation didn't mean you'd be allowed to walk out with anything.

With its white walls, limited stock, and wide-open

rustic wood floor, Glory wasn't much to look at from an outsider's point of view.

Nothing phenomenal, really.

The objects Glory housed made her special. Gave her mystery. Magic. Even the cheaper items entrusted to me were special.

One of a kind.

Any interaction with them had to be supervised. Meaning my brother had to be here. Not that he paid much attention to my work, but still.

It was one of my father's laws.

Father had a gifted eye for discovering precious pieces. In art collector circles, they lauded him as a genius.

Renowned the world over for obtaining the best treasures, Gavriel had no trouble expanding his business with the move from New York to the UK. He had a loyal clientele and a thirst for knowledge.

If you asked me, though, I'd say we mainly moved so Father could live closer to his inner circle of supernatural occultists. Or, as I called them, his sect. They were the privileged who had access to the exhibition hall hidden behind the façade of this shop.

The more superstitious members believed that Father possessed objects touched by higher beings. Items once owned by angels themselves. Others were plucked directly from hell.

For most, those were nothing but rumors.

Not for me. I didn't doubt their existence. Quite the contrary.

Aside from my Shadows, I had *seen* things. Plenty of things.

My first brush with the abnormal happened very

young. I remembered robed figures brandishing swords at a lone person screaming in the center.

Micah had found me before Father saw me and told me they were trying to help the person. He had been possessed by evil. I never saw the end. Gripped by my first taste of terror, I'd never dared speak of it again.

Years later, my father had found a sacred book in Egypt, written in a foreign language. He spent night and day trying to translate it himself. He'd never dare ask for help from a professor and give a stranger access to such a valuable manuscript. So, he'd finally allowed my brother and I to help. We eventually cracked some of it.

A part of the text claimed human contact with the items of higher beings carried extreme consequences. The intense powers of those pieces could bring about insanity or even instant death.

That was all the information I'd needed to glean to decide the book held many truths. It made me question if I'd accidentally had a run-in with an angelic piece from Father's collection when I was younger.

It would explain some things.

Following in my father's steps, I'd decided to study art history in a select program offered only in London. A program that admitted less than forty students. Privileged kids and guys only, aside from me. Women were a rare sight in those exclusive classes. Even in the twenty-first century.

It did come with many perks like my access to certain off-limits books, so long as we read them in class or in the private library.

Through these courses, I'd discovered which era our various Glory objects came from, and the history behind them. It became my obsession.

My father's fame among art historians probably weighed in the balance of my acceptance. Much to my fellow students' chagrin, it seemed.

The sound of the chime above the entrance snapped me out of my thoughts. A customer walked in, navigating around the shelves as if seeking a particular item beneath the glass plating. His back was turned to me, clad in a long black jacket. A sixties hat covered his hair.

I left the counter, my footsteps creaking on the worn floorboards until I stopped beside the customer. He'd stopped to observe a golden medallion with a dragon head engraving. Micah had found it in a cave in Indonesia, and it had taken me days to remove the dirt and rust from the grooves.

"That's a beautiful piece," I told him.

Without glancing my way, he sidestepped to another item.

"Is there anything I can assist you with?" I offered.

He slowly turned his chin my way. At five-feet-four, I craned my neck to meet his eye. He had at least a head and a half on me. The black sunglasses he wore hid half his face. I had no idea where he was looking, but somehow, it made me uneasy.

An alarm rang inside my head, as if warning me to get away.

The silence stretched under his thorough inspection.

"Hopefully," he finally croaked in the rusty voice of a man far older than he looked. I'd guessed late twenty or early thirties from what I could see. His skin didn't wear any marks of age, although he dressed like my mother's grandfather.

I managed a tight smile despite the tension spreading throughout my muscles.

"I've been searching for a very old item," said the stranger. "I'm not certain what outer appearance it might have adopted with time. Perhaps a box, or an orb, or even an image on a frame."

My face scrunched. "That's a little...vague." I wasn't clairvoyant, despite some of the loftier expectations Father's clientele had of me in the past, believe it or not.

"Yes, unfortunately," he conceded. "It's a family heirloom. It's been hidden exceptionally well."

Cannot fall into the wrong hands.

I spun toward the new voice, almost a growl spoken barely above a whisper. Yet, I'd heard it as if the words were murmured in my ear. My heartbeat raced. A shudder of fear wracked my spine. I glanced across the shop, only to find it empty. God, I was losing my mind more each day.

I twisted back, once again under the odd client's scrutiny.

Oh crap. I didn't need witnesses to my episodes. Especially not a potential customer who might be an acquaintance of my father's.

"I'm very sorry. I thought I heard something." I fumbled to explain, my hands tangling together.

I shifted from foot to foot and found my voice. "Since you're unsure what it looks like, maybe you can tell me the object's purpose. Is it used to bring fortune or maybe protection? Knowing that could help pinpoint which section to search."

His prolonged silence wore away at my nerves. I fought the urge to fidget again.

"Perhaps I've found something just as precious," he murmured, taking a step closer to me.

Instinctively, I took a step back.

One random customer every blue moon, and I get saddled with a creep. Totally my luck.

A fight-or-flight alarm clanged inside my head.

I wasn't one with sharp intuition, but if my instinct spoke to me, I listened.

The stranger slowly withdrew his hands, bigger than my whole face, out of his pockets, and placed two fingers on his dark shades to remove them.

I screamed, stumbling back in terror.

His eyes.

No hint of whites or pupils. Just pitch-black orbs. Eyes I'd only ever seen in the yellowed pages of ancient manuscripts.

Demon's eyes.

Chapter 2

I'd thought I was a believer.
I was wrong.
Touting belief in God, angels, and demons was one thing. Facing tangible proof was entirely different. No one had prepared me. Not for this.

I'd read about demons in many books. I hadn't given the matter much thought. Hadn't taken it seriously enough. My expert family never mentioned any reason to be worried, so why would I? From what I had gathered, demons haven't roamed the earth in ages, and if some did, there was no one left to speak of it.

I didn't register the look of pure shock on his face, too trapped in my own terror. Despite my shaky legs, I somehow made it to the back door without stumbling over my own feet. Heroics weren't on my talent list yet. I was far from those paranormal characters in those shows Isabelle loved to watch.

I pushed the heavy metal door, bouncing it against the brick wall, and landed straight in the bulky arms of my brother, Micah.

What a timing.

"Whoa, is there a fire, or did you miss me that much?" He mocked until his ocean-blue eyes landed on my face. I probably looked like I'd just seen a ghost. Well, technically, a demon, but that fell in the same category.

"What is it, Nyssa?"

My fingers dug into his arms as I glanced over my shoulder. The demon hadn't pursued. "This is going to sound insane, but…" I panted as if I just ran track in the Olympics.

"What?"

"A demon. In the shop," I whispered.

If we were a normal family, I would have expected Micah to laugh it off and dismiss my fears as crazy ramblings.

But we knew better. Or maybe the fear leaking out of my pores infected him. Either way, he pushed me straight behind him. Yeah, like big pecs make a difference against a demon.

"Go wait in the truck," he demanded, without looking back at me.

I squeezed his forearm. "Don't go in there. We don't know what it can do." From what I could recall, every demon possessed unique powers. "Come on," I urged, tugging harder. I hated to admit it, but we might need Father. My brother didn't move an inch.

Micah twisted and took me by my shoulders, halting my miserable efforts to move his two hundred pounds of muscle. "Can you for once just do as you're told?" he whisper-screamed at me. My eyes widened in shock. I dropped my arms to my side and took a step back.

"Go in the truck, Nyssa," he said, voice softening. "Lock the doors. I'll be back in a minute." I wanted to point out that locking the doors probably wouldn't keep a demon out, but Micah had already stormed into the store.

I did as I was told.

Settling in the back of his Volvo, I even locked the door for a false sense of security.

Had I really seen a demon? Was I hallucinating? Micah had believed me.

Then again, we'd been raised to believe in the unbelievable.

In myths and legends. In gods and angels. In Heaven and Hell.

In art objects hosting powers of the divine. I mean, what's a demon after all of that?

A lot more than I had ever seen. That's what.

Studying the unbelievable or faith in it changes a person. Still, to be in the supernatural's presence was terrifying.

I bit my nail while shaking my foot. Two bad habits that arose whenever I was anxious and alone. The wait was nerve-wracking. What if Micah needed my help? What if he was hurt?

I had to go back inside. Help him somehow. God, surely one of those backroom items could come in handy. Right?

I left the safety of the car and slowly crept through the heavy metal door wedged into the brownstone. Gathering my courage, I'd wrapped my fingers around the handle when it slammed open, almost knocking me on my ass. Micah walked out, his gaze homing on me.

"Nyssa." He wrapped me in his arms. We may not be blood-related, but he was my family in every way that mattered.

I briefly hugged him back, soothed by the *home* scent he carried with him, before pulling away.

"What happened? What did you do? Did he say what he wanted? Did he try to hurt you?" I bombarded him with questions.

His eyes bounced around my face, searching, concerned. "Nothing happened. There was no one there, Nyssa."

I frowned, backpedaling. "He was right there. I spoke to him. He came searching for an old object. He told me himself."

Micah gently nodded. "Did he say what?"

Feeling a sudden chill, I briskly rubbed my palms on my legs. "Not exactly. He didn't know what it looked like. It was odd. And then." I stopped myself. I wasn't about to make myself look even crazier and tell Micah about the voice or the demon's unsettling comment.

He narrowed his eyes at me. "Then what, Nys?"

"I don't know." I lied. "But I saw him."

Micah's head tilted; affectionate gaze locked in place. His annoying parental look, like I was two. "How could you be sure it was a demon?"

I shrugged a shoulder. "Easy. His eyes. They were black. Like *all* black."

He went taut as a violin string. His next nod jittered in stops and starts like a rusted machine.

"You do believe me, right?" I said, retreating another step.

Micah was quiet a moment too long.

"Oh, my God. You don't! You don't believe me."

"I didn't say that."

"Not with words!"

I tried to storm off, but his fingers wrapped around my arms. "The door of the shop was locked from inside Nys. Maybe you were dreaming or–"

"I was not! I left it unlocked."

Micah stayed silent for another beat too long. "Demons haven't been seen in centuries, Nys."

"It's not because we don't see them that they're not here." That's what I've been taught about God my whole life.

"I'm worried about you, that's all. Can you blame me?" We both knew what gave that question weight. It was a low blow but also all he had against me. "Have you been sleeping, Nys? The few times you aren't out for your walk till sunrise, I hear you toss and turn all night. That can't be healthy."

I bit the inside of my cheek. "Plenty of people have insomnia. They aren't being accused of imagining things."

My dear brother didn't deny it.

"You've been alone too long lately. That's my fault. Are you remembering to eat? You know that can mess with you," he ventured.

"I can take care of myself," I growled through my teeth. Maybe I hadn't missed him that much, come to think of it.

"Maybe we should see a doctor," Micah pushed.

How dare he?

Irritation flared like a match. I yanked my arm free and marched back inside the store. I studied the two aisles. They were empty. Nothing out of place.

I ignored my brother's approaching footsteps and sat back in my chair. I opened my schoolbook and pretended to read the assignment I'd already failed to focus on before the demon invasion.

I heard him sigh. "Nys, I didn't mean—"

I threw up a hand, cutting off any other false excuses. "Save it. What? You didn't mean to imply I'm imagining things? That I'm delusional because you're not there to tuck me in like a baby?" Without giving him the opportunity to reply, I answered, "Yes, you did. We both know it. It's fine."

I had confided in a teacher once. A long time ago. About hearing the music.

It hadn't ended well. Not for me, at least. I should have learned my lesson. I'd just foolishly thought we were past that.

"It's not. I'm a jerk. I just figured since you haven't had a good night's sleep in…" He paused, searching for the right words with a sigh. "You don't sleep well, Nys. And your night walks worry me." He passed a nervous hand through his light curls. "I want to be sure you're doing okay."

Of course, I'm not okay.

I'm probably cursed.

Hearing things.

Seeing things.

Going out to meet darkness.

Seeing demons.

Total nutcase. Beyond help.

"I'm fine."

I kept my nose in the book, reading the same sentence for the third time without comprehension. Micah hadn't made a sound, but he still breathed down my neck.

A moment later, he said the last thing I wanted to hear. "We have to tell Father about this." Micah didn't believe me, so what he meant was he had to tell Gavriel about my hallucination.

"Of course." Bitterness coated in my tone. "*I* don't have to tell him anything, but you go right ahead.

Maybe he'll finally take some interest in our everyday lives."

Fantastic.

Gavriel Lewis didn't deserve the title of father. Donor suited him better. At least in Micah's case. I didn't actually share his bloodline.

Gavriel treated me accordingly. Like a stranger.

He acknowledged my existence only when I could be useful to him—safeguarding Glory or a menial business task he entrusted no outsider to handle. Despite our lack of biological ties, he'd choose me over anyone who didn't live under his roof.

Other than that, I was nothing more than my mother's daughter. And he had been her husband. Not a good one either, if I might add. Not that anyone cared about my opinions. To his credit, he did keep me after she passed away. Probably for Micah's sake.

"Sarcasm doesn't suit you, Nys." Micah's voice brought me out of my little hate trip.

Listing all Gavriel's flaws had no real reward, but God, did it make me feel better about myself.

"Sucking up to your father doesn't suit you, but you're still about to run off to tattle, aren't you?" I snarled back.

"Nyssa." My brother was about to defend him. He always did. Only God knew why. Gavriel sure as hell didn't deserve it.

I shook my head, interrupting him. "You do what you have to. Tell him. Don't tell him. I don't care. But please don't feed me that crap about him doing his best. We both know it's a lie. He does nothing but the bare minimum."

I'd never received a hug or any show of affection

from Gavriel. Neither had I witnessed Micah receive any. No matter our achievements, not a single compliment crossed Gavriel's lips.

I peeked at my brother through the curtain of my hair.

His shoulders slumped, sky-blue eyes begging me to see things from his perspective. This was a weekly debate. One I didn't wish to rehash. We'd been in each other's company for less than fifteen minutes, and we were fighting. Must be a new record.

To my surprise, Micah dropped it. "Let's close the shop. I'll drive you home."

I didn't need to be told twice. It was almost five anyway. I shoved my stuff in my bag and waited in the truck while Micah locked up.

I kept my lips sealed the entire drive home, watching the buildings fly by us. Micah stayed tense, waiting for me to glance his way or give him a sort of sign to wave the white flag.

My eyes stayed glued to the road, totally avoiding the situation.

I wasn't in the mood. Being called crazy sucked. Especially when you already doubted your own sanity.

Unfortunately.

Fast enough, we reached our house. After months in England, I still couldn't get used to how different it was from New York.

Classy, sure, but too spacious. We lived in a prestigious four-bedroom townhouse with six bathrooms. My father's genius in the art world came with some benefits. But I mean, who needs more bathrooms than bedrooms? Or four bedrooms with only three occupants? More like one, most of the time.

Me.

"Will you be all right home alone?" Micah asked, snapping me out of a daze. "I won't be long. Why don't you go visit Professor Jones and Isabelle?"

Although my father didn't appreciate my childhood friendship with Isabelle, he couldn't say much about it, considering her father was one of his most important colleagues. Isabelle had been dragged along across the ocean each time Professor Jones came to visit my dad. And vice versa. We became inseparable. She became my rock.

Now they lived down the street. Thankfully. But I knew she had plans for the evening. She might have already left.

"Yeah, maybe." I opened the car door.

"Be careful, Nyssa," said Micah before I'd stepped out. "No late walks tonight. Okay?"

I twisted at the waist, my emerald eyes narrowing in on Micah's sunglasses' reflection. "Why not? Isn't it all in my head?"

Pushing Micah's buttons didn't make me feel better. It's not like I was planning on going out. Without any malintent or conscious effort, he had compounded my insecurities.

I wasn't going to tempt fate. I fully intended to keep the little sanity I had left by staying home, as far away from darkness and lurking demons as possible. Even if it meant staying away from my Shadows.

Chapter 3

The words on my textbook pages made less sense than earlier today. I read the same sentence for the umpteenth time. My eyes kept drifting to the wall-length window overlooking the street. Night had arrived.

Teasing me.
Testing me.
Tempting me.

After my little encounter earlier, no way was I stepping outside. I wasn't stupid.

Was I?

Yet, against my better judgment, staying in drove me totally crazy. Left me antsy. Maybe because I could see *them* through the glass.

Dancing around.
Expecting me.
Waiting for me.

A resounding loud thud echoed when I shut my book and placed it on my bureau. I grabbed my laptop and attempted to write my essay without reference instead. The subject should have been simple for me.

Write about anything supernatural.

Easy, right? Daughter of a famous mystic art collector.

Hearing music in empty rooms.
Seeing things no one else saw.

Encountering a demon.

My preoccupied brain gave me nothing. No words manifested on the screen.

Father and Micah weren't back home yet. Neither had bothered calling or texting me. You'd think they could at least check in on me after today's debacle. I mean, I did have an encounter with a demon.

But I supposed if Micah didn't believe me, there was no way Gavriel would.

I paced the white velvet carpet of my bedroom for about three minutes before giving up. I'd never be able to relax. Taking my phone and bag, I made my way down the long, narrow stairs. At the bottom, I crossed beneath the chandelier in the prestigious entrance.

Like, who hung a chandelier in an entrance?

Weird people, that's who. Though I spent the most time here, I'd had no say in the cold, aristocratic decoration. Too British for my taste.

Snatching my coat from the closet, I put on my rain boots, and walked out into the fresh night, welcoming the cold for once.

I inhaled deeply, my apprehension almost forgotten.

The night. The dark. It soothed every worry. Appeasing. Nourishing.

That pleasure in the night's isolation couldn't be normal for someone approaching twenty, right?

Although I was never alone.

I shook myself, redirecting my feet. I didn't come out for my Shadows. No. I'd gone out to see Isabelle.

I walked on the sidewalk, illuminated by the dim glow of the streetlight. That small luminescence prevented them from coming closer, and kept their implausible existence at a reasonable distance. I tried not to glance their way. I knew they wanted me to.

A few houses down the road, Isabelle's house stood illuminated by a cascade of bright lights. I felt my noncorporeal companions draw back, almost believing I heard their irritated sighs. My chest rose, filling my lungs with fresh air.

It's okay, Nyssa. You should be happy.

I peeked sideways above my shoulder. They waited on the opposite side, incapable of keeping still in their eagerness to greet me properly. The three black shades jumped around.

A baseless guilt weighed on my shoulders.

I continued forward, facing Isabelle's porch and pushing open the small gate in the white picket fence. My boots had tapped on the paved alley when the sound of a slowing engine halted my steps. I pivoted to see my brother's SUV brake alongside the sidewalk. At the same time, I heard Isabelle's front door open.

Micah had his window completely rolled down, his arm hanging from it like it was a hot sunny day instead of this dreary, wet cold. The type that wrapped around your bones. I tugged my coat closer.

A faint but hesitant smile graced the corner of his mouth when he caught my eye. My own lips stretched, burying the invisible hatchets I'd raised in my mind. Staying mad at him forever never crossed my mind. I couldn't cast too much blame. Not many would have bothered charging into the shop after my 'seeing a demon' claim.

Especially given my history.

"Were you planning on coming in or would you prefer to just stand there?" My eyes shifted to Isabelle, but she'd already started gawking at Micah, as usual. She couldn't help herself.

"Come straight home after, Nyssa Bear. No wandering around," Micah warned.

I gave him an army salute. He raised an eyebrow.

"Be good," he called as he drove off.

Isabelle sighed like a lovestruck princess. "Does he get sexier every day?" she asked as I met her up on the porch. "I suppose it's good he never spares me a glance. I was drooling all down my front."

Disgusted, I scrunched my face in a grimace. "Could you please not go there?" *Again*, I finished for myself.

She feigned a swoon, falling against me, her forehead laying on her arm.

"How do you do it, Nys? You must be a master of self-control. If I'd lived under the same roof as Adonis, I wouldn't be able to resist him," she said in dreamy tones. "I'd sneak into his bedroom night after night."

"He's my brother."

"Only by name, Nys. Only by name. Thank your lucky star. You should take advantage." She straightened and winked. "Or I will."

I held my tongue. She wasn't the first to daydream over Micah. Sure, he was an attractive guy. Just not one I looked at that way.

"Can we drop it, please?"

She laughed, making her red curls bounce lightly as she took a seat on the white bench swing attached to the little overhang. It reminded me of the one we had at our lake house in the Hamptons. Out of place here, but whatever Isabelle wanted, Isabelle got. "Sure, let's drop the fact that you're probably the most beautiful girl in the country, living with the sexiest guy I've ever seen. I mean, how can the universe be so cruel to the rest of us?"

A half smile tugged my lip. Isabelle will do well in acting.

"What do you think my chances are?" she continued.

Zero.

"Only God knows."

I've never witnessed my brother showing interest in any girl. Sometimes, I questioned his sexual orientation. Although, we shared the same lack of interest for the opposite sex.

"Are you done talking about my brother?" I asked while taking place beside her.

Using one foot, she pushed off the floor, rocking us. "Yep, I'm done. For tonight, anyway. Just remember, you are welcome to invite me for a sleepover anytime."

I couldn't help but laugh.

"Yeah, our fathers would be thrilled."

She waved it off. "They'll be way too busy to care. Trust me, with what's happening around the city, mine would rather have me at your house than wandering the streets."

My head jerked around to face her. "What do you mean? What's happening?" I told myself to calm down. It wasn't related to my mishap in Glory. That'd just be crazy.

Isabelle returned my stare, her brows pulling together. "Haven't you heard? Didn't your father warn you?"

My heart started pounding. "Warn me about

what?"

She glanced around and leaned closer as if sharing the world's deepest secret. "Demons are in town."

Oh, good Lord.

So, my sanity remained intact. I didn't know if I felt relieved or frightened.

"Like proper ones," Isabelle continued, oblivious to my inner torment. "Can you even fathom? I always reckoned those books were all balderdash." My heart threatened to pump out of my chest, pounding in my ears so I barely heard her next whispered words. "Word has it, their master's climbed free from the underworld and a whole lot have tagged along."

I froze, and the sound of my Shadows on the move, like leaves in the wind, reached me. I couldn't resist glancing their way for a second. Blacker than the night, their thick, shapeless forms flew around in mini tornadoes, mirroring my rising anxiety.

"How would you know all that?" My voice was composed. Somehow.

I mean, I did believe demons existed somewhere on the other side, but I also never believed I'd face one.

If the tales were true, though, they came for the dark souls. Offering power and money in exchange. Things I'd never lusted after and thus had nothing to fret over.

I never truly paid too much attention because my father didn't. I'd assumed if the stories held nuggets of fact and were still around, Gavriel would have been curious. He would have investigated. Sent Micah in search of an object to prove their existence. Least of all, inform me.

I'd put too much faith in a man who cared only for

himself.

"I overheard my father on the phone." Isabelle brought me out of my pity party. "I confronted him, and he admitted it. He wants me to stay home. To be safe." She inspected her flawless nails. "Not that I'm going to listen."

As her stare met mine, a spark of curiosity ignited in her eyes. "Did you come because you've changed your mind about tonight?" Voice tinged in delight, she glided her gaze from my head down to my rain boots. "I've got a change of clothes for you, no worries."

I hurriedly shook my head before she got the wrong idea. "No, I needed to get out of the house, but… what are the demons doing here?"

She shrugged like it wasn't a big deal. "Bargaining. Or that's what's going 'round, anyway."

I thought they only came for the dark souls. "Why would anyone want to bargain with a demon?"

Her brows shot up. "Come on, Nys, even you must want something you can never get."

No. Not really.

"I suppose, but at what cost?" I put my legs up to my chest, trying to warm myself.

"Depends on the favor. Small favors, small payments."

"Like what?" I wondered, more curious than was wise.

"A feeding."

"A feeding?"

She rolled her eyes, annoyed by my questions or my ignorance.

Probably both.

Isabelle crossed her arms over her chest,

attempting to fight off Mother Nature's doing. "Seriously, Nyssa. Aren't you the daughter of the leading expert on everything gods and demons?" she grumbled. "A feeding means blood."

I almost facepalmed. Of course. Demons needed blood to survive. I was still trying to wrap my head around this whole demon thing.

"But the bigger the demand, the bigger the price."

Yes, I remembered now, a favor or your soul.

"Who'd be foolish enough to trust a demon?" I mumbled to myself.

Isabelle stiffened. "Some don't have the luxury of a choice, Nyssa. Have a little compassion. Your life isn't the standard, babes."

She threw her legs off the bench, but I grabbed her arm before she could stand. "Whoa. What's up with you? All I'm saying is demons can't be trusted. Even regular people who weren't raised in our world know that."

She'd never directed her fury at me before, but I suddenly got a full blast in the face, hot enough to singe eyebrows and melt off lipstick. "See, Nys, that's just it. Some people are willing to risk it because, unlike God, demons answer prayers, at a cost." Clearly, I had offended her. "And unlike you, not everyone is a flawless genius who has everything handed to them like they were God's favored." Before I mustered an apology, she jerked her arm back. "I've got to go. You can find your way back." She dismissed me, stalked across the porch, and slammed her front door behind her as if a demon were on her tail.

I rocked on the unbalanced swing, stunned. What the hell just happened? I'd known Isabelle since our tricycle days. She'd never acted this emotionally over nothing.

Maybe she was hormonal, I thought, using Micah's favorite excuse for any exaggerated behavior of mine he couldn't explain. Since I took that road, I'd continue on it. No point in chasing after her. I'd let her sleep it off.

I strolled to the sidewalk, scanning the opposite side where my Shadows impatiently waited. Going home would be the smart thing to do.

I wasn't in the mood to be smart.

As I stuffed my hands into my coat, I headed across the street toward the dark, glossy mirror of Hampstead Heath pond. Isabelle's newsflash about demons invading the city still echoed in my mind. Micah had to know something. He must have heard the rumors by now. Perhaps he'd known all along. But if so, why make me feel like a nutcase?

Isabelle's accusations played in my head, setting my chin at a defiant tilt. I wouldn't take it back. Anyone who sought to bargain with demons was nothing but desperate. As if agreeing with me, the Shadows brushed against my jacket. The smallest of the three rested on my forearm like a perch, stretching its dark shade to my collarbone.

I strode into the woods, seeking refuge from reality, until I reached the water's edge. The biting wind cut through me. Little white clouds puffed out of my mouth with each exhale.

I didn't let the cold ruin it. Darkness was here. I dared admit how I'd missed it. Missed them. Was it wrong?

My eyes shut, listening to the music of their

whispers, and enjoyed the wind of their touch.

They'd kept me company for as long as I could remember. Long before I comprehended their abnormality and began to fear why I was seeing them. The danger of the unknown. It was probably even before I could walk or speak. In a way, I was happy I'd gotten to appreciate their presence uninhibited by societal fright for a while.

I now sought their presence. Why did I find their company more comforting than that of my peers? Why did they calm me instead of terrify me?

No one knew about them. I'd be locked away in an asylum with padded walls if they did.

As I continued my midnight walk through the veil of the night, they busied themselves dancing around me, my constant companions. They moved in tempo with my actions, caressing my skin. I'd been scared the few times I'd wandered into the night without their company. Although they never left me long when I felt unsettled. Almost sensing my distress. Whenever I felt restless, they came.

They were the least of my worries right now. With demons and their boss in town, real trouble was brewing. I was relieved my Shadows had shown tonight. Truth be told, the midnight strolls Micah worried about were for them because they comforted me in ways no one else could.

They made me feel safe.

They kept the panic attacks at bay.

I guess if I had to live in complete madness, I might as well enjoy the ride.

Chapter 4

Wandering around town was at the top of my hobbies list. But after the demon invasion at Glory, the rumors Isabelle shared, and my earlier argument with Micah, I thought it was best to come home after an hour.

Besides, it was cold.

Unsurprisingly, I arrived at an empty house. Yet, I couldn't help the pang of neglect that hit me. Micah had to know, if not earlier today, he knew by now. He hadn't bothered to wait and share the news with me. To apologize for thinking I had seen things, or at minimum, to warn me.

I almost felt like continuing my walk out of spite.

I didn't.

I headed to my room, intending to get some sleep. I had an early class. Taking my cell, I plugged the charger in and checked for messages.

Nothing.

I turned to put it down on the nightstand beside my bed. My hand froze midway, transfixed by a basket filled with new seashells resting on top. An attached white note reading *Jordan* declared their origin.

The corner of my mouth tugged at the sight, fulfilled by an incomprehensible sense of peace. I didn't question it.

I tamped down the urge to send a text to Micah and

battled for sleep instead.

****

Holding a bag half my body weight in both arms, I ran like a mad person through the university hallway in a miserable attempt to make it to class on time.

When sleep had finally claimed me, early morning light had touched the edge of my duvet. My alarm didn't ring, or I'd forgotten to turn it on. I was functioning on a pitiful amount of sleep lately, and it had caught up to me.

I barged into the room, probably looking like a mess. I usually climbed the auditorium rows as far as possible so as not to be seen, but that'd be impossible now.

Professor Gerard barely glanced my way as I finally slipped into the empty seat closest to the door. Next to Mike. Great.

He leaned close, cloying my space with his rich perfume. "Trying to catch my attention?"

"More like catch my breath."

Douchebag.

Being late to class wasn't an option for a student in my position. A position that wasn't just handed to me despite what my pair believed. I'd fought hard for my acceptance letter. Aside from the basic exams. Being a girl made it…difficult. The Art History Department, with the Dark Art content, didn't think they needed the feminine touch.

Which also meant I needed to work twice as hard to get my work appreciated.

But I had.

I listened, took notes, studied facts, and came up with strong arguments. I even offered free tutoring to any student for extra credits. A girl could never be too careful. If one of those old snakes decided to flunk me just because they could, I'd have another leg to stand on.

That was if I succeeded in finding a student to tutor. The main issue with that was getting students to make an appointment. Few even looked my way, much less struck up a conversation. They would rather pay for the services of a B student male than have free tutoring with me. An A student.

However, today I wasn't worthy of the grades I'd earned. My focus escaped me, zoning in and out multiple times. Of course, my current state could be blamed on this demon invasion my family totally kept me out of. Or perhaps the fact that Mike's gaze was glued to me instead of up front.

Anything to get on my nerves.

Also, I knew for a fact that most of these professors, as members of my father's circle, were aware of the truth of our world. The scary truth currently walking freely outside.

It baffled me that they weren't more afraid. More worried. If it came down to a fight, they'd flee like cowards.

Instead of sitting here, covering the boring technicalities of paintings and the meanings behind them, we should be working on a plan, finding ways to protect our own. Not discussing painters inspirations and blah blah blah.

I mean, who cares? Demons were back and walked among us like they owned the place. Yet, we all went to class and acted like nothing had changed.

Well, it had.

These professors were specialists in cults, gods, and demons. They knew the danger awaiting us. Yet, they'd kept this information confined to the inner circle.

I wished I knew why. I also wished I had the power to share that kind of information without risking being locked away. Unfortunately, no one would believe the loner American. They'd brush it off and move to juicier gossip.

So here I was. In a front-row seat. Beside Mike. Soaking in my loneliness and frustration. Unable to pay attention to the useless words being spoken in my least favorite class of the program taught by my least favorite teacher in the universe.

"Miss Lewis, please, can you tell us what you see in this painting?" Professor Gerard asked, interrupting my inner monologue.

My head lifted to meet his disapproving gaze, his little glasses sitting on the bridge of his nose. His thin lips pressed in a tight line. He never tried pretending he liked me. I was the furthest from one of his golden students.

Regardless of my grades.

Regardless if I gave all I had.

Regardless of the fact that he was one of my father's closest allies, along with Professor Jones, Isabelle's dad.

Paintings weren't my forte, either, which did nothing to gain his approval. But I should've earned points with him for my efforts by now. Today aside, my track record was impeccable.

I held my breath, caught beneath the magnifying glass of the entire class's scrutiny. Being the center of attention? Really, not my thing. I sank a little deeper into the chair, wishing I could blend in with the shadows. Internally, I pledged to arrive fifteen minutes early to every class in the future.

I studied the painting on the projector. A bare, muscular chest on display for all to see. Stunning, wide, white wings stretched proudly from either side of his back. His brown reddish curls rustled by the wind.

I couldn't see his whole face, half hidden by his forearm, as if trying to shield himself from the world's judgmental gaze. A sentiment I could relate to right now. A tear brushed the corner of his striking blue eyes, the pain that brought it about almost tangible.

And it did…unexplainable things to me. His intense gaze transfixed me, as if he sought to penetrate in the depths of my soul. My breath caught in my chest. My throat tightened. The weight of his grief crushed my heart. Tasted like my own. A consuming agony. It held me captive, more real than my own reality.

It was binding.

It was suffocating.

It was agonizing.

"Miss Lewis? How long are we to wait for you?" Professor Gerard's annoyed voice broke the hypnosis.

And for the first time in daylight, my Shadows drew near. Responding to my distress. Because for unknown reasons, I wasn't feeling well.

Really not well.

Inside.

Like someone punched a hole through my chest and held my heart in their fist.

This painting…it touched me in ways nothing else did. I wanted to shield him away from those prying eyes. From those brainless students who saw nothing past the reflection. From this professor who couldn't see past his glasses perched on his nose.

"Miss Lewis!" he barked through a scowl. "The painting. Get on with it. Daydream on your own time."

I cleared my throat and sat a little straighter, pushing back the eruption of feelings fogging my brain.

"When I look at this painting…" My voice had a different cadence. Smoother. Lower. Calmer. "Really look at it…Beyond his obvious beauty, I see a being misunderstood. Trying to hide, to protect himself from the judgment of all who can't grasp the extent of his grief." The classroom went dead silent as I talked. "I see loneliness. I see the disappointment that goes beyond a banal disagreement. I see anger and barely contained frustration." That crystalline blue gaze arrested me again. "But most of all, I see real, raw pain. The type that scars you. The type that never leaves. The type you carry forever."

The classroom stilled, the silence stretching. From my peripheral vision, I spotted Mike, mouth parted. I sank a little deeper in the chair.

After a few beats, Professor Gerard was the first to recover from his shock.

"Better late than never," he muttered into his book. "This is the classical image known as the Fallen Angel. However, most interpretations aren't quite as…dramatic as Miss Lewis' emotional rendition." He put emphasis on "miss" as if the feminine title explained everything anyone needed to know about my opinion.

That earned a round of laughs from my classmates. A bunch of ignorant pricks, agreeing with that sexist loser of a teacher. "Although she was spot on about the anger. Scholars agree this is a tear of rage. Of fury. Because the angel couldn't usurp the throne of the sky. Because he couldn't defeat his father. God himself. This painting depicts the first Fallen Angel cast from Heaven to the underworld. This is said to be the moment before he was reborn as the King of Hell and unleashed his wrath on Earth." After toting his own opinion as fact, he dismissed the class with no room for rebuttal.

The students gathered their belongings, getting ready to leave. I hadn't moved an inch.

"Just play along," Mike murmured, as if sensing my intent. "Make it easier on yourself. Blend in. Do what's expected."

I ignored him. I'd make it on my own as myself, thanks.

The muscles in my jaw clenched so tight, my teeth ground against one another.

"This isn't about a throne." I heard myself say in a cold, clear voice. The opposite of the demure mouse's squeak this school used to get from me. Mike shook his head.

The icy stare of Mr. Gerard landed on me. "Class is dismissed." He bit out the words, as if it'd make the undergrads move any faster.

I remained sitting, waiting for my fellow students to empty the classroom. My gaze shifted from the teacher, who was busy gathering his stuff into his expensive leather bag, to the angel in the painting.

"You have no idea what he felt." The words came out before I'd processed them.

Professor Gerard stopped shuffling his papers, his gaze snapping to meet mine.

"Excuse me?" he asked, astonished.

I couldn't stop myself now. Something about the way he'd spoken about the angel just rubbed me the wrong way. My Shadows knew it, too. That's why they'd come.

I folded my arms across my chest and leaned back in my chair. "The painting. You're wrong. It isn't just anger. There's real pain. He's wounded. Broken." It baffled me that he couldn't see it. "And he didn't do it for a throne."

Professor Gerard seemed to snap out of a stupor, round face turning red. He straightened his spine, giving him maybe an extra inch on his five-foot frame.

"Listen carefully, young lady. The only reason you're here is your father's pedigree, but let's get one thing straight. I will not hesitate to fail you if you can't follow my curriculum. Got it?" His chest heaved rapidly. I was almost afraid he'd stroke out on me. After all, he had to be in his sixties.

Yeah, I got the threat. Yet, I couldn't keep my mouth shut for the life of me.

"I thought we were entitled to opinions and discussions in the classroom," I said sweetly. "I don't see why I'd fail a class simply because I don't share your views on a subjective interpretation. Unless the artist put it in writing, you can't possibly know the intended meaning. You weren't there to witness its creation or the event it's depicting. This painting speaks differently to me than your simple description."

I couldn't claim to know what Mr. Cabanel thought when he painted it or what the angel felt at that particular moment either, but I wasn't closed-minded.

"Out! Everyone," Professor Gerard ordered the few

lingering students. They rushed out under his wrathful stare. Mike included. Gerard then turned back to me. "Miss Lewis, I strongly suggest you learn your place. Perhaps the regular art program may be more suitable for you if you're looking to share your opinion." He picked up his bag in such a haste, papers fell on the ground. "The ancient art program is reserved for the few deserving of its caliber. Remember that." He exited at a fast pace, leaving his mess behind in his fury.

The door shut with a loud bang.

I ignored his outrageous behavior. It wasn't new to me.

I sighed. Still staring at the image. I sauntered to the front of the class. My fingers brushed the painting, unable to peel my eyes from his until the door opened to admit the next class.

I picked up my book, shoved it in my bag, and stormed out.

This was my only class of the day. Thank the Lord! My brain was malfunctioning. I blamed it on the stress of meeting a demon.

At my locker, I dropped my books, grabbed my coat, and headed outside. It was cloudy and raining. Again. Another day in London.

God, I missed the sun.

Chapter 5

As I heaved open the onerous door of the university, I bumped into Isabelle. Any trace of our little disagreement had already vanished from my mind.

"Hey, where have you been?" She usually waited at my locker before heading to her second morning class. "Wait until I tell you what happened in Professor Gerard's class. That creepy coot can't stand me. He's probably going to fail me."

My rambles died out when I got a better look at my friend. She'd piled her light red hair atop her head in a messy bun. Her flawless face was bare of its usual, carefully applied art. Her chocolate eyes were swollen and red, like she had been crying. Her lips trembled.

"What is it?" I asked, my muscles tensing.

She threw her arms around me and sobbed. Not once in our entire lives had Isabelle ever broken down. Not when we'd bid each other farewell before returning to our respective homes across the ocean. Nor when we were punished for our misdeeds. Not even when her mother fell ill. No cracks.

Never.

"Isabelle, you're scaring me," I whispered into her hair, my arms wrapping around her.

I held fast until she regained her composure. My hand glided up and down her spine. After a while, Isabelle pulled away, wiping tears with the back of her hand.

I gave a weak smile.

"I'm sorry, Nys, I've got to run."

She tried pushing past me, but my hand shot up, gripping her wrist.

"Wait, Isabelle. Talk to me."

She glanced around and whispered, "I can't."

"What are you talking about? You can tell me anything. Everything. Who do I have to kill?" I joked.

Her lips twitched for half a second.

"As if you could kill anyone."

My lips drew into a sideways smile. "Never underestimate what people will do for the ones they love. Besides, that's why I've got a brother who can. What else would he be good for otherwise?"

Truth was, no matter what, she stood by my side. After an unexplainable event that happened when I was young, before the hospital, I decided it was best to keep people away from me. Isabelle never took a hint. She never cared. She had stayed. Even when I refused to respond, we'd be in my room, and she'd play dolls as if I was participating. She never changed. I couldn't help but let her in the armor.

Her smile faded. "I've got to leg it, love."

My grip didn't falter. "Wait. Tell me what you need me to do?" I insisted. I wasn't going to leave her in this state. "You always have me in your corner, Isabelle. No matter what."

She pulled her wrist back, but not before I saw the tattoo. Isabelle didn't have a tattoo, or at least, she didn't yesterday. It looked more like a weird scar—red and swollen lines depicting a circle with a five-pointed star inside.

Isabelle backed away from me with tears welling in her eyes. "I really am sorry, Nys. I just need you to drop it and leave me be for now. Until I figure it out." With that, she left me there, ogling in disbelief.

One of my few talents was handling Isabelle. I could handle pretty much all of her personality. Crazy Isabelle. Fun Isabelle. Trouble Isabelle. Raging Isabelle. But this new one I couldn't quite grasp.

I took out my phone.

—I'm a call away whenever you're ready. We've got this. Love you.— I sent her the text.

Our little friend mantra: no matter what, we had this. We'd promised it to each other a long time ago when my mother passed away. I intended to deliver on that promise.

With my bag on my shoulder, I walked home, leaving Isabelle the space she needed.

For now.

Patience wasn't my greatest virtue. I held out until after supper. I had hoped she'd at least respond to my text message. I got nothing.

My brother and father were still MIA. I was used to it, but considering the new demon trouble, I was offended.

A warning would have been nice. I mean, I was still in danger. Sort of.

Being me and living up the street from Isabelle's house, I decided to show up uninvited, as I'd done dozens of times in the past.

Only, this time, I wasn't welcomed inside.

Professor Jones answered the door and informed me his daughter wasn't available. He provided no explanation and promptly closed the door before I could bother him further. Though it was obvious Isabelle was avoiding me, I couldn't help but sense something off with Professor Jones as well.

With a heavy sigh, I trudged home, my Shadows looming at an oddly safe distance. I wondered what was going on with them, aside from the fact they shouldn't exist at all, much less have typical, chartable behavior.

Just when I thought the madness had reached its summit, I heard it.

Again.

Louder.

The music.

I mean, it had always been there. Sort of like a super soft white noise machine I tuned out on the regular. Now, it was making itself known. My feet halted, rooted to the ground. My heart palpitated.

I had been doing good. So very good. Well, good for me. It was *almost* gone.

Almost.

I glanced around, praying it was coming from a house or a car, when deep down I knew the answer.

It was everywhere.

So nice and gentle. A mixture of instruments and elements. The type of harmony to comfort and warm your insides. Almost like arms engulfing me.

I felt the Shadows brush against me.

My eyes opened.

I didn't realize I had shut them. The second I opened them, the shadows retreated further, and the music dropped to its customary, ignorable volume.

As if it were never there.

I glanced around again. The air changed. The temperature seemed warmer, and the night suddenly became…too quiet. I got the impression of being observed. Yet, there was no one in sight. Against logic, I wasn't afraid. Not like I had been when the demon pulled off his glasses.

No. Instead, I was nervous with anticipation.

I shook it off quickly.

God, I was losing it more with each passing day.

Walking at a quicker pace, I stared right ahead. Not daring to glance around or above my shoulder. On a mission.

Get home.

The moment I arrived, I quickly locked the door and leaned against it, panting heavily as though having jogged a mile. Despite my attempts to calm my racing heart, the unsettling giddiness persisted.

I moved to the narrow window by the door and pushed aside the thin curtain. My eyes settled on a man standing across the street on the sidewalk, facing my house. I couldn't see anything other than his shape, but I would've sworn his eyes were locked right on me. Fixated and unwavering.

I blinked, about to back away, but he was already gone.

Perhaps he'd never been there to begin with?

Oh, sweet mother of Jesus! I needed to talk to a shrink.

It was getting out of my control. Or maybe I should talk to Micah.

It had to stop.

In the kitchen, I chugged down a nice glass of cold water to shake off the nerves.

It didn't work.

I went upstairs and did my nighttime routine, doing

my best to forget my momentary lapse of sanity.

I admitted I'd let the madness go too far, craving the darkness, ignoring the music, befriending the Shadows. But now, the music was out of control, and I'd relished it. Not to mention the man standing outside my house, who was likely a figment of my wild imagination.

I showered, brushed my teeth, dried my hair, moisturized my face, and hit the bed. The house was quiet. No one around for company or protection. No one to grill over the state of the city and how much Father's sect knew about it.

I glimpsed at my phone again. Nothing.

Not even Isabelle deemed me important enough to confide in.

The thought of Isabelle's frazzled state kept me wondering. Whatever the trouble, it must be with her mother. I rolled to my side, stretching to shut off the lamp on my nightstand.

Once my room fell into total darkness, they came.

It was the first time they'd dared come inside. Hence the night walks.

I decided to ignore them. Ignore that figure or figment on the street. Ignore Isabelle.

But when a key turned in the front door bolt with a snap downstairs, there was no way I was going to ignore that. I pushed the blankets off, jumped off the bed, and rushed down to find Micah sneaking into the kitchen.

"Hi, Nyssa Bear, why aren't you sleeping?" He yawned, taking a bottle of water from the fridge.

Mouth parted in furious disbelief, I stalked over and snatched away the bottle.

"Maybe I would be sleeping if you'd bothered telling me demons were in town and, I dunno, gave me some assurance. I *know* Father is aware, therefore you're aware, but you left me in the dark, *purposely*!" I shouted.

My brother supplicated me with a raised palm facing up, his brain stuttering for a moment. "You saw one in the shop. You knew." He had the nerve to reply casually, walking to the fridge, where he grabbed another bottle.

My eyes threatened to bulge out of their sockets.

The jerk!

I tipped my arm back and threw the water bottle at him. He tried dodging, but it clipped his shoulder.

"The demon you thought I invented! Or did you forget?" He stood there in shock. "You implied I was crazy! That I was imagining things! You…you…jerk!"

"By all heavens, Nyssa, what's the matter with you?"

Hearing music. Seeing Shadows. Seeking darkness.

Oh, and a man stalking me.

Plenty of options to choose from.

I narrowed my eyes at him. "What's wrong with me?" I repeated. "Oh, nothing really. Only my family doesn't think I matter enough to warn about demons moving into town. I'm not surprised Father didn't include me." He never did. "But I am hurt *you* didn't." With that, I ran to my room, shut the door, and locked it.

Out of pure spite.

I saw my handle shake under his weak attempt at entry. If he wanted, he could easily break it. It wouldn't be the first time. Only, he didn't. He didn't send me a text either. His utter disinterest in reconciliation pissed me off even more.

Asshat.

My eyes might have shut for a few minutes or mere seconds before I jolted awake in my bed. Mixed with the heavy rain hitting my window, the echoing boom first sounded like thunder. Then I recognized the steady rhythm of a fist banging wood. I glanced at the clock beside my bed. 3:06 a.m. Who the hell was at the door?

Surely, Micah could bother answering.

If he was still home.

What if it was the demon from yesterday? Oh God. I wouldn't survive. My self-defense was very basic. As in nonexistent beyond chucking the nearest objects at someone's head. But maybe it was important. I mean, it was past three a.m.

Hell! I gathered the little courage I had and clambered out of bed. Micah had put a baseball bat between my bed and my nightstand when we first moved in a year ago. *In case.*

Picking it up, I made a mental note to thank him later.

Whenever I'd forgive him.

The Shadows were still here. They seemed agitated. Moving fast and brusquely. Perhaps it was a sign for me to stay in my room.

The sound didn't stop. On the contrary, it became louder, more urgent.

I walked downstairs, slowly, looking through the window at the shadow of the person manhandling the door. On tiptoe, I checked the peephole to see…Isabelle.

Chapter 6

In my haste to unlock the door, I dropped the baseball bat. It clattered away as I flung open my home to Isabelle. She stood in the pouring rain, her wet hair clinging to her face. Her swollen eyes had puffed up even worse.

I stepped aside to admit her. Without giving me a chance to shut the door, Isabelle grabbed my shoulders. "I messed up. I need help." Voice soaked in desperation; she glanced over her shoulder at the street. "He's coming."

Without hesitation, I shoved her deeper inside, slammed the door, and turned the lock.

Could it be the same man from earlier? Pushing aside the curtain, I glimpsed into the street. Everything seemed…normal. Aside from the rain, nothing was out there.

"What the hell is going on, Isabelle? Who's coming for you?"

She couldn't even look me in the eyes. Tears streamed down her doll face as she studied her feet.

"Isabelle," I urged.

Her gaze lifted to mine. "A demon." She trembled.

It all came together and slammed into me like a fist. I stumbled back, a hand over my mouth.

"No. No. No, and no. Tell me you didn't," I whispered.

Her sheepish face said all I needed to know. Isabelle had messed up. Big time.

"What have you done?"

She took my hands in hers. "Nys, please, I'm desperate. Daddy can't find a way to help me. The council is refusing to assist us." She meant my father, the head of the cult, had refused them aid. "Please, I need you."

"I don't know how, Isabelle." It wasn't like my father would hear any of my pleas. "You need to tell me everything, and we'll figure something out."

She nodded. My shadows didn't like it. Not one bit. Agitated, they zipped around the walls and across the floor with alarming speed. Almost as if...they didn't like Isabelle or her proposition.

I ignored them and guided my friend to the living room.

I opened the small glass doors of the fireplace and carefully arranged the wood and papers inside. Once done, I opened the trap and lit the kindling. "I'll be right back." I headed to the laundry room near the kitchen. After a quick search, I found a dry hoodie and joggers and brought them back to Isabelle.

While she changed, I grabbed the thick blanket from the couch.

"Put this on. You're shaking." I wrapped the blanket around her shoulders and guided her to a seat near the fireplace.

"I went to Peccatta," Isabelle croaked.

I gasped. Those debauched clubs weren't places girls like Isabelle and I were allowed to even think about. People gathered there to drink their problems away, gamble their life savings, or have a one-night stand with a nameless stranger. The ideal place for demons to meet sinners.

Oh crap.

"You made a deal."

She lowered her head, picking at her fingernails. "Yes."

"What were you thinking?" I said, harsher than intended.

Isabelle abruptly stood, dropping the blanket on the floor. "See, that's exactly why I didn't want to say anything to you." Her gesticulating hands tossed accusations my way. "You just don't get it. How could you?" She shook her head, water droplets falling from her hair. "You can't. You never could."

Clearly.

"You're right. I can't understand why anyone would want to bargain with a demon. No one should have everything they want handed to them. There's always a price to pay. There are plenty of things I want but don't have. I won't go strike a deal over it."

She huffed, her sneer scathing. "What do you want that you don't have, besides a diploma?"

Was that really all she thought of me? Yes, I wanted my diploma, but I longed for so much more.

To have my mother back. To belong somewhere. To chase away loneliness. To be cared for. To matter.

Although I'd never said any of that out loud, she ought to have known I had more layers. She was my best friend after all.

I pushed down the irritation her words awoke. "I am not the subject of discussion. I'm not the one that needs help. How about instead you tell me what happened so we can find a way to break this deal."

Her shoulders sagged as the fight left her. Folding her torso, she picked up the blanket and sneaked closer to the fireplace. She sat, holding her knees to her chest. Despite the warmth of the room, Isabelle shivered.

"When I eavesdropped on my dad, I also overheard what demons could grant. Limitless possibilities for a price." A small detail she'd cleverly left out when she first told me about the demons dropping in town. Although, it's not the first time I heard of it—The books had mentioned it. "He said they hung around Peccatta. After you left, I went there." Isabelle had omitted to tell me where and why she was going out. She hugged the blanket closer. "I met him there. The demon. They all live nearby from what he told me." She watched the dancing flames, a sad smile tugging her lips. "You should have seen him, Nys. He was so charming. Good looking. Not how I imagined a demon at all." Her eyes were almost dreamy. "He listened to me. He cared about my problems. We danced. We laughed." She turned her gaze back to me. "In those few hours, I felt connected to him." She paused.

I figured that sensation came from a demon power of some kind, but that wasn't what Isabelle needed to hear right now.

"He offered to heal her, Nyssa. My mom," she whispered. "How could I walk away from that?"

I swallowed my next breath.

I totally got it, now. Isabelle's mom had a rare autoimmune disease. Her days had been numbered for the past six months, and every day her state worsened.

To have her well again was a huge temptation. One that struck home. If I was honest with myself, I might have considered it, too, if mine were still alive.

"I jumped on it," she confirmed. "I didn't realize he'd already set a cost until it was too late. Even then, I thought maybe a feeding or a favor." She shook her head. "He wanted more."

"How much more?"

She stared at me, broken. "My soul, Nyssa. And I gave it to him. I'm damned." She sighed, tears in her eyes.

I crawled beside her, put my arms around her shoulders, and pressed her against me. Isabelle's hands wrapped around my waist, engulfing me in the warm cover.

"I'll never let that happen. I'll find a way, I promise," I vowed in her ear. I needed to talk to Micah. Where the hell was he when I needed him, anyway?

She took my hands, and her sleeve lifted, revealing the weird star tattoo I had seen at school.

"What's this?" I traced the raised lines of the five-pointed star inside an angry red circle.

Her eyes drifted downward with reluctance. "He branded me."

The bastard.

"Micah's going to help us." I searched around for my phone. "Wait one sec." I returned to my room, unplugged my phone, and scrolled to Micah's name.

—Where are you?—

I'd reached my door when I heard it—the eerie sound of fingers rubbing against a surface. In one frantic heartbeat, my fear reached a new summit. To make matters worse, my shadows had fled, peeved by my dismissal of their concern. The source of the incessant noise seemed to come from my window. My unease heightened, pulling my muscles so taut I could hardly turn to look. My neck creaked around…to find the white blinds drawn.

My gut knew what hid behind them. Part of me wanted to go pull the cord to prove my imagination wrong, but I wasn't brave enough to satisfy my curiosity. Instead, I sent one last message to my brother, praying he'd hurry.

—He's here. Hurry.—

I rushed downstairs, clutching my phone like a lifeline and glancing over my shoulder every few seconds, expecting the monster to walk through the wall.

I turned down the hallway leading to the living room. Isabelle was still crying, but she wasn't alone. A strange man hovered over her prostrate form on the floor, a hand wrapped around her neck.

Acting on pure adrenaline, I charged the man and threw my weight on top of him, wrapping my forearms around his neck. I summoned all my strength, managing to pull him away from Isabelle. He fell backward, using my body as a cushion, crushing me with his weight.

"Isabelle, run!" I yelled, tightening my grip on the man. My legs secured around his waist. Or so I thought. It didn't last long.

He bucked his spine and sent my head crashing onto the hardwood floor. Hard. My vision blurred, and dark spots danced before my eyes. My hold on him loosened.

As I rolled to my side, my eyes focused on Isabelle's body. She'd curled into a ball, her back pressed against the wall, sobbing hysterically.

The man crouched into my vision, his slender fingers grabbing my face, forcing my eyes to his. They were completely black.

A demon. Go figure.

And now he was a pissed-off demon.

All thanks to me.

What could I say? I'd found a new skill to add to my repertoire.

With nostrils flared, each heaving breath sent his anger rolling off his skin like a heatwave. I gulped when his free arm reached for me, but it suddenly stopped. His head jerked toward the hallway.

That's when I heard it.

Never had I been so happy to hear the annoying creak of the front door. Seizing the opportunity, I rolled away from the demon and stood on wobbling legs. That's when his head twisted my way again, and a vicious smile spread across his face.

Not good. Not good at all.

I grabbed Isabelle by the wrist and pulled her up. Forcing my legs to work, I rushed down the hallway, dragging my friend with me. I tried to make a break for the back door, but we'd barely made it to the kitchen before an unimaginable force yanked me back.

My grip on Isabelle slipped as I was suddenly hurled across the main floor, my feet no longer touching the ground. I wasn't much more than dust in the wind.

My back collided with the mirror hanging in our hallway, shattering on impact. My breath caught in my throat. Shards of glass flew everywhere as I crashed onto my ass. An intense pain erupted from my shoulder. A piece of glass as big as my hand was lodged in my flesh. Warm liquid flooded down my arm and pooled in my palm.

My eyes shut. My body ached. My head spun.

"Don't move, pet, while I take care of the interruption."

"No need. I'm very interested in that one," another voice responded with authority. One I recognized but couldn't quite place.

"That bitch deserves nothing more than to be reminded of her rank in the food chain."

A growl resonated off the kitchen pans. "You seem like the one who needs a reminder of his rank. Consider yourself lucky you found something interesting enough to distract me from your inability to retrieve a weak human. Now go, take her," he ordered. "She's mine."

When I peeked from the curtain of my hair, a new man stood beside Isabelle, his arms behind his back. He had gotten his minion to do the dirty work. I couldn't catch his face. My vision blurred worse.

I tried shaking it off, sending a shift in the air. The atmosphere had weight. And I felt *them*, swirling all around me. I couldn't begin to describe the relief. The air in my lungs passed a little easier.

Until the demon grabbed my arms. A scream echoed through the house.

One of pure pain. One of pure suffering. It sent shivers of terror down my spine.

My gaze fixed on the demon before me. His mouth gaped open as his skin began to turn a sickly mottle of gray and orange. His features contorted in agony, convulsing as he collapsed to the ground. I pushed away with my feet, but my back hit against the wall.

And poof. The demon shattered into thousands of miniscule ashes.

I searched for Isabelle, but my body tilted to the

side, unbalanced by the pain coursing through me. I fought to keep my eyes open when the entire room spun.

The new demon and Isabelle were long gone.

So was I.

Chapter 7

My eyelids peeled open one at a time to find Micah's face inches from mine. He lay on his side atop my comforter, eyes closed. He always looked undeniably beautiful, but like this, without the severe angles and serious expressions that plagued him in wakefulness, he looked almost fragile.

It reminded me of a time in our lives when Micah and I slept together every night. Sometimes because my nightmares had made me cry out, others because of his own anxious need to watch over me. More often than not, though, we simply enjoyed each other's company. He'd read to me each night until I'd learned how. Then I read for us. We'd talk and laugh.

Until it wasn't 'proper' to do so anymore.

My fingers moved on their own, pushing his golden hair off his face. His blue eyes snapped open, and just like that, his expression steeled. Gone was the fragile façade.

"Nyssa. Heavens, you scared me to death." He pushed up on his elbow. "Are you okay? What happened?"

The memory of last night came crashing back. The throbbing radiating from my shoulder developed into a searing pain, barely tolerable. My mouth felt like a desert. My head throbbed like someone had struck me with a hammer, feeling like dead weight.

I tried sitting and failed, wincing.

Micah came to my rescue. His arms encircled my shoulders and waist, propping me on the pillows with care.

"Thanks." I swallowed, aching for water. "Isabelle. She came. She was crying. We got attacked by a demon and another one showed up."

Micah tensed. "What demon?"

I ignored him, recalling the exact minute before losing consciousness. When one of the demons tried taking me. He'd combusted…

Oh, my god. Had my shadows done that? Or had I imagined it?

No, the image was vivid.

They'd been there. They'd protected me.

But the other demon, he took her. "He has Isabelle. She…" I bit my lip, hesitating.

"She what?" Micah urged.

I grabbed my brother's hand, searching his face. "I'll tell you everything but you gotta promise me to not tell Dad. No matter what."

From his flinch and troubled blue eyes, you'd think I'd asked the world of him. It still baffled me why he trusted his father so much.

"Fine," he grumbled.

Not good enough.

"People are only as good as their word." He'd drilled the phrase into me a hundred times. "Promise me." I held out my pinky.

Micah rolled his eyes. "You're kidding, right? We're not ten years old anymore."

"Right, but I know you." And everything a silly pinky swear had come to mean for him and me.

"Promise. Let me know I can trust you. That it's still you and I against the world."

I didn't miss the flash of hesitation. After a beat, he tangled his pinky with mine. "I promise. You and I against the world. Forever."

I gestured for him to come closer. He leaned until I felt his breath on my cheek. "Isabelle. She made a deal with a demon." Micah's eyes hardened to cobalt gemstones. "To save her mom," I added in a rush before he could toss out blame. "She came to me, hoping I could find her a way out of it."

Micah stiffened, pupils dilating. He stood so fast my eyes barely registered the movement. He threw a bunch of curses at no one. I'd never heard him cuss in my whole life.

He kicked my desk chair, breaking the leg and making me jump. "You should have stayed away from that girl." His finger jabbed in my direction. "She's nothing but trouble. She's stained, Nyssa. You're just too good to see it."

I gritted my teeth. My fists clenched on my bed sheet. "She's my best friend. My only one, if you must be reminded." The only one I'd trusted with my unstable past. "I won't leave her hanging. Her father can't find anything to help her, but he doesn't have all of Glory's resources."

Micah's feet stopped pacing. "With a friend like that, you don't need another. Every time she's in trouble, which is always, she comes running to you. Whether it's for schoolwork or for an excuse to go out."

I opened my mouth and closed it. How the hell did he even know about that?

"I'm not stupid, Nys. I see. I pretend I don't. I let

most slide for your sake. But she's reached the limit. I won't let you risk your life for her."

I kicked off the blankets and rose out of bed, chest heaving with pent frustration. "That's not your choice to make. The demon asked for her soul." A plea shook my voice. He had to understand. "She'll be worse than dead."

"She didn't have much of a soul to start with."

All rational thought left me.

"Like you'd know!" He'd never bothered getting to know her. "You don't want to help me, Micah? That's fine. Just stay out of my way. I'll find something myself." I stormed to the bathroom, holding my aching shoulder, and slammed the door in his face.

"It's not you I won't help. It's her," he shouted from the other side.

"It's the same thing!" I shouted back, going to the vanity.

I looked even worse than I felt, which I hadn't imagined possible. Dark circles had formed under my eyes. My brown hair stood up in static strands as if I had stuck my finger in a socket.

I pulled down the strap of my tank top to inspect my wound. Around the white bandage covering the worst damage, the swollen skin had a bluish tint.

To be safe and keep the bandage dry, I settled for a bath. Washing my hair without the use of one hand proved more of a challenge than expected, but I managed.

Untangling my hair with a brush remained impossible. Instead, I turned the nest into a high bun, clipped it, and went back to my room in a towel.

Micah had vanished from my personal space. I

couldn't decide whether I was relieved or upset.

I threw a loose, white, long-sleeved T-shirt over my head and, like a gymnast, passed my arm through the right hole. I considered it my exercise of the week. After wriggling into black leggings, I ventured toward the main floor.

As I reached the bottom of the stairs, I heard muffled voices coming from the closed study. I kept my footsteps light and quiet as I crossed the living room to the door.

I recognized Isabelle's father's voice. I couldn't distinctly understand all the words, but "please" and "daughter" stood out amidst his tone filled with deep concern.

However, my father's clear voice slashed like a scythe through Dr. Jones' murmurs.

"We will do nothing." Father didn't scream. He never did. He didn't need to. His words were king. Unarguable. "She put Nyssa in danger by coming here. Your daughter made a choice. Now she lives with it. Each is accountable for their mistakes." No hesitation. No help offered. Nothing.

And he knew everything about Peccatta and the deal. If I had any doubt about the amount of information Dr. Jones had shared, it disappeared after Father's third sentence. No one hid secrets from Gavriel for long.

"If I may, perhaps I could look into it," said a feminine voice. It could have only one owner in that cult of men: Professor Maryssa Vero. She taught in my program. She also happened to be one of my favorites. A woman of few words, but she never judged me. On the contrary, she appreciated my intellect.

I didn't hear the answer. Knowing my father, he'd never take Maryssa's offer. He hated her. Thought she was evil. Only he knew why.

I didn't stick around for their petty arguments. I'd gotten enough of what I needed. They'd stand back and do nothing. Well, I planned on doing everything I could for Isabelle…despite my pitiful state.

Chapter 8

Being the brilliant person that I was, I decided to visit the only place where I might have a chance to find Isabelle.

Peccatta.

I made the Uber pick me up at the corner of my street. If worse came to worse, and I couldn't find her, maybe I'd be lucky enough to recognize the demon that took her. Not much to go on, but it was all I had.

It seemed pretty simple when I went over it in my head. The same couldn't be said once I'd reached my destination.

As I stood in front of Peccatta with my stomach in my throat, I almost regretted not telling Micah about my crazy idea.

People dressed to impress, flaunting platinum cards and stacks of bank notes, crowded the velvet rope queue. I had twenty pounds nestled in my jacket pocket, an injured shoulder, and my trusty cell phone. I stared at it for a moment. The rational part of my brain implored me to inform my brother. I ruled against it and shoved it in my pocket.

Micah had made it clear where he stood concerning Isabelle's situation.

I, however, couldn't stand idle while Isabelle suffered, so I'd come to the birthplace of her deal.

God, did I wish I'd picked a better outfit. I stood

out too much, underdressed for a place that screamed to be seen. With no makeup, a baggy T-shirt, and a tangled bun, everyone would notice the second I stepped foot inside.

Dammit.

I cursed all the demons in my head–wishing they had stayed in whatever hole they'd been hiding–as I entered the crowded establishment. The strong scent of alcohol invaded my nose as soon as I pushed open the door.

I'd never been curious about nightclubs, bars, or gambling houses. Still, the initial impression astounded me.

The center of the room pulsated with alternating flashes of white and red lights while the deafening beat of music reverberated through the air. Revelers chatted and imbibed, adding to the frenzied atmosphere. At a distance, two imposing red doors with the word "Games" emblazoned on them loomed, embedded in the onyx wall.

I rose onto my tiptoes, scanning the place in a desperate search for Isabelle. It was a long shot, but what did I have to lose?

The place crawled with demons, walking around without qualms or a shred of self-doubt. So many that I took an automatic step back, doused by a wave of fear. If the one I was looking for recognized me and attacked, I had no means of defending myself.

Ordinary humans mingled among them, flirting with danger while wearing oblivious smiles. Didn't they realize? The more they interacted, the more they shared, the more the demons could sniff out the weaknesses they'd use to tempt their prey.

The people behind me huffed and sighed, annoyed by my presence in the middle of the entrance. Some shoved past, shooting me dirty looks.

I cupped my injured shoulder for some protection, and against my better judgment, dared to advance a couple of steps. At least, enough to let the impatient horde reach the path to the bar.

This was probably the worst idea. Like ever.

I'd barely gotten a glimpse of the demon who'd kidnapped Isabelle. I had no real shot at recognizing him in this chaos. I could barely see past the pain.

Besides, I doubted he let his captured souls walk around freely.

Another idea formed. Maybe the lodging? That's why they came around her, right? Busy debating myself, I jumped when a voice interrupted.

"Are you lost?"

My attention slid to my right, and every nerve ending jolted to life. I struggled to control the rapid beat of my heart as I turned to find myself face-to-face with the most stunning guy I had *ever* laid eyes on. The Hollywood Chrises had nothing on his chiseled features. A deep scar cut through his right eyebrow and down to his jaw. I barely paid attention to it, languishing in striking blue eyes.

Not a regular shade of blue, but the drown-your-sorrows kind.

The kind that could read the depths of your soul.

The kind that means nothing but trouble.

The kind that broke resolutions.

The kind I didn't need.

I mentally shook myself and answered as coolly as possible, "No. I'm just looking for someone."

His head tilted sideways, his eyes gliding over me. I couldn't help the heat that rushed to my face. I knew I wasn't much to look at in my current state—a thought that had never occurred to me in all my previous nineteen years.

And he smiled.

A killer smile—a knee trembler. The type you damn a soul for.

Good God, I was about to. My insides tightened.

"And who may that be?" That voice. It made me shake...inside.

I forced my eyes away from him, refocusing on my mission.

"My friend." Rising on my tiptoes, I scanned the sea of bodies tangled together on a dance floor. If you could even call that dancing. A shiver of disgust ran through me. Demons wrapped themselves around defenseless humans, lost to sensations that probably weren't their own.

"You won't find any friends here."

My head snapped to meet his gaze. If only he knew how right he was. No one who came here would find a friend. Or anything of worth at all.

A human could *lose* plenty, though.

"Now tell me, what does someone with your..." The stranger paused, staring into my eyes. I arched my brow, waiting for him to complete his sentence.

He didn't.

"This isn't a place for someone like you," he finally said in one breath.

A not-so-subtle jab I didn't need after getting tossed around by a demon. Let him try it; see how he and his tailored, all-black suit ensemble fared. Still, he hit me right in the self-esteem.

"And how would you know who fits in here?" I snipped. He didn't quite fit in either. For opposite reasons.

The corner of his lips stretched. "Trust me. Reading souls is sort of my expertise."

I returned his smirk. "Really?" I gave him a scathing full-body scan of my own. "Now you tell me, what does a human with a…" I pretended to think while he arched a brow. "… a soul is doing in a place like this."

That wiped the smirk right off. I wondered how aware Peccatta's patrons were of the current demon situation and why they weren't running for the door the second they saw those abyssal eyes.

The stranger cocked his head once more, his eyebrows creasing together. "And how would you know that I possess a soul?"

I shrugged my good shoulder. "It's sort of my expertise." Hoping to get him off my back, I casually added, "This place is crawling with demons, you know." He'd probably think I was right down crazy.

Instead, he put a palm against his lapel. "Sam."

"Nyssa." He must've thought it was a joke.

"Well, Nyssa, you just made this boring evening extremely interesting." He eyed me with open curiosity that soon sparked a new gleam inside his pupils. One that might have excited me under other circumstances. "I'll tell you what—if you can identify three demons in this whole place, I'll allow you to stay."

"Allow me to stay?" I snorted.

Sam powered on. "I'll even help you find your friend. If you win, consider me your personal servant for the evening." His lips quirked when he added, "Many would kill for that privilege."

Something else clicked. Not only had he absorbed my demon comment without a flinch, he'd mentioned them without a hint of sarcasm.

"You know," I whispered, "about demons."

"That knowledge was forced upon me, unfortunately."

Anyone aware of demons and still hanging around an establishment like this one meant one thing.

Problem.

"I don't need any help, thanks." I tried sidestepping him, but he blocked my path. He waggled a finger, refusing me access.

"You're wrong. Demons can scent how pure you are. How...precious. They'll be attracted to you like wolves to a lamb. I'm your only chance of keeping them away."

Pure? Did he mean, in the virginal sense? The heat rushed to my face.

"And before you think you have a choice in the matter, you don't." He grinned. "See, I own this place. You aren't allowed in unless I decide otherwise. So, what do you say, precious?"

The heat crawled back to my neck at the pet name. I glanced around the luxurious demon nest. "You own this place?"

"I do."

My eyes narrowed on him. Aside from the fact that he seemed barely older than me, why would a human agree to make his business a demon hub? Unless it was imposed on him. I pushed the thought aside. Not my problem.

"And why would you decide to help a random girl?" Either way, if I didn't play along, he wouldn't let me stay, as he'd so politely put it.

He leaned forward and murmured in a dulcet baritone, "I wouldn't, precious."

"Am I supposed to feel special?"

He laughed. It was as rich and depthless as those eyes. It unraveled me. "You are, but that isn't why I offered you this little bargain. See, I'm not the helping type." Sam lazily draped his arm around my shoulders, tugging me close to his side. I ignored the strange feeling filling my stomach and winced at the pain he inflicted unknowingly.

I pushed his arm off, holding my throbbing shoulder, and fought to swallow a cry.

Damn him.

"What did you do?" Sam must have seen the brief confusion on my features because he gestured with his chin. "The shoulder."

"Clumsy."

He moved closer in one big step. "Liar," he said, midnight eyes on mine.

"How did you get the scar?" I asked back.

"My brother." God, I hadn't expected brutal honesty from a wolf like him. "What happened to your shoulder?" Sam insisted.

I caved. He believed in demons, so why not? We could be nutcases together. "I got tossed around by a demon who invaded my house. Nothing like a mirror shard to the shoulder. His buddy kidnapped my friend." Because I felt self-conscious, I added, "It explains the look."

If I hadn't been preoccupied with nursing my

bandage, I might have noticed the change in Sam's demeanor. How his whole body froze as if trapped in ice. How the muscle popped in his jaw. How his breathing went ragged.

A gravelly "What?" escaped him. With spikes of pain shooting from my shoulder to my fingertips, I missed the anger.

"If you aren't the helping type, why did you offer it up as a bet?"

He folded his thick arms over his chest, revealing forearms adorned with ink. "Because there's no way you can identify any demons."

Oh, good God, he couldn't be right. Right? I prayed they weren't in my head.

Swallowing hard, I managed a weak nod. "If I do, will you hold up your end of the deal?"

"I always honor my deals."

Somehow, I believed him.

I let my gaze wander around the place, grasping at sanity amid an insane task. Dread owned my being.

I gestured with my chin toward the nearby bar. "See that bulky guy with the long ponytail drinking a beer?" Under the flashing lights, his black eyes stood out. I didn't dare check Sam's reaction. I was too much of a coward. Instead, I silently prayed that I wouldn't come across as completely mad in front of the first guy to ever pique any sort of interest. "And the girl on the dance floor with the tight black dress, grinding on a man old enough to be her father."

I heard Sam mumble something along the lines of "judgy little thing."

My eyes roamed, settling on another demon standing close by, staring straight at Sam and me. So much for not attracting attention to myself.

"Crap," I mumbled under my breath. "The guy near the door with the platinum hair." I paused, then whispered, "Watching us."

I twisted at my waist back to a speechless Sam. He stared like I had grown a second head, full lips slightly parted.

Sure, he owns the Club of the Damned, but I'm the one with issues.

Just when I wondered if I had gone mad, Sam snapped out of his trance. In a breath, he stood mere inches away from my face. His chest brushed mine as he placed one hand on the back of my head and the other under my chin, both feverishly warm. His long fingers restrained my movement. The touch was firm but surprisingly gentle. The contact of his skin against mine awoke a need I thought I'd been born without. His piercing eyes scrutinized my face, his brow furrowed with concern.

Unconsciously, my back arched slightly toward him.

"Let me go." My whispered demand sounded almost like a plea.

I was afraid. Not of him. Of *this*.

Sam's frown deepened. "How are you doing it? How are you..." He selected his next words cautiously. "Seeing the damned?"

I swallowed. Hard. "You mean the demons?"

"Yes."

"I don't know. I thought everyone could see them." Or that I was simply losing my goddamn mind. One of the two.

Then something else clicked. "How do you even

know I'm telling the truth? That they're really demons?"

He shook his head slowly, not answering me but releasing my chin. Almost aware that I wouldn't move an inch. His hand brushed the hair from my face as he coaxed me closer with a hushed croon. "Let me in, Nyssa."

His hold on my head softened, and instead, his fingers tangled in my hair, rubbing my scalp. Something in his tone was...enthralling. His russet hair fell to the side, and I had the sudden urge to run my hand over his cheek, close my eyes, and do exactly as he asked—to just let him *in*.

Isabelle. I needed to find the demon that took Isabelle. Fast.

"Let me go. Now," I demanded, my voice cutting through the fog in my head.

As fast as he had grabbed me, he was gone. A chill enveloped me.

Without warning, Sam seized a passing man by the collar, spilling his drink all over his suit. "What about him, then?" Sam asked, shoving the helpless stranger toward me.

I took a frightened step back. Sam wasn't all there either. He matched my crazy peg for peg.

"Hey, man, what's your problem?" The guy fought against Sam's grip, but when Sam leaned in and spoke too low for me to hear, he stopped struggling.

"What are you doing?" I asked, shifting from foot to foot.

"What about him?" Sam repeated.

"What about him?" I echoed. "Leave him be. He hasn't done anything."

"What is he?"

My brows pulled together. "Human. Now let him go." And he did exactly that, never taking his eyes off me. It was unnerving.

Surprisingly, the man walked away without a word. Like a zombie.

This was a whole new level of weird. Even for me. My gut knew I wouldn't find any clues here. I had wasted time Isabelle might not have. I turned on my heels, ready to leave this place and Sam.

My face met a hard chest. When my eyes lifted, the demon I'd caught staring at Sam flashed me a big smirk. A shiver of fear wracked my spine.

"Well, well. What do we have here?" My heart came back to life in my chest, revving like a race car. I stepped back only to bump into another chest of steel. I blinked, and I was facing Sam's black suit. A much more comforting sight.

Somehow.

"Sorry, Nat, she's my guest. Move along," Sam ordered the demon. My heart did a flip. Did Sam realize he was talking to a demon? Or that demons all had some sort of powers he needed to watch out for? Not that I was an expert on it, but my knowledge was better than most regular humans.

"He's a demon," I reminded him in a whisper.

I peeked around Sam's arm. The demon seemed shocked. "You're kidding? I must have heard wrong. Your guest?" he mocked with a muffled laugh.

I heard a rumbling sound. So close to a growl, I figured a little more of my mind had just fluttered away.

Sam held his ground. "Move it, I said."

The guy lifted his arms in surrender with a sneer. "I'll leave you to it."

Sam turned to me, took my hand, and led me into an elevator.

"Where are we going?" I asked as he pressed level two.

A smirk grew on his face. "To talk. Don't worry, I won't eat you." Sam stepped closer to me, into my personal space. "Unless you ask nicely." He winked.

And I forgot how to breathe altogether.

Chapter 9

The ding of the elevator jolted me out of shock. The doors glided open on an equally opulent but less flashy floor.

Sam gestured for me to slip out with a gallant, "After you." But I had beaten him to it, running on a noxious mix of fear, emotional turmoil, and frayed nerves.

My feet met a slick floor composed of one massive onyx marble tile, run through with streaks of silver.

Sam's dress shoes clicked all the way to a dark door. I trailed closely beside him, my sneakers silent. Once we pushed through the door, a familiar scent assaulted my nose: a mixture of firewood and crisp winter air. The same eau de parfum that clung to Sam's skin.

"Here, let me." When I gave Sam's extended hand an interrogating look, he clarified, "Your jacket."

"No need. I won't be staying."

Another smile. Without insisting, he led us further into an office.

A small gasp escaped my lips.

The cream-colored walls provided a gentle backdrop for a stunning decor collection that screamed of power and new money worthy of a magazine spread. A massive desk stood between two windows bigger than cars. On the opposite wall, a magnificent fireplace dominated the space, casting a warm glow across the room. Luxurious, dark leather couches with gold accents beckoned me to sink into their plush cushions. And beneath my feet lay a thick, golden carpet.

Sam walked over to what I assumed was an antique bar. He examined the wall of thick liquor bottles displayed behind the bar top.

"Are you more of a wine girl?" he asked, turning from the impressive collection and walking to a glass-fronted cellar embedded in the wall.

"I'm more of a water type of girl. Thanks."

He shot me a wink and said, "Could have fooled me." He tugged the pressure-sealed door and soon walked back out with a bottle of wine.

I was growing annoyed. Why had I even followed him here? Time was running out, as reminded by my phone vibrating in my pocket. I glanced at it.

Micah.

—What are you doing out of the house??? Forget out of the house. How about out of bed? You should be resting.—

I rubbed my temple with one hand. The one not in constant pain.

I lifted my eyes to Sam uncorking the bottle.

"Listen, if you can help me, by all means, please get on with it." After all, I needed it. "Otherwise, I'm headed out. I'm kinda working against the clock here." I had no clue about the rules of soul collection, but I guessed the quicker I found the contract-holding demon, the better my chances.

"Why did he take your friend?" he asked.

I opened my mouth, then closed it again. Technically, the demon in question had sent a crony to retrieve Isabelle, then shown up when I'd caused trouble. I was uncertain of how much to share. "It was a misunderstanding."

"She made a deal," Sam guessed.

I couldn't deny it. Even if the truth left a bitter taste in the back of my mouth. "Yes. Only, he took her soul. I need to find the demon holding the deal."

Sam picked up two crystal glasses from his trophy wall. "What if you find the demon who took your friend's soul? What then?"

I felt my brows draw together. God, what then? I had no freaking idea.

"I…"

His cold, blue gaze met mine. "You haven't thought that far."

I hadn't.

I crossed my arms over my chest. "I was hoping to ask him to end the deal. Undo it or whatever."

Sam chuckled loudly. The jerk even wiped a tear from the corner of his eyes. I gritted my teeth hard enough to chip them.

Gathering my dusty pride scattered all over the floor, I turned on my heels, heading straight for the exit. I blinked, and Sam stood in front of me. His nose brushed mine, and his big hand cupped the back of my neck.

"Do you realize how foolish that would have been?" His breath brushed my mouth, and my brain stopped functioning properly, overridden by my hormones. "Demons have powers. Some very awful ones. Some can control your mind. Others are invisible and much, much worse." I knew all that, but I was desperate. "And demons don't undo deals. They can't.

Only a few high-ranking ones can, and trust me, they don't."

"So all I have to do is ask a higher demon?" I'd read about summonings somewhere.

Sam suddenly let go of me, taking a step back. "That wouldn't be very wise, Nyssa. It's as good as a death wish."

Sam swiped my phone out of my hand and typed in something. I heard a ring, and he took out his phone and silenced it.

"You have my number now. I know a lot of demons. I'll ask around about your friend. See who made the deal and if the terms could be lightened. That's the best anyone can do for her."

I threw my arms around him impulsively. "Thank you!"

He froze under my hug. "Don't thank me yet. I haven't done anything."

I nodded, backing up to my spot, embarrassed. And then I thought of one thing. "How do you know a lot of demons? I thought they just started showing up."

Sam's smile didn't reach his eyes. He wore it with arrogance. "Says who?"

Right, says who?

"Text me your friend's full name." He continued, "And please call me if you find anything?"

"Why?"

He shrugged. "I promised I'd help if you identified three demons. You did. I always uphold my promises. A man is only as good as his word." Strange to hear the saying from anyone other than Micah. "And despair often leads to bad choices, so call me." Sam handed me back my phone. "I took the liberty of ordering you an

Uber back home."

"Right. Thank you." My heart squeezed in my chest.

Possibly because I couldn't do more for Isabelle right now.

Probably because Sam was sending me home.

Sam escorted me down the elevator, but the same icy-blond demon, Nat, I thought, stopped us. He spoke in hushed tones to Sam, who asked me to wait for the Uber inside.

Unwittingly, Sam and his information had helped me much more than he knew.

I needed a high-ranked demon to call off Isabelle's deal. I needed to find one, and I needed leverage. And I had a good idea where to hunt for answers to both problems.

The cold night welcomed me. Strangely, my shadows weren't there.

The black Fiat Uber stopped in front of Peccatta. At the same time, a Volvo turned the corner onto the street. How the hell did Micah know where to find me?

He parked his truck partially on the sidewalk, blocking my path to the Uber. My brother barrelled out of his truck, leaving his door open, and walked toward me with his deadliest glare. "Get in," he ordered in a barely contained snarl.

The young Uber driver got out.

"Miss?"

Micah's head snapped to him. "She's coming with me. Be on your way and charge the full fare."

The guy shuffled on the asphalt, reluctant. "I was ordered to make sure she gets home safe."

Well, thank you, Sam. The thought of Sam caring

enough to give those instructions triggered a weird twist in my stomach.

"Get. Lost," Micah said, stretching each word. I'd never seen my brother this menacing. I came to the poor driver's rescue.

"I'll be fine. Thank you." I hopped in Micah's car, hoping to avoid an escalation. He let it go and took his place behind the wheel.

"How did you know where I was?" I asked once he started driving away from the club.

Micah seethed in his seat, knuckles white on the wheel, totally ignoring my question.

Tough luck. I wasn't going to apologize for trying to help Isabelle.

The problem was, I couldn't have Micah upset at me right now. The plan I'd formed, thanks to Sam, wouldn't see daylight without my brother's help.

I placed my hand on top of Micah's hand, which was resting on the shifter, and squeezed lightly.

"I'm sorry I got you worried." I meant it. I didn't want him to be concerned about me. But if I had told him, he would have prevented me from going.

Micah intertwined our fingers together and gave a reassuring squeeze back. We always forgave each other quickly.

I twisted toward him, earning a wince from the pain shooting in my arm.

Micah side-eyed me. "You're in no condition to be out, Nyssa."

Tell me something I don't know.

"I overheard the council talking about Isabelle," I said. "They won't do anything to help. Father won't allow them."

A heavy sigh left him. "We can't get involved, Nyssa. She knew. She made her choice."

"To save a life!" I shouted.

Micah's mocking laugh filled the car, igniting my fragile fuse. "Yeah right. We're talking about Isabelle. It wasn't selfless, or she wouldn't be in that position. Trust me. She gained something in return."

I twisted to the window, taking deep breaths to tamp out an explosion. "You don't have to agree with what she did." I didn't either. "But I won't stand back and do nothing." My chin turned to my brother's profile. "So, you can either help me or let me be. Either way, I'm doing this."

He didn't answer me, and I didn't push it.

Until we got home.

The silence that followed us up our walk broke when Micah pushed open the door. "Tell me, what do you have in mind, Nys? What can you possibly do?" Thanks for pointing out my uselessness. "Tell me it's not completely irrational and dangerous, and maybe I'll consider it."

Of course, it was dangerous and irrational. My plan banked on me acting like I was made for the field, like Micah, when I was really the bookworm.

A bookworm without a library card to the one place I could research my strategy. I couldn't simply walk into Glory and borrow whatever I pleased.

Unfortunately.

I needed access to the forbidden backroom. Obviously, Father wouldn't have something as normal as a key to open a simple door. Nothing I could borrow either.

Why make my life easy?

Instead, you needed to speak a code into a microphone hidden inside some weird symbolic design on the door. A code Micah knew.

So I was prepared to go into full begging-sister mode while praying Micah could be trusted not to run his mouth to Father.

When it mattered, he would stand beside me. It was, and always would be, him and me against the world.

"It might be a little irrational to attempt on my own, but with you, it'll work."

As if reading my mind, Micah warned me, "As long as it doesn't include anything with Glory or demons."

Damn him!

I threw my hands up in the air, forgetting about my injury and regretting it in the same second. "Of course you'd say that." I faced him, my fingers wrapped around my shoulder. My eyes welled up. Not sure if it was from emotions or my physical condition. "Listen to me, just this once. I need you to trust me." I took his big hand in mine. "Please. I need you. All I ask is for the codey thing on the door at Glory. I need ten minutes max with the books. I won't take anything, I swear. I just want a spell to locate Isabelle." I patted his knuckles to better plead my case. "And you need to keep quiet about it."

Not an easy ask. Micah didn't hide anything from Gavriel. Strange behavior for a twenty-five-year-old, but Micah carried a blind trust for his father like a torch. Not that Gavriel ever earned that kind of devotion, but what did I know? I wasn't exactly part of the private circle.

My brother passed a hand down his face. "Nyssa, you shouldn't get involved in demon business. If we don't hear from her in a day or two, we'll meet again."

I groaned, annoyed. "We're talking about my friend. My *only* friend. The one who would jump through fire for me. I will not stand back and do nothing," I said, one fist clenched at my side. I wasn't backing down on this one. "All I'm asking is for you to be quiet about it. I need time to find Isabelle."

"And the code to the door."

I inhaled patience. "Yes. Please, Micah, I need you."

I stared into my brother's baby blues, fully aware I wasn't going to win this one. He clenched his jaw so tightly that his muscles twitched.

"Fine. I'll figure it out on my own." I turned on my heel and ran up the stairs two at a time. I slammed the door behind me and threw myself onto my bed.

If my brother didn't want to help, I'd figure out another way.

Chapter 10

The other way meant one option. Taking my phone, I swiped the screen up. My contact list was limited enough that I easily found Sam's name.

My fingers hesitantly hung in space on the dial button for a moment. We had just met, but what other option did I have? I opted for a text.

Yeah, much easier for someone like me.

—Hi.—

Anxiously, I waited for what felt like an eternity as the three gray dots flickered at the bottom of my screen, my insides twisted in knots. After twenty long seconds, the dots continued their ominous dance, teasing my nerves.

—Hi.—

Much too long for a simple hi.

—What you up to?—

—Not much. Why?—

I rolled my eyes.

—Why does it have to be for a reason? Can't I just be wondering what you're up to?—

—You were here like an hour ago, so…no?—

My gaze shifted to my seashell light hanging from the ceiling, casting a gentle, ambient glow in the room, before I replied.

—Fine. You still want to help?—

—I've already started asking. I should have

something conclusive very soon. Till then, I suggest you hang on tight.—

—I can't.— My fingers typed fast before my courage vanished. —I need you. For something bad. Sort of illegal.—

I pressed send. Oh lord, maybe I shouldn't have sent it as a text message. Was I leaving clues already? Criminal life really wasn't for me.

—Ohh…You came knocking at the right door, precious. Exactly my type of mission. Where do I meet you?—

My stupid heart somersaulted inside my chest.

Before I could answer, Micah barged into the room. A determined expression on his face.

He leaned his massive body against the door.

I arched a brow, waiting for him to speak.

"Gavriel will be busy all evening. We can go tonight." And I jumped on my feet, grabbed my bag, threw my phone in and I was ready to go when Micah pushed himself off the white frame and stood in my way. "Listen carefully, Nyssa, I'll get the door open. You're going to find the spell to locate Isabelle, where you'll have a maximum of five minutes to do. If you don't find it. You *will* leave it be. Are we clear, Nyss?"

I knew what he was asking.

"And let's pretend you do find a way to locate her, you won't go without me." He continued. "You won't push it and put yourself in unnecessary danger, promise? Those are my conditions, and they aren't negotiable."

I rolled my eyes. "I'm not ten anymore, Micah!"

He crossed his arms on his chest, brows arching. "Still haven't changed much since. You're careless when you want something. I could name many occasions."

I narrowed my eyes on him, biting my tongue. "I. Am. Not."

He tapped his mouth with a finger. "Let's see, the time I hid all the cookies in the tree house and pulled the latter up so you couldn't come in and eat all of the supplies. What did you do?" He didn't give me a second and he continued. "You found a stick and attached a hammer to the edge. Being the smart kid you used to be and obviously still are, you smashed the hammer on the wood sticks holding the structure and destroyed the tree house. While I was in it, if I may add. Almost making it crumble on you. You just turned eight."

"But you took all the cookies!"

"See! That's exactly what I mean." He was shaking his finger at my face. "It amazes me how someone as good as you are can have such a strong will."

"What can I say, I'm a girl of many attributes." I tried joking. Micha's lips stayed in a straight line.

I put my hands up in front of me. "Fine, I promise that if I can't find something to locate Isabelle, I won't go looking for her."

"And if you do, will you take me along for the ride?"

"Yes. I promise."

He stared at me for a while. With a heavy sigh, he exited my room. I quickly followed suit, hastily slipping on my shoes and jacket before we both went in his car.

My bag kept vibrating. I searched and picked up my phone.

—Send me the location.—
—Hello?—
—Just so you know, I've never been ignored in my life, and I find it extremely frustrating. Especially after your last message.—
—Nyssa...I don't find you funny. I will turn on find my friend on your phone to stalk you whenever I please or when you pull things like this, if necessary.—
—Nyssa! You're making me become my worst nightmare.—

All those from Sam in the span of nine minutes. Surely, he never got a taste of what he probably did to a hundred girls.

—So I'm already on your friend list?— I replied.

The gray dots appeared. —A point we have to work on it seems. Friends answer each other's messages. Are you all right?—

—Yes. Sorry. I'm fine. My plan A came back to life. I GTG. TTYL.—

—Plan A...Are you telling me I was only plan B? I'm hurt.—

A laugh shook my body.

"What's funny? Who are you texting, Nyss?" Micah's voice brought me back from this back and forth. I shoved my phone into my sweater pocket.

"Someone from school about a project. No worries."

My brother stayed silent, but I didn't fool him one bit. Not about the phone, anyway. "And don't think I forgot you went to Peccatta. Want to tell me what that was about?" Micah asked, parking the car in the back of the shop.

I wasn't getting out of that one and we had no time

to waste. "Isabelle said that's where she met him. I thought I could maybe find him there."

I heard him hold his breath.

"Not one of my finest ideas, I know." Sam and I went through this already.

I got out of the car, shoved the door, and went to the store.

"I'm happy you realize it," my brother said.

I twisted to him. "How about you tell me how did *you* know I was there?"

"I know everything, Nyssa."

That's not an answer but I dropped it. For now. Or else, he might just change his mind about opening that door if we start arguing.

When we walked inside the store, Micah gestured for me to leave the light closed. In case I presumed.

"One more thing." My brother told me.

"What?"

"Once you get in, you do not touch anything other than books. Got it?"

"Are the items from higher beings?" The ones who can kill or make you lose your mind.

Micah passed a hand on his face. "Yes. Some dangerous ones. Don't touch anything. Books only. Okay?"

"Yeah."

My brother walked to my forbidden entrance and shut his eyes. He pressed both palms on the door and started chanting in an ancient language.

Probably one his father taught him. I hadn't gotten the honor of such knowledge. Not yet.

But I will.

Once I finished first in class with the diploma,

Father would have to admit I was just as good, if not better, than his group.

Smarter. Sharper. More knowledgeable.

Where Micah's hand rested, a strange golden light appeared, and started slowly rotating until it formed a shape that resembled a sword, or so it seemed. Intrigue, I squinted my eyes and stepped closer to examine the peculiar manifestation.

On each side, half of a wing and half of a heart flanked the sword. The sight was beautiful. Suddenly, with a loud click, the door magically opened.

"Hurry, Nyss." Micah rushed me. "Do not touch anything other than the books. I'll watch the door. Hurry." He didn't have to repeat. Heard him the first few times.

'I ran in. There was no time to stop and be astonished by the sight beyond, but that's exactly what happened. Nothing could have prepared me for this. Items were shining from all corners.

Singing to me. Almost hypnotizing me to go explore them.

Touch them.

Analyze them.

Connect with them in some way.

My feet took me to a shining bow emitting a mixture of bright white and blue light. It stood on its own, slightly above the ground. Next to it were arrows, seemingly suspended in mid-air too. As if they were floating weightlessly in space.

My right hand lifted when I felt *them*. Only for a brief second, but enough to snap me out of my trance.

What in the world was this? Was it what the ancient book from Egypt referred to as the Call of

Angels? I didn't linger on it.

Instead, I ran to the bookshelves and started searching for titles. I wasn't looking for some silly spell to locate Isabelle because even though I was dying to know where she was and if she was fine, it wouldn't free her from her contract.

Unknowingly, Sam guided me to the only way possible to save her.

What I truly needed was someone strong enough to unbind her. Someone who could control a demon. I was thorough in my research. Who better than the one they answered to? A high-ranked demon meant little to me.

I scattered through titles as fast as humanly possible. As if an invisible hourglass sand clock was on, which technically it was. Most books were written in old, forgotten languages. A few were in Latin. Those were the ones I was seeking since they were the only ones I could read.

I picked up a Latin book. "King of Hell." Here we go.

He was the one in charge of the demons. From what I had gathered over the years, if one summoned a demon, as long as he was kept in a demon trap, he wouldn't be able to escape or do anything to harm the summoner. Once the offering was paid, he'd vanish back to wherever he came from.

A paragraph gained my attention. One that had nothing to do with the summon but the Devil's interest in an object he lost a long time ago. One he'd supposedly move heaven, hell and earth to recover. He had tried for centuries without any success.

"Nyssa, one minute," Micah called out from the other side.

Crap.

Quickly going through the pages, I tried to locate the solution. *Voila!* Got it. I ripped the pages I needed, hoping it'd be enough, folded it in four, and shoved it in my bra. I'll be in so much trouble the moment my father discovered the missing pages, but that was an issue for another day. One I'd never hear the end of.'

I ran to the door a second before Micah shut it closed. A bright golden light with a shining ember hovered before disappearing.

Chapter 11

We got home in record time.

"I'm really sorry, Nys. I understand why you wanted this. I know your heart is in the right place, but this goes beyond us. Now you leave it be, Nyssa. You don't go looking for her. Okay?" The implied finality irked me to no end.

"Yes, I get it." A deal was a deal, and a man is only as good as his word. Or a woman, in my case. Of course, I had a loophole. I didn't plan to go looking for *Isabelle*.

"But I do want you to update me on the new meeting. Promise?"

"Good girl."

"You'll tell me," I persisted.

"Yes, I promise." He scratched the back of his head. "Now that you mention it, I've got a meeting to go—"

"What?" I interrupted. "I thought they'd put the issue to rest for a couple of days?"

"Yeah, me too. Seems like something came up."

Yes, my unwelcome interest. I was almost certain of it.

"What came up? Did they find Isabelle?" I pestered him with my concerns, keeping my other doubts at bay.

Micah shook his head. "No, there's still no sign of her. I'm not sure what it's about. Father doesn't talk about those things over the phone."

Of course not. Father had way too much to hide, and he was paranoid about technology. Not the type of man to evolve with the rest of humanity.

"Promise me as soon as you find out anything, you'll keep me posted."

His light eyes found me. "I will. And you stay home, all right?"

Yeah, right.

"I'll lock you in your room if I can't trust you."

No, he wouldn't.

"Don't worry. I won't look for Isabelle. I gave you my word, and I intend on keeping it." The one strength our sham of a family possessed? We didn't make promises we couldn't keep. Even Father. That didn't mean we didn't play around with the words we used. Quite the contrary. We were all experts at manipulation.

Micah's shoulders relaxed, and the tension in his jaw loosened. He gave me a half smile. "Be good."

Oh, I planned on being really bad, actually.

Absolutely reckless and irresponsible.

Very unlike me.

I waited until I heard the front door shut and his engine roar out of the driveway.

Perfect. Pulling my shirt open, I grabbed the stolen papers secured in my bra. More like borrowed. I planned on returning the sheets if the opportunity ever presented itself.

I sat on my carpet, unfolding the papers with care. Latin was my favorite ancient language. Easy to learn. Similar to Italian.

The first thing one needs to do is build up the energy in your astral body, the first line read.

Oh great. Who had time for this?

While there are many ways to do so, the preferred methods are as follows:

—For a period of seventy-two hours before the ritual, fasting the body on nothing saves water.

—Preserve your sexual energy by practicing abstinence for a minimum of seven days before the ritual.

Perfect, being a virgin came in handy in this case.

The list of ingredients was simple enough for me considering they were mostly things I had access to at Glory.

As long as I didn't go in the locked room, Father didn't care about me popping by to get some work done whenever. I could always tell him I forgot my homework or a book.

—Dark ashes
—Six black candles and one red candle
—Dagger
—Clothed fully in black
—A bone
—Wax to draw a protective circle and pentagram on the floor
—Two incenses
—Blood

I almost shouted a victory cry. Most of these items were available in my own basement. I wouldn't even need to go to the shop. Only the bone had me worried for a moment. Grabbing my backpack, I emptied it on my bed and went down to gather the stuff. There were no bones in the trash but...I did have a tribal necklace that Micah got back from a trip to Congo. I could only hope it'd do the job.

The second I stepped outside, the silent night came to life. Like children reunited with their mother after a long time apart, my Shadows danced erratically around me. For a second, I wondered if they could sense my apprehension. Or if they could sense what I was about to do was wrong. And dangerous. And stupid.

I found myself doing what I've never thought I would do in my life. Summoning a demon. And not any demon—the most powerful one of all—the king of Hell. My knowledge on the matter wasn't as expansive as I'd have liked, but more than most, I'd assume.

Given my upbringing, one might assume that I'd always been aware of the presence of demons and other creatures roaming the earth. But I had never given it much thought as a real, tangible fact until this week. If the cult took such things as more than ancient history or religious symbolism, they never let it show. To me.

The idea of encountering a demon had never crossed my mind before one strolled into Glory.

I still had a hard time digesting what Isabelle had done, how she'd wound up with a demon's seal burned into her wrist. And it was now up to me to figure out a way to change her fate. Somehow.

For her, I'd awaken the wickedest of all evil.

One powerful enough to dissolve Isabelle's contract. I didn't have a choice. Hell was a place of madness and torment for eternity. To leave Isabelle there…I couldn't. It wasn't fair. Isabelle didn't have a condemnable soul. She hadn't killed or harmed anyone.

This wasn't my expertise. My interest in the domain wasn't for the dark arts and demonic temptations.

It was about the objects and their secrets. It was

about fitting in, following the family legacy.

My late mother had imparted the importance of recognizing good and bad. She cautioned me against excessive greed and encouraged me to appreciate what I had. If I wasn't satisfied, I had to work to fetch more.

While the easy way might seem tempting, the momentary release of a burden would never be worth the price you pay for it. There were other ways.

Her compulsion to repeat such admonishments got me wondering, now, if she'd known more. If she'd known about this hidden world.

Maybe one day, I'd gather the courage to ask Gavriel about my mother's involvement with his sect.

I picked up my pace, pulled up my hood, and crossed the street. At this hour, the park was empty. I walked through the forest leading to the water. On the edge of the trees, I sat between the river and the woods.

Thanking my lucky star the wind was asleep, I started emptying my bag.

First, I lit the six big onyx candles. I took out a bowl and poured the fireplace ashes in it and set it aside.

Then I lit the vanilla incense, praying it was good enough. I picked up a candle with my shaky hands and made a protective circle big enough for a few people. I finished with the star inside.

As per the book, the Devil was to appear in the pentagram in the middle of the circle, and I must stay within the outer circle to remain safe before banishing him. No harm could come to me if I followed that rule.

Very comforting.

I also needed an offering for when the demon showed. In other words, I'd have to give him blood.

That was the purpose of the dagger at my feet. And to reassure me, in case the whole thing went wrong. Not that I possessed any sort of skills to use it.

Steeling myself, I laid my tribal necklace in the bowl. Then, I grabbed the dagger and pierced the tip of my finger, letting drops fall on the bone.

I inhaled, preparing for the next step—reading the ancient text.

I started chanting in Latin.

The air crackled like static, startling me. I paused for a moment, scanning the area. Nothing. At least nothing visible to the naked eye.

On edge, I read quicker, repeating the last paragraph over and over as indicated.

Until the dim light of the lampposts trailing the park path to the distant road suddenly went out all at once.

I shivered, tugging my jacket closer to my body, although tonight's chill had no bite. The tiny hairs on the back of my neck stood straighter than a porcupine's quills. I managed to stand, despite my shaky legs.

"I know you're here," I whispered, feeling a cold wind kiss my nape.

Raw fear gripped me. Gathering some scrap of courage, I slowly turned my body, taking cautious steps. The circle was empty.

My mind was playing tricks on me.

My shoulders slumped. In relief or defeat. I wasn't sure anymore.

The reality hit me. I had failed. Isabelle must be somewhere terrified, and I was powerless to save her.

I picked up my bag, fighting the lump growing in my throat. I started gathering the stuff on the grass.

It had been silly to think I could accomplish this on my own. I walked toward the first candle, ready to go to my father and grovel, when all my candles blew out in one gust, leaving me with nothing but the dim light of the stars. I'd never feared the dark.

Until now.

What once was a friend had turned on me, teeth bared.

Maybe the absence of my Shadows added to my discomfort. Perhaps it was simply because the Devil lurked nearby. I turned another frantic half-circle.

I sensed a presence and thought I saw a darkness blacker than the night, obscured in the bushes. Too sturdy to be my ever-swirling Shadow friends.

The wind, which had been nonexistent minutes ago, kicked up a fuss, blowing my hair back. My nape bristled again, warning me of the approaching threat.

"Show yourself," I ordered, squinting into the night. My voice remained low and steady. Demons feed on fear and I wasn't looking to be anyone's meal.

Why hadn't he appeared inside the wax symbol?

"It has been a very long time since I was last summoned," said a voice behind me…coming from the pentagram. "I can't even recall." It wasn't the rough growl I had expected. It wasn't dangerous or frightening.

It was…inviting.

Charming even.

Softer than the fresh wind on my skin. Warmer than the summer sun.

Without even facing him yet, I knew trouble had found me. A danger I'd be lucky to escape whole.

I took my time to turn and face him. Whether it

was to mentally prepare myself for my demand or for seeing him, that'd remain a mystery.

I was startled to find two blue eyes staring right at me, barely an inch from my face. Just like that, my fake courage vanished, and a scream escaped me as I stumbled back and fell right on my bum. Quickly backing up with my feet until I reached the edge of the line, I hurriedly stepped out.

I reassured myself that I had trapped him within the pentagram.

"I knew you were up to no good." My eyes narrowed as the implications of a past relationship rattled me to my bones. Had I not been this frightened, I would have placed him already. But in heavy darkness, his features smeared. All save the midnight blue tint of his eyes. They shone bright in the night.

Almost...glowing.

Then he advanced, coming toward the lowest point of the star. The moonlight shone upon him for a second, revealing his unforgettable beauty. His scent attacked my senses, a mix of wildfire and fresh wind.

My already pounding heart took off speeding, its revving pace resonating in my eardrums.

"You."

Chapter 12

Sam tilted his head, curious eyes roaming my body.

"I must say, I didn't think you had it in you to do something this…foolish." In two big strides, he closed the distance between us, separated by the thin wax point of the pentagram. "Being wrong is a new experience for me. It's very unpleasant. On rare occasions, someone's managed to surprise me, but that hasn't happened in, oh"—he tapped his chin—"a thousand years."

I nearly thanked him for the unexpected compliment.

I mean, it was a compliment. Right?

Not like I could ask the Devil. He might get offended.

Or not. Afterall, wasn't he the same Sam who wanted to help me? Who'd gained my trust in one evening? Me, the girl who kept everyone away.

He waited with penetrating calm, standing in all his splendor, far too close to me. My breath caught in my throat. Not at all what I'd pictured when I prepared for this summoning. Sam seemed the furthest thing from demonic. If anything, he was…angelic.

Powerless not to stare at Sam's flawless face, a rush of desire washed over me.

Right then, I understood why people damned their soul into his care. Maybe just to please him. Or to have him acknowledge them even for an instant. Sam's tousled curls cascaded down his chiseled jawline. I ached to pass my hand through them. To scrape their softness through my fingertips. My gaze shifted to his.

And the Devil smiled. A devilish smile. Almost as if he were reading my mind and pleased with my thoughts.

Instinct urged me to take a step back.

I didn't. It wasn't time for weakness. I stood my ground despite the icy tendrils of fear creeping down my spine. I lifted my chin a little higher in a meek attempt to prove I wasn't intimidated.

"Then let me return the compliment. I never expected *you* to appear before me." I crossed my arms on my chest, trying to hide the shiver running through me. "The book said I was summoning the ruler of Hell."

The wind blew harder, pushing back my hair as if nature herself were begging me to retreat and reconsider.

My mind struggled to reconcile the impossible truth and searched for a more logical solution that wouldn't make him my enemy. Maybe because when I stared into Sam's eyes, I saw the deep blue of a warm night, not a soulless black pit.

But he owned a club infested with demons. He knew more about them than anyone I knew, aside from Gavriel. His silence rattled my nerves.

"You aren't a demon," I said, hopeful. "Your eyes. They're blue."

Was I so desperate for a connection that I'd ignored the signs? Or was I that interested in him in particular? Of course, the only guy to ever capture my interest would turn out to be a demon.

"I'm special, precious. My fellows recognize me by my essence. I lack the attributes of lower demons. Easier to tempt the wayward that way." His words struck me harder than expected, knocking me back a step. The disappointment hit home in my ribs.

"You've fooled me."

His brows pinched together. "No, Nyssa. I didn't. Everything I've said to you was the truth. From the second we met."

A nervous giggle left me. "And I'm supposed to believe you? A demon? *The* demon?"

Sam's fist clenched at his side. "You obviously don't know much about me. I. Do. Not. Lie. I plan on finding out who bargained with your friend like I promised."

"Why? It's not like we had a real bargain." Not in the regular demon world anyway.

He was silent for a minute, holding my nerves by a thread. "Besides the fact that I vowed to do so at my club?" Sam asked, as if I'd forgotten. "It's my duty to locate him. If your friend is half as pure as you are, no demon would be free to take her soul. There are rules. Especially surrounding damnation and surrendering a soul."

"Rules?" I echoed. I'd never heard of rules, and I knew more than most. Demon deals never favored humans. They sought only to benefit themselves, leaving their victims in the dark and helpless. How many innocents had been deceived by their false promises? How many had suffered because of their greed?

I expected their king to be the same, if not worse.

Only this king wore the face of someone I had just met and yet considered a friend.

"Yes. Rules," he replied, sliding his hands into his coat pockets. "Why did you summon me, though? I'm curious."

I gestured to him in exasperation. "I didn't know I was summoning *you* specifically. As in Sam. My rescuer from Peccatta."

He arched a brow. "Rescuer?" His lips stretched into a grin. "I like that. A lot. Very suiting."

I shot him a glare. "So not the point. I was expecting a demon with horns, red skin, and a tail or whatever. Not you."

Sam threw his head back and laughed. "You've been watching too much television. I'm genuinely interested."

I huffed. "I don't watch TV." As if I had time between the store, university, and this new demon invasion.

He tipped his head to the side with an incredulous stare. "What are you talking about? Everyone in this world watches TV. It's one of humanity's greatest inventions for passing time on earth."

"I don't." Actually, I did whenever I stayed at Isabelle's. She was a Netflix fan.

Sam's eyes widened. "What do you do then?"

"Cultural things."

"So, boring stuff?"

"Educational stuff. Mature stuff. Responsible stuff."

He smirked. "Yes, I was merely summarizing. Boring stuff."

I pulled at my scalp. "Coming from a demon, I'll

take that as a compliment."

"Hmm. Debatable."

"Aren't you going to ask about my demand?" We needed to move onto a more constructive path. Although, he'd gotten me curious about a few things. Isabelle's words echoed in my head: *The word is, their master's climbed free from the underworld.*

Had Sam been locked down? What changed?

His smile vanished. "I already know what you want, and the answer is no."

Of course, he knew. He'd given me the idea.

"I want to make a deal."

Sam soured. "My answer stays the same."

"Fine, if you won't do it then I'll summon another higher demon who will."

Sam looked like he'd swallowed a handful of needles as he coughed dramatically. "Are you threatening me?"

No one was stupid enough to threaten the Devil. I was certainly no exception. "No?" I mean, it wasn't a threat, it was a fact. "I just…want to make a deal," I repeated, nervously tangling my hands together.

"Really?"

I answered in a breath, "Really."

"You could have summoned a regular demon for a deal. That's what they're here for. Most don't dare ask me for anything. They want to give me things. Willingly." He took another step, crossing my lines as if the trap didn't exist.

My mouth dropped open.

"You weren't supposed to be able to cross into the circle," I said, my breathing accelerating.

Sam wore a smug smirk. "If you want to cage me,

you'll need a much stronger trap. This one may have held a regular demon. Not me."

Gosh, I was probably missing important pages. If only I'd had more time in the back room...

"I already told you. I'm not a regular demon, precious," he taunted, closing the distance until there was no space left. The warmth of his body chased the cold away. Sam cocked his head, studying me. "Why summon *me*?"

Something in my gut told me he was more interested in how I'd performed it.

I inhaled.

A mistake. A big mistake. His scent was addictive. A mix between hellfire and heaven. Not like I'd smelled either. Yet, I wanted to wrap myself in the scent and let it consume me. Let it devour me whole until there was nothing left but my burning desire.

I mentally gave myself a good slap. It wasn't time to daydream about the most menacing creature roaming the earth—who happened to be Sam.

"You know why. You basically gave me the idea."

He seemed lost.

"Remember? I need a high-rank demon to undo a deal. So, I summoned the Devil because you're the highest in the food chain. You must be powerful enough to reverse a deal." I hoped to flatter his ego before cutting straight to the chase.

The blue of his eyes darkened. His stance went rigid. "Deals aren't made to be broken," he said in a voice colder than ice buried under the glacial winter of the north.

Most would cower away. God knew I wanted to. The thought of Isabelle rooted my feet to the soil. "I understand. But you could if you wanted to."

"And here I thought you simply preferred my presence to one of my soldiers." His sigh swirled melodrama with amusement.

So, the Devil was bipolar. How comforting? I ignored his shifting mood.

"You really didn't expect me to be the one to show?" he asked, head cocked.

I threw my hands up in the air and winced. I held my shoulder and cursed in my head.

"You want to be careful with that," Sam said.

"I'm not that stupid," I growled, ignoring his play at concern. "If I'd known who you were, don't you think I would have sent a text message instead of setting up this whole summoning circle?"

"Hmmm. Good point."

Sam had no idea what I went through to get the book pages or that I'd be dead the instant Father found out I'd ripped apart one of his priceless items.

Taking courage, I attempted to explain my current situation better. "Isabelle was tricked into—"

His finger went to my lips, cutting my words short. I should have been insulted, but my brain went fuzzy at his scorching hot touch against my mouth, clouding my mind with other stuff. Inappropriate stuff.

I shouldn't have been surprised. Afterall, if the stories held the slightest truth, he seduced humans into sin and falsehood. I totally got how.

A metallic taste tickled my taste buds. I wondered if that was the taste of his skin.

"There are' no tricks," he rasped. "Demons aren't allowed to lie to a business partner. It's forbidden." I'd read that but didn't think it'd be true. "Your friend

Isabelle knew the exact cost of her demands. I will make sure her reasons were selfless like you claim, but don't come here spreading rumors about something you know nothing of."

Great, now I *had* offended the Devil.

Fantastic!

He removed his hand, almost reluctantly.

"I didn't mean—"

"Don't lie. We taste the lies. Demons feed off them as much as fear," Sam advised as if he cared. "Were you there when the bargain took place?"

"No."

"Then you know one version. Your friend's. Remember, there's always three sides to a story." He paused, watching me. "Her side, his side, and of course, the truth."

The Devil's words of wisdom.

"Perhaps that's true. But I guarantee she didn't fully understand the implications of her deal," I said, thinking back to her description of the night, floating on air, intoxicated as if by a supernatural power. "She wouldn't have gone along otherwise."

His gaze locked on me, almost like he was searching within me.

"What are you willing to give for this bargain to disappear?" he whispered slowly, his stare holding me captive.

I didn't hesitate. "Anything."

There it was again; his eyes tinted a dangerous onyx and his anger was palpable, as if I hadn't responded the way he had hoped.

"Revealing there's no limit you wouldn't reach. Nothing you wouldn't give. You just showed your hand, your weakness, to a demon. That's the biggest mistake you could have ever made."

My brows pulled together. "Yes, but you aren't any demon. You're the Devil." And my friend.

Oh Lord. We'd met last night, and already, I was acting like clingy Caroline.

"Which makes it even worse. My price is higher. My demands, wider. My greed, stronger."

That's not how it felt. A sense of familiarity whispered otherwise.

"You said you were going to help me," I reminded him.

He passed a hand down his face. "And I am already doing that. You're the one who cheated in hopes of making a deal to save your friend. No one is that honorable."

Honorable seemed a strong word. "I guess you're wrong, 'cause here I am."

He slowly nodded. "Yes, here you are. You've made a mistake trying to bypass me and conduct a summoning. Now it'll cost you." My heart jumped at his words. He still studied me. "Are you afraid?" Sam asked, as if he'd felt my pulse buzzing erratically.

"No," I murmured, taking a step back.

Sam took one closer. "Liar."

Leaning to bring his mouth to my ear, he whispered, "I'm feeling charitable, so I'll give you a chance to take it back. Ponder whether your friend truly deserves such a sacrifice. If the roles were reversed, would she do the same for you?"

My voice trickled out. "I'm not doing it because I'm looking to gain something. If the roles were reversed, I wouldn't want her to do what I'm doing. I'm neither blind nor foolish."

He sniffed my neck. My head moved slightly to the side, granting Sam access to my body's own accord.

"You smell different." Sam's hand gently went to rest on my hip, knotting my stomach.

My body almost arched toward him. "In a good way, I presume?" I found myself answering.

I felt his lips stretch against my collarbone. "For someone who can see harbingers of death, you smell…of life. You almost remind me of…"

"Of what?"

"Heaven," Sam whispered, threatening to buckle my knees. "You should be flattered," he continued, inching away, making me exhale the breath I hadn't realized I was holding. "Sadly, there's nothing in it for me. Charity isn't one of my many traits, unfortunately for you."

My mind cleared. "I offered you a deal," I replied in a barely contained tone.

"Not interested."

I had hoped to supplicate him with a bargain. Now I had to manipulate him into one. And I didn't like it. Not one bit. Even less knowing him as Sam first.

"I hear you're looking for an object you lost many lifetimes ago." I held my breath, dangling the bait.

His mask did not crack one bit. Maybe the book was wrong.

"What may that be?"

That was the real tricky part. I had no clue what the object was. God, I wasn't even sure it existed. All I knew was that he had supposedly searched every corner of the earth for it.

Sam didn't wait for my reply. "Don't bother

yourself with it." He withdrew. "I'll see you soon, Nyssa." My name rolled off his tongue. He savored it, enjoyed it.

"I'm willing to make a bargain for the object." I spoke as if I already possessed the item.

He gave me a lopsided smile. "You aren't making any deals, precious. You're lucky enough to get free help. Take it."

But he wouldn't break Isabelle's contract.

"Sam I–" His finger pressed against my lips.

"Don't, Nyssa. I'll forget about tonight's incident. I'll come find you tomorrow once I know more." All my brain understood was the tremor brought on by his finger against my lips.

"I don't recall agreeing to meet you."

"I don't need you to agree. I was informing you."

"I may avoid your calls."

He chuckled, putting his nose back to my neck for an instant. "I could never refuse a challenge." His lips nipped my earlobe. My insides tangled. "Just so you know, you can never escape me now that I've found you, even if you wanted to."

Was that a promise or a threat? Before I could utter a word, he turned to the street. The lights came back on.

"Oh, before I forget. What are you planning on giving me?"

I was lost for a second. "Giving you?".

"Yes. When you summon the Devil, you need to have…what's the appropriate word?" He feigned searching his memory bank. "Yes, an offering."

Oh crap. Oh crap. Double crap on a crabcake.

I had forgotten for a moment.

To offer blood to a demon I'd never met was

stressful but achievable.

To offer blood to Sam...Sweet Lord. The thought heated my blood to lava.

Sam's smile reached new heights as if aware of my inner debate.

The jerk.

"Since you lied about who you were, how about we call it even?" I dared to say.

"Like I've said, I never lied."

"You've omitted, which is the same as lying." Then a loophole occurred to me, putting the confidence back in my stance. "Besides, you weren't trapped in the circle."

Sam arched a brow. "And?"

"And you don't need the offering. Isn't the offering to free the demon from the circle?" And to keep the summoner safe from harm.

He took a step so closer to me, his nose brushing mine. "It is. But you still owe me one. I haven't harmed you. Have I?" Dammit! I couldn't catch a break.

"I won't take your blood." The pressure dissolved a fraction in my chest. *Here's to small favors.* "You should never offer it to anyone. Ever. It's more precious than humans realize."

"Thank you." Still, he remained way too close for my nerves to settle.

"With pleasure, precious." He gave me a sly grin. "A kiss will do just fine."

I barely had time to process his words.

Process a clear thought.

Process an answer.

His lips had already brushed mine—surprisingly soft for the ruler of Hell. His mouth gave mine the barest caress, almost testing my reaction. Telling me without any words to take the lead if I had the desire to do so.

I became grounded to the earth like one of the restored light poles. I blamed it on the shock of my lips getting devirginized in a dark park late at night. Such a romantic picture. Only I was exchanging saliva with the Devil. Well, not saliva per se since he wasn't pushing it further and my brain had momentarily stopped functioning.

Before I had a chance to push him away or pull him to me, Sam stopped. He put enough distance for his gaze to meet mine. My heart jumped out of my chest.

"Can you drive me?" he asked, unbothered by the kiss. Probably business as usual for him. That had the effect of a bucket of ice. My hands curled into fists at my sides.

For the first time, I genuinely wanted to punch someone other than my brother. I followed Sam's lead, acting like it meant nothing. I should've been happy he offered me the opportunity to ignore whatever that was.

"I don't have a car." My brows furrowed. "Can't you just…poof into a place or something?"

Sam chuckled. "No, Nyssa. I can't physically poof anywhere unless I'm summoned. Although I could physically be somewhere while sneaking into other places in my mind."

As if to prove a point, his eyes clouded over, seeing another space or time instead of me.

"That's—"

"Impressive?" he suggested.

"Creepy."

He laughed again. "First time someone dared call

me a creep. At least to my face. So, can you order me an Uber? Seems like my phone didn't follow me for the ride. I'm actually surprised I'm clothed."

Oh Lord. As if I needed to picture him unclothed. Thanks a lot.

Chapter 13

Wasting time in a miserable attempt to find sleep didn't even cross my mind. Meeting the Devil didn't exactly put a person at ease. That was without adding the fact that his lips touched mine. Oh, and that the Devil is actually Sam.

The thought made my body shudder. Instead of letting the turbulent mix of emotions overwhelm me, I took a quick shower.

Then, I tried to do an online search for any valuable information about the Devil.

Pure crapshoot. The truly trustworthy manuscripts were vaulted up tighter than a bank. The code they used was impossible to replicate. There was no point in trying; I'd only waste time Isabelle didn't have. Asking Micah a second time wouldn't fly.

I threw my phone on my bed, fed up with the internet's wild stories. One suggested to sacrifice a virgin and drink her blood to have the Devil worship you, and that wasn't the craziest suggestion I found.

With a groan, I left my bedroom. To have all the necessary answers so close yet so far was maddening. A life hung on the line!

Sneaking into Father's secret trove a second time was as possible as Sam doing me and Isabelle any favors. Just thinking of her predicament twisted my insides.

My stomach grumbled. I couldn't recall the last time I'd eaten. As I rummaged through the fridge, I picked out a freshly pressed juice that Micah tended to prepare when he was home. I settled for toast to go with it.

After cleaning my dishes, I headed to the stairs to gather my school stuff when I noticed my father in the sunroom. He sat with his notepad in his lap but stood up the second he saw me.

"Nyssa. A word, please."

Not a good morning or a "How are you holding up?" or even "Be careful when going out."

I shouldn't be surprised.

It didn't lessen the disappointment that churned my stomach.

I bit the inside of my cheek to hold back an "At your service, captain."

His glare made me gulp. Hard. If I had to take a bet, I'd say Father was upset. Very upset. But the list of things I'd done lately could trail the floor. So which part had he uncovered? My blood pressure skyrocketed.

"Yes?"

"Sit." My father was a copy of Micah. He hardly looked over forty, and I hated to admit, he was a good-looking man on the outside. It must be a genetic thing.

Where was Micah? He always made these *talks* more bearable.

The outcome was inevitable. I'd get blamed for whatever had set Gavriel off—only this time I wasn't exactly innocent—then Micah would drum up excuses and calm his father. The same boring pattern.

And from the look in Gavriel's eyes, I needed my brother's help. My feet carried me to the forest green armchair opposite him, and I sat down in his looming shadow.

"You're grounded."

My head jerked back to meet his cold gaze. My heart skipped a few beats as my fingernails dug into each side of the armchair. "Excuse me?" I couldn't have heard right. The concept of grounding never existed in my house. No one cared enough about what I did.

"I will not repeat it."

I stood, my hands curling. "That's rich coming from you. Trying to act like a real father now, are you, Gavriel?" An arrogant chuckle left me. "I'm an adult. You can't tell me what to do." I folded my arms on my chest.

Gavriel's eyes, already cold, turned icy. I'd never behaved this way. Too busy trying to please him. He closed the short distance between us. "You will do as you're told, Nyssa."

Not that easily, though. I stood my ground. "I haven't done anything to deserve grounding."

Actually, I'd done plenty, but I prayed he wasn't aware of half of it.

His lips tightened into an even thinner line. A display of his irritation. "Lying is a sin, Nyssa."

I tried to keep eye contact. I had to keep the show going now. "I'm not lying."

Father's head cocked slightly to the side. "Very well, Nyssa." A small smile formed on his lips that filled me with dread. "Let's ask your brother, shall we?"

I swore I felt the room move around me. My determination slipped through my fingers as if they were coated in oil.

Micah had always tried to protect me, but it seemed he couldn't shake his habit of spilling his guts to his father. Maybe, just maybe, he could for something this important. Something he pinky swore to keep secret.

As if summoned by an invisible link, the sound of the front door stretched Gavriel's smile wider. Soon, his son walked in.

My gaze clashed with Micah's, begging him to side with me. I needed him. Yet, the way his piercing blue eyes avoided mine told me everything I needed to know.

Micah couldn't keep his mouth shut. He had already told Father about the store. About my fake plan to find Isabelle. The bitter taste of betrayal filled my mouth. I averted my eyes, unable to stand the sight of him. A knot formed in the pit of my stomach. My throat was so tight that even my saliva didn't pass through.

"Right on time, Micah. We were talking about why Nyssa has lost the privilege of doing as she pleases," Father said.

"I'm an adult," I still managed to say in a controlled tone.

My father's lips tightened in a thin line. "You surely don't act like one. You went to one of those sinner's dens."

I frowned, not getting it right away. I'd been too caught up in the store situation, and I had forgotten about my little outing. I glanced at Micah, and he gave a quick nod.

The weight lifted from my shoulders. The air in my lungs passed freely again. I had been quick to assume. This was the best-case scenario, considering...everything else.

"I was trying to find Isabelle," I told Gavriel.

"So, you acknowledge you've done something to warrant losing your privileges."

I threw my arms up. "No, I don't. At my age, everyone goes to nightclubs. I've done nothing wrong. I went out and looked for Isabelle, which is less than most girls my age do in places like that, for your information."

Not that he cared.

He clasped his wrist behind his back. "Who did you ask for authorization to wander around places created by evil?"

Oh God. The speech about sinners and God's expectations.

"I didn't realize anyone cared!" I shouted.

He never had. Never even bothered getting to know me.

"And I'm almost twenty years old, for crying out loud," I complained. He was old-fashioned to the extreme, as if he lived in another time. "Since you and your *colleagues* decided to abandon Isabelle, what other choice did I have? We can't leave her like this, Father." I tried to appeal to his good side. If he had one.

Father's clever eyes narrowed on me. "Isabelle got what she asked for, and that's the price to pay. You will not get involved. There are rules you can't even begin to comprehend." Rules like Sam mentioned? Gavriel's knowledge knew no boundaries. Why did no one tell me anything?

"If you wanted to, you could help her and her family."

He didn't deny it.

"We help those who deserve help."

"You help no one," I hissed through my teeth.

"Even when you have the power to."

Gavriel decided to ignore me. He considered the discussion closed. "You are not to leave this house."

My chin dipped. A part of me had been wired with the desire to please Gavriel ever since I could remember. To have him approve of me, my choices, and my achievements. To have him be proud enough to acknowledge me as his daughter.

Yet, another part of me, a growing part, wanted me to stand firm. Keep my chin up and defy him.

I landed on a middle ground. "What about school and the store?"

Gavriel's brows drew together. He hadn't thought that far yet. Of course, he wasn't a regular father figure. I was astonished he knew what "grounded" meant.

"Ah, yes, you've taken an extra interest in the store of late, haven't you?" Gavriel's smug smile and sudden glance Micah's way struck me down.

And I knew, he knew.

All thanks to my dear brother. I should have known better.

Micah came to my rescue, probably out of guilt. Not that I wanted the help of a traitor.

"Those aren't part of it. You will still go to school and work at the shop."

Gavriel's eyes swiveled to Micah. He seemed to consider it, but it didn't last more than a few seconds. Then I could see the disagreement in the way his jaw popped. Micah must have seen it too. He closed the gap between him and Father, his hand stuffed nonchalantly in his pockets.

"She still needs to pass her classes, and we need her for the store. Those are essentials. Everything else will be on the line. She comes directly home after." Micah shot me a stern look as he said, "No going out after sunset."

I bit the inside of my lips hard enough to taste copper. My fingernails lodged so deep into my palms, I broke the skin. I had to restrain myself from flipping Micah off and storming out of the room, but I needed that diploma and everything it represented.

Although, my motives surrounding completing my program had gone fuzzy recently. Maybe it was to prove to Gavriel that I could do what even Micah couldn't.

"That's settled," Gavriel finally agreed.

I wasn't happy. Far from.

I refused to look at Micah. Indifference always worked better against him than screaming. I turned the bitch switch down.

"Can I go?" I asked.

Gavriel nodded, and I rushed out, going to my room two stairs at a time.

"Nys, wait," Micah called when I reached the top.

I didn't bother turning. His steps drew closer. I almost ran to my bedroom. I tried to shut the door with as much force as I could, hoping to smash it in Micah's face, but he slid his foot into the frame.

Jerk.

"Nys, I didn't—"

"Save it. I don't care. Leave me alone." I rammed all my weight against the door.

He braced his hand on the other side. "C'mon, Nyssa Bear. I just want to talk for five minutes."

With a little scream, I mustered all my strength to keep him out, but with one effortless push from him, I ended up on my ass, hair in my face, and my shoulder throbbing.

The nerve of him.

"How dare you!" I fussed my hair away from my face, holding my pulsing shoulder and warding off all its horrifying reminders.

Micah shook his head and offered me a helping hand. I'd rather stay on the floor. "I didn't tell him about the store. With his code on the door, he just…knew."

"How? What? He has some kind of private alert?"

Why would Micah agree to open it, then?

"You have no idea how spot-on you are."

I barely acknowledged everything behind this simple sentence. "And the club?" I asked, standing on my own.

His chin dipped.

"Why do you tell him everything? At my expense." I pointed at my chest. "Don't we mean more to each other than that?" I had to ask because I was hurt and confused. "The only reason you pinky swore after I got stabbed is because you knew Isabelle's dad had already spilled everything to Gavriel. Or that he would sooner or later."

Micah had fooled me. Well, not exactly, but he'd played his cards like a pro.

A deep sigh escaped his lips. "You don't understand, Nyssa. I don't want to…I just. I have to."

"I have to," I mocked. "Thanks for showing me why I can't trust you." Gripping the handle, I held my bedroom door wide open. "Now get out."

It was evident he wanted to say more, but I wasn't in the state to listen. Micah hesitated. My anger ratcheted up a notch. "Get out before I say things I may regret and can never take back."

With another loud sigh, he walked out.

I shut the door behind him loud enough to shake the mirror on my wall. I sat on the bed as my phone vibrated. A positive distraction would be welcome.

My heart skipped a beat when I saw an email notification from the school. Oh God, I hoped it wasn't about that awful Professor Gerard and the humiliating incident with the painting.

Uncertain, I opened it. To my surprise, the email informed me that I had a new student to tutor. My list of students went from zero to one.

Finally, good news!

Extra credits, here I come.

I furrowed my brows at the name Altar Brilliant. It wasn't familiar.

Strange. I'd made it a point to know all the students in my program. The perfectionist in me demanded it. If you weren't the best, then who remembered you? I was already invisible enough. I wanted to leave a dent somewhere. What better place than the university, right?

Wait, 5 o'clock today? I checked my watch. Already 4:20. Did they think all tutors lived on campus or didn't have lives?

It was fine. I needed this. Since it was for school, the grounded rule didn't apply.

The house was dead silent when I reached the bottom of the stairs. I checked around the main floor. Everyone was gone. Great! Who would even check if I respected my punishment? Totally outside my father's expertise.

Anyhow, I got to school in record time. I made it to the library, only to find it empty. All students met their tutors here at the time of appointment. My student didn't show. Probably a prank from a privileged douchebag.

I was so over it. Only I had other things to do now.

I tightened my grip on my bag, ready to leave when I got an email notification from Mr. Brilliant. Talk about a name. His parents had proclaimed him excellent to the whole world.

Of course, he wanted to change the meeting location. It was sunny enough to have it outside.

Great. Just great. It might be sunny, but it was humid. I'd like to stay dry.

Extra credit, Nyssa, I repeated like a mantra. A minimum number of hours were required to collect, and I wasn't even close to the target.

Grinding my teeth, I retraced my steps to meet Mr. Wonderful outside. I wondered who his rich daddy was. He had to have one, making demands like a lowly tutor ought to just be grateful he was alive and breathing the same air.

As soon as I walked out, an icy cloud of humidity sank into my bones. I scanned the campus and noticed a guy sitting on one of the picnic tables. He gave me a small wave.

He was dressed entirely in black, including dark sunglasses, with his platinum hair pulled back. I took a deep breath to compose myself before walking toward him. I'd never seen him before in my classes. I'd remember someone with his stature and that bright, icy hair. Impossible to miss.

Yet, as I trudged over, I got an odd sense of

familiarity, like a different name was sitting on my tongue.

"Altar?" I asked when I was close enough.

His head fell back in a loud belly laugh.

I frowned.

"The one and only." My student flashed me a smile. His technique probably worked with a bunch of girls. I wasn't one of them. My interest in the other gender, or anyone really, had been nonexistent until very recently. Actually, since he happened to be the Devil, he didn't count either.

I pulled my jacket closer, giving him my fakest smile.

"Great. I'm Nyssa, your tutor. Can we please go inside?"

"Why? Are you cold?"

Yes, I was frozen.

"I don't want my papers flying all over campus."

Altar rose from the bench and walked toward me. "But are you cold?" he insisted as he stopped barely an arm's length away, his head cocked to the side.

"Yes."

"I could warm you up?" he suggested with a smirk.

I took a step back. "I'll pass, thanks."

He closed the distance, nudging me on my injured shoulder. I held a wince as he told me, "You don't know what you're missing."

"Listen, do you want my help for class or are you just here to waste my time?" I barked. It was out of character, but I'd had a long week.

Offense dragged down his features as if I had cursed him, or worse.

In the awkward silence, I took my phone out to

check the time or if anyone cared about my whereabouts. It was fifteen past five. I had no calls or texts from anyone.

Splendid!

Altar still hadn't answered, and if I hadn't needed those credits, I'd have been long gone. Instead, I prayed for patience, tried to smile, and took the lead. "Let's go inside. The faster we get this done, the faster you could go do…" I stared at him for a few seconds. "Whatever gym bro things you do."

He muffled a laugh.

"You're a handful, you know that?"

No, I didn't. Boring was my more common descriptor. I rolled my eyes. "Can we go?"

I turned on my heels, hoping he'd follow like a good student. Instead, I blinked, and Altar stood in front of me. I gasped. "How? You were…" My head swiveled between where he'd been and where he was now.

He put his hands on his shades, giving me a sense of déjà vu. That's all it took for me to know.

He wasn't a simple student.

I'd found myself cornered by the demon Sam had ordered to get lost back at Peccatta.

Chapter 14

Instinctively, I stepped back. His black eyes pierced mine. My heart pounded frantically against my ribcage as fear threatened to overtake any rational thoughts.

I quickly glanced at the door, evaluating my chances of ditching this demon. What had Sam called him? Certainly not Altar.

"Why can't I get inside your head?" he asked through a perplexed pout.

Hell if I knew, but, good Lord, was I glad he couldn't. I didn't need witnesses to the craziness locked up in there, especially not a demonic witness.

Altar continued with his monologue. "You aren't a higher demon. You're clearly mortal. How are you immune?"

Reciting a Hail Mary in my head, my hands gripped the pepper spray hidden in my pocket. Courage wasn't one of my main qualities. Terrified, I took it out and pressed it right in front of Altar's face, spraying him and myself. He fell back, rubbing his eyes and cursing.

I took off sprinting, ignoring my burning eyes and wishing I had gone to more than one self-defense class this year. I threw the door of the school open and rushed through the empty corridor. Pounding steps grew closer, closer, closer until I nearly died of terror.

How mad would the demon be once he got his filthy claws on me?

Night classes had already started; I just needed to reach a classroom. The thought barely finished formulating when a hand clamped my mouth, an arm circled my torso, and my feet were dangling in empty space. I tried to kick and scream, but that only earned a chuckle from my captor.

The demon suddenly pushed me into a janitor's closet, and I stumbled, knocking over a broom. I knew what people my age did in here between the sweeper, mop, and cleaning products.

Real classy.

Now, it was my turn, only for a very different purpose.

I did a one-eighty and faced the demon, warning in a shaky voice, "Don't touch me."

I tried to push down my fear, but its grip remained unyielding.

Altar crossed his arms on his chest. "Why? Have you got another one of those canisters? It could have done some serious damage if I wasn't—"

"A demon?"

He smirked. "Awesome."

Oh God. Did all demons have a superiority complex?

"What do you want?" I asked. Was he here to finish the job the demon at my house couldn't? "Are you planning on killing me and leaving me for the janitor to find?" That would really be a crappy way to go.

He laughed so loud, I was sure it echoed through the whole hallway.

"Watch a lot of movies?"

Ugh, they were impossible.

All of them.

I crossed my arms on my chest, staring into the darkness of his eyes. "So, if you aren't going to kill me, what do you want?"

He lifted one shoulder the size of my head and dropped it carelessly. "To be frank, I was...curious about you. So, I decided to come and check you out."

I must have heard wrong. "Curious about what?"

"Nothing you gotta worry about." He appraised me. "You're...not what I expected. You're harmless."

Gee, thanks.

"Can I go?" I didn't plan on staying in this closet forever.

He nodded. "I'm Nathan, by the way."

"Glad to know Altar Brilliant didn't exist."

Nathan gave me a sideways smile. "But what a name, though."

My own lips tugged up. "Yeah."

I put my hand on the handle and looked over my shoulder. "I'm guessing this means you don't actually need the tutoring, right?"

That was a shame. I really needed those credits.

Nathan's head tilted to the side, observing me. "Why? Do you want me to need it?"

My lips tightened together. What was I gonna do? Ask a demon to keep pretending to be a student so that snobby Professor Gerard couldn't ruin my life by deciding to fail me? Please.

Yet, I found myself bouncing from one foot to another.

"I do need the extra credit?" It sounded like a

question, like I doubted it, but in the end, what did I have to lose? Maybe he'd even find it in his dark heart to help me out. Who knew?

"Oh, Nyssa. Of course, you do need them," he said dramatically, winking at me. "I shall be the hero you need. I'm here to stay to help you achieve your greatest dreams." He leaned in a little, although we were already in a confined space, not to mention alone, and whispered, "Even if you have some very boring dreams."

Granted. My dreams weren't dazzling for most.

"So, will you be my tutor, Nyssa?"

I took him in. His eyes were back to their original brown. I read right through his little game. "Right. I'm not bargaining with you." I went to pull open the door, but Nathan's hand was quicker, resting above my head to keep the door shut.

"Who said anything about a bargain?" he wondered.

I puffed. "Yeah, like there's no cost to this sudden generosity. You're a demon, you always want something."

"True."

"You can forget about it." Whatever he wanted, I had nothing to give.

Nathan continued as if I'd said nothing, twisting me around to face him. "But I'm not going to offer you a bargain. Who even brought up a bargain? You did," he said matter-of-factly. "How about a friend helping a friend out?"

I couldn't help but roll my eyes. "You're not my friend."

Nathan put his hands on his heart. "Nyssa, I'm

hurt."

"If you're done with your little act, can you let go of the door, please? I have things to do."

"Like what?"

A friend to save.

A family to avoid.

A Devil to beg.

"Important things."

He narrowed his eyes, donning a perplexed expression. "But you still don't know what I want in exchange."

"Whatever it is, I doubt I'll agree." And then realization dawned upon me. God. "You could force me, couldn't you?"

He gave another shrug. "Nah. Not my style."

That was sort of...honorable.

Well, for a demon anyway.

"Fine." I caved. "What do you want?"

He smiled. "I just want to get to know you. That's all. No deals. No bargain. Just two honest people getting what they want. You get your credit and I get to spend an hour with you a day, and we just talk."

My lips parted. "Get to know me?"

"Yes." His lips stretched. "You are fascinating. I've never really had a human friend. I'm not asking for much. And you keep me as a student."

"Why?" There was nothing interesting about me.

"Like I said, I want to get to know you."

At this time, I had no interest in questioning him further. Overall, it seemed like I got the bigger end of the stick. Besides, I felt a headache racing toward me.

I sighed. "Fine."

"Is that a deal?"

And because my brain was functioning at less than a quarter capacity, I answered. "Why? You'd like to have a taste of my blood or kiss me?" Demons sealed deals the same way they took summoning offerings.

Nathan stared at me as if I had spoken a forbidden language. "A kiss?" he echoed. "That's not a way to seal a deal. You don't have your facts straight, little one, clearly. I'll have to take over your education."

I said nothing. I mean, what did I know at the end of the day? What Sam had told me? *Trust the Devil*, I thought sourly. Maybe it was a method exclusive to the King of Hell.

Nathan opened the door for me, and I didn't wait to storm out.

"Oh, and, Nyssa. Get another bottle of pepper spray. Not everyone is as cool as me."

Chapter 15

The strange meeting with Nathan didn't bother me. Not like it should have, anyway. I wasn't afraid. Strange. I suppose he was decent—for a demon. My mind had been too preoccupied to acknowledge the reality of what he represented.

I glanced at my phone. Again. Neither Sam nor Micah had tried reaching me.

I was out of options.

Actually, I hadn't exhausted *every* available option. As I walked the halls of the university, a new idea formed. One probably just as bright as summoning the Devil. On second thought, nothing could be as bad as summoning the Devil.

My feet led me to Maryssa's classroom. This might be the sign I'd searched for. Yes, this could work. She was a Glory insider with access to all the information I needed, but Father kept Maryssa at arm's' length. She might understand my plight.

I'd wait for her, then unburden myself in the hopes that she'd take pity on me. If anyone knew about the secret item the Devil sought and would be willing to share it with me, it would be her.

I knew Sam could reverse Isabelle's deal. He had admitted so himself. I was certain he didn't lie. I didn't know how I knew, but I knew. The same way something told me Sam wouldn't reverse this deal regardless of its parameters or my begging.

So, I needed a way to force his hand.

Oh God, just that thought sent my heart back into a panic.

Forcing the Devil's hand?

If it wasn't so crazy, it'd be laughable. Either way, it didn't mean a method existed to bend the Devil to someone's will. And if there was, it didn't mean Maryssa had the answers. And if she did, it didn't mean she'd help me.

Way too many ifs for my liking.

I paced the hall, biting my already nonexistent thumbnail. I kept glancing at the big clock above the massive entrance.

God, time moved like molasses, slow and sticky, each second stretching endlessly. I peeked through the narrow window on the door of Maryssa's class. They were all taking notes.

Come to think of it, this wasn't one of my most brilliant ideas. She could run to Gavriel and tell him everything, but desperate moments called for desperate measures.

A few minutes later, to my great relief, students started barging out of the classroom.

My anxiety skyrocketed.

I cowardly waited for the last one to walk out.

Breathe in. Breathe out. I repeated my mantra three times before I peered inside the classroom again. Maryssa sat at her desk writing in a notebook. Her long raven braid slid down her blouse, tickling the oak surface.

I gulped. Maybe I should have gone to Micah. Then I remembered I couldn't trust the traitor. Damn, talk about bad timing.

Micah could have easily weaseled more information from the circle, whereas Father's buddies always looked at me down their noses. As if they had some divine spark I didn't. Even Professor Jones, Isabelle's dad, hadn't bothered calling me to share anything about his daughter. Of course, he thought I was useless, but as a courtesy, he could have kept me in the loop.

I refused to stay on the sidelines like everyone wanted. I just needed a chance to prove my worth.

"Are you going to come in or just hover out there?" Maryssa's voice made me jump. "I don't have all day. If you've got something to say, then make it quick." I tightened my grip on my backpack strap. With a deep breath, I walked the center aisle.

Professor Vero leaned back into the plush leather cushion of her chair, her elbows on the armrests and her hands intertwined together in front of her heart. Her cold gaze never wavered. She might have been a tiny woman, but there was no denying the power in her presence.

After all, wasn't that the reason I'd thought of her? She stood up to Father in ways I never did.

"Professor Ve—"

She lifted a hand, interrupting me. "I already know why you're here, Nyssa. You've wasted your time. Unfortunately, there's nothing I can do for you, child."

I blinked at her, mouth parted. Could she read thoughts?

She huffed. "I'm very good at deduction. The stubborn old fools are keeping to themselves, like always." Pushing off the desk, she stood and gathered some papers into her bag. "Isabelle is missing, no one wants you involved, but you're trying to help." Walking around the massive wooden piece of art, she met me. "You'll get yourself killed. There's nothing you can do, no matter how noble your intentions."

"You don't even know what I want and yet, you're ready to refuse me?" I asked, stunned. It had taken her less than a minute to deny me.

Maryssa didn't answer. Instead, she walked past me.

I followed, snatching her arm in a rush of anger. "I'm not useless!" I shouted, my fingers gripping her. "There's plenty I could do." I raised my chin in defiance. I'd already done more than all of them.

Maryssa gave me one of her strange looks. "Can you?" She glanced at my squeezing hand, and just like that, I dropped her arm. She strolled onward without having the decency to wait for my reply. It almost felt like she was taunting me. If that was the case, it was working beautifully.

"Yes," I yelled after her. "I can see them. The demons. I can see the darkness of their souls in their eyes." I shared the secret with Maryssa not because she'd earn my trust—quite the contrary—but to prove myself an asset to her team.

Professor Vero halted her steps, slowly turning to stare at me. Her mask didn't crack. If she was surprised, she didn't let it show at all. Her cold blue eyes speared me.

"That's impossible, dear."

With all the conviction I could muster, I said, "You're wrong. I see them. Their eyes are black, as if they have no souls." My heart pounded a desperate plea in my chest. "I can prove it to you. I. Do. Know. The same way I know you have your own ways of finding Isabelle and you could help me if you wanted."

She arched a brow at me. "Do I, now?"

I advanced with a confidence I was far from feeling. "You do. My Father may know a lot, and he may have the bigger collection of priceless artifacts, but he'll never use any of them. Not to help Isabelle." Or anybody other than himself. "We both know that." I paused. "And I know he must keep you close for good reason, despite his obvious dislike for you." She had to be of use to him somehow. "You could help me. You have decent resources and equal know-how." I gathered my courage on a breath. "So, what do you know about the Devil?"

In three long strides, she closed the distance between us. Her hand cupped my face, her pointy fingernails brushed my skin while her eyes narrowed on me as if seeking lies or truths written in my pores.

The corner of her lip upturned. "I always knew you were so much more than a pretty face." She let go of me, dropped her bag to the ground, and shut her door.

She twisted back to me. "Why do you ask about the Devil?"

I bit the inside of my cheek. There were limits to what I'd be willing to share. After all, the Devil was Sam. And Sam had been nothing but nice to me. I didn't want anyone using anything against him.

Other than me.

Maryssa didn't actually let me answer. "A lot of stories have been told about him over the centuries." She rested the backs of her thighs against a student's desk. "They say he's pure temptation, that he lures souls into eternal cages with smiles on their faces."

Her words turned my stomach. I'd read many stories about him. All before we met. For unexplainable reasons, her condemning tone when speaking about Sam didn't sit well with me.

My jaw became so tight my teeth ground against each other. Sure, Sam was tempting in a bunch of different ways, but he didn't seem like the type to try and attract people. He seemed indifferent.

She continued speaking, unaware of the storm she'd awoken inside me. "The Devil is an enchanter with control over darkness. A deadly mix. He could end anyone in a second and devour their soul. He's an opportunist. His beauty made him vain. A—"

"Stop," I ordered, shaky with anger. "You. Know. Nothing." Sam was none of those things.

Maryssa smiled. "Those are only stories." Her lips stretched further. "I never said they were true." She crossed her arms, observing me strangely.

"Then why mention them?"

She arched her brow. "To test you?"

"Test what?"

Again she didn't answer but went on. "The Devil was the favorite of Heaven. The most complete being created by God. The word perfection was created to describe him. Some stories claim that he fell because he thought of himself better than God. Others say his hunger for power knew no limits–"

"Those are lies." I had no idea why I spoke. I knew nothing and yet, *inside*, I did. Something was definitely wrong with me.

Which earned me another smile. "Perhaps," she said. "Do you know what Samael lost the day of his fall?"

I thought about it. "Access to Heaven."

She absently nodded. "Yes. But he lost so much more than that. He lost his family. His brethren, even though most had turned on him. He lost his Father. He lost his song. And yes, he lost Heaven, but he lost himself, too. I don't think he ever found his way back." Maryssa looked lost in thought. Her gaze, though glued to me, seemed to be elsewhere.

She shook it off. "The truth is, Samael did something he shouldn't have. He lost something else in return. The only thing he valued." Yes. That was it. What I needed to know.

"What did he lose?" I urged. I couldn't help but wonder if I got it back for him, would it give him closure? Would it heal the sorrow he harbored beneath that beautiful face? Why did I care?

"Everything." She pushed herself off the desk and picked up her bag. "And unfortunately, time sometimes plays against one. It has been a very long time. Long enough for his heart to freeze over in the underworld. Long enough for his pride to become his second sin. Long enough for his anger, fury, and wrath to burn him from within. Long enough for him to roam the earth and envy those who share something that, once upon a time, he didn't even know he longed for. Long enough for him to relish in the sorrowful comfort of drink until he was too lazy to do more," she said, walking slowly toward me. "Long enough for him to stand again and collect himself in hopes of filling the hole within."

My heart hammered against my rib cage. We'd gotten off the subject. I simply needed the object. I shouldn't be worried about Sam or be interested in his history.

Yet, I wanted to know more. Everything.

"It may be time for him to remember who he once was."

Something bothered me. Actually, plenty bothered me about the story, but my curiosity snagged on one thing. "Why are you telling me all this?"

"You earned the right to know," Maryssa said, making me stand taller. "From what I understand, Samael punished himself more than God ever could have done. Many don't believe God would have cast out his favorite, and yet, he became the first Fallen Angel, nonetheless."

I'd never seen Sam for what he truly was. The angel from the painting. The painting that unraveled me.

A second later, Maryssa's words fully settled in. I frowned, confused. "But God is the one who did this to him."

"Did he now?" she asked me before turning toward the exit. "Meet me at my store in two nights. Nine o'clock sharp. Come alone. Do not tell anyone about it. Not a living soul." She paused a moment, then spoke over her shoulder. "Or I'll know, Nyssa, and you'll be on your own."

"Two nights is too long," I complained.

"It's what's needed to gather the one item that can help your cause."

I frowned. "I haven't told you what I want." Finding Isabelle wasn't the goal for now. Even if her location were revealed, I'd still have no way of helping her yet.

"Don't worry. I know exactly what you need. You

want the item Samael seeks, and while I do not have that, I may have the perfect thing meant just for you," she told me before vanishing into the crowd of students in the hallway.

Exhaling my nerves in one breath, I took support from a desk. What did she even mean by "meant for" me? And her store? I wasn't one for gossip, but if what I'd heard held even the tiniest truth, it was a witch store.

Why there? But what other option did I have?

Chapter 16

For a change, the house wasn't empty when I passed the door. Micah was sitting on the stairs facing the entrance with his elbows resting on his knees. His finger intertwined under his chin. His blue eyes that brought me so much comfort in my life clashed with mine.

Isabelle and my brother were all I've ever had. I didn't want to be in a place where I couldn't rely on him. Only, that's exactly where *he* brought us.

"I was at school. I've got a student to tutor now," I said, defensive. I couldn't begin to picture being stripped of my right to go to school. "In case you report to your father." I continued on the same path, my tone dripping with sarcasm.

I took my boots off, then hung my jacket in the closet.

Micah didn't even acknowledge my little outburst. Good for him.

"I'm so sorry, Nyssa Bear."

My eyes shut, my body still facing the closet. The sincerity in his voice urged a part of me to throw myself in his arms and forget about the betrayal.

The rational part of my brain knew Gavriel would have found out sooner or later. He had a tad to know it all. I never hide anything from him anymore.

First, because my life was boring and there wasn't

much to hide. Aside from my Shadows, but those were part of my issues. Not a secret. And second, because Gavriel always found out about my misbehave. Whether it was ditching a class, which I only did once but heard of it for months, or going to a house party.

I twisted at my waist, fighting to contain the hurt in my voice. "I trusted you," I whispered, my words barely audible. "I guess it's not you and I against the world?" The realization swept over me like a sudden gust of wind on a calm day, leaving me reeling and struggling to keep my footing.

In two long strides, Micah closed the distance between us and wrapped his big arms around me. The familiar scent of peppermint enveloped me.

"It will always be you and I against the world, Nys. In this life or the next." He vowed his warm breath on my hair. "I didn't have a choice. He already knew too much of it." It might not change anything but Micah did confirm Gavriel's doubts. And because I knew it was the truth, my arms circled his waist as I pressed my face against his chest.

"I hate when we fight," I admitted.

His arm tightened a little more. "Me too. Don't let him drive a wedge between us, Nyssa Bear. I always try my best for you."

I nodded, pushing against him. I cracked my head to look at him. "Any news on Isabelle, though?"

He shook his head.

"Will you tell me? If there's any development whatsoever?"

His lashes touched his cheeks.

"What is it?"

Micah hesitated for a moment.

"Please, Micah."

"Isabelle's mom...she's gotten better." A miracle considering she had weeks at most left to live a few days ago. "She was able to get out of bed, eat, shower. Perfectly healthy again."

It didn't come as a surprise to me. "I told you Isabelle made a deal and that's what she asked for."

His lips pressed together in a thin line. "Yeah, well, her state started deteriorating again. Scarily fast too."

"What? How? Can a demon go back on his deal?"

He shrugged. "It could but it's unheard of."

And then it struck me.

Sam.

Maybe he forced the demon to end the deal. While I did feel relief, I couldn't push down the guilt I felt for Isabelle's mom. Nor the guilt for what I asked of Maryssa.

I needed to call Sam without tripping in apologies.

My brother kept talking, unaware of the storm he woke accidentally.

"I'm going to meet Father at Glory. We might not have a choice to get involved after all. He's losing the trust of his people."

About goddamn time those old fools wake up.

"Right."

Micah reached into his coat pocket and retrieved a petite book. He outstretched his arm and I took his present.

"Protection against demons." I read and gave my brother a puzzled look.

In one heavy breath, he spoke. "In here there are' ways to keep demons out of your head. Ways to defend yourself." He gave me a stranger look. "I know you. I won't be able to leave you out of my sight if I can't be at least a little reassured that you can protect yourself to a certain degree."

I can't get in your head. Nathan had said. How? I didn't even know about ways to keep them out.

"Do you still have that pepper spray?" Micah asked, taking me out of my questioning mind.

No, I used it on a demon, which also happens to be my new student.

"I lost the one you gave me."

He reached into his other pocket and gave me two more. "Make sure to keep one in your pocket and one in your bag at all times."

"I will." Even Nat had suggested the same. "Thanks."

"Not sure it'll do anything, but better than nothing. I'm going to try and find you something else. Okay?" He leaned forward and kissed the crown of my head. "Stay put, Nyssa Bear. Text or call if anything."

"Yeah. Be careful." And he was out the door.

Frantically, I snatched my bag up the floor and rummaged through it in search of my phone. With trembling fingers, I hastily texted Sam.

—Did you break the deal?—

I rushed upstairs. If Sam broke the bargain, why was Isabelle still missing?

I glanced at my screen.

—As much as I'd love to be efficient, I'm unfortunately still seeking the demon who made a deal to start with. Besides, I don't recall agreeing to break anything. I said I would look. Try to keep up, precious.—

My finger typed faster than my mind registered. —

Isabelle's mom became healthy and suddenly today, she's back to being sick. What does that mean?—

The three gray dots appeared. —It means your friend didn't hold up her end of the deal.—

—That's impossible. The demon took her!— She couldn't invent that; I saw it with my own two eyes.

—I wasn't aware you were an expert on demon deals.—

I groaned. —Fine. If he has Isabelle, how is it possible she didn't hold up her end? What does he have to do to own her soul?—

—Not much. I'm going to find out what went wrong. Get some sleep, precious.—

Yeah, right, as if I could sleep. —I want to come.—

—Can't do.—

Arghh. He's infuriating. —Is there a way for you to lessen the bargain? Keep Isabelle's mom healthy without taking Isabelle's soul?—

—Yes.—

I chewed on my lower lip. —Will you do it?—

"It's not because one has the power to do something that he should."

So no, Sam wouldn't do it.

Hell be damned.

People like Sam couldn't understand why it mattered so much for me. I had been so lonely, whether it was because I pushed people away out of fear or because I was cataloged as weird, the result remained the same.

But Isabelle, she chased away some of that loneliness. I was in my first year of elementary school the first time the Jones stayed over for a few months.

Isabelle attended school with me. On the first day, I got the usual greeting, some pushing around, called names when Isabelle stepped in. She pushed back. She threw some threats and invented how her dad was a secret agent 'who'd kidnap anyone who dared attack us. It worked. I never got bullied after that.

Or when I cried each time she left, Isabelle managed to leave something of her behind. A teddy, a coloring, a clip, so I could bring it back to her.

She wasn't just a friend. She was who stood by me through sticks and stones—it was time to return the favor.

I threw my phone on the bed before doing the same to myself. I guess all I had now was Maryssa and using something to control Sam. Oh God, I felt the panic rushing back to me. Instead of drowning in it, I picked up the book Micah gave me.

Given what I had planned, I guess I'll need protection against demons now more than ever. After all, my plan pitted me against the Devil himself.

Sam would be furious when he'd found out. Or betrayed. The mere thought of Sam's reaction made my stomach turn with unease. I didn't want to betray Sam.

Truth be told, I doubt I could bring myself to use the one thing Sam still cared about against him. Even to help Isabelle. And that alone made me question my sanity. Why did Sam impact me enough to question what needed to be done to help my best friend?

I started reading and even though the source had to be reliable since Micah gave it to me, it still sounded ludicrous. *Believe in God. Pray to the one you believe in.*

Yeah, as if he ever listened before. I highly doubt

he'll listen if a demon tried killing me. Oh yeah, it happened already, and I had to fend for myself.

I turned the pages. *Use anything pure like salt.* Okay, that may be useful. *Wear the holy object.* I glanced down at the little cross hanging on my neck. Micah had given it to me when I was young. He wore the same one. Maybe that's why Nathan wasn't able to get inside my head. Then again, thousands of people wore these.

The words started dancing in front of me like I was under a spell. Next thing I knew, when my eyelid opened again, it was daylight. I must have passed out. I glanced at my clock.

Oh crap, three p.m.

I rushed to shower. I had my first official tutoring lessons with Nathan in an hour.

With my hair dripping, I grabbed the first pair of dark Levis and a long-sleeve hoodie. I put my wet curls in a messy bun sitting on my head, and stopped by the kitchen. I grabbed the sea salt, poured some in a small glass bottle that I slipped into my pocket and I was out of the house.

I reached campus right on time.

Nathan was already there. Laying down on a picnic table near campus. He had dark shades on and was soaking in the sun as if he was on a beach in Mexico. To be fair, the sun was out and bright, a rare sight for the London weather, I supposed.

"Don't you prefer the shade? Being a demon and all," I inquired, going to sit on the bench at his table. That was part of our little agreement. We'd pretend to have a tutoring class and we'd…talk. I guess.

He gasped, turning to me. "Shade? How am I

supposed to maintain a decent tan in the shade?"

I arched a brow. "You're a demon. Why do you care about the color of your skin?"

His hands flew to his heart as if I physically just injured him. "By all hell, Nyssa! Do you think because I'm a demon I do not care about my appearance? That I have no worries? Of course I care about my skin color. I do want to look my best. I'm that vain." He put down his sunglasses on the bridge of his nose, his eyes roaming my figure. "You should start caring a little more about your own skin. You're as white as snow."

I rolled my eyes at him. "Jeez, thanks. I could blame it on my best friend disappearing. Or demons crashing the city. But hey, no need to give a girl a break or anything."

"I wasn't going to."

"That was clear."

Nathan sat back down without commenting.

I guess I needed to ask. "Why are you even here? There's really nothing interesting about me." I pulled out my phone to check if Micah had called or texted.

Nothing.

However, I did stop answering Sam last night and he wasn't happy about it. A smile tugged the corner of my lips at his last message.

—I swear to all Hell, Nyssa, I've never been ignored in my entire life and it's very unpleasant. STOP DOING IT.—

Nathan hopped off the table, clapping his hand as though I had just granted him his greatest wish. "I'm so glad you asked, Nyssa," he said, going toward a backpack on the ground. "As much as I do enjoy your company, I didn't come here solely just for the sun and your pretty face, or to hand you those extra credits on a golden platter. I have some questions for you." He rummaged through the green bag, adorned with logos of rock bands, and pulled out a file.

"How will you even get the extra credits? You aren't a student here." It didn't occur to me before right now.

"Don't worry. It'll be in the database," Nat said.

"It will?"

Nathan winked at me. "I'm that awesome, I know." He placed the file in front of me with a loud thud and sat on the table, his feet on the bench beside me.

I frowned, confused. "What's this? A human interrogation for a page in the Demon daily news?" I mocked.

"There's an idea. But no. This, my ignorant friend, is a file."

I shot him a look. "I know what a file is. I mean, what's it for?" It was thicker than any books I've ever laid my eyes on and that's saying something.

"Open it. Take a peek."

I eyed the file. My gut knew that whatever that file held, I wasn't going to like it.

Nathan grabbed it, put it on his knees and opened it.

"Nyssa Prima, now Nyssa Lewis. Born June 11th 2002. Daughter of Marina Prima, now deceased, adopted daughter of Gavriel Lewis." He stopped to give me a strange look. "Oh, you have a brother. Sorry, step-brother. Not blood-related. Lucky him. Ever had extra feelings? Was he the one who gave you that smile earlier while looking at your phone?" He wiggled his eyebrows suggestively, working my nerves. Nathan didn't give me the chance to reply or react.

"You're an A student. Way above average from your peers. You managed to get an entrance into the art program at London's, which is very impressive and, let's be honest, unusual for a girl." He lowered his sexist eyes on me, tilting his head. "And I doubt even your father has the power to make the system agree. Those old owls cannot be forced unless with grand persuasion. Care to share how you managed that one and have your soul intact?" His dark eyes narrowed on me as I opened my mouth, but Nathan continued without giving me a chance. "Anyhow, some of those professors even consider you a genius. Quite remarkable. But see," —he leaned closer to me to whisper— "How does one with such an impressive resume end up locked up in a psychiatric institution?"

I stopped breathing altogether.

Stunned.

As if he just punched the air out of my lungs. It didn't last long, though. I stood and ripped the folder from his grasp so quickly, the demon's stunned face was almost comical.

"How dare you!" I said through my teeth. Holding the folder, I shoved it in my bag and walked away fuming.

No one, and I mean no one other than my immediate family, knew.

Not even Isabelle.

Micah and Gavriel had done everything to get me out, but when you're a kid and you go tell a teacher about hearing voices, you fall into a system. I stayed there for thirty days. The minimum required by the government of America when they suspect schizophrenia in a child. My mouth got the best of me back then because I didn't know better. But sue me, I was only ten years old.

I heard his fast step behind me. "Nyssa, wait. I didn't mean—"

"Oh please. That's exactly what you meant to do. You went snooping into my life. How did you even get this? It's private information. Not to mention intrusive," I shouted over my shoulder.

I was so pissed.

He grabbed my shoulders from behind and turned me to him. I struggled to break his grip. "Stop it. Yeah, it's intrusive but I'm a demon, what do you expect?"

I tried yanking myself away. No. It wasn't happening. "An apology would have been better than this stupid I'm a demon excuse."

"You're right."

I waited for the words.

"I'm sorry," he gritted as if the words physically harmed him.

"Did that kill you?"

Nathan looked like I poured acid in his mouth. "Almost."

I huffed. "Where did you even get this?" Could anyone else find this? That thought had my nerves almost unhinged. "And why? What's so interesting about me that you had to go dig into my past?"

He shrugged, letting go of me. "I can hack into pretty much any system. As easy as a child's game. That's how the tutoring will appear in your university's database."

"I guess I'm not the only brain here." Nathan shot me a wink but he still hadn't answered my question.

"Why though?" I insisted.

"I need to know something."

I rolled my eyes, throwing my hands up to the sky, earning a reminder of my injured shoulder. "No, I'm not crazy nor medicated."

A smile grew on his face. "That's not what I wanted to know, although your state of mind is debatable." It totally was. Nat became serious again as he glanced around and back at me. He whispered, "Do you still hear it?"

I felt my insides twist at his words. So he knew. He knew it all. I felt my head spin just thinking of it. My heart accelerated. The air started passing less and less. My heartbeat was out of control. The panic attack was close. I needed to get a grip on my emotions.

I didn't want to admit it. I never stopped hearing it. I simply pretended it didn't matter. Like background soothing sounds. White noise parents put for their baby.

"The music, Nyssa, do you still hear it?" he specified as if I wasn't aware of what he was referring to.

Yes. Unlike my Shadows, the music was always with me.

I inhaled deeply, counting in my head. One. Two. Three. Exhaled. "Who cares? Want to know if I still have my sanity? Clearly, I don't if I'm standing here talking with a demon."

He shook his head. "I don't care about your sanity. Tell me if you hear it."

Just then my phone vibrated.

Thank you, God!

I rushed in my bag, praying it was Micah who got some news on Isabelle. I could feel the frown on my face.

—If ever you're in a mood to answer, precious. I found something. You're up for it?— '

Still, the perfect excuse to ignore Nathan. —Sure what is it?—

—Meet me at the Peccatta. I'm already here.—

—On my way.— I sent my reply. Ready to take off when Nat's hand held me back.

"And where do you think you're going? We had a deal. Not one of my regular deals but a friendly deal. You can't walk out. I give you the credits you desperately need, and we talk. You haven't answered me yet."

"You have a car?"

Nat's thick brows creased together. "Yeah?"

I gave him one of my sweetest smiles. "Great, I need a ride. I'll answer you when you drop me off."

His mood dropped. "I'm not an Uber driver or a private chauffeur."

I stepped closer to him. "No, but considering you want answers from me and you literally sneak into my privacy and hack a private institution to get it, I'd say it's the least you could do."

He took his key out, narrowing his eyes on me. "I'm not doing the UK's turn. I have a certain commitment I need to take care of. I can't be late."

"Commitment? Like what?" I asked while he stopped in front of a very normal Civic. A white one, if I may add. Not that I was complaining. It was better than my way of transport.

"Yes, like a favor I'm making for a friend. Hell, Nyssa, we live in the same world. Most of the time, anyway."

"Why are demons even back? Is it new? Were they always here?" I asked.

"It's complicated but yeah, demons were always here but…it got out of control recently."

"Why?"

"Not my place to tell."

"Does it have anything with the Devil escaping Hell?" I pushed.

Nathan's mouth parted. "He didn't *escape* Hell. He rules over the underworld, but yeah, his time to go up arrived."

"How? He couldn't come and go as he pleased before?"

"Not exactly."

Right. It's as good as I was going to get for now. "To Peccatta please," I told him, buckling up.

He twisted to me so fast, I jerked back. "Why in all hell would you go there, Nyssa? The place is crawling with demons and sinners. So not for you. They'll smell you a mile away," he said, shaking his head.

I gritted my teeth. "I have a father and a brother with a life mission of keeping me away from *everything* lately, so please. Just go. I'm meeting a friend there."

Nat mumbled under his breath about stupid ideas and reckless humans. He gave me a last look I couldn't quite place before starting the drive. After a couple of minutes, he broke the silence. "So?"

"So?" I repeated.

"Do you still hear the sound of the music?"

Getting comfortable in the cushions, my head tilted to the side. His hair was tied in a hightail. He looked like a guy from *The Godfather*, only his hair was light. "I'm curious, Nathan. Why would a demon be interested in my issues? Why are *you* so interested? You've made it clear it's not about concern or caring. What is it then?"

He hit the steering wheel with one hand, making me jump on my seat. "Hell, Nyssa! I'm done playing this game. Yes or no?"

I sank into the cold leather seats. "No." My voice came out small. For a second, I had forgotten Nat wasn't a regular friend giving me a ride. But a demon. A bargain.

"Liar."

Of course, he detected the lie. "Fine. You win. I hear it, okay. All the freaking time. Happy?"

"Ecstatic." His knuckles had turned white from the tight grip on the steering wheel.

He didn't sound ecstatic.

He sounded sarcastic.

The car was roaring under Nathan's maneuvers as if we had multiple lives instead of one. Yet, he still turned his head to stare at me. Like we were having a stroll instead of a race. Well, maybe a car accident wouldn't kill him but at this speed, it sure as hell would kill me.

One hand on my bag, the other gripped to the side handle of the door. "Can you watch the road and not drive like a maniac? I'm not a cat. I have one life."

With that, he loosened his foot on the pedal, and the engine sounded as relieved as I felt.

"Sorry. I got carried away."

We stayed quiet for the rest of the road. Nathan looked lost in his thoughts while I kept glancing at my phone. Still nothing from my brother.

I decided to text him. —What happened at the

meeting? Any news on Isabelle or her mom?—

Before I knew it, the car stopped in front of Peccatta. At this time, I got a better view of its look. The place seemed much quieter. Instead of a lineup of debauched, the two big black doors, ornamented with gold on the edge, screamed prestige and luxury.

"Thanks for the ride," I said, picking up my bags and opening the door.

Nat cut the engine and got out of the car. As I got out, he was in front of me. "I'll walk you in."

"Don't." I didn't need to be seen with a Demon.

I stepped around him when he called me. "Nyssa."

I twisted at my waist to look at him.

Nathan was leaning against his car. "What happened when you were five?" he asked.

His question unraveled a ball buried deep in the pit of my stomach. The thought alone felt like he cut my legs from underneath me. The answer was a very complicated one. The reason I kept people away. The reason I felt so lonely. I couldn't unbury that part of my past.

Nathan's now brown eyes were staring at me, waiting for my response. Demons sensed lies so I cut the apple in two.

"I'm not exactly sure." I fully faced him. "Do *you* know what happened when I was five?" I returned his question.

"All I know is there's much more to you than this file will ever tell me."

I frowned again. "I'm not sure what this"—I gestured between him and I—"is all about but you won't find anything good. Besides, I'm nothing special."

I'm just crazy and in urgent need of therapy probably until the day I die.

"On the contrary," Nathan said. "You're exceptionally different."

"Different how?"

"That's exactly what I'm trying to figure out." He walked around his car and opened the door, his head lifted to me. "You, be safe in there. See you in a few days for our tutoring." And with that, he settled behind the wheel and drove away.

Chapter 17

I pushed open the heavy black door, leaving outside the strange moment Nathan and I had shared. The knowledge he had acquired about my past. The music. The hospital. What happened when I was a child. Nothing I wanted to acknowledge.

As soon as I walked in, the overpowering stench of alcohol assailed my nostrils. From the street, the place had seemed quiet, but inside, it was bustling even in the early evening.

I still felt as out of place as the first time, despite the invitation to come meet the Devil himself. From the entrance, I scanned the room for Sam, but he was nowhere to be seen. I sent him a quick text to let him know I had arrived.

Since waiting by the door would draw more attention, I headed to the bar. The onyx, velvet high-top stools were filled with people facing the wall mirror, so I took a seat at the far end, away from the mingling, interspecies crowd.

With my elbow resting on the glass smooth surface of the bar, I rubbed my eyes with the heels of my palms. My nerves were brittle icicles. I had no news from Isabelle. Maryssa's little story lesson shook me in an...inexplicable way. And Nathan had mentioned the music.

My music.

I'd learned to live with it. To appreciate it. Even love it.

It didn't mean I wanted anyone aware of it.

God, I'd thought that part of my life was sealed for good. That, maybe if I never spoke of it, it'd just disappear.

I guessed you never escaped your past. No matter how hard you try.

I'd heard the music for as long as I'd seen my shadows. The melody remained the same.

Lost in my thoughts, I didn't notice the bartender until he placed a slender glass in front of me. White bubbles pervaded the liquid, bobbing the herbal leaf he'd dropped on top.

"Here, beautiful. Looks like you need it." His eyes were a comforting, average brown. A normal guy.

Well, not entirely. Tattoos and piercings took up every inch of skin. He even had a thin chain hanging from his lip piercing that connected to the gauge in his ear. It swayed when he gave me a friendly smile.

I eyed the glass suspiciously. "What is it?"

"A special house concoction to make you feel better." He inclined his head and moved to another customer further down the bar.

My eyes settled on a man who shared the company of a young girl. He had one of his big hands clasped on her hip. There was nothing wrong with the picture per se. Only, the man looked older than my father, yet there was nothing fatherly in the way his tongue slid over his lower lip and his fingers dug into her side.

Was she even of legal age? Did she have any idea of what was going on here?

None of your business, Nys, I told myself

Yet, my eyes couldn't look away.

She looked even more out of place than me. She was skinny enough her collarbone stuck out in that tiny blue dress, which left nothing to the imagination. Sallow cheeks gave her a pitiful, malnourished appearance, and her eyes looked…like the light was shut off. Zoned out.

Her fluid, dreamy gaze found mine. Her pupils were blurry. I couldn't be sure if it was from unshed tears or illicit substances.

She mouthed one word to me.

Help.

Her lip trembled as the man roughly grabbed her by the jaw and spoke to her. I felt my blood boil. He might not be a demon, but his sinful intent put a few I knew to shame.

My lips curled in disgust. What was I supposed to do? I had no idea. But I couldn't just sit there and do nothing.

Taking the drink in my hand, I threw my head back and slugged it down. I needed liquid courage. And I recited a Hail Mary in my head.

A small part of me whispered to mind my own business. I shut it up rather quickly. She needed help. Powerless as I felt, I refused to be a coward.

The sound of my chair grinding against the black shiny marble didn't attract one glance with the music booming.

I walked toward them, each step imbued with deliberate false confidence.

The man spotted me first, licking his lips while his gaze glided down my body shamelessly. He had no idea how wrong he'd assessed this whole situation.

"Let the girl go," I ordered, as if I held any authority in here.

She lifted her head, and the spark returned to her eyes. Aglow with hope. She really had no idea. She needed a way out. An exit. And I was the answer.

The real evil beside her tightened his grip on her hip and smiled, revealing perfect white teeth. He reeked of money, with his tailored blazer and silk shirt. That didn't make him any better. Not far from his Rolex, he wore a wedding band.

Gross.

"Why? You don't have to be jealous. You can join the fun." His wetted lips glistened like slugs in the blue-green pulsing light. "I'll have a bunch of customers for a fine specimen like you. What's your name?" When I said nothing around my rising vomit, he offered, "I'd rename you Emerald. For the eyes."

My fists clenched at my side, wishing I were stronger, then I could throw a mean left hook. With that ability unattainable in the next five seconds, I shifted the wish, hoping Sam would appear and come to the rescue.

"I'm joining nothing." I jutted my chin at the high schooler. "Neither is she." I took her hand in mine. "Come on." She stood, ready to follow my lead, when the man pushed her behind him and popped up to tower over me.

My heart skipped a beat. I hadn't expected him to put up a fight. Especially not in a public place, but I guessed a place like this didn't really count.

"How about you mind your own business before you turn up on a flyer? Understand?" he threatened in a low tone.

I had no idea where I mustered the courage to stand taller, but I did. "The only thing I understand is how much bad publicity can ruin someone in the public eye." I dropped my eyes to his hand. "I also understand you wouldn't want your wife or kids to know about you trying to get with a minor. Course, no matter what the world thinks of you, when you leave it, you're ending up in a place much worse than your darkest nightmare, you soulless bastard." I lifted my chin, letting a small smile pull my lips. "How I wish I could be there to witness it."

The man grabbed my arms with bruising fingers, vanishing my courage as fast as my Shadows disappeared in daylight. I barely held back a yelp as fire raged down my shoulder.

"Then I guess I'd better make sure you keep your pretty mouth quiet." With a devilish grin, his grip tightened, digging to the bone. A whimper escaped me. "I have the perfect place for you." I tried yanking free, but that only made his smile grow.

Real, paralyzing dread took hold. Much bigger than when I first realized Sam was the ruler of Hell. Even bigger than when I encountered Nathan on campus. This man was the definition of evil.

"Is there a problem here?" the pierced bartender asked, voice sharp, and my assailant roughly let go.

"Yes." I swallowed. "He's holding that girl against her will." I turned to the bartender, crossing my fingers he was aware of the secret world half his patrons hailed from and wasn't going to think I'd lost my mind as I said, "There are rules. No matter which side you stand on, they must be followed. Sam wouldn't approve of this." Maybe throwing Sam's name around wasn't my finest idea, but what could I say? I panicked.

The guy looked over my head, beckoning to someone.

Oh great. Just freaking great.

I was going to get kicked out in the cold with no jacket, no phone, and no way to let Sam know.

Bloody hell! I couldn't catch a goddamn break.

Two muscled beasts flanked us. "Take the girl home," the bartender said. To my surprise, he didn't mean me. He meant the other girl. "And take out the trash."

The rich man threw a hissy fit, shouting at the top of his lungs when a bulky bouncer took his arm. "Do you know who I am? You can't do this to me. I'll have this place closed." His voice died down as he was dragged away to a back door.

The young girl grabbed my hands. "Thank you. I-it wasn't…We met online. I didn't know."

"I know."

"I'm Jen."

"Nyssa." I looked at the waiting bouncer assigned to escort her. "Make sure she gets home safely, please. I'll be sure to confirm that you did with Sam."

He nodded while she gave me a bright smile. "I'll see you around," I told her.

I went back to my original seat. The bartender gave me something else.

"To help overcome the shock," he explained.

It was a shooter. Actually, there were six. Three facing him. Three facing me.

"What you did back there was—"

"Stupid?" I suggested. "I already know that."

He laughed, shaking his head. "No. I was going to

say brave. Really brave." I've never been called brave. Reckless seemed more suitable right this second. "Most would have ignored it and gone about their own business."

I gave him a look.

"Like you did?" I challenged.

He flashed me a lopsided smile. "No. Despite what you may think, I wasn't going to let him leave with her, but he actually needed to say or do something wrong. You accelerated the process. As you so politely mentioned earlier, there are rules."

He took a drink, and I copied him.

"Cheers." He clinked my drink with his and gulped it down. I did the same. After twenty years of being good and all the craziness of the last few days, I'd earned the right to be a little bad.

Chapter 18

In less than fifteen minutes, I felt lighter than I had in my entire life. The burdens of the past few days no longer weighed me down.

I've learned that the bartender's name was Max, he came from Edinburgh to find work and help his sick sister pay for her cancer treatment. Behind the ink and hoops, he was one of the good guys.

Somehow, I found myself dragging him to the dance floor.

"Nys, I can't. I could lose my job." I ignored the weak protest.

"You won't get in trouble. I promise." That somehow convinced him. As if I had any say in here. I laughed at the thought.

I had no idea how to dance but once we stood in the middle of the dance floor, I followed the tempo. I threw my hands above my head and swayed my body along the music. The pain in my shoulder, forgotten. Max's delightful drinks had the effect of what I expect a valium mixed with a strong painkiller would. Only ten times better.

Max had a smile on his face as he moved me along with him, one hand resting on my hip. My head fell back as I drowned in the music.

I didn't feel like myself.

And it felt God damn good.

Without warning, Max's hand was ripped away. My eyes left the ceiling and locked with midnight blue ones. Only this time, the shade seemed mixed with the color of flames. His pupils appeared vertical as he took me in.

Perhaps my vision wasn't very good tonight.

Yet, I clearly saw how Sam didn't wear his usual smirk. Instead, pure rage deformed his perfect features. He was wearing it like an anchor. It poured out of him. His lips were tightly pressed into a line.

Maybe if I was in my right state of mind I would have been frightened. Or I would have been worried for Max.

Not tonight. Tonight, I was neither.

Instead, my lips curled up. "I'm really happy to see you," I told him, swinging my hips. "You missed the show."

I turned my back to him and continued dancing when I felt his arm slip around my waist. His palm, flat on my belly, sent butterflies in my stomach. Sam crashed my back to his chest. A shiver of excitement ran in my blood. My hand went above his.

"Seems to me like I arrived right on time for the show."

I laughed. "Nah." I meant the other scene.

"What do you think you're doing, precious?" he whispered in my ear in a husky voice. I tilted my head a little to meet his eyes.

Maybe it was the drinking that gave me the courage I thought as I slipped my other hand above my shoulder and touched his cheek. God, he was so…hot. My lips brushed his jaw. I felt his whole body shudder at my touch. Could it be I wasn't the only one 'whose hormones were over the roof?

My lips tugged up at the thought as I whispered back to Sam, "Living a little."

His scent was addictive. That's all I could smell.

His whole body became statuesque before he replied. "I'd say you lived enough for now."

I spun fully to face him. I took his hand in mine, lacing our fingers. "I haven't even started living." I laughed. "Dance with me." I put his hand on my hip and closed the small gap between us. Every inch of my body was against him. Somehow, it wasn't enough. I wanted more.

The effect his palm had on my hip reminded me of when you knew you shouldn't eat too many cookies cause they were bad for you but couldn't help it.

I felt giddy.

My arms tangled in the back of his neck. Never, in my right mind, have I ever been so bold or so close to a man. Any man. And to be this close to a specimen like Sam was almost impossible when I was my normal boring self.

In this state, it was inconceivable.

My lips touched the space between his collarbone and his jaw as I inhaled the firewood and fresh wind. It was making my head spin. Like poison running into my blood. The aroma was so addictive. My hips kept swinging gently against his.

Sam stayed of steel, and I heard him mumble something along the lines "This is the worst idea." I couldn't be sure with the music blasting in the back.

"You always smell so good. I've never smelt anyone else with that scent."

Sam's hand gripped my hip tighter, I couldn't be

sure if it was to stop me from moving or to keep me in place.

"Precious."

My head tilted sideways. "Why do you keep calling me that?"

His eyes never left mine. "You've never asked about it before."

"No." I was too much of a coward to ask. "Why tough?"

"Because you are. I've never met anyone like you in all my years and, trust me, I've met lots of people."

And I might have died right there.

"I like you," I told him. "You're nice."

My little confession made him laugh. It was the nicest sound I've ever heard. And I became jelly.

"You've got it wrong. I'm not nice."

I pushed off a little with my hands trying to steady the movement with Sam's shoulders and failed. Sam's hand automatically went behind my back, rescuing me from the embarrassment of falling.

"I've heard theories about you," I blurted out.

"Don't believe everything you hear," he warned, his eyes glancing between my mouth and my eyes. I nervously licked my lips.

"Some think you're frozen. Inside." One of my hands slipped from his shoulder to his chest, my gaze followed the movement. "That you can't feel. That you've forgotten." I lifted my eyes to his. "I happen to think the opposite."

Sam stayed quiet, but the storm of emotion reflecting in his eyes kept me going. "I think you're burning with emotions you haven't let out and you lost control of the fire and got burned so deep, you haven't recovered from the scars." My hand lifted to his cheek. "We tend to forget that sometimes, the deepest scars aren't visible for the eyes to see." Before I touched his face, Sam gently stopped me, taking my wrist in his hand.

"Time's up, precious."

Before I realized what he meant, Sam wrapped one arm behind my knees, the other on my back, and I hung my face upside down, with my body hanging from his shoulder.

I tried to pull myself up and failed horribly. "Hey!" I shouted. The world was turning around me. "Are you out of your mind? Put me down this instant!" I ordered. Sam kept his pace unbothered by the curious glances we got. "I said, put me down!" I screamed. He walked into a small space of an elevator, pressed a button and only when the door shut in my face, did he place me on my feet.

Frustrated, I pushed the hair away from my face and shot him a piercing glare. "That wasn't very nice."

"I told you I wasn't nice," he answered, arms crossed on his chest. He leaned on the opposite wall of me. As if he needed the distance.

My fingers wrapped on the ramp to stay steady. "Are you trying to convince me?"

"Have you considered that maybe you're just wrong?"

Not really.

His question reminded me of an important point from earlier. "I realized something tonight."

He scoffed. "Drinking is bad?"

I laughed, shaking my head. "No. Drinking has been good to me, actually."

"Let's see if you feel the same in the morning."

I ignored the sarcasm. "I realized that pure evil isn't always found behind the ones wearing tattoos and ripped clothes. It could be found behind the expensive suit and the nicest smile. And no matter which you wear, evil can't be hidden."

He stared at me curiously before nodding as if he was already aware.

"This place isn't what I expected," I said out loud. "I'd love to go back. I was having fun. Talking and dancing. I made a friend!" Sam had no idea how exceptional that statement was. "Come on, Sam." I begged like a child, taking his arm.

He huffed. "Yes, and you would easily become easy prey for anyone in there. You should thank me."

"Since when does the devil care?" I taunted.

"Who said I cared?"

I nudged him. "Admit it. You do care."

"I don't," he contradicted.

"Fine, I'm going back."

Sam pushed himself off the wall. "No, you aren't." The door of the elevator opened. He gestured for me to go first.

"I thought you didn't care?" I said with a grin.

Sam inched closer, causing my neck to stretch upward. "I may have lied. Just this once," he admitted, sending my heart right into a frenzy. "After you, precious."

I stumbled out, but before my face planted on the marble floor, I was lifted off the ground. "Hell, how much did you even drink?" Sam asked, walking us into a hallway with only one onyx door at the end.

"A couple? Max is a really good bartender. He

deserves a raise. Did you know he moved from Scotland to help pay for his sister's treatment?" I rambled, spluttering.

"He's fired."

I smacked his chest. "Stop. You can't. He saved me."

His steps slowed as his eyes came to meet mine. "Saved you?"

"Yeah."

His beautiful face was confused when he asked, "From what?"

I nestled my face closer to Sam's chest. "From the real evil. He was going to take a girl, Jen. A minor. He threatened to take me. Said he'd have customers for me. I wish you had been there to see him. He was bad, Sam, like real bad." I rambled as a shiver of disgust ran through me. "He could have taken us and no one would have known."

My cheek pressed against Sam, suddenly boiled as if his body temperature went up a couple of degrees. "Wrong. I would have known. And I would have searched for you till I found you." It sounded so much like a promise. "And I will make him regret ever laying eyes on you."

I think my heart skipped a beat. My stomach fluttered. "How?"

A muscled throbbed in his jaw as he said, "Don't you worry about it. But know that I will see him, Nyssa. And he will pay. I will make him pay."

I wasn't sure what he meant, but we stopped in front of the doors. Sam didn't take a key out. He mumbled words in a foreign language, and they opened. So much like at Glory's, it was scary.

He walked past an astonishing living room with windows so high that I had to crane my neck back to see the end. I barely had time to take in the sight when Sam turned past multiple doors until he went to a bedroom identical style to the rest of the apartment.

Sam walked to the bed with four black posts sitting in the center of the room and gently put me down on the blankets. My head rested on the pillows.

"I got to go home. I wasn't even supposed to go out. I'm grounded."

"You're in no condition to leave. Send a text to whoever. I'll take you in the morning." He pulled half away from me when my fingers gently wrapped around his bicep.

"Sam?"

He hesitated, almost as if he knew he wasn't going to like what came next. "Yeah?"

"Do you always kiss the person who summons you?" I had tried not to think about our kiss. A part of me wanted to know if that was part of the routine. From what Nathan had said, it was unusual when making a bargain and I didn't dare ask about it. "I know it doesn't happen a lot. The summoning thing." I licked my lips nervously, my fingers freeing him. "But when it does. Is it something you do…a lot?"

"No." No hesitation. No pause.

My heart jumped.

"Is it because only men summoned you in the past?" I mocked.

"No, Nyssa. Actually, women tend to do more summoning than men."

A smile stretched my lips. "So…was I the first?"

"Yes. Now sleep, Nyssa. You're going to feel ill in

the morning."

He straightened away from me when my hand grabbed his wrist and the words poured out of me before my brain could comprehend anything.

"Stay with me."

He inhaled deeply.

"I can't, precious."

I pouted. "Please?"

He shut his eyes briefly. "I'm doing this for you."

"I don't want to be alone."

Sam laughed. "Trust me. Being alone is better than being with me."

I shook my head, my curls dancing in front of me. "No. That's not true. Please. Stay."

"I can't, Nyssa."

"Why?" I insisted.

"Because." He raised his voice before inhaling deeply.

"Because what?"

"Because I won't be able to resist temptation and you, precious, you're a whole bundle of temptation wrapped up just for me to take. And I won't let myself take from you. I won't do this to you."

In the state I was in, I still managed to stand on my knees. I tripped on them, but Sam steadied me with one arm going around my waist. He cupped my cheek with his other hand, a thumb landed on my lower lip.

I lifted my eyes, and his intense gaze was already on mine. "How could this be possible?" Sam asked me in a whisper.

"What?" I replied in the same tone.

"You. How could you be real?" he said in wonder. "You're a vision. You're so pure and yet you wear the lips of a sinner. You're more virtuous than an angel, and yet you wear the face of a vixen. Your calls are so innocent, yet your song is as compelling as a siren." He continued rubbing my lip. "Yeah, you're temptation in its greatest form, and even one with the strongest will couldn't resist you. And I'm far from one of those." He breathed out, his eyes now fixating on my mouth.

Sam made me feel like I was the most precious piece of art he wished to stare at all day. And slowly I pressed myself onto him, not leaving a silver line of space between us. I boldly pressed my mouth to his, hoping he'd *respond*.

Instead, I think he stopped breathing all together.

"Nyssa." He said my name almost like I was the answer to his prayer. It was soaked in desperation. Anticipation.

I spoke against his mouth. "I don't want you to resist," I whispered. "Don't resist it," I repeated, this time, like a plea. "I want you to take what I'm willing to give you."

"Nyssa." This time when he repeated my name, there was a warning to his tone. Like a parent calling their kid's name when he was about to put himself in danger. Right now, the danger was so appealing, it was all I could think of. "Don't tempt me, Nyssa. I'm a demon. I'll take until you have nothing left to give." He warned.

"I don't believe that."

He let out a nervous chuckle. "And that makes you incredibly naïve. You have no idea how wrong you are. I'm the Devil for a reason."

"I saw…I felt.. the wicked and evil tonight. That's not what I feel with you. Quite the opposite."

"I'm the Devil, Nyssa." He repeated, as if it could engrave those words into my head.

"And I think you're an angel disguised as the Devil," I murmured.

Sam shut his eyes as if in pain. My hand brushed his face. I wanted to ask him why. What caused him pain? I wanted to wash it all away with one touch.

"Just let me in your armor." He didn't react.

So, I did the only logical thing. I let my lips meet his mouth. His lips were soft but unmoving. I pressed a little harder. Sam didn't respond to my invitation.

The rejection sunk in. I pushed myself off a second before his hand buried in my hair, pulling me back to my original place on the pillows, and Sam's mouth was back on mine.

And, oh boy, was he moving. Moving like a man who'd been denied water longer than one could survive and finally found the watering hole. His mouth was urging, demanding as if he would never get enough of me and I was about to vanish. My arms wrapped around his neck as I dragged him closer on top of me.

Good lord, nothing prepared me for this. His body was molding onto mine. My legs wrapped around his hips. The heat emanating from his body tempted me to rip my clothes off.

Sam lifted his weight for a moment. His now completely dilated eyes fixated on me. "I will not take you, Nyssa. Not tonight. You will wake up as pure as you are right now." The deception of his words shook my insides. "But I'll make you a promise."

"What?" My tone, raspy.

"If it's still what you desire in the morning. I'll gladly comply."

Gripping his shirt, I pulled him back to me.

I was seeing stars. Actually, I wasn't seeing anything at all. There was only him and the wildfire he ignited within me. I was drowning in a never-ending whirlpool of dizziness.

Not in a good way. Without warning, my stomach turned. I pushed Sam off and, as if knowing what was coming, he picked me up, ran to the bathroom and I emptied my stomach into the toilet bowl.

Sam's hand held my hair, and he witnessed my most embarrassing moment.

He gave me the time I needed then helped me back up. Sam gave me mouthwash before carrying me back to bed. My face nestled on his chest, my hands tangled on his shirt. My eyes were closed as I spoke. "Sam?"

"Yeah?"

"Why can't you just be a normal guy?" I asked in a sleepy voice.

Sam didn't answer. I didn't think he was going to. I was getting rocked by each inhale and exhale of his chest. His fingers were gently brushing my hair.

"Why do you want normal? Is it because you realized I'm evil?" he half mocked.

I gently shook my head. "No. You aren't evil."

"Then why ask for normal?"

"Because it'd be okay to like you without feeling like I completely lost my mind and myself in the process," I whispered. "I can't be lost." I'd never be found again.

The repeating movement of his hand against my head and my ear pressed against his chest was weirdly soothing.

"I'd still like you, precious," he whispered back.

"Lost or not."
    That made me smile. "Me too."

Chapter 19

The pounding in my head ripped me from slumber. My neck ached from lying on a hard, scorching pillow. Desperate for relief, I tried shifting into a more comfortable position, but the hard surface was unyielding. I peeled an eye open to discover I lay not on a brick-stuffed pillowcase but a chest. A very naked chest. A man's chest.

Oh, good lord.

I bolted upright as if I'd snuggled a venomous snake now rearing to bite me. My head spun as I scrambled back, only to land on my butt.

Way to wake up on the wrong side of the bed.

Sam's head peeked over the edge of the mattress. "Good morning, precious. Are you well?" he asked in a sleepy voice.

Oh crap on a cracker.

Was I well? No, I wasn't well.

Heat crawled up my face. I'd used *Sam* like a body pillow. Had I drooled on him? His midnight-blue stare gave me a shiver.

Why did he have to look like he was getting ready to pose for a boxer commercial?

"I could get used to waking up to this view." His eyes roamed my body.

I looked down to find the hem of a man's shirt riding up my hip and my white cotton underwear on display. I gasped and stood, pulling down on the shirt. The room swayed for a second. Shutting my eyes, I brought a hand to my forehead.

Oh, this was bad. *Real* bad.

My stomach churned. I was going to be sick. Words stuck in my throat. I took a sharp inhale, one that almost cut through my lungs. "Did…did…"

I opened my eyes and found Sam arching a brow at me, patiently waiting. He was going to make me finish this sentence.

Of course. How lovely of him.

I clenched my jaw, feeling the pressure of my teeth grinding together. "Did something happen?"

He feigned ignorance, putting an arm under his head. "Something? Plenty happened, precious. You need to be more specific."

He enjoyed watching me squirm.

The bastard.

"Did…" My hands tangled together. "You know."

The corner of his lip turned up. "As in did we—"

My arms shot out, making frantic waving motions to interrupt him. "Yes. Yes. Please do not say it."

Next thing I knew, an arm snaked around my waist, and I was lifted from the ground and pressed against the sheets. Sam's perfect face hovered above me, barely an inch from mine. His little move bottomed out my stomach.

A second later, his nose found the crook of my neck. My hands gripped the sheets on either side of my legs. I could swear, he…smelled me.

Such bad timing. I felt like a corpse. Probably smelled worse.

His body was scorching against mine. A little voice

inside urged me to nestle against him. To let the warmth swallow me. A shudder slithered down my spine. I wasn't sure if it was of anticipation or surprise.

His deep voice spoke in my ear, his breath making me shiver for a reason I couldn't deny. "I may be a demon, Nyssa, but I'm not one to take advantage of this kind of situation." Of course not. Afterall, I'm sure there was a lineup of gorgeous girls waiting to throw themselves at him. "And you can be certain that when it happens, you won't be left doubting. You'll remember every second and will beg me for more."

I just died of embarrassment. Or maybe excitement.

My insides twisted with the desire to apologize. To say I didn't mean it like that, but the words got stuck in my throat as he stood in his splendor wearing only black boxers, his back to me.

It was covered in tattoos. Two huge wings arced out of his shoulder blades and covered every muscle down to his hips. The ink looked so real; I could see each feather. My gaze shifted to the center, where a verse bridged the wings together.

From the light it chose darkness.
From love it chose loneliness.
From good it was born, to be reborn in evil.
With no regrets, I shall continue the path I chose.

My hand reached for Sam before I knew I'd moved. My fingers brushed the words as if hypnotized. He flinched at my touch but didn't move away.

"What does it mean?" I asked him, barely above a whisper.

He covered himself with a shirt and turned to me. A moment passed in loaded silence. "It's a reminder,"

Sam finally said.

"Of what?"

"That we each build the path we take." It was far from what I wanted to know, but the discussion closed as he passed me some clothes. Men's clothes. "That's all I have. Yours are being washed. We've got to go. I'll drive you."

That brought me back to the reason I'd shown up here.

"Wait, you said you found something yesterday. What is it?"

Sam walked to the bathroom without answering.

Great. Just great.

I heard the noise of cupboards opening, water running, and he came back to the room, a glass of water in one hand and Tylenol in the other.

"Here, for the headache. Go shower. You need to look presentable for your family. We'll talk after."

"Thanks." I took Sam's offering, suddenly doused in self-consciousness.

"How's the shoulder?"

Funny he should ask. I moved my arm. "Actually, pretty good," I told him, surprised.

He nodded.

I rushed to the bathroom. When my reflection stared at me, I wanted to punch Sam for not saying anything.

Dear Lord. It was worse than I expected. I looked like I'd slept outside in a hurricane. My hair was a nest of curls pointing in all directions. My eyes had huge dark bags underneath. My hand went up to my swollen lips like I'd been kissed all night.

And I remembered. My boldness. The sense of

power. The desire.

And Sam's righteousness.

He didn't *take* when I begged. No. He'd controlled himself through the wanting. The memory of his body sharing my desire reddened my cheeks. The promise he'd made me whispered still. That if I wanted him in the morning, he'd willingly *take*.

Oh, good Lord.

I wasn't sure if I was grateful or upset about Sam's behavior. Either way, I was mortified. I couldn't recognize the person staring back in the mirror.

It took me less than ten minutes to wash up.

When I got out, Sam was already dressed and showered. His curls were wet, and he looked ready for the runaway.

My hands tangled together. "I wanted to thank you for…"

He arched a brow.

"Being a gentleman."

A chuckle escaped him. "You've got it all wrong. I'm no gentleman, precious." In two big strides, Sam closed the space between us, waking my sluggish heart. His hand cupped my neck and my stomach clenched as he whispered, "I'll confess that I'm happy you didn't want me to take you this morning. You've awoken a beast, precious, and once the chase starts, you'll have nowhere to hide. I will chase you to heaven if I must, but you will never escape." His face advanced, his lips brushed my jaw. "And you'll love every second of it," his lips promised against my skin. My knees wavered, ready to buckle from underneath me.

My mouth opened, but no words came out.

Sam took a step back, all business again, his hands

in his suit pockets. "I couldn't find your friend's name in our books."

I let myself sit on the edge of the bed before I collapsed. It wasn't time to get swept away in daydreams of Sam. Isabelle took precedent.

"Book?" I repeated.

I swore a new fire burned in Sam's blue eyes. The way he looked at me was…different. The very hunger roaring in my chest shone in his eyes.

He cleared his throat and averted his gaze. "Yes. We need to keep tabs of bargains and their terms. I couldn't find Isabelle's name anywhere." His voice was deeper. Huskier. Sam passed a hand over his face.

"What does that mean?"

He sat on the chair between the window and the bed. "It means the deal wasn't sealed or I'm missing something, which is highly unlikely."

I stood. "If the deal wasn't sealed, how is she still missing?" My hands played with the shirt Sam gave me.

"There's more out there than demon deals to blame for your friend's disappearance."

"I saw a demon take her."

"Yes, but that does not mean he still has her. And if he does and doesn't respect the rules, I will take care of it."

"And if she's not with him?"

"Then it's out of my control."

"Let's say the demon doesn't have her anymore." Which I was certain he did. "If we make a deal, you and I, can you make everything go away? Can Isabelle keep her soul and her mom healthy?"

Sam's expression turned to ice, and I quivered in

the chill rolling off him.

I blinked, and Sam stood in front of me. His fingers on my chin, tilting my head back. I inhaled his unique aroma.

"Do you not have any value for yourself at all?"

My heartbeat thundered in my eardrums. "This has nothing to do with me."

"Why would you think she matters more than you do?"

Maybe because I never felt like I ever mattered. "Does it matter?" I asked back.

"Yes. It does. Because from where I stand, no one would be worth you." That swallowed my next breath. Sam's eyes swapped from blue to orange, his pupil becoming vertical. His gaze shifted from my eyes to my lips.

"How would you define someone's worth?" I murmured.

The corner of his lips tugged up. "Trust me, precious. I've seen plenty of souls, none compared close to yours."

"Does that mean you'd be willing to be more lenient with my deal?" Considering my soul was purer?

That wiped the smile right off. "What do you think that would cost you?" Sam asked me. He tried to sound careless, but he couldn't hide the anger behind his question.

I had hoped it would cost something reasonable considering we were sort of friends, but from the look in his eyes, I wasn't so sure anymore.

"You tell me."

"Nothing you'd be willing to give."

My eyes narrowed on him. "We've already

established that I'd be willing to give it all to save her." Then it dawned on me. It wasn't the unwilling participant. "This isn't about me. It was never about me," I voiced aloud. "This is about you."

His brows drew together, and the midnight blue in his eyes darkened in warning, but I no longer cared. "You're the one who isn't willing to take whatever I'm offering."

His face came so close to mine, our noses touched. "Are you that eager to lose everything that makes you, *you*?" he asked against my mouth before abruptly letting me go. "I'll figure out what happened. You get to keep your soul another day, precious."

"Why do you care so much about my soul?"

Sam's fist clenched at his side. "The real question is, why don't you?" With that, he went and picked up my bag. "Come on, I'll drop you off at home."

And he was out the door.

I chased after him. "You haven't answered, Sam. You're a demon. Why are you trying to help me? Especially when I'm offering you the biggest prize that your kind seeks and since it's so special, huh?" After all, demons weren't known for their virtue. Sam didn't even bother turning around.

"If demons aren't following rules, they have to face punishment." He studied me over his shoulder. "That's one reason, anyway."

"Why else?"

"I want to help a friend."

My steps halted as I took in Sam. "Like a *real* friend? Like how humans define friends? As in someone you actually like?" I asked, stunned. Demons didn't have friends, did they?

Instead of being insulted, he laughed, and it warmed me to my core, deep and rich as a vat of toffee. "Well, maybe not to the degree you feel about your unfortunate friend and the pickle she's in, but yeah, someone I don't wish to die."

The corner of my lip twitched. "The pickle she's in, huh?"

He shrugged one shoulder. "I've picked up some human lingo."

We both resumed our walk down the hallway. Gosh, this place was huge. "Right. So, you want to help this friend. Who you don't actually care for in any meaningful way besides preferring her alive?"

He smiled. "You got it, precious."

"All right then. For a second, I thought you were going to tell me demons could actually love," I joked.

His feet halted, and he twisted around at the hips.

"I never said we couldn't. I said I preferred not to see *that* particular friend dead or hurt."

My heart jumped. "So demons could love? Like love *love*?" I asked, the thought wheedling in and planting irrational hope.

Sam seemed to ponder my words for a moment. "I'm not sure if the word love accurately describes a demon having strong feelings for someone, but yes, contrary to common beliefs, demons do have feelings. Very strong ones, I might add. Probably stronger than anything humans have ever felt."

I waited for him to make one of his sarcastic jokes.

"You're serious?" I said, speechless.

"Yes." His cold, blue eyes met mine, glowing with a new fire—a slow-burning ember at the heart of his pupils. "But our love is fierce," he said, leaning in, "possessive—some might even say obsessive. That's why they don't call it real love. Because humans categorized true love as altruistic. Our love is the opposite. It's selfish, demanding, and..." He paused, making my breath catch in my throat.

"And what?" I murmured, hypnotized.

"Inescapable."

Sweet baby Jesus, save me now.

He continued walking.

I trailed him like a duckling. "That sounds—"

"Terrifying?" he suggested as we made it to the elevator.

My mouth felt as dry as the desert. "Actually, yes." My voice was raspy. I licked my lips. "But also..."

He tilted his head, inviting me to finish.

"Promising."

Oh Lord, I wanted to smack myself for daring to say that out loud.

"Promising?" he repeated the word slowly.

"Yes," I breathed out, stepping into the elevator to hide my embarrassment.

Sam followed closely, staying silent until the door opened to an underground parking garage. "Nyssa, if anything happens and you can't reach a phone, all you have to do is think of me very hard. I'll know where you are, and I will come to you."

"You're kidding right?"

"I never kid. Think of it like praying to God, except I'll actually answer you, Nyssa. Always."

My gaze lifted to his. I believed him.

We walked to a sports car I had never seen in my life. Sam flashed me an arrogant smile. "You like?"

I shrugged. "Cars aren't my thing."

"Cause you've never been inside one as classy as this baby." He opened the door for me. I sat. He was right. It was luxury to the extreme. And while I appreciated the beauty and comfort, I didn't care beyond that.

"You're probably the only living being in this world or beyond to not be impressed by this car." Sam sounded amused.

My gaze drifted outside. I was in a fight with myself. A part of me wanted to be upset at Sam for refusing to bargain. He had the power to help and chose not to. That stung.

The other part of me believed he wouldn't take my soul because he cared.

Perhaps I was wrong, seeing only half the picture. Waiting wasn't a luxury I could afford, though. I had no time to puzzle him out. I needed action, or I'd have to eradicate distraction.

"Can you drop me at the corner, please?" I didn't need Micah to see Sam. What a blowout that would be.

Sam looked like he wanted to say more. Lots more.

I put my hand on the handle, ready to walk out.

"Nyssa."

I twisted to him.

"Just remember. If anything happens, just think of me really hard. Okay?"

"Yeah, okay."

It'd be much harder *not* thinking of him.

Chapter 20

No one was home. Not one missed call or text. Yeah, I was officially a loser. Gone for twenty-four hours and not a soul noticed. I wondered how long it would've taken for my family to report me missing, if that creep at the bar had made good on his threats.

I bet Sam would have realized before them. There was no time to throw myself a pity party. I dialed my brother, pacing the main floor.

No answer. I dialed again. And again.

After the fifth time, he picked up.

"Nys, are you okay?"

No, I'm far from okay. My best friend is missing, her mother is dying, and I may have a thing for the Devil. Far from okay.

"I'm fine. What news do you have?" I bit my thumbnail, pacing and hoping he'd found something useful. Praying Isabelle was fine.

"It's not good," he said in one breath.

I sat on the edge of my bed.

"Not good how?"

I heard Micah exhale a heavy breath. "Isabelle isn't back, Nys."

"Her mother?"

"She's gotten worse."

It made no sense. "How? If she sealed a deal, the demon can't go back on it. And if she didn't, then he should've brought her back. They're bound by the rules."

A silence followed. "How do you know about their rules, Nys?"

I held my breath. *Stupid.* "I read it in a book somewhere."

Another silence answered. My heartbeat accelerated. Micah was annoyingly skilled at analyzing me. He knew me better than anyone. He didn't need a demon's ability to know when I lied. He read it on my face or peered into my heart somehow. I never had to speak a word.

"What book?" Of course he'd insist.

"Who cares!" I snapped. "Where is Isabelle? What does any of this mean? Did anyone from the cult say something?" My brother knew what I meant, but I could practically hear him frowning about the cult label.

"They think Isabelle didn't end up holding her end of the deal. There was more to it than her soul."

Very similar to what Sam had said. "Like what?"

"That's the big mystery."

"Why are they suddenly interested? The cult. Father can't be saving face over losing followers." Opinions of sheep never mattered. "So why's he wish-washing all of a sudden? He made it clear he didn't care about whatever happened to Isabelle."

Another silence. My annoyance was growing with each breath. "Of course. You can't tell me," I finally said.

"Nys—"

"Don't worry, Micah. I'll figure it out all on my own." I ended the call.

I had class to prepare for, and I dressed while ignoring the non-stop vibration of my cell phone.

I walked to school and ignored Mike and his followers as I entered my first class. Settling in, I brooded on a plan I didn't particularly fancy.

In my defense, I had no other option. Finding the item to bend Sam's will was all I had, and I didn't like it.

Not one bit.

Not only for the most obvious reason—I mean, who was crazy enough to force the Devil's hand—but also because we'd developed some sort of...*thing*.

I had no other more appropriate word to describe it.

When class ended, I shut my blank notes window, closed the laptop, and aimlessly wandered campus. I couldn't risk going home and having my brother thwart the only plan I had.

Maryssa.

After an hour of roaming, I found myself across the street from her store. I sat on the bench, debating.

"Why are you sitting here all alone?" a tiny voice asked.

When I looked up, I found Krista, the kid who lived on top of Glory, blinking at me from beneath a beanie crammed over blond curls. Her mother had buttoned her wool jacket tight to her neck.

"Hey, kiddo."

"Why are you sitting alone?" she asked again.

I gave a small smile. "I'm just...thinking. What are you doing here alone?"

She gave a small shrug. "Getting some air. Can I sit?"

"Sure." I scooted over to give her space.

"What's bothering you?" Her round, pale face and light eyes looked genuinely curious.

I twisted to her, a small smile tugging my lips. "What makes you say I'm bothered?"

She shrugged. "You have the look of someone bothered."

Hmm. Fair enough.

"Have you ever done something you didn't want to do but had to?"

She hadn't. She was only eight.

"Why do you have to do it if you don't want to?"

I tucked my hands in my jacket. "My friend needs my help but…it'll be at the expense of someone else."

She tilted her head slightly. "Another friend."

Not even. At the Devil's expense.

"Not exactly, but someone I…I sort of…you know." I couldn't find the right word.

"You like?"

Good God, yeah, I liked Sam. A lot.

"Someone I care for," I corrected. "And I just…I don't know." I'd officially gone insane. Why did I care so much? I was sure the Devil had done much worse and for lesser reasons.

Krista's tiny hand touched my arm.

"Does he care about you?"

Did he?

"I think so."

As much as the Devil could care, I guess.

"Then he'll find it in him to forgive you."

Would Sam?

"And if he doesn't?"

Her lips curved into a small smile. "Then he wasn't worth your worry." She nudged my shoulder with hers.

"You know what I think?"

"What?"

She stood, slipping her hands in her wool pocket. "Something tells me that he'll surprise you. You wouldn't be so worried if he wasn't worthy." She shrugged. "Do what feels right. Instincts don't lie." *How is she eight?* "I got to go, but promise you will tell me how it went?"

"I will. Be careful."

Krista followed her way back to her home.

I stood, aware of what had to be done.

Despite myself, despite knowing better, I'd go to her.

Once my racing brain slowed, I realized how foolish it was to have gone to her in the first place. There was no way Maryssa had agreed to help without expecting to gain something in return. Father hated her, yet she kept her position in their tight circle. That wasn't done without threats and pressure.

Gavriel's daughter seeking her help was the perfect opportunity for her. She'd thrown a lure, and I was going for the bait.

We both knew I had no other option. Isabelle's time was running out. I needed something to force Sam's hand. God, force the Devil's hand. It was truly laughable. Beyond that, guilt ate at me. Sam meant…more. More than he should. A part of me didn't see him as a demon. Even less as their leader.

Desperate times called for desperate measures. But I was as good as dead the second he found out about this. Or maybe, like Krista said, he'd forgive me, and it would all be worth it.

Gathering the little courage I had, I crossed the

avenue. I stared at the green door, and with one breath, I pushed it open and walked inside.

A heavy scent of incense floated in the air. Candles illuminated the wares in soft halos. Which also meant it was dark enough for my Shadows to drift in after me but still provide enough light for me to inspect the shop.

Thanks to Father, I was well-accustomed to the bizarre, but this place gave me the creeps. Terrifying objects occupied the shelves, from skulls to jars of eyes and other unidentifiable substances. Upside down crosses and the devil's star hung scattered throughout the store as macabre wall decorations. Clumps of herbs, weapons, and strange lumps I didn't wish to identify dangled from the ceiling.

I had entered a house of evil.

My heart raced, sending a deafening rush of blood through my head. My courage evaporated, and I stumbled back, ready to make a run for it. As I turned to flee, Maryssa appeared, making me gasp in surprise.

"God! You almost scared me to death!" I told her, panting, a hand on my poor heart.

Her lips didn't even twitch. "I must say, with a fifty-fifty chance of you coming, I was ready to hedge my bets you wouldn't show."

I couldn't guess if she was happy or not.

She gave me more credit than I deserved. The chances of me showing were much less than that, but here I was.

As if reading my thoughts, she explained, "It's that selfless soul that gets you into trouble. More trouble than a dark occultist by far. That big heart blinds you to danger. Otherwise, you would have stayed away for sure." I almost felt like a child getting reprimanded for talking to a stranger. "Were you about to leave? Already?"

I was too petrified to answer. I had no idea what I was doing, going against the prime evil. How had it gotten on my bucket list? My life might have been boring and lonely a week ago, but it was mine, nonetheless. I'd chucked a bomb into it.

I spotted a whirlwind of movement behind Marissa. And another on my left. My Shadows were still here, and just like that, I released the breath my terror had caged. They drifted closer, reassuring me.

Marissa slightly cocked her head, intensely watching me.

"No, I was…I was checking the place." I was safe now.

Her eyes narrowed on me longer than necessary.

"Follow me."

She brushed past me and headed to a back door.

I still hadn't moved. She halted and spoke over her shoulder. "I don't have all night, and I don't like wasting time."

Inhaling deeply, I followed.

We entered a stock room filled with boxes, a rickety table, and a nasty surprise leaned back in one of the seats. Nathan waggled his fingers at me, balancing on two chair legs. Maryssa was consorting with demons? How naïve I'd been to trust him. Did he share that file with Maryssa or was she the one who'd given him the information?

This was the worst idea—*ever*. Again, I prepared to bolt.

Nathan stood, black eyes pinning me. "Don't, Nyssa. Everything is fine."

"Fine?" I glanced between him and Maryssa. "Why are you here?" I wanted to ask if he shared the secrets he'd dug up about me.

"Is this a trap?" I asked instead, my fear growing big enough to swallow me.

Nathan frowned. "Of course not! I'd never hurt you."

My arms folded on my chest. "Says a demon to a defenseless human."

Marissa laughed out loud. For the first time since I'd known her.

"What's funny?" I wondered.

"Do you honestly think of yourself as a defenseless human?" she asked, a finger tracing the wild flight pattern of one of my Shadows, dark eyes bouncing between all three. No, impossible.

They were in my head. Weren't they?

Nathan rescued me without knowing it. "How do you do all this, Nyssa? How did you even know I was a demon that first night at Peccatta?"

I shifted my weight from one foot to another. Those onyx eyes were impossible to ignore. Yet, Sam made it clear, the feat should've been impossible. He had never mentioned it again and neither had I.

Perhaps, this was Maryssa's test. "Your eyes are pitch black. It's difficult not to notice." His mouth opened. My Shadows left their perches along my arms and swirled, agitated.

A sign, maybe?

"You can see my eyes in their demon form?"

I nodded and glanced back at Maryssa.

Interest turned her face more feline. "You were telling the truth."

"That's impossible!" Nathan exclaimed. "Only the damned can see demons. Unless you—"

"That's enough," Maryssa interrupted. "Nyssa came here with a purpose. Not for an interrogation." Her defense surprised me. "I have what you've been looking for." She inclined her head, dipping her shoulders into the gesture. My brows creased deeper.

What on earth was going on? Did she just bow to me? She left before I could utter a word, leaving me alone in the devil's shop with a demon.

God help me.

The Shadows calmed down, hovering around me like a barrier wall.

"I promise, I won't harm you. It was never my intention." Nathan's eyes flicked upward, landing right on my Shadow's inky, ever-shifting forms. "But please, keep those things away from me. They give me the creeps."

"Yes, he'd never dare try and harm you," agreed Maryssa, walking back with a black box in her hands.

One shadow slunk toward Nathan, and he sank deeper into his seat, shrinking away.

"You see them," I whispered more for myself than anything else.

He looked at me like I had lost my mind.

Perhaps I had.

"Duhhh. They're very difficult to miss." And I swear, I heard the inspecting Shadow growl. "Sorry. Sorry. Not that you aren't lovely to behold, of course."

"Oh, my God." I needed to sit.

No no, I needed to flee.

Wait! I pinched myself, sipping air through a straw-sized airway.

Ow! So this was real. I mentally gave myself a good slap. The Shadows fed on my agitation, whipping around like banners in a storm.

Marissa came up beside me, alarmed enough to shield herself with my body. "You need to relax. Just like demons, they sense when you're afraid." Her eyes jumped around the room. "Only they seem to become"—she searched for the word—"*upset* by your distress." She scrutinized me. "How long have you been able to see them?"

A nervous laugh left me. "I thought…" I shook my head.

"What?"

My eyes met hers as I whispered, "I thought they were in my head. That I was imagining them. Because seeing Shadows is crazy, right?"

Even for me.

Nathan laughed from his seat. He still wasn't moving. "Trust me, doll. They are very much real. Remember I told you there was just something about you? This is one of those reasons."

"Nyssa, how long have you been able to see them?" Marissa insisted.

A nervous giggle left me. I passed a shaky hand through my hair. How long? She must be kidding.

"This isn't funny, Nyssa. Quite the opposite. We need to know how long they've been around you," Maryssa said. "To know if you're in danger of any kind."

"Danger?" I was more concerned with her or Nathan hurting me than my Shadows.

Another titter bubbled up as I crouched on the floor and hugged my knees to my chest. "They've been with me for as long as I can remember." I thought back before lifting my gaze to Maryssa. "I've seen them my whole life."

The room went dead silent. I couldn't believe I'd confessed. To a witch and a demon, no less. But they saw them. My shadows.

While that made me feel less crazy, it also awoke new worries.

Nathan walked closer to me, or he tried to. A shadow blocked his path, the most imposing one of the three.

"Hell, Dell, what's your problem? I won't do anything. Please move out of the way." A growl answered.

"Dell?" I echoed.

"Yes, they have names. All three of them. Dell, Blaze, and Fury."

"They never told me," I said, more for myself.

"They've spoken to you?" Nathan said in a shriek.

I didn't react, mainly because I wasn't even sure they had, aside from that odd warning when the demon walked into Glory looking for a mystery object. The same one I was now seeking, I'd wager.

"Do you know what they are?" Marissa questioned.

I studied the one Nathan called Dell. "I call them Shadows."

My Shadows.

"Have they ever tried to harm you?"

It was my turn to give them a puzzled look. I rose slowly off the floor. "No. Never. Why would they want to harm me?"

A nasty laugh escaped Nathan. "Because that's what they do. What else would they do with you?"

My fists clenched at my sides. "They'd never hurt me. They keep me company," I said more irritated than I rationally should be.

"Bullshit," Nathan said.

Once again, they growled.

Nathan showed them his hands and murmured under his breath, "Well I'll be damned."

"You already are," Maryssa reminded him.

"Wait," I said. "How do you see them?" I asked.

Nat shrugged. "I'm a demon." He glanced at Maryssa. "She's…special." He didn't elaborate, but she must be a servant of the underworld to own this place. No wonder Father kept her at arm's length.

I twisted to face Nathan. "Does that mean your boss sees them too?"

"When you say—"

"I mean Sam."

Nathan stared at me as if I'd just lost my mind. Little did he know I'd misplaced it a long time ago. Actually, he and his damn file probably did know.

"Sam?" he slowly repeated. I felt the heat crawling up my neck under his narrowed eyes.

"Yes?"

"Why do you call him Sam?" Nathan asked.

I fidgeted on my feet. The Shadows became a tornado.

Nathan put his hands up in surrender. Again.

"That's what he told me to call him." Had I done something wrong? What was with the interrogation? "You haven't answered, though. Does he see them?"

"That, he does," he said with a laugh. "He's their master. They only answer to him."

Marissa stepped in. "But, Nyssa, you have no idea

what they are?"

They're my friends.

And I was ready to defend them. I wasn't some clueless girl. Sure, before this exact moment, I hadn't been totally sure they were real, but now that I knew, there was no way I'd let anyone speak ill of them.

"Here is what I know that counts. They've been with me through everything. Whenever I was afraid as a child, whenever I got hurt, or whenever I've been suffocating with anxiety, they've always been there." My chest was heaving with each breath, faster and faster. "They appear when they feel my need for them. They defended me when a demon tried taking me. They are *my* Shadows. Mine." All three of them flew around me, making Maryssa suck in a breath. One brushed my shoulder, his shade acting as a volatile sleeve for a few beats.

"They're my light in darkness, and that's all that matters." As if agreeing with me, the two other ones shaded my sides and curled over my shoulders, their touch intangible. "Now, can we get this over with? I'd like to be on my way."

Maryssa and Nathan exchanged a look before she nodded. She deposited the small box on the round table and gestured for me to sit.

I walked to the chair on the opposite side of Maryssa, with Nathan seated between us. She gently pushed the box in front of me.

"Open it."

Something twisted inside me.

Something illogical.

Something irrational.

I was the one who'd gone to Marissa and begged

for help. This was the answer to my prayers.

But I held the pandora box in the palm of my hands, unsure. Once I opened it, once I peeked inside, there'd be no going back. The King of Hell finding out my plan was merely one consequence. This step meant more than that. It meant entering a world I'd been shunned and guarded from, but entering it from below, sneaking inside through unsavory means, not walking through the front door with a key.

"Is this the item Sam has been searching for?" Another weird exchange took place.

"Not exactly."

I frowned. "Then what exactly will this do?"

"It will make him accept anything you ask of him," Maryssa told me. "But only if—"

"If what?"

"If you're the one meant to be opening this."

Oh crap. So, it wasn't a sure bet. "And if I'm not?"

She just stared, her silence a challenge.

I gulped. "How will I know if it worked?"

She gave me a small smile. "Trust me, you'll know."

Summoning my courage, I placed my hands on the shiny box. The cold material bit my skin as I lifted the top.

A bright white light blinded me. And then, before my surroundings could return, everything went black.

Chapter 21

My eyelids peeled open. The familiar seashell light on the ceiling absorbed the ray of sun coming from the window. I sat up. I was dressed in the exact same clothes I'd worn to meet Maryssa. I had no recollection of how I'd gotten back home. Much less in bed.

I felt...different.

Changed. *Inside*. My soul felt shattered. Like a vital part of me had been torn away, leaving a raw and gaping void. Oh, God, what was in that box?

I rushed to the bathroom vanity, bracing my hands on either side of the mirror. My legs, barely able to carry my weight. The same big green eyes. The same brown caramel hair. The same heart-shaped face.

Yet, not the same person. As if the girl in the reflection had stepped out of a faraway memory, dangling an inch from my fingertips.

No trace of my Shadows anywhere.

Without warning, the music crescendo. Only, to a different tune.

The notes were heavy, loud, heartbreaking. The shattering I felt exploded. My hand grabbed my chest, holding my shirt in my fist, and a pressing grief knocked me to my knees.

The heaviness in my chest made it difficult to breathe, each inhalation a laborious effort. A persistent ache gnawed at my core. It wrapped around me like a suffocating cloak, isolating me in a realm of desolation and despair.

My music wasn't a soothing background symphony. It was screaming to be heard. To be understood. Tears welled up.

I gripped my hair at the roots with my free hand, rocking my body back and front.

My throat got tighter.

A panic attack was near.

Breathe in. Breathe out.

You're okay, Nyssa.

Breathe in. Breathe out.

"Stop it. Stop it." I couldn't take it. The music surrounded me, *broke* me. As if my heart were ruptured glass, exploding out of my chest in slicing shards.

"Stop!" I screamed.

And it did. It all died down. The pressure in my chest lifted. A little.

The air passed more freely, although I panted like I'd just ran a marathon. I stood, my legs trembling, using the vanity as a crutch.

That box had done something to me.

I felt broken inside.

I'd signed up for power, for leverage, and gotten a crippling weakness.

Maryssa had some explaining to do. She'd better know what went wrong. Figuring she'd be at the university, I didn't bother with a shower, just brushed my teeth, threw on fresh bottoms, tossed my hair in a bun, and barreled out the door.

I made it to the university in record time, panting hard. I shoved through the sea of annoying people glancing at me like I was a specimen from another world.

Considering my time had been divided between finding the demon who'd kidnapped Isabelle, summoning the Devil, and seeking a way to force his help, I'd say I'd earned a break from the judgment.

I wondered if the box had even worked. If Sam would suddenly be more inclined to chase down every demon until we found the one that held Isabelle's contract and ripped it apart.

If this pain was the price to pay...could I handle it?

I tried rushing in before class began, but when I finally trudged to Maryssa's door, she was already speaking to a crowded room.

For God's sake, I couldn't catch a break. In agony, I gave zero fucks about etiquette and tapped on the door with my knuckles.

Her head snapped to meet my gaze, along with every student in the classroom.

"Miss Lewis, please shut the door on your way out."

Of course. Like she'd take a minute to come see me in an emergency. She was one who'd shoved that pandora box on me with no real warning.

I was being dramatic. She hadn't *made* me open it; I'd sort of begged for it.

Still, I'd obviously fainted, and she'd just tossed me in my bed. She could have kept me with her to check on me. She owed me answers, and I wasn't going to back down.

"I need a minute of your time. It's sort of urgent." In front of so many witnesses, I couldn't keep the blush off my face. Maryssa just stared back with her icy blue eyes.

Oh Lord, say something. Anything.

Right when I gave up and started to shut the door, Maryssa dropped her screen remote and made her way toward me.

"Read the next three pages," she commanded her class. "I'll have questions about it." She pushed past me, and the moment I ducked out with her, she closed the door and crossed her arms.

"Someone better have died if you're interrupting my class."

I opened my mouth and closed it. Twice. "You're kidding, right? What the hell happened last night? I don't remember anything."

"You collapsed."

I threw my arms up. "Yes, that part I guessed. Did it work? Did I gain Sam's favor? Will he listen to me?" I bombarded her.

A little smile tugged her lips. "Well, dear, you're still standing here breathing. I'd say that box was for you."

My brows drew together. "But you're not sure."

"I'm as sure as one can be, considering our unusual situation."

So *not* an answer. Maryssa already had her hand on the door handle, ready to leave me hanging here with more unanswered issues.

"Wait." I grabbed her arm. "I think the box did something to me. Something *bad*."

"It probably did."

God, so it was the price to pay.

"Why didn't you keep me with you last night? Who brought me home?" I asked her.

Good God, I hoped it wasn't Nathan.

She twisted at her waist. "The Shadows wouldn't let me come near you."

I nodded, understanding. If my Shadows frightened a demon, I understood why Maryssa hadn't taken her chances testing them.

"Either way, your brother unexpectedly showed up at my store. Let me tell you, I didn't have a choice in the matter."

"What?" How in the world had Micah known where I was?

Marissa pulled her lower lip between her teeth, looking hesitant. "Be very careful, Nyssa. Sometimes, the most fearful monsters wear the face of a friend or family. Not every evil announces itself." With that warning, she stepped back into her class, leaving me standing there with more questions than when I came.

Did she hope to turn me against my brother? I didn't even bother checking my phone for answers from Micah about last night. Tugging my coat closer to my body, I walked to the exit. The crushing pain still lingered, but it was more manageable.

Until without warning, an incredible heat ran in my veins and burned all the morning's discomfort away. My heartbeat picked up at an anticipatory pace. The tiny hairs along my nape all stood at once. My eyes lifted from the ground, and I froze at the sight of Sam. Casually leaning against a tree trunk, a foot propped on the bark, he folded his inked arms on his broad chest.

Oh, good Lord, have mercy on my soul.

My knees almost buckled. What in the world was wrong with me?

Technically, my chance to find out if Maryssa's black box was worth the trouble was standing a few feet away. All I needed to do was reach him. Sam made that decision easier, strolling toward me without a care.

I wanted to stop him.

I couldn't see him in this state. I wasn't myself. God, I was about to throw myself in his arms, tangle my legs around him like a baby panda, and beg him to take all of me like I should have yesterday.

I was debating my next move when Sam suddenly stopped. Staring at me as if…in awe. So still, he might have stopped breathing. Could the King of Hell die from lack of oxygen?

Then his whole stance shifted. His hands curled into two balls; his piercing blue eyes scoured the campus like a wild animal sensing an immediate threat. They even seemed to glow when they snapped back to me, and then in five decisive steps, he reached my spot halfway down the steps.

Something changed in his demeanor. God, he looked furious. Ready to unleash Hell on Earth and eliminate anyone in his path.

I gulped. My heart threatened to jump out of my chest. Was he pissed at me? My eyes roamed the campus searching for another culprit before landing back on a very upset Sam, locked in on me.

Yep, definitely the target of his anger.

And being the smart person I am, I did the only thing I found plausible, given my current predicament.

Backing away, I twisted, pushed back through the school's front door, and I ran.

I ran like Hell was chasing me. Its king was the next worst thing, anyway.

I'd barely made it to the intersection of the hallway when I bumped into what felt like a rock wall and fell straight on my ass.

Damn, that hurt. A pair of shining black shoes planted in front of me, framed by perfectly tailored pants. I dared peek up at the Devil, looking more beautiful than ever, glaring at me with fire in his blue eyes.

"Nyssa," he said like a teacher about to scold his student. It irritated me to no end. "You've been a busy little bee, I see."

"I—"

His raised hand cut me off. "No, no, it wasn't a question."

Rude. The Devil was rude. How shocking?

He bent down to my level, his arms on each thigh and his hands intertwined between his knees. "Do you have the slightest idea what you've done?" he murmured in a charged tone that rattled me to the bone.

I tucked my hair behind my ear as a nervous chuckle escaped me. "Gained your favor?"

I hoped.

He laughed. It was rich, deep, and *hot*. Like sultry music. "If only."

Oh God, I burned head to toe, my blood flowing thick and searing as lava. To my great relief, I didn't combust before the discomfort subsided.

"You never needed to do anything to gain my favor, Nyssa." His hand, gentle as his tone, hung in the air between us, fingers extended for a caress that never came before he settled it back on his thigh. "And now, you've gained Hell."

I wasn't even listening.

His words were gibberish.

I was in a trance. Mesmerized. Totally

mesmerized.

My breath caught in my throat.

What was in that box? I ached for the touch he'd denied, yearned to claim it, even as I sat paralyzed by his proximity, examining every hair, every line, every micro expression as a work of art. I'd never felt so utterly out of control.

All I wanted to do was lift my hand and meet his skin. Would it be soft like velvet? Scorching like hellfire or cold as the lake of ice in Dante's ninth circle? I wanted to discover all those answers, and this time, I wanted to remember every detail. To cherish those memories like my most precious treasure. All I needed to do was lean in and reach him.

"That'd be a very bad idea, precious. The game just changed. A game without rules. You need to keep your focus." He stood too far in a blink. "Get up," he ordered, his eyes never leaving mine. The pain returned, stabbing my heart through my back.

Had the temperature just gone up thirty degrees? It was his voice that lit the kindling; he needed to stop talking. My thoughts were scattered. Enchanted by the Devil's gaze. My brain fogged.

"I think something is very wrong with me," I mumbled.

"You think?" I barely noticed the sarcasm.

"What have I done?" Was it some kind of love spell? To make me infatuated with him? Zero what I bargained for.

"Nyssa, we can't stay here."

I couldn't control the smile that grew on my lips. "I like it. I like it a lot."

"You like what?" he asked, confused.

"The way you say my name."

Sam pinched the bridge of his nose and inhaled deeply, as if trying to calm the storm that took life in his eyes. I realized I wasn't alone in my current state. Whatever this was, it clawed at Sam, too. Only, he was much better at controlling it. Clearly.

"Get a grip. You've made yourself a giant target for any powerful being. Do you even understand what this means?"

Something in his voice was urging me to move.

To think.

To snap out of it.

"No, I don't understand."

"Unfortunately, we don't have time to talk about it at the moment. You're coming with me. *Now*." His barked order shocked life back into my limbs. "I need you to tell me everything. Where you've been. Who you were with. Everything. Am I clear?" I stood slowly, using the wall for support.

Then I saw one of my Shadows, on the wall across me, ever so slowly creeping toward us.

My brows creased together. It was daytime. They never showed up in daylight. Never.

"Something is wrong," I repeated, my anxiety skyrocketing. "They shouldn't be here."

"Everything is fine, Nyssa. You have to trust me. Please."

Trust the Devil. Was that not the most foolish idea ever?

Crazier, I wanted to. To blindly follow him.

Insane. I'd officially lost the scrap of sanity I had left.

I needed an escape route. And as if God answered

my prayers, or maybe Hell had, I spotted Nathan from the corner of my eye, leaning against a door frame. And my legs came back to life. I peeled myself off the wall and sprinted to Nathan.

I had no idea what was the matter with me, but I knew I needed to get away from *him*. I tangled my arms around Nathan's chest like he was my savior instead of a soul eater. The pain in my heart grew exponentially until it blocked air from my lungs. I held my chest.

"Hell, easy, Nys. I know I'm a real woman magnet, but I wasn't expecting you to be *that* happy to see me." His teasing grin faded as he pushed me back for a full-body scan. "What the hell happened, Nyssa?"

What? Did I look that bad? Well, I felt much, much worse. Before I could interrogate Nathan about last night…I felt him.

Sam.

Without looking back, I knew. The little hairs on my neck tingled in his presence. Nathan stiffened, and I hid behind him, clutching his shirt.

"I can exp—" Nathan began.

"Silence." Sam didn't scream, but the Antarctic fury billowing off him like blizzard clouds was so much worse. When I dared to peek from my hiding place, Sam's eyes burned with a rage I'd never seen on any living creature. I ducked away like a coward, tightening my grip on Nathan.

"I will deal with you later," Sam threatened. "Move away from her."

Nathan sidestepped, but with my hand tangled in his clothes, I was pulled along.

"Let go of him, Nyssa, or I swear you won't like what I'll do." Sam advanced a step but made no real move to extract me.

"I'm not scared of you."

Lies. I was afraid but for so many other irrational reasons. I inched from my spot enough to see his brows furrow.

"I'd never hurt you," Sam finally said.

Again, I knew that. I knew it in my bones.

His eyes latched to the demon I currently held captive.

I felt Nathan's next breath hitch before he spoke. "Nyssa, if you don't want me sent back to Hell, or worse, let go. Please."

"Much worse," Sam confirmed, jaw tight.

I released, and Nathan distanced himself, leaving me to face the angry Devil. Yet, Sam still wasn't looking at me.

"Do you see it?"

"See what?" I asked.

Nathan briefly glanced my way. "Yeah. It's hard to miss."

"Heaven be damned!" Sam's voice raised for the first time. "Do you know how?"

The demon's eyes lowered to the ground. "Maryssa, she—"

"Maryssa? She's responsible for this?" Sam asked.

"She wanted to give you–"

Sam advanced on Nathan, grabbing him roughly by the collar. "Shut up," he snapped. "You don't speak of this to anyone. Not a soul, not a demon, not anyone. Or you'll be wishing I sent you back to Hell. Am I fucking clear?"

My hands encircled Sam's forearm. "Stop it. What are you even talking about, Sam? See what?"

When he turned to me, crimson stained his eyes. With a gasp, I dropped his arm and backed away.

"Don't move, Nyssa." His blood-red irises flicked to Nathan, still hanging above the ground. "You're going to get Maryssa. You will both fix this. You will meet me. I'll send you the details." He dropped Nathan like a rock. "I have to hide Nyssa." I retreated further, but sensing my plan, Sam turned to me and said, "I thought you realized by now that running won't help you." My hands gripped the strap of my bag tighter. "Running will only make me chase you down, and although I enjoy a good chase, right now isn't the time. I'll be most upset, Nyssa."

I glanced between him and the exit, evaluating my chances.

"Very bad idea, precious. Either way, you will be coming with me."

Blame it on fear or complete lack of judgment, but I dared answer, "Or what?"

"I'll punish you, Nyssa."

My chin rose. "I'd love to see you try."

In three long strides, he closed the space between us. I almost had to break my neck to look into his eyes.

"I'd never touch you." He paused, reconsidering. "Not to harm you, anyway." A chilling grin spread over his face. "But I could do much worse." He didn't even give me the opportunity to wonder. "Isabelle will be forever bound by her contract, and my demons will do more damage than you could ever imagine."

My heart almost stopped, and my head swiveled to Nathan. He kept his gaze down.

The stupid box didn't work at all.

Dammit.

"Don't look at him. He can't help you," Sam snapped.

My head jerked back to his burning eyes. I didn't need to have visited Hell to know Sam borrowed the color from the flames of the pit. Never had I seen him this mad. Yet, I didn't cower in fear.

"How about instead, you play nice and do what I want?" I challenged, using courage I didn't know I had. This was my last card.

The familiar shade of blue leached back into his irises as he gave me an interrogating look, tilting his head.

"Free Isabelle of her contract. Do it now, and I'll come with you." I wanted to pat myself on the shoulder. A shiver ran through me at the mere thought of being alone with him.

As if he knew the kind of power he held over me, he smirked and leaned to whisper in my ear, "Fun as this may be, I'm not known for my patience, little bee, and I've doled out more for you than I've given anyone else. You're walking on very thin ice, precious."

Ignoring my body's reaction to his proximity, I pushed my hair back. "Then I'm not coming anywhere with you."

I moved past him and spoke over my shoulder to Nathan, whose jaw dangled while his eyes jumped from Sam to myself. "You coming?"

I felt pretty badass walking away. Until I pushed open the school door and fresh wind smacked my face. A little group of people were coming up the walkway. To most, they looked pretty normal. But I saw their true, empty eyes. Demons all, and they were heading directly for me.

Chapter 22

I halted, watching the four demons' fan out as if to circle me. The distance between us closed too swiftly. Ten feet, then five in one stutter of my heart.

"Hell, that was fast," Nathan muttered at my side. "Maybe they're just curious about the essence?" He almost sounded hopeful.

"They're attracted to her," Sam answered.

I twisted to him. "Not her as in me, right?"

Sam ignored my wishful thinking and grabbed my shoulders, yanking me behind him. Shielding me with his body.

"I highly doubt they're here only to satisfy curiosity," he informed Nathan as if I didn't exist.

"God, Sam. Do you mean they're really here for me?"

He turned to me. "No one's ever called me God before." He winked at me. "I kind of like it."

I shoved the heel of my palm into his spine, but he didn't budge. "I am serious, Sam." His head twisted to meet my gaze. "Tell me they aren't here for me."

"They aren't here for you."

I threw up my hands. "You're lying."

"No, I merely obliged to your demand."

I clawed a hand through my tangled hair. Stress compressed my chest. The world was upside down, and I couldn't get a straight answer from anyone.

"I won't let any harm come your way, precious. You stay put. I'll take care of this."

God, so he did mean me. I knew I felt different. What had I done? Become a demon magnet?

"I'm not a dog," I still managed to hiss at Sam.

His eyes raked my body from head to toe, and his familiar grin returned. "Trust me, I am very aware of that."

"Are you guys lost?" I heard Nathan ask the new demons. Sam's attention went back to the action. I peeked through both of their wide shoulders. "You wasted your time. There's nothing to see."

Besides the black holes for eyes, the group didn't look like much. The standout was an Asian girl dressed like she'd come straight from boarding school with her navy skirt, white polo, and ballerina flats without socks. Her assets were on full display: long, wavy hair; silky skin; and curves any man would fight to keep.

Did demons not feel the cold?

A blond guy dressed completely in leather—he was only missing the bike to be cast in *Sons of Anarchy*—answered. "We were curious about the new essence. Odd, but it reminded me of—"

"Don't worry yourselves about the essence," Sam interrupted. "I strongly suggest you go back to wherever you came from." He paused, letting his gaze slide to each of them. "Or I'll be forced to send you back."

The youngest guy of the bunch, I'd say barely eighteen years old, was the only one whose confidence faltered at the threat. He slunk closer to the fourth man, who wore elegant gray suit pants with a dark shirt, his hair quaffed like he was headed to a photo shoot for

CEO of the year.

He flashed Sam a glistening ivory smile and stepped forward, hands in his trousers. "I must inform you, Master, the new boss has other plans."

Sam didn't even twitch, unbothered by the threat to his position. Perhaps it was a common occurrence in Hell. "I don't need to be informed of plots that will never come to fruition."

The smile vanished from the demon's face. "His view of our future is much more appealing than the restraints you've forced upon us. We support him."

Sam sized them up, and his lazy smile found them wanting. "Do you, now?" he asked, low voice laced with an undeniable power. "That's very foolish."

Nathan gave a loud belly laugh. "They want a democracy, Boss?" He clucked his tongue at the CEO-looking demon. "Too bad you're talking about the underworld. Strength alone wins Hell's crown. Maybe you need a reminder of why he's king." Nat finished with a growl that left me thankful to have him in my camp.

It had little effect on the demons, though. The CEO gestured to me with his chin. "We just want the girl. No need for dramatics."

Sam's back tensed and...stretched? His fists, too, expanded into balls the size of honeydew. "I will crush you before you even dream of touching her, but not before you tell me who wants her." Sam's clothing started ripping right off his skin as I watched in stunned awe. He grew two feet taller, his muscles bulking at an alarming rate. A cloak of darkness, threaded in veins of crimson thread, covered his golden skin.

I was rooted to the ground. The youngest of the

four interlopers was smart enough to see he stood no chance and fled.

I wished I could do the same.

The scandalous schoolgirl was the first brave enough to take a step forward. Or stupid enough depending on who you asked.

She propped a hand on a cocked hip. "She's not worth a fight, Master." Her melodic voice sang like a siren. It was enthralling. "Come to me and leave her to her fate."

Sam's laugh sliced through the air like razor blades. "That's cute," he said, voice rougher and deeper in his new form. "You forget your tricks won't work on me no matter how old you are, succubus."

Now the outfit made sense. I'd read about succubus—sneaky, manipulative creatures who used their bodies as tools, enslaving humans to act out their whims.

Her nose wrinkled, and she hissed like a snake, her whole face metamorphosing into a hideous, deformed creature with two thick horns curled above each brow. Her eyes glowed a neon green that cut through the last of her glamor.

The biker-looking demon said, "I much prefer her other form."

"No," the suited demon countered, appreciative eyes roaming the succubus. "Like this, she's so...wicked."

"Clearly, you need to upgrade your taste," said Nathan.

The succubus sauntered toward Sam, hips swaying. "I could have made all your dreams come true, Master." Her fingers slowly trailed from her neck, down her cleavage, past her belly button, all the way to the hem of her low-rise skirt. "Like the old days." My stomach knotted, a new emotion bubbling within me.

My hands curled into fists reading to swing. I couldn't help myself. "You reek of desperation. It's real classy."

I don't know why I felt the need to comment. Bad idea. Maryssa's box of horrors had fried my brain. The demon's head snapped to me, and she smiled, uncovering black teeth.

"Come to me, little girl," she sang. The tremble of her final note vibrated in my core. It stirred up desire.

Desire to please her.

Without warning, the music inside my head turned up a notch or two, erasing the succubus' song. My fear faded with it.

Sam's big hand covered my whole forearm. My eyes lifted to his red ones, and everything else vanished. A compulsion, a thousand times stronger than my music and the succubus combined, thrummed through my torso, radiating from his touch.

I was lost to him. The pain I'd felt all day disappeared completely.

I was the rational girl, never guided by hormones and emotions. If someone had told me that one day I'd forget my own name just looking at a man, I would have laughed. Yet, I forgot that and more. Our predicament, the demons, Isabelle, everything but him went away.

The feeling that had enthralled me earlier when I saw Sam on the lawn came back like a hammer smashing my head, only I wasn't seeing stars; I had eyes only for him. His touch…it was scorching, injecting one thought like a poison. I wanted to press my curves to his. Feel every muscle. Inhale his scent until my head spun.

Sam's pupils dilated under my gaze, and he inhaled sharply. He almost looked pained. He shut his eyes, shaking away the spell or curse or whatever this was.

He dropped my arm, and I felt…rejected.

I ached.

Again. Only ten times harder. Like someone just punched a hole through my chest, ripped my heart out, and stabbed it with a knife.

I'd strangle Maryssa the next chance I got.

When Sam opened his eyes again, whatever we'd shared was gone.

"You stay where you are. She'll make you believe you want to go with her. She'll play with your head. Do not let her."

A chuckle almost escaped me. The only one with the power to play with my head was him.

Thankfully, Sam's warning had broken the last trace of the trance to pieces. "Trust me, if I wasn't going with you earlier"—Despite my whole being begging me to give in to his every wish—"do you think I'm stupid enough to go with the evil siren of hell?"

Sam's eyes widened in disbelief.

Nathan mumbled under his breath about powerful essence and will or something.

The succubus gasped, her sharp nails like a star on her chest and her flashy eyes on me. "How did you deny my demand, mortal?"

I'd be keeping my guesses about that to myself, thanks. I still had some lingering sense of pride left somewhere.

"Maybe it had nothing to do with me. Maybe you've just lost your touch?" I suggested.

Biker guy laughed. "Hell, Rebecca, leave the human and the Master to us. Go for the soldier."

The succubus hissed like an aggravated panther. "You are nothing more than a human whore!" she shouted my way.

"Soldier?" Nathan repeated with offense. "I'm hardly so basic." He twisted to Sam. "How haven't they heard of me?"

I couldn't care less about Nathan's quibbles, too busy nursing my own outrage. How dare she!

"That's rich coming from *the* whore of the underworld. Why don't you stay out of this and lie down on your back. That's all you're good for."

"I'll make you swallow your words."

I shrugged as if I could hold my own against a demon. I couldn't. "I'm sure you'd be the best at teaching to swallow."

Nathan muffled his laugh. "I like this Nyssa. Can we keep her this way?" he asked.

"Enough nonsense," Sam snapped at him. "Concentrate on their next move. Defend Nyssa. Send them back to Hell." Malice coated his next words like hard candy. "I've got great festivities awaiting them."

Nathan didn't look ready to let it go. "Easy for you to say. They all know who you a—" They didn't let him finish his sentence. The succubus charged us. Or should I say me?

Her cherry-red nails became claws as she swiped at my face. Sam was faster. His hands—the size of melons—wrapped around her throat.

"Very poor choice." He heaved her through the air

like a shotput. She smashed into a dumpster, ripping a hole through the metal.

From my peripheral vision, I saw a dark fog sneaking out of the earth, forming a sort of trap around the three demons.

Next moment, they moved together, aware of the threat.

Was it coming from Sam?

"Nathan. Take Nyssa and run," he ordered. My mouth didn't have a chance to formulate a complaint before Nathan hoisted me off the ground in a bridal carry.

"You heard the boss," Nathan said when I squawked. He ran through the university, mostly empty with classes in session, thank God.

"Where's the next exit?" he asked.

I saw the cafeteria coming up. "Turn right, second corridor to the left. There's a back parking lot."

As Nathan sped through my directions, I couldn't help but glance behind us. "What about Sam?" He was alone against three demons. "Will he be all right?" I just had to ask.

Nathan chuckled. "Yeah. He'll be peachy. You should be far more worried about us."

"Why? Aren't you technically immortal?"

He rolled his eyes at me. "There are things much worse than death, Nyssa. I'm loath to imagine the eternal fate Master would cook up for me if I lost you or let you die. He's very creative with his torture instruments."

I huffed. "Yeah, right. I think you're in the clear; Maryssa's got it all wrong. Her box didn't work. Sam's not enamored with me or bound to me or whatever that thing was supposed to do."

His gaze lowered to mine. "You really are clueless, aren't you?"

"No? It really didn't work."

"You're cute. Like a kitty cat."

"What's wrong with you?" I snipped.

"Much less than with everything that's wrong with you."

Clearly. That was a fact.

"I could walk," I finally told him.

"And you could fall and break your neck. We've already established what Boss would do to me if his precious gets hurt. So please, cut me some slack and follow my lead." Nathan pushed the exit door open with his back.

The cold hit me at the same moment my eyes landed on the young boy who I'd thought had fled. He leaned against one of the parked cars, his raven skin glowing. Nathan's steps halted, and a low growl vibrated his body. The boy never flinched, weaving a coin through the knuckles of one hand.

Nathan put me on my feet and whispered, "You're going to have to run back to the boss, Nyssa."

I frowned over my shoulder.

"But he's just a kid," I told Nat, twisting to face the boy.

Nathan's nose creased. "Don't be fooled by appearances."

The boy flashed me a genuine smile. "You like?" he asked me in a teen's cracking voice, gesturing to himself. "I got him this morning just for you."

Confusion toyed with my expression, and he threw his head back and laughed. "If I had known you'd befriended a lower demon, I would have taken him as host instead." He sized up Nathan. "Boss must not be happy about this."

If I hadn't been working to make sense of his words, I might have realized Nathan was priming himself for a difficult fight, inching in front of me with a dour expression.

"Doesn't make a difference now," the boy sang. "You are right where I want you."

"Why?" I was nothing special.

"Why?" he repeated with a blinding smile. "Because you, my dear, are the key to the throne of Hell."

"Run!" Nat shouted, pushing me back.

The young boy's peal of laughter peaked in a shriek of madness. "As if there's anywhere for her to hide. Anyone can smell her miles away."

I didn't stick around to find out what that implied. I ran back inside the walls of the university. The demon screamed with a siren wail, loud enough to break the windows. Glass shards shattered inward, chasing me down the hall. I glanced over my shoulder, forcing my feet onward, and saw Nathan fighting the demon. Only, he no longer wore the young boy like a suit.

I recognized his true form.

The demon I'd met at Glory.

Chapter 23

My heart jumped out of my chest. My lungs burned from exertion. My legs cramped. This was a nightmare.

Demons were after me. Me! A nobody.

At least this place was crawling with occultist professors in my father's fan club. One was bound to help me. At least, I hoped so. Professor Gerard's class was just ahead. I threw open the door to find him alone.

Thank God.

He glanced up from his desk at my entrance, leaning back in his chair, glasses perched on his nose, undisturbed by my obvious distress.

Doubled over, I rested my hands on my thighs, trying to catch my breath.

"Miss Lewis," Professor Gerard droned. "I'd say it's a wonderful surprise, but we both know that'd be a lie."

We had no time for his petty grievances with me.

Lifting my head, I cut straight to the chase. "Where are the weapons to kill demons?" My father stashed them everywhere—surely I'd find some here. Otherwise, none of those professors would be brave enough to come to work every day. If Micah's book taught me one useful thing, I needed pure iron soaked in salt and holy water.

Professor Gerard finally raised his head from his work, his mouth blubbing like a fish. "Miss Lewis, in case you need a reminder, you aren't part of our circle."

Nostrils flaring, I closed the distance between us and yanked his chair around to face me. I leaned close, putting both hands on each side of the armrest. "Save it. You don't like me? Good for you. Demons are here. The school needs help." I needed help. "So I'll repeat the question. Where are the weapons to kill demons?"

Gerard's pasty complexion when downright snowy. "Demons are here?" he squeaked.

"Snap out of it. They smell fear. They're attracted to it." He knew that. "Where are the weapons?" I repeated, patience running thin.

"I...I...Most are with Gavriel." Of course they were.

"And the rest?"

"In the basement."

I straightened my spine. "Come show me. We need them. Now."

Professor Gerard seemed glued to his chair. I tapped his cheek a few times. "You have to get a grip. He's—"

The grating whine of claws scratching metal cut me off. A shiver of dread ran down my spine as a man's tenor crooned, "Ohhhh Nyssaaaa. I can smell you. Come out, come out, wherever you are."

"Shit."

The door flew open, and the teen sauntered in wearing a jogger suit and sneakers. The dread in the pit of my stomach grew exponentially. I prayed Nathan was okay. Snoopy demon or not, I'd hate to think my troubles had brought him to harm.

"Here you are," the demon said, his smirk not matching the innocence of the face he wore.

"Here I am." I stepped in front of Gerard.

The demon's smirk grew. "I must say, I never expected you to fall out of the sky the way you have. Like a gift wrapped up just for me." He paused, reconsidering. "Well, maybe not exactly for me, but I'm still very thankful, Nyssa." He gestured to the door with his head. "But the fun's over now. Time to go."

I took a step back.

The smirk disappeared. "Trust me, you don't want to ruin my mood," he warned.

"Stay away, demon!" Professor Gerard cried, a cross held out in shaking hands.

I was far from an expert in demon battles, but I doubted a cross trinket could hold up to much. To prove my point, the demon simply snapped his fingers, and Gerard's head turned in a one-eighty on a stationary torso, jutting his neck bone out at a horrific angle. He fell with a loud *thunk* to the floor.

My hand flew to my mouth, holding back a gag.

"Stop, you couldn't stand the old fart. Don't pretend to care. We both know I've done you a favor." My head snapped to the demon. "Come on now, let's get going."

My legs turned to jelly and glued me to the ground. I stood there trembling, neither defiant nor obedient, swallowed whole by fear.

"You will come now, Nyssa. Or I will kill every human in this university," he threatened. A real demon trait. He succeeded in snapping me out of my stupor. Instead, I boiled with a newfound rage.

I walked toward him slowly, working open the bottle in my pocket. He stepped aside, ushering me through the door, but instead, I planted my feet, adrenaline pumping, and tossed the bottle of salt in his eyes. The demon screamed, scratching his face, and I took the opening to ram my knee into his crotch.

Fragile as any human male, he dropped to his knees, holding his package. The shock written on his face was worth it for half a second—until his gaze snapped to mine. The smirk was long gone, and the fury in his eyes promised a punishment worse than death.

Terror whipped me into a full sprint. I barely made it to the entrance of the cafeteria before I was knocked from behind and thrown a few feet in the air. Must be another demon thing.

Gravity yanked me back down, and I hit my head on a corner of a lunch table. My hand reached up to the pulsing knot on my head. When I brought it back to eye level, my palm was painted red. I felt the liquid slide down the side of my face.

"That wasn't very nice, pet," he scolded.

I blinked, and the demon materialized in my blurred vision, closing the gap between us. Skidding back on my butt, I fled the echoes of heavy steps.

But...they weren't his. They were down the hall, getting closer.

Sam.

All I needed to do was hold on for another minute. But my back hit a wall.

The demon cursed. "Come with me, and I'll let your friend go," he said in a hurry.

My head jerked to him. "You mean Isabelle? You hold her deal?" The way he tilted his head and smiled told me I'd reacted too eagerly, and he had me exactly where he wanted.

"Yes, and I will let her go. I will even restore her

mother's health. All you have to do is take my hand."

I knew demons were wicked creatures, but this is what I'd been searching for. I had failed with Maryssa. Sam wouldn't grant me what I wanted. Well, whether he couldn't or wouldn't remained a mystery.

He wanted me to be patient and put my faith in him. Perhaps I would have if it didn't involve Isabelle's soul. Only, it did.

The demon had just offered up my wish on a platter, and in exchange, all I had to do was go with him. Not stay. Just go.

I'd figure out a way to get free one way or another.

He slowly bent to my level. "Say yes, and it's done. No tricks." He extended a hand.

"Are we sealing a deal, or is this a simple agreement between two honorable people?"

He laughed. "You should listen to your demon friend. Do not be fooled by appearances. I'm not doing you a favor. I'm doing myself one." Yeah, like I didn't know. Still, I had hoped to not enter a deal with him.

"All I have to do is come with you?" I clarified. "And Isabelle is free, and her mom is healed?"

"You got it."

"Why?"

His eyes darkened. Just when I thought he wasn't going to answer me, he did. "Because no one, and I mean *no one* has ever earned a sliver of Master's attention since he's taken control of Hell. And you managed to make him lose himself. I'll give it to him—he's got taste."

Okay. This demon had completely lost his mind.

"The first time I saw you at the store, I knew there was something different about you."

Who was I to burst his bubble and reveal how wrong he is? Still, a strange coincidence for two demons to make similar assumptions about me.

"How do we seal a deal?"

His smile stretched to his ears. "Well, usually, I cut the palm, exchange blood, all the usual fun, but with you, my dear"—he leaned in inches from my face—"a kiss will do just fine."

Back pressed against the wall in more ways than one, my stomach churned with the ugly truth.

I'd go with this asshole. I'd make the deal.

But I wouldn't let him kiss me. As crazy as it sounded, I'd rather exchange blood with him. As if agreeing with me, the pain that had afflicted my heart when I woke this morning returned in full force, making me wince.

The words lodged in my throat as the demon ducked his head, advancing on me. My hand instinctively shot up to stop him, but I didn't have to. The next moment, his body exploded into a thousand little beams of inky particles. When my eyes looked beyond the hazy residue, Sam emerged from the gloom.

A very *enraged* Sam.

Chapter 24

Wobbly, I slid up the wall to keep my balance. Sam's crimson eyes were on me like a hunter on his prey. His chest rose and fell inhumanly fast. His nostrils flared. He looked ready to go for the kill. Only, I was the one person left breathing in the room.

"Did you kill him?" Did that free Isabelle of her contract or bind her forever?

A muscle in his jaw popped. "Why? Sad you missed the chance to be kissed by another demon?" he said, colder than winter.

So he'd heard.

Then, it dawned on me. "Are you…jealous?"

The word almost got stuck on my tongue. I mean, how ridiculous did I sound? To assume Sam, the King of Hell, may be jealous over me.

In a breath, Sam stood right before me. His hands, flat on the wall, held me captive. A paper's width separated our chests. If I moved even the slightest, we'd touch. Not the smartest idea considering what had happened when he'd grasped my arm earlier.

"In my world, jealousy means envious of rivalry or intolerant of unfaithfulness. It implies I fear anyone else could gain my possession. So no, I'm not jealous, because no one would ever come close to making you theirs." That admission made me swallow my next breath. "But in your human terms," he rasped, "I guess the right answer is yes, Nyssa. I'm very jealous."

My heart somersaulted, and a shudder of excitement ran through me.

I licked my lips, which had suddenly gone dryer than an eczema rash, and Sam's eyes darkened, fixating on my mouth. His pupils became vertical slits. My brain stopped working altogether. The only thought left drifting through my head wasn't about Isabelle, or demons, or Gerard.

It was all about Sam.

His hands around me, his soft lips on mine, his warmth, his smell. It was driving me insane. His head inclined, and my heart almost exploded in anticipation. His nose brushed mine, all I had to do was rise on my tippy toes and take.

"Hell, I just found a body," Nathan's voice boomed through the cafeteria. "More demons are about to crawl from the pit and chase us down for that essence. Yet, you guys look ready to rip each other's clothes off?" He chuckled. "Love it. Please, don't be bothered by little old me. Just keep going at it. I always enjoy a good show."

My face burned from embarrassment. Yet, Sam didn't budge, and I couldn't escape without touching him. Again, a very bad idea.

I tried chasing away those thoughts. "Is the demon dead?"

"Nah, he's the kind that's impossible to get rid of. A real pain, if you ask me," Nathan answered.

Sam's arms dropped to his sides as he turned to Nathan, and I took the opportunity to slide away, going to a table to get a paper towel. Sam didn't seem particularly pleased, following me closer than my own shadow.

"Where do you think you're going?" he asked.

I pointed at my head. "I'd like not to bleed to death. It'd be most inconvenient." At least for me.

"You have no idea," Nathan chipped in with a laugh. "But your cut is closed already."

My eyebrows squished together as I brought my hand up to my wound. The bleeding had stopped, and the pain had vanished.

"I could have sworn I needed stitches. It was gushing blood," I said out loud. Even weirder, perhaps, I rolled my shoulder without the slightest pain, lips parted in amazement.

Nathan gave a shrug. "Head wounds always bleed the most. No stress."

I dropped it and bit my thumb nail in a nervous tic. "The demon. He killed Professor Gerard."

"Yeah, I saw. He made a real mess," Nat confirmed.

I hadn't fancied Gerard, thought he was closed-minded, but no one deserved to die the way he had.

"Are you all right, precious?" I lifted my eyes to Sam's blue ones. A part of me wanted to find comfort in his arms. To erase the last day.

I nodded. "It was…awful. The way he…he…" I couldn't finish my sentence. Sam took a step toward me before halting like he'd hit a glass barrier.

"What will the police think?" I added.

Nathan pulled his platinum hair back, combing it with his fingers before tying it in a tail. "No one will find anything. I got people to clean this mess up already."

"Clean up? As in—"

"Disappear, yeah. Kinda out of options here."

Again, that was awful. Gerard must have a family, people who loved him. They'd be worried. Forever wondering if he'd up and left or gotten into an accident, never getting an answer. That was cruel. Although, the truth wasn't any better.

"We've got to go," Sam told Nathan. "Find Maryssa. You know where to meet us."

"What?" I said. "I have to go home. I can't just come with you. Be reasonable."

Sam inhaled, pinching the bridge of his nose.

Nathan chuckled at our side. "You've got your hands full, Boss."

"Sorry, precious, but we've got no time for this debate." He turned to Nathan and barked, "Get her."

The room tipped as Nathan tossed me onto his shoulder. My head hung upside down for the second time this week. Only this time, I didn't feel dizzy—I was furious. Arching myself to glower at Sam as he strutted close behind, I found a murderous grin on his face.

"Are you out of your freaking mind?" I yelled, offering a show to the clueless students who had finally decided to walk out of class. "Put me down this instant!"

And out of nowhere, we stopped.

I didn't think I had that much power.

"Oi, mate! Put 'er down, yeah? She ain't lookin' to go with you," said a man's voice. One I knew.

Mike. The idiot. I hadn't taken him for the courageous type. Sam stepped forward. Using Nat's shoulder for support, I twisted in time to see Sam put a hand on Mike's shoulder with all the authority of a general.

"You saw nothing," he commanded. "And as for Nyssa." Sam glanced my way for a second. "Are you listening?" Mike weakly nodded as Sam's gaze shifted to his. "You don't look at her. You don't talk to her. You don't think of her. She's taken. Got it?"

Rich boy Mike wouldn't take kindly to orders. A fight was bound to break out. It'd be ugly. Very much so.

But Mike nodded dreamily and walked past us without looking at me.

"Fool." Nathan laughed while Sam shot me a glare.

"How? What did you do?" I asked.

"I took care of a problem," Sam snapped, and we resumed the walk of shame.

I flopped back down, abs tired. "You're going to regret this," I warned as the outside chill hit my face.

I felt the vibration of Nathan's laugh. "I've got to tell you, I'm really going to enjoy this." I couldn't be certain if he was talking to me or Sam.

I didn't have time to scream some more, or react at all for that matter, before I heard the sound of a door, and I was shoved inside a car without grace. The window almost smacked me in the face.

Then all hell broke loose. I kicked, screamed, and hit, but the door was locked from the outside.

Both the demons were busy talking and completely ignoring me. If I'd had a part of my brain still functioning beneath my raging hormones, I might have been smart enough to stay quiet and eavesdrop. By the time I finished my tantrum, Nathan had trotted off to obey Sam's orders like a good little soldier.

I'd have to deal with Sam alone.

Traitor.

My eyes followed the Devil as he rounded the car and settled into the driver's seat beside me. While I seethed.

Sam's eyes met mine for a moment, and I almost forgot why I was upset. How did one barricade their heart against angelic perfection turned temptingly sinful? When Sam grinned from ear to ear, my face burned. The car roared, and we sped out of the university's parking.

"How did I know you were going to make this difficult?" he asked, navigating between lanes to pass cars.

"How dare you blame me for this!" I fumed. "I haven't done anything."

Total lie, but did my indiscretion even count it if it didn't work?

One perfect brow arched. "You've done plenty, precious. Surely you can take some responsibility for this mess."

Of course, he knew I'd lied. Demon heart rate detector or what not. A walking polygraph machine. How annoying.

He sighed at my stubborn silence. "It may not seem like it, Nyssa, but I am trying to help you. You don't understand. Those demons, back there, that's just the beginning."

"Help?" I mocked. "As far as I know, Isabelle's soul is still on the line! Oh, by the way, her mother is getting worse, not that you care about your minions messing up the lives of innocent people." I didn't give him a chance to reply. "Or are you helping me by threatening to have your demons take more souls if I don't cooperate with whatever you've got planned at Maryssa's? Just the beginning, huh?" I scoffed, outraged. "You want to help? How about you forbid demons to make any deals at all?"

Sam's nostrils flared. As he turned to me, fire raged in his eyes. "So you've got it all figured out, don't you?" he snarked, his tone as heated as mine. And I didn't like it. Not one bit. "Tell me, precious, would you rather I let you roam around with a target on your back for anyone with a grudge against me? Trust me, that's a very long and scary list." Just like I'd done, he powered on, giving me no chance to react. "And you want me to stop the deals? Would you prefer I let them feed by killing whoever they want? Let them devour souls at their discretion? Tell me all about your brilliant ideas on the subject."

I sank deeper into the leather seat. I hadn't thought that far. Humans with souls had rules to follow to keep the world in order. Demons needed boundaries just as much. Shame crawled on my skin like ants.

He sighed. "I know. This isn't perfect, but it's balanced. As balanced as can be. Deals are a choice humans make. Most of the time, not the good type of humans either."

"How about the ones that came to the school?"

"Not everyone falls in line easily."

I changed the subject. "I'm still confused as to why you kidnapped me."

"I'm not kidnapping you. I'm protecting you."

"From where I sit, you're the only one I need protection from."

After a few minutes of tense silence, Sam asked, "Did you know there's always a chance for redemption, even for the damned?"

"Really?"

"Really. That's why they can roam around up here. If they don't respect the rules, if they cross the line, they're sent back to Hell, but they are given the chance."

"Why are so many of them up here now?" Nathan hadn't shared much.

Sam glanced my way. "Some are rebelling against my rule. They've come here to distance themselves from my throne."

"Why are they making deals?" I had to ask since presumably some of the demon interlopers were with Sam.

Sam shrugged. "Humans, too, are tested. It's a business. Some will go up straight away, others will go down. The ones who earn their place don't ascend, but they'll live comfortably in the underworld."

"You can live happily in Hell?"

"There're many worlds in Hell, Nyssa."

Did he mean the nine circles? Had Dante truly peeked into Hell?

Sam's head turned my way. "How do you know him?"

I was completely lost for a minute. "Who?"

"The demon you ran to at the school."

My lips turned up at the corners, and I arched my brows suggestively. "Oh, Nathan?"

His jaw clenched as he checked the road. "Yes."

My smile grew wider. "When you refused me, I looked for an alternative."

Sam's head snapped back to me. "Refused you? I've never done such a thing. Say the word, precious, and I'll make you mine right here. Right now."

Oh sweet Jesus. My insides tightened at the mere thought.

I shook it off, clearing my throat. Sam smirked, totally aware of the effect his proposal just had. It made me wonder if he would have gone through with it.

"He offered me a deal," I clarified. "We're still negotiating the terms, but I'm sure we'll come to an agreement that satisfies us both."

That wiped the grin right off. Sam's grip on the steering wheel intensified until I thought it would break.

"I forbid you to make a deal with anyone. Is that clear?"

I laughed. "Oh good. I wasn't aware I needed your permission. Thanks for bringing the light into my life." As those words left my mouth, I got an odd feeling of déjà vu. I stretched my mind, reaching for what felt like a foggy, farfetched memory.

"Where are you bringing me?" I asked, turning to find Sam straight and rigid as a steel blade.

"A special place. It's where I spend all my free time."

I didn't have a say in the matter. We stayed quiet. Relaxing seemed next to impossible, yet before I knew it, my eyes shut.

I stood surrounded by darkness. The heavy smell of burning wood lingered in the air. I searched around for my Shadows. Instead, I found a small town in the middle of a valley. Some of the brick houses glowed with dim, flickering candlelight. North of it rose a mountain, and along its ridge, dozens of people stood in an unwavering line. I squinted, trying to make out more. A wide shape hung from all their backs. I had to be hallucinating because I could've sworn they all had wings.

Chapter 25

My eyes shot open inside Sam's car. My heart sped faster than a racing Thoroughbred. The dream stuck to me like sweaty clothes, vivid enough to stamp itself on my mind and body.

I sat straighter on the leather seat. We weren't moving, and we weren't in the city. Crashing waves echoed from a shore I couldn't see clearly in the darkness. Sam's seat stood empty. My new grief-stricken agony lingered at a lesser, tolerable level.

The car handle clicked under my hand, and the door opened.

My feet wedged into the sand. After a few careful steps, my Shadows came to me. I couldn't see them per se, but I sensed them dancing around my skin, like tickling breezes.

"Where is he?"

My hair danced with the wind as I turned, finding a source of light. I stepped forward, comforted by their presence. A magnificent arch made of shimmering, multicolored seashells greeted me at the entrance. The intricate arrangement formed a perfect curve, as if meticulously crafted by hand.

I crossed the threshold and was greeted by cool, damp air. The smash of waves against the rocks outside grew muffled.

I stepped further. Why had Sam brought me here?

He couldn't possibly know about my obsession with seashells. A lucky guess? A coincidence?

I took a step. And another. A mosaic of seashells arranged in a beautiful, swirling pattern covered the entire structure, floor to ceiling. The dimmed light of the moon filtering through the door danced across the shells' contours, casting a cool, silver glow over everything.

I reached the center where an open skylight let the moon peek inside like a fairy-tale illustration. I'd stumbled into a secret treasure, hidden away from the rest of the world.

Neck craned toward the moon, a warmth caressed my neck and back. The shiver that ran through me told me *he* was near. I twisted to my right. Sam stood there, leaning against the wall and staring at me.

"Do you like it?"

"You're kidding, right?" A smile stretched my lips and I twirled, my arms outstretched. "I love it. This is magical."

So magical, I'd forgive the little stunt he pulled. For now, anyway.

Sam smiled back, his blue eyes...warm. "That makes me happy, precious. It took me a very, very long time to make," he said, pulling the words like taffy.

Planting my feet, lightheaded from my spin, I twisted to face him. "You? You did this."

Of course, the Devil had to be perfect.

Perfect for me.

He nodded sluggishly, closing the distance separating us with the slow, cautious steps of a stag approaching water—not playing the predator for once. His watchful eyes gauged my reaction.

"Why?" I whispered.

Seashells had lifted my spirits since I could remember. When I shut my eyes and put them to my ear, I was connected to the ocean. All my anxiety disappeared. And they offered a saner method of peace than the Shadows.

I needed normal. To feel like I belonged.

"Tell me, Nyssa, do you know who I am? Who I truly am? What my *real* story is?" he asked instead of answering me.

I wasn't sure what to say or what he wanted to hear, so I gave the most basic answer. "You're the Devil."

He halted his steps. And although we both knew it was the truth, a sickening lump formed in the pit of my stomach as my heart squeezed. The need to apologize arose, although I couldn't pinpoint why.

"Yes. I am." His lashes touched his cheeks, and the knots tightened inside of me. "But I'm so much more than my title."

He totally was, but he gave me no chance to confirm it.

"So you have no idea who I truly am."

I hugged myself, uncomfortable. "Do you mean…" I bit the inside of my cheek, hesitating.

"Tell me," he almost pleaded. "Tell me anything you think. Actually, I've been dying to know your theory or if you believe the same story that's been told for hundreds of years."

I shook my head.

"Don't be afraid, precious. You can tell me anything."

I wasn't afraid of him hurting me. If anything, I

was afraid of my words hurting him.

"Do you mean the story of your fall from Heaven?" I murmured.

Sam reached me. His fingers tucked a curl behind my ear.

"Yes," he whispered back. "Only, my fall didn't come from my indiscretions. It's so much more complicated than that. I didn't follow the rules, and God handed me a punishment. I refused to comply."

"What rules did you break?"

His piercing eyes stayed on me. "Plenty. But only one that mattered. One that changed everything."

Deep within, his words unraveled me. My mouth dried.

I wanted to know the crime that changed everything.

I wanted to know why he did it.

I wanted to know if there could have been another way.

I wanted to know if he regretted it.

But what I burned to know above all else. "Was it worth it?"

A grin stretched his mouth. "More than words can tell."

My hand reached out for his face and froze midway when Nathan's booming, "Honey! I'm home," interrupted us.

Sam mumbled under his breath about timing and sending him back to Hell. I dropped my arm back to my side.

The demon joined us, chipper as ever. "I've always wanted to say that. They do it in movies all the time."

Sam rubbed his eyes with his thumb and index.

"The husband says it to his wife. Not an employee to his boss."

"True, but considering I'm unlikely to marry, I seized the opportunity." Nathan winked at me.

Behind Nathan, Maryssa entered the grotto with her back pin straight. Her stride lacked her usual confidence.

Once she reached Nathan's side, she bowed.

Sam wasn't having it. His whole demeanor changed. He stalked toward her, the picture of a raging king on the brink of ordering an execution, and because I hardly recognized myself anymore, I grabbed his arms, holding him back from doing anything incredibly stupid.

A gasp escaped Maryssa, muffled behind her hand. Was I not supposed to save her from his wrath?

"Yeah, very unusual. I agree," crooned Nathan. "Our king is evolving. I've witnessed much more affection with these little eyes. I sort of liked it."

I bristled, dropping my hands, letting them curl into claws at my sides. Oh, he did not dare.

"Shut up," Sam snapped. Nathan took the hint and moved clear of Sam's path to Maryssa.

"I want to know what you've done," Sam seethed in the cold tone I'd always associated with him until moments ago. "Every single detail."

Maryssa bowed a little deeper. "We thought we were helping you."

Of course! She hadn't agreed to help *me*. No, she agreed to my proposal because she thought it would benefit Sam.

"We?" Sam repeated, his brows pulling together.

Nathan's eyes dipped to the seashell ground. I

shifted my weight from foot to foot, realizing that Sam hadn't had any clue about Nat's involvement in the scheme until right now.

Maryssa froze, at a loss for words.

"Don't make me repeat myself," Sam threatened. He'd throw a fit the second she dropped Nathan's name. Maybe even send him back to Hell.

I intervened. "They haven't done anything. You denied me help. I sought it elsewhere." His head jerked around, shriveling my unwarranted confidence.

"I didn't deny you anything. I refused to bargain. Two very different things."

I rolled my eyes. "Sure. However you want to put it. The point is, they only did what I begged of them."

Not entirely true, not entirely a lie.

Sam's eyes shifted to a shame-faced Nathan, who refused to look up.

"I will deal with you later. You seem to have forgotten who leads and why." His warning held the promise of unimaginable torture.

Nathan humbled himself, murmuring a weak, "Yes, Master."

"No, you won't do anything," I said louder than intended.

Sam turned to me so fast, I almost stumbled back.

"I will do whatever pleases me."

"You won't."

I made fists at my sides.

A muscle popped in Sam's jaw.

"Watch me."

"I swear, Sam, you better drop this and drop it now. We have more important things to deal with like my best friend's deal or rebel demons chasing me," I reminded, hoping he'd care. "And if you're petty enough to waste time that we don't have to satisfy your ego, God be my witness, I'll never speak to you again." My breathing accelerated with the secret wish tucked behind the threat. If his feelings mirrored mine in the slightest, it'd be enough for him to drop it.

In my next breath, Sam towered over me, chest heaving.

"God hasn't cared to be anyone's witness in hundreds of years, precious. He won't change that for you."

"You're missing the point."

Our gazes held in a combat of wills. I could almost hear Maryssa and Nathan hold their breaths.

"You win, precious."

I exhaled an impulsive sigh of relief. My eyes found Nathan's. His lips stretched into a smile as he mouthed a thank you.

"Don't look so happy," Sam told him. "It's only until all this is dealt with."

Well, that was a battle for another day. I'd learned at an early age to appreciate the small victories.

Sam's eyes whipped back to Maryssa's. "You made her open the box I gave you to protect, didn't you?"

"I did."

"Who gave you the right? You know what it could have done to her."

Maryssa's lashes lowered. She took a moment before letting out a weak, "Yes."

"Yet, you did it anyway. Knowing it could have killed her."

Killed me?

Nathan thought it was a good time to step in. "Yes, but it didn't. We only wanted to help you."

Sam's eyes were turning crimson. "This doesn't help me."

Confusion scrawled across Nat and Maryssa's features.

"But—"

"Don't. Don't say more," Sam advised before shifting his ferocious attention back to the professor. "Now, you're going to fix it. I don't care how, but you will. You've made Nyssa a target. You will repair your mistake, or you will pay the price."

What was Sam even talking about?

I stepped in. "Listen, what we did was wrong. I was trying to…" I bit my lip while Sam's brow arched in an invitation. "…gain your favor."

His gaze glided over me. "You didn't need that to gain my favor, Nyssa. I thought helping you made that very clear. You had me in your corner—a one-of-a-kind position. Why couldn't that be enough?"

Shame crept in. I hadn't realized how much a simple, termless promise had meant for Sam.

"Yeah, because he talks to no one, he likes no one, and he definitely helps no one," Nat confirmed from behind me.

"I'm sorry. I didn't realize I was already favored." I should have. "How have I made myself a target? What does that even mean?"

"Master, if I may," Maryssa interjected.

Sam never turned from me. "Yes?"

"We can't stay here much longer. I could mask our scent for the next few hours at most, but I need my things at the store." Her tone harshened when she added, "We sort of left in a hurry."

Nathan warded off Sam's glare with raised palms. "In my defense, you gave the impression of a life-and-death mission. *My* life or death, if I may add. I didn't think further."

"You've been doing lots of that lately."

"I don't have a scent," I told Maryssa, offended.

"The essence, Nyssa," Sam said. My head still couldn't wrap around the whole idea. What was an essence, really?

"I got it because of what we did last night?"

I didn't miss Maryssa's hesitation or the glance she exchanged with Sam. She seemed to weigh her words carefully. "When you opened the box, it released the essence within, yes. Now anyone with sharpened senses can pick it up." So demons. "The more powerful the being, the easier they can sense you. So, I'll mask it so we leave no trace of your presence, making it almost impossible for anyone to track us down. However, this spell has its limits, and it won't last forever. We need to move quickly if we want to stay ahead of whoever is after you."

Her gaze shifted to Sam. "For what it's worth, I had no idea how this would turn out."

A moment stretched into a lifetime before he slowly nodded. She turned back to me. "I had no intention of putting you in danger. For that, I'm sorry."

"You did what I asked. There's no reason to be sorry, but thank you."

Maryssa gave a small nod before she chanted a spell in a foreign language. Deep down, I'd always suspected she was more than she let on.

"It's done," she confirmed.

"Let's go," Nathan said.

Tucking my hand in his, Sam led us out in the cold night. Even the sound of the ocean couldn't calm my tangled nerves.

I didn't know what Isabelle's demon wanted from me, but I was determined to put a stop to this whole madness. To get anything done, I couldn't have a bunch of them attracted to my essence. Whatever that even meant.

Chapter 26

I blinked at a familiar street sign a block away from Maryssa's store. It seemed we'd just left the seashell grotto, yet an hour had passed. I hadn't paid attention to the country roads or crossing city lines. Sam and I had stayed quiet for the ride, both preoccupied in our own minds. But I had questions that required answers, or I'd snap under the anxious strain of this essence debacle.

"Sam?"

"Hmm?"

I tangled my hands on my thighs. "What Maryssa's going to do..." I bit my lip, unsure. "Will it get rid of the essence thing?"

The silence stretched. I couldn't control the hammering of my heart.

"It's not that big of a deal, right?" I said, more to appease my nerves than anything else. "But she'll still get rid of it? I mean, it would suck to have the whole demon race chasing me forever." I frowned. "What do they even want with me though? It's not like I'm the first essence in the world?" I was rambling, talking about subjects I didn't understand, pretending I had a basic grasp.

Without warning, the car jumped the shoulder, skidding through pebbles and dirt, jerking me forward. My seatbelt caught, digging into my collarbone.

"What is wrong with you?" I shouted in a breath. "I am human; I only have one life. Are you trying to end it?"

Sam twisted to me. "No. I didn't mean to frighten you." That was as close to an apology as I was going to get.

Sam exhaled deeply, rubbing his eyes with his thumb and index. His scar scrunched and stretched with the circular movements.

"I've explained how any demon can recognize me without ever seeing my face before."

My brow creased. "Yeah? They scent you or something."

He nodded. "Yes, but it's a little more than that. Angels and demons don't have a soul. They—"

"What!" I interrupted. "Like real angels? With big white wings?" He nodded, and I gaped. "You're telling me the guardians of the human race don't have souls?"

A dry laugh escaped him. "Don't look so surprised. Angels are far from the pictures of virtue humans have painted them to be. And they don't guard humans; they just…watch. Or they used to." He shrugged like it didn't matter. "Anyhow, they have an essence."

"Like demons?"

"Exactly like demons, except a demon's appears dark, while it is believed that angels' appear white."

"Right." I dragged out the word. I still wasn't sure what he was getting at in terms of my problem. "So, demons recognize each other by the essence."

"Yes, and they can identify angels, too."

"Angels are here?"

He cocked his head, a playful arch to his brow as he gestured at himself.

"Yeah, I mean you're here, but you know...the ones that..." *Didn't fall.* "...still have white essence. They're here, too?"

"Some."

"So why aren't they doing anything to fight demons that don't follow the rules?"

Sam laughed. "Well, that's my burden to carry. Either way, my brothers wouldn't get their hands dirty. They have rules of their own. A balance is always needed."

Crazy collided with reality, jumbling my brain with wreckage I couldn't piece back together into a satisfactory frame. Even with my background and all I'd seen lately, true belief in the stories felt very different.

Some people believed in ghosts, but they'd still probably pee themselves if they came face to face with one.

"Are you okay, Nyssa?" I must look baffled. "It's...a lot."

"I'm dealing."

My eyes clashed with his as I whispered, "You didn't, though." I swallowed, nervous without knowing why. "Follow the rules."

An intake of breath. "No. I didn't."

"Why?"

He opened his mouth, then closed it again.

"I won't tell anyone," I vowed.

His eyes flicked toward the clouds through the windshield. "Have you ever wanted something so much that the sheer thought of being denied it left you in physical pain? To the point where being without it for just a moment made you want to close your eyes and never open them again? To have a hole inside your chest that only that thing can fill? To feel hollow? Empty?"

Yes. The description defined how I'd felt ever since opening the box. Perhaps I'd experienced something akin to it long before that, but I had no idea why or what I sought.

I wished the box had contained the item Sam lost eons ago. Not to use for manipulation to save Isabelle, but to give him the closure he deserved. To make him whole again.

I wanted to take his hand in mine. Chase away his pain and emptiness.

His piercing eyes locked with mine. "I refused to exist that way. I decided to fight for what I believed mattered more than the rules that felt wrong."

"That's so—"

"Reckless?"

I shook my head, my curls brushing my jaw. "Human." I paused. "Brave. Honorable." My curiosity wasn't satisfied, so I pushed further. "What's the item you couldn't live without?"

"Something irreplaceable."

Sam wasn't going to share that part, and I respected that.

"What rule did you break?"

Sam studied the road, face hard. "We were meant to be watchers, but watching wasn't enough anymore," he said, glancing back at me. "I wanted more without caring if the 'more' I sought would be worth it."

"Change is always..." I searched for the right word. "Uncertain. Most prefer to stay in their comfort zone rather than attempt it. The unknown is scary."

He gave a sad, deep laugh. "Most think I was very stupid."

"Most *are* very stupid." I resisted my urge to take his hand off the wheel, to offer physical support. "I don't see how that got you cast out, though." His eyes shifted away again. I guessed that wasn't a story for tonight. "For what it's worth, I think it makes you worthy."

Sam held his breath. "Thank you, Nyssa. Coming from you it means…everything."

"I'm biased, though. Not every day does the Devil offer his help," I teased. "So, how do you recognize each other's essence?"

"Imagine someone wearing a passport stamp on their shirt, only it gives us more information: the type of demon and their rank. An exceptionally strong essence sends out signals for miles around, making itself known to everyone. And it's as quick as an iPhone's face recognition or a fingerprint ID." He stared at me before dropping his bomb. "And now you have one, too."

"But I'm human." I didn't want to have this beacon on my chest forever.

Sam threw his head back and belly laughed. But he wasn't amused.

"Oh clearly, and I'm an angel. Yet, here we are."

"This is so screwed. It'll go away once Maryssa does her thing, right?"

Sam laughed again. "She can't help you fix that. None of them can."

Oh God. My hands trembled. I should have never trusted her. "Why would she do this to me? I sort of thought she liked me. Well, as much as she likes anybody, anyway, but I thought she disliked me less than the rest, if you know what I mean." I shut off my cell phone's vibration. It was going nuts, jangling my nerves even worse.

Micah was officially going to kill me. I had no idea how I was going to get out of this one.

"I think you're impossible not to like."

My head jerked to Sam so fast I got whiplash.

His eyes sharpened, pupils dilating. "And she didn't give you the essence."

I probably looked like a fish, gawping at him, still hung up on, *You're impossible not to like.*

Okay, I became a puddle.

Wait, a neuron connected. Maryssa hadn't given me the essence? "But you said I had the ess—"

"You do. But Maryssa didn't give it to you. She removed the veil hiding it, making it visible to any upper being. It was already there, just concealed."

I shook my head confused, still fantasizing about the implications of Sam saying I was impossible not to like. I fought to push it aside for more important puzzles, like how the hell did humans get essence? And how had I obtained one?

"I don't have a soul?" I wondered.

"Oh, you do, precious. And yours is..." He inhaled, not completing his sentence.

I passed my tongue over my dry lips and asked, "Is what?"

"Don't do that." The way he stared at me made heat crawl up my thighs and start a bonfire in my gut.

Putting my lip between my teeth, I asked. "Do what?"

His eyes glued to my mouth. "That."

"Why?"

"'Cause it's taking everything I have not to take you. Take all of you and never let you go. And you doing that is tilting me over the edge."

Oh, sweet Lord.

"I'm sorry." Or not. I was about to beg him to take me right here, too.

Sam's tone rasped just above a whisper. "Don't be. You're perfect. Pure. Real. One anyone might wish to own. One anyone would die for. One anyone would kill for. Me being the first."

And I stopped breathing altogether. My insides knotted, tangled in the desire written on Sam's face, but then he pulled himself together, quick as a rubber band snapping back into place, forcing his gaze straight ahead. The car came back to life with a roar, and Sam drove us to our original destination.

To my immense disappointment.

Chapter 27

Maryssa's store was exactly like I remembered it. Creepy. Dark. Scary.

As if sensing my inner turmoil, Sam stuck as close as a shadow but cautiously avoided any physical contact. I wondered if that *urge* would go away once Maryssa fixed whatever had gone wrong. Not that I'd ever asked Sam that. Or anybody for that matter, but God, would I like to know.

I couldn't decide if it was because I wanted to keep this—whatever it was—or get rid of it. Probably the first. The spell had dug deep, shaping my thoughts.

"Why did you make me open the box?" I asked Maryssa once Sam was out of sight.

"You presumed I knew what you were looking for, but even you had no idea."

I should have known. How in the world could anyone know what I wanted when my vague understanding of it had come from a torn page of an ancient book?

"I knew the second you met him which side you'd take," she continued.

"You know nothing. This isn't about sides. I wanted him to help me free Isabelle. You knew this box wasn't going to coerce Sam into helping me. You took me for a fool."

Maryssa's lips parted in genuine surprise, emoting

harder than I'd ever seen her. "You didn't gain blind cooperation, true, but you did gain a champion. The Devil is fighting with you. For you. It's more than anyone could ever wish for. It's more than I've ever witnessed and trust me, Nyssa, I've seen a lot."

If only. "It's because of that essence. Not because of me."

She blinked a few times before shaking her head. "He didn't tell you," she murmured.

Oh no.

"Tell me what?" I asked the moment Sam and Nathan both returned.

Maryssa turned to her candles as if I didn't ask a question. My Shadows slithered through the wall's cracks and zipped around the room in erratic circles.

"Calm down, boys. She needs this," said Sam. Their flight patterns stilled, leaving me speechless. "Dale,"—he snapped his fingers at the largest—"stay close to Nyssa."

Dale purred. Yes, purred, and settled on my shoulder, covering my whole left side.

Nathan's nose wrinkled. "That's a sight I will never get used to. Why do they love her so much? They love no one." He elbowed Sam. "I don't even think they like you, and you're their Master."

"They don't have to like me. But just so you know, they do." Sam assessed Dale curled around me with a pleased smile.

"Are they like shadow cats?" I asked. Dale lifted halfway off me. Nathan laughed so hard he gasped for air, earning a loud growl from the smallest of the bunch, Fury.

"Sorry, buddy," Nathan told Fury. "But come on,

she said cats!" Between laughs, he turned to Maryssa. "You don't have cameras in here by any chance? This is one moment I want to capture. Seriously hilarious."

She speared him with the glare she usually reserved for students not paying attention. Nathan writhed in its uncomfortable intensity like a regular frat boy, despite his demon blood. Maryssa was much more than a university professor or a cult member, that was for sure.

Gavriel's reasons for keeping her in the inner circle became much more obvious now.

That got me wondering. Did Gavriel know about Maryssa's extracurricular activities, associating with demons? Perhaps it was the side she fought for he disagreed with. I'd love to ask Micah, only I couldn't trust he'd keep my curiosity to himself or that he'd even answer me, for that matter.

Maryssa shut off the storeroom's dim light, leaving us in the flickering glow of a dozen candles. She came over to where I sat.

"This won't be easy, Nyssa. It's a whole different type of magic. A spell used only once, before it ceased to exist a very long time ago. You carry the essence as the result of that one instance. A single decision." Her hands trembled as she reached for me. "You need to relax, and let me in."

"Just so you know, that didn't help me relax." Instead, my stomach knotted. "So, you basically have no idea what you're doing?"

Her sharp eyes narrowed on me. "I know more than anyone else would."

Not really an answer, but the best I was going to get.

I shut my eyes, trying to control each inhale and exhale, holding five seconds in between each.

She spoke a foreign language. One I didn't understand but recognized.

I let my eyes peek at her. Her palms cupped my ears, and she dipped her head as she chanted. It was too dark for my human eyes to see Sam or Nathan, yet, I knew exactly where Sam stood. And that his eyes were latched onto me.

Without warning, the whole room warmed up, and I felt...energy. It thrummed in the air, thickening it to a silken soup. When my eyes lifted to Maryssa, a pale gold aura glowed around her body.

I started feeling dizzy. Almost like the energy had slipped under my skin and applied a small pressure on the back of my head.

The sensation skyrocketed my anxiety. The dense air didn't pass through my lungs as smoothly as a moment ago. I held on. I couldn't spend my whole life worrying about demons chasing me. Right?

I inhaled for a five count and exhaled for another five. A small price to pay. Hang on, Nyssa, I told myself. And then, the pressure in my head grew to the point my eyes watered. I grabbed my skull. In my panic, I tried standing, only to discover I'd gone numb below the hips.

"Why can't I move my legs?" I asked, fear spiking in my voice. Maryssa didn't even glance up. "I don't feel well," I told her with my heartbeat pounding in my eardrums. "It hurts." I moaned, short of breath.

The pain reached a level so high that I forgot for a moment I was paralyzed from my waist down. I felt like she was melting my brain with acid.

I yelped. "Stop!"

What was the point of removing this essence if I died in the process?

Maryssa ignored my request. Pushing off with my hands on the armrests, I tried to stand again, but my behind stayed glued to the chair.

She chanted louder, and the enormous swell of pressure throbbed in my eyeballs until I couldn't bear to keep them open. I doubled over, hugging myself, as the agony spread down my spine. "Stop!"

Nathan and Sam weren't responding. My Shadows weren't moving.

My anxiety reached the point of no return. "Stop," I begged her again. "Please." My heart was about to beat out of my rib cage. Tears swelled in the back of my throat. Tears of boiling fury.

Why was she doing this? Why was nobody helping me? Why was I even expecting them to? They were demons after all. But the betrayal *hurt*. More than it should.

And then my music blared over the drumbeat in my heart. Its usual calm tempo had accelerated into a gritty rock beat. It fanned my anger, surrounded me in comforting heat. It secured me.

It answered my call for help when no one else did.

I clutched my shirt and lifted blurry eyes to Maryssa. "Stop!" I bellowed, this time a command that cut through the energy barrier in a powerful wave—weaponized power chords. The whole room illuminated with a bright white light. I traced the source of the beam back to my chest just before it erupted like a supernova.

The ripples sent Maryssa and Nathan flying across the room. They hit the shelves of creepy items. The sounds of shattering glass and crashing objects backed my music. They both hung suspended above the ground, pinned by the pressure still gushing from my body.

I saw Sam. He inched his expensive shoes over the floor, arms out to carve through the gale-strength force coming from me. The light solidified into a white-hot shield, keeping him back.

"Nyssa!" he yelled, making me frown. No reason to shout, other than interrupt my music. "You're not in danger, precious. I'm right here with you. Put it away!"

I had no idea what he was talking about. But then, with a pang, I realized *he* had been in the room the whole time. And he'd done nothing to stop Maryssa from hurting me.

"You were here," I accused, swallowing the lump in the back of my throat. The light of the shield brightened. "You didn't stop her!" As my anger rose, so did the wind, blowing my hair all around me. "I should have known."

I was on my own. On my own in my home. On my own with my pathetic goal. On my own to help my best friend.

Always on my own.

Sam took what appeared to be a very difficult step toward me, as if fighting against denser gravity. "I'd never let any harm come to you, Nyssa. This has to be done, or they'll find you."

My spirit tore between the desire to believe and the need to protect myself.

"You're lying," I finally growled, and the music swelled. The wind howled, lifting me off the ground, raising my glowing shield with me. The bowl shattered, papers flowed all around, candles were blown off, the wind twirled.

There would never be me and anyone else against the world.

I'd always fought alone. Me against the world.

The air changed again as the force grew stronger. My gaze met Sam's eyes. They weren't blue, not crimson either. They were white. The wind had forced one arm above his face, reminding me of the painting in Mr. Gerard's class.

His other arm stretched out in front of him, his fingers opened wide as if fighting the power or…absorbing it.

The shield dulled to a silver. I weakened, feet drifting back toward earth, shoulders drooping. The music turned down a notch. Then the energy slipped from my fingers all at once, snuffing the light. Nathan and Maryssa fell with a loud *thunk* along with the mixed objects.

My feet touched the floor.

"That's it, precious, let it go. I've got you." Sam's voice drew closer, but when I tried to focus on him, the room spun, creating four wavering Sams.

Warm arms picked me up before I lost my footing. I didn't lose consciousness, but my eyes were too heavy to open. My tongue was glued to the roof of my mouth. My body was exhausted as Sam nestled me closer to his chest. His scent of wildfire and fresh wind comforted me in ways it should not. Especially after he'd let Maryssa inflict such atrocious suffering on me. As if I needed a third party to make our relationship more messed up.

"Anyone want to tell me what in all hell that was?"

Nathan asked. God, I was dying to know the answer. I was human; it couldn't have been me. It must have been that box.

Flipping pages and approaching footsteps were the only answer. Sam and Maryssa seemed in no hurry to reply.

"Did it work?" Sam asked instead. His tone was new to me. Hesitant. Worried.

The silence frayed my nerves, making my uncooperative body restless.

"Only halfway."

Sam's grip tightened around me, pressing me closer to him. "Which way?"

"Demons will still be able to sense her essence. The veil is back up for the sky."

Nathan stepped in. "What does that mean for her power? I must say, she surprised me. Hell, she's strong."

Seconds passed.

"I'm not exactly sure," Maryssa finally answered.

"The essence and its powers are part of her," said Sam. "Veil or not, it's always been in her, but when you pulled the barrier back, it awoke. She's too strong now. The connection started. It won't allow any harm to come to her. Neither will I." His warm fingers moved my hair off my face. "I'll protect her."

"If I may," interjected Maryssa, supplicating Sam. When he gave no reaction, she pushed on. "You know they'll use her against you. And it'll work." Maryssa cringed. "Samael, I beg of you. We must think of a different solution. You haven't told her." She fiddled with her fingers, but her jaw stayed firm. "All this time, I've stayed here, waiting. I've allied with despicable people so I could be ready for this moment. To help you when the time came. That time is knocking at our door. But you need a different plan. This will backfire, and I'll be damned alongside you if I let it happen again."

Samael? That was the first time I'd heard someone call him that.

"Forget it. This isn't up for discussion."

"Brother—"

"Don't," he snapped, and Maryssa's supplicating hand pulled back. "Nathan. Go find her friend's contract. I want to have it, and I wanted it done yesterday. Do not come back without it. Am I clear?"

"Yes."

Sam rose with me in his arms, and I shut my eyes against the wooziness, letting him carry me wherever. I was glad he wasn't leaving me behind with the witch who'd attempted to fry my brain.

I couldn't help but wonder if all I'd done up to now in my quest to save Isabelle had been for nothing. Right now, weak and foggy and hunted by far more demons than I'd intended to find, I seemed further than when I'd started.

Chapter 28

By the time my body decided to cooperate, I'd been sucked into the most comfortable couch on earth. My fingers dug into the dark velvet material as I glanced around without moving and recognized the fireplace of Sam's place. The memories crashed into me.

Maryssa's storeroom.

The pain in my skull as she tried to restore my old, normal, boring self.

Sam stood back to watch as I begged her to stop.

My Shadows. Who'd simply disappeared or ignored my cries of pain and fear. That was the hardest part to digest. My whole life, I had relied on them. They were my pillars of fire, guiding me in my darkest times. And they'd just…overlooked what Maryssa did to me.

I felt betrayed. By all of them.

Yet my music had rushed to my rescue.

Had called to some raw power. I had no idea where that energy had come from, but it was the invisible hero that swept me off my feet and saved me from the magic holding me down.

I threw my feet off the couch, ready to take my leave. I'd lost track of time, and I could just imagine the bombardment of missed calls and text messages from Micah.

If Gavriel found out where I'd gone, I was in big

trouble. The real type. He might even take away my chance at a diploma.

Oh God, I'd lose my only means to make my family proud, make me worthy of reception, into the inner circle like Micah. My key to helping other people. People like Isabelle.

I searched the floor for my bag, hoping Sam brought it back with us. I stepped around the couch, and down the long hallway, I saw my dark green bag hanging from the hook beside the double-door closet. With determined steps, I charged for it, eager to get out of here as fast as possible when the Devil suddenly appeared in my path from the kitchen.

Shirtless.

Of course.

He held a glass of what looked like thick orange juice.

"Good, you're finally awake. I was starting to get worried, so I read a little." His eyes glanced down as his free hand raked through his hair. "Yeah, I do read sometimes. You aren't the only one with boring habits. One book recommended intake of freshly squeezed juice for better vitamin intake. I had one of my demons collect all the best organic fruits and vegetables to make you all shiny again. I even added hemp seeds. It took me forever to figure out the procedure of the machine." The Devil wouldn't simply read the manual. "After a few shots, I got it working perfectly. Here." Sam handed me the glass. He seemed different. Nervous. Rambling wasn't one of his traits. I had that one covered.

My gaze bounced between him and the glass. "That's...very thoughtful."

His brows grew together, displeased.

"But I got to go." I tried passing him, but he put one palm flat on the wall, blocking my path.

"Where do you think you're going, if I may ask?"

I shifted from one foot to another. "Home?" God, why did it sound like a question? I cleared my throat, hoping to sound firm as I continued, "Look, my family must be worried. I'll probably be grounded for the rest of my life."

Sam frowned. "I can't let you go home alone. Not with demons wanting you. I'll come with you."

Oh God. The thought alone almost gave me a panic attack.

"You can't. My brother will most probably kill me. And then kill you."

Sam laughed at my words. "Like any of them could dream of killing any of us."

"Us?"

"Yes. Us. You saw what you did. Do you know what some would do to have access to that kind of power?"

Not a thought I wish to entertain.

"Sam," I said more seriously, "I have to go home. Alone."

"I'm sorry, precious. It's too dangerous."

I threw my arms up in annoyance. "I can't stay here forever."

"Why not?"

My heart stopped. Was he kidding?

"You are infuriating. I have a family. I have to go home. They're probably worried sick." If they even realized I had been gone. "I also have to change, shower, eat, sleep, go to school. Human stuff."

"That's not it, is it?" He read my thoughts.

My jaw tensed. I didn't want to go there and instigate a fight, but since he brought it up, no point in hiding it.

"You did nothing," I said, voice sharper than a butcher's knife. I couldn't keep down the bubbling emotions. The energy that awoke earlier rushed back, at the tip of my fingers.

He passed his free hand through his hair again. "It had to be done, precious. Besides, I'm sure you noticed that you didn't need me to do anything. The essence, it protected you."

That didn't make me feel any better. An irrational part of me wanted him to have come to my aid.

"Thank God."

"More like thank me."

I massaged my temple. "How did the essence do that?"

For a brief moment, a hint of embarrassment flashed across his face. "Technically, you did that with the essence."

Nathan barged into the entrance, startling me. Not bothering with simple manners like taking off his shoes or simply saying hi, he walked past us and threw himself on the couch. I was torn between relief and the urge to strangle him. "Found out the info you were looking for," he told Sam. "I wonder what you'd do without me."

"I'd probably be much calmer," Sam groused.

"And?" I asked, impatient.

"Well, seems like her friend made a deal with Bael."

"Fuck." That one word from Sam's mouth carried a

mix of anger and annoyance.

His fervor perplexed me. I'd read about Bael. He was a pretty well-known demon—a big player in the Key of Solomon stories. Still, he wasn't anywhere near as terrifying as others. Like the Devil for starters.

"What does it matter which demon she bargained with anyway?" The king should trump them all, right?

Both pairs of eyes settled on me. Nathan walked over and lazily circled my shoulder with his arm. "Nyssa, sweet pea, sometimes I forget you're so—"

"Human?" I suggested.

"Naïve," Nathan corrected before turning to Sam. "I get why you want to keep her. Never a dull moment with this one." Before anyone could snipe him with a comeback, Nathan plowed on, "I'll give you a crash course in the underworld, darling, don't fret. Just know you're a set above the rest already with me in your corner." He stretched out of his arm. "And the boss, of course."

"Splendid, a class about Hell. Just what I wished for." I massaged a growing headache.

Sam walked past us to the apartment's luxurious bar, and I watched him pour himself a drink. A red drink. I wondered if it had a magical component to give demons a high like I'd felt in the club. Or maybe I just had a low tolerance for alcohol. More specifically, I wanted to know if Sam might lose control the way I had.

His hair was still wet from his shower. His shirtless body offered a view impossible to tire of. The ink on his back sparked a heat to rival Hell between my thighs. My hands begged to touch what God had gifted Sam. I licked my lips, which felt dryer than a desert.

Nathan snapped his fingers in front of my face, blocking my view. "Hell to Nyssa!" I blushed under his gaze. My brain was fried. Either from the effect of the box or staying away from the opposite sex too long.

My hormones were playing with my head.

Oh, and I was hosting a feral essence that might be provoked at any moment.

Nathan glanced to where Sam stood, now staring at us, and my whole face burned. Nathan threw his head back and laughed.

He then leaned in close to my ear and whispered, "And to think you scolded the boss for being petty about me because we had a lot on our plates, and yet here you are absolutely unable to think in his vicinity."

"Yeah, well, he's not wearing a shirt."

Oh, sweet baby Jesus. Had I just said that out loud?

Nathan laughed, a loud belly laugh. I gave him my deadliest glare.

He put his hands up. "I saw nothing. I heard nothing."

I didn't have the courage to look up at Sam.

"So, like I was saying, imagine having to go to your human courthouse and dissolve a lawful contract. One without escape clauses. Would you rather deal with a nice old grandma or a shark of a CEO known to eat little minnows like you for breakfast?"

"I see your point, but it's not like we're dealing with Beelzebub, Leviathan, or Lucifer himself."

Nathan tsked at me. "I'd take Beelzebub or Leviathan over Bael any day. I doubt you can even grasp one percent of what's really happening."

I narrowed my eyes at him. "So, it's not good."

"It's worse, precious," Sam said from right behind

me. I looked over my shoulder, and his scent was enough to make me dizzy.

Head in the game, Nyssa.

"How much worse?"

"If you'd asked me to pick the one demon who hates me the most, I'd say Bael. He'd do anything to see me deposed."

"Why?"

"Oh, because he picked me over him as his second," Nathan said with a sinful grin. "He's known to hold grudges."

I tried to wrap my head around that. "He won't break the contract."

"If only that were our main obstacle," Nathan said.

Sam nodded. "If he finds out I'm trying to help Isabelle, he will—"

"Try and manipulate our king to hand over the crown or worse," Nat finished for him.

I had to sit. I plopped back onto the velvet couch. "So, unknowingly, I've made things worse for Isabelle because now that he knows about the essence, there's no way you could…" I stopped talking, feeling like a laughingstock even saying it out loud. Sam would let Isabelle die before he gave up Hell to a mad demon, whether he liked it or not. It'd damn us all.

Sam shook his head. "Maybe Bael doesn't know my personal interest in Isabelle's bargain. Maybe he has no idea about the essence connection. But even if he did, I could never bargain with him."

I nodded, feeling even more stupid knowing he'd read right through me. "I get it."

"No, you don't. If I were to agree, Bael would free Lucifer, who would unleash Hell on Earth. The balance would be broken. Angels would have to intervene, and God knows how pleased they'd be." Sam didn't bother hiding his sarcasm. "It'd be chaos."

My eyes searched his. "How could you be the Devil and think of others' needs? Really not demon-like."

He grinned at me. "You've got it wrong, precious. Trust me, I'm the Devil because I've always thought of only me. My desires. My needs. Me." Sam put two fingers to his chest.

"I don't believe that."

He sank onto the couch, his fingers wrapped around his crystal highball. "And that makes you very trusting of people. Not in a good way."

Nathan jumped in. "Bael won't ever change the bargain. We can forget about that. It's no longer an option."

So all was lost?

Nathan spoke as if I'd voiced my thoughts. "We have to find the contract. There might be a loophole. Hell knows he's gotten lazy over the decades."

My head swiveled back to Sam. I had almost forgotten about the incident at school.

Sam and Nathan couldn't help Isabelle, but I could. The thought had escaped me between this whole pulling back the essence veil thing. "He offered me a loophole. Said he'd take me with him."

"Who?" Nathan asked. By the way, Sam went rigid beside me—he'd already figured it out.

"The demon. At the university. He said he held the contract."

Another series of curses left Nathan. "He borrowed a vessel and glamored his essence. The bastard."

Sam rapidly popped out of his lounge and loomed over me, back straight. "What were his exact words, Nyssa?"

I couldn't recall the exact words, but I summarized. "Only that if I went with him, he'd free Isabelle of her contract." A chuckle left my lips. I blamed it on my fragile nerves. "He even offered to heal Isabelle's mom without any extra cost. All I had to do was go with him."

"Fuck."

It wasn't a secret per se. I'd just failed to mention it.

Nathan strung together an impressive list of swears. "Bael knows."

I stood, feeling antsy, and Sam followed close on my tail. I swear he had no concept of personal space or hyperventilation. "That's not an option, Nyssa. Do you understand?"

Another wild giggle found its way out. "No, I don't understand. Or maybe you don't. My best friend's future is on the line. I just had to go with him, Sam, without giving up anything important. I would have found a way to leave. There was nothing specific barring me from leaving once I got wherever he wanted to take me." Thinking back, I had been stupid to let the opportunity pass by me. "It's my one chance to save her now. How can I spit on it knowing even you won't be able to help?"

"I never said I wouldn't be able to help. Just that it'll be a little harder than we first expected. Don't tell me you really think you could simply walk away from him?" Sam grabbed my shoulders. "He would have held you prisoner in a place out of reach even for me,

Nyssa. You can't go with him no matter what. Promise me," Sam urged, Adam's apple bobbing and his frown, dare I say, frightened.

"Why?"

Sam's gaze dropped. My heartbeat kicked up a rumba, certain I wouldn't like his answer.

"I'll leave you guys to it. I have, eh, a contract to find," Nathan said, then practically fled the place.

"Tell me what's going on before I start imagining things worse than reality," I half-joked, trying to ease my tension. Sam didn't laugh. "You do understand that if me going with him could save Isabelle and her mom, it's a chance I'll have to take."

Sam's sharp gaze snapped to mine. "You can't, Nyssa." His words were final.

"Why?"

"Your essence..."

I frowned, not seeing where he was going. "Yeah? What about it?"

"It's mine."

Chapter 29

I think I stopped breathing. I must have heard wrong. I was born with this essence, right? He'd said so himself. And we'd just met recently.

"There's one good thing," Sam continued. "Maryssa partially restored the veil. Angels won't be able to see it."

A nervous chuckle left me. What did I care about angels? Demons could see it. Could see me.

Sam kept talking, unaware of my skepticism or growing cynicism. "And demons can't tell it's mine. That's a win, precious. They sense your essence, but it's indistinct." He seemed to reconsider. "At least, for them it is. They'll never know you carry my touch." He advanced, and I took a matching step back.

"What are you even talking about?" My breath shortened. "How is any of this great?" None of this made any sense.

The heartache inflicted by the box came back full force. I doubled over with a gasp.

"Why do I feel this grief?" I panted, teary-eyed. "How do I have your essence? You said I had to be born with it." I couldn't hide my agony, clutching my chest harder.

Sam mussed his hair, combing it with rough, nervous fingers as he danced forward one step, then back two, reconsidering. Instead, he paced the room.

"You weren't supposed to find out like this. The memories would've come back." Sam's jaw tensed. "Or at least, they're supposed to."

Something awoke at his words. The scenery changed in a blur of color. I startled, finding myself back in that village where winged strangers looked on from the mountain.

They were still there, staring down at the empty village streets. Standing like statues. Angels. The watchers Sam had spoken of.

I turned on my heel, facing the opposite side, beckoned by waves. The sun was bright when I stepped onto a new scene, but my throat clogged with a nightmare's scream.

A girl wearing my face stood facing Sam, only this version of him had white-feathered wings hanging from his shoulder blades and trailing the sand. His hair was long and loose on his shoulders.

I stood in total awe. I had thought it impossible for Sam to look more perfect.

I was wrong. So, so wrong.

With his wings, Sam looked…magnificent.

The girl smiled. Just for him. Demure and rosy-cheeked, she tucked a strand of hair behind her ear.

"Hello." She slowly lifted her gaze. And God help me, I wanted to walk over there and snatch him away from her. Claim him as if I had a right to.

"Hello," he answered, holding his hands behind his back.

"You are new in these lands," she said. "Where hast thou been hiding?" She was braver than me. Far bolder than she looked.

I burned with envy.

Sam smiled right back at her, and I felt…betrayed. "I have remained before you, yet leagues away."

I wanted to punch him in the face.

She blushed the color of strawberries and introduced herself. "I am Lily."

Despite myself, I liked her name. It suited her face. My face.

Sam took Lily's hand in his, bending to kiss her knuckles. "I am Samael." He'd never introduced himself with that name since we'd met. It got me wondering why. Wasn't I as special as her to him? He'd implied I'd garnered favors unavailable to anyone else. Could it be because of my uncanny resemblance to this woman? My heart gave a pang.

Lily smiled, showing a row of white teeth. "Your answer tis very—"

"Angelic?" Sam suggested.

"I thought to say poetic." That earned her a laugh that drove the knife in deeper. "Pray tell, what does your pretty riddle mean?"

Sam's spine had straightened, but he still held Lily's hand, and I couldn't look away.

"It depends who you ask."

"Well, whatever your meaning, I shall thank thee for brightening my day."

"Nay, it is thee who burns with the sun's glory."

She laughed. "No, believe me, tis I who spoke the truth. I shall need thee to come around often. There is never enough light for me."

"Never before have I been called light-bringer. Most find me too…severe."

"They do not see past the shield."

"Then I shall bring you the finest light straight

from Heaven."

"I shall be delighted."

The way they spoke. The way they flirted. I fell on my knees. This…couldn't be real. The hole in my chest stung, the edges raw. The scenery shifted like a teary mirage. I was back at Sam's house. He knelt in front of me, his features deformed with worry.

"Oh my God," I said in one short breath.

"It's okay. It changes nothing, precious."

My eyes snapped to him. "It changes everything." Tears formed in the back of my throat.

I dug my nails into my chest, hoping a fresh pain would dull the other's bite. "It hurts, Sam," I croaked.

He shut his eyes, almost sharing my pain. "I know. It's the essence. I'm sorry you have to carry my burden."

I frowned, not getting it. "Why…Why did I see you with a girl that looks exactly like me, Sam?" I questioned. "You seemed…" I shut my eyes, trying to push the memory away.

"I seemed what?" he asked, studying me.

"To care," I whispered. Oh God, the pain was unbearable.

A sad smile appeared on Sam's lips as his eyes drilled into mine. "I did," he said, striking a killing blow. "I still do. I will always care about you, Nyssa. No matter what name you carry."

I froze, the weight in my chest lifting. "We've met." His midnight blue eyes squeezed shut in answer, giving me the courage to keep going. "It was me. Before. In another…" Aloud, it sounded ludicrous, so I choked it down.

"In another life. For you, yes." His eyes were

searching for a sign in mine. "So, you know. You remember?"

No, I knew nothing.

Neither did I remember.

But I felt everything.

My thoughts scrambled to unravel the truth in the face of blind agony that burned so hot it gave the world the surreal haze of a mirage. I hugged myself tighter. Sam's palms cupped my cheeks, his thumbs erasing the trickling tears. His touch, it made me feel whole.

"Don't cry, Nyssa."

I couldn't help it. I was drowning in sorrow.

"I don't know why I feel so sad."

Sam inhaled deeply. "We're bonded. We feel each other's pain. When the veil hid the essence, it also hid the bond. When Maryssa removed it, the bond awoke. The essence you bear wants to be reunited with its other half. The same way we did."

A piece of me had always been shattered. Always been missing. It started to make sense why.

My gaze locked with his, and the intensity behind it evaporated all inhibition. He looked at me like *I* was the answer to his prayers. Like I was what *he* had been waiting for. Unconsciously, so was he. The next second his lips crashed into mine because it was the only logical thing to do. My brain still didn't understand how any of this was possible.

But my heart. My heart had recognized Sam the second I saw him at Peccatta. My body had responded to his presence in ways I'd never considered possible. My lack of interest in men ended the moment Sam stepped into my life.

Our lips were responding, craving one another. I

drowned in it.

In the comfort of his scent.

In the warmth of his body.

In the softness of his embrace.

In the familiarity of his touch.

I tugged him closer to me with a hand tangled around his shirt, allowing his lips to devour mine. The world outside might be chaotic and unpredictable, my memories might be messy and missing, but there was no denying that this, whatever we shared, was real.

When Sam pulled back to allow me to breathe, I had forgotten everything aside from him. He plucked me from the floor, and I wrapped my legs around his waist, crashing my lips back to his. My arms crossed behind his neck, and Sam walked us to the bedroom I had slept in the night of my first drink.

He moved away, resting his forehead on mine. "You need to rest, precious."

"I'll rest later," I said as he laid me down. "I need you."

"You always had me, and you always will."

I held his shoulders, keeping him with me. "Make me better."

He shook his head. "I can't believe I'm saying this, but now is not the right time."

Taking his hand in mind, I brought it to the hem of my pants, inviting him to continue.

"Please."

His eyes shut under my demand. "I can't take you. Not like this." When they opened again, his gaze clashed with mine. "But I could give."

His hand took me upon my invitation, earning a loud gasp from deep in my chest.

"That's it, precious, let it all go." He kissed my neck, my jaw, my face while his fingers unfolded me. Giving me a taste of pleasure I'd never discovered before. I came undone. I felt Sam's desire for me and his restraint. I wanted to return the favor.

Only when I tried to travel my fingertips lower, he stopped me. "This was all about you, precious. You've given me enough. I promise." He lay beside me in the bed.

Multiple questions plagued my mind, yet I didn't expect the first one that came out.

"You weren't punished because you moved from the watching place," I declared with full certainty. "What rule did you really break to deserve such punishment?" I whispered close to his face.

I didn't remember everything. I had pieces I attempted to stick together now. But my heart, my soul, it remembered. The emptiness. The hollow.

Sam's flawless face was above mine, and his eyes…they held so much *pain*.

"One I'd break a thousand times over given the choice."

His head touched my pillow, his knuckles petting my cheeks.

"I want to know what happened. Your real story."

He shut his eyes briefly.

"Angels were watchers, and like every other being, we had rules to follow," he began. "We were denied any interactions with humans. I never cared. They couldn't see us either, while we watched through everything. No matter what, we could not intervene in their lives unless given an order. No order ever came." His hand played on my legs like I was an instrument.

"So, I watched, without ever moving. Through it all: the wars, the famines, the illnesses, the pain, death. And I didn't care. I felt nothing. I had duties, and I followed without question. Until one day…" His eyes took a photograph of me. "I refused to stay still."

I could feel his heartbeat beating against mine.

"Because of me?"

"No, precious. Because of me. I was tempted, Nyssa, so tempted that rules were the last thing on my mind. Yes, I saw you," he admitted, a small smile affixed to his lips.

"But you didn't become King of Hell because you stopped watching?"

He slowly shook his head. "You piqued my interest with the smallest things. Your kindness for souls in need. You found happiness in watching the sunset, picking seashells. You fascinated me. My eyes followed you for days. Until it wasn't enough," he said against my mouth. "I moved from my guarding spot to watch everything you did up close. When you slept, when you cooked, when you ate, when you laughed, when you danced. I simply watched. Until watching up close wasn't enough either."

My world stopped. My heart and mind came to stuttering halts. A sleeping piece deep in my core began to vibrate, ready to wake.

"And the most incredible thing happened," Sam continued.

My heart pounded loud enough for anyone in a one-mile radius to hear. I was torn between the desire to know or to block it out. Scared out of my mind.

"You looked back at me," he murmured in awe. He smiled brighter than I'd ever seen. "A miracle, or so I thought—humans couldn't see the higher beings. And I lost myself completely. It was the best thing that ever happened in my entire existence."

When Sam's forehead pressed to mine, the view changed once more.

I was by the water, walking barefoot in the sand with a big bowl in my hands. Every few feet, I'd stop, bend over, and search the shore. Only I was watching as if it were a favorite movie and I knew every move the actor would make, because she and I were one.

I was looking for seashells.

"Will you leave those and come lay with me?" That voice. The same voice that now shook me to my core. I'd recognize it anywhere. My face turned to find Sam lying on the beach.

His smile was blinding. The girl who wore my face smiled back. God, I don't recall ever looking so happy. She, or should I say I, walked to him. Once I stepped within reach, Sam took my waist, laid me on the sand, and hovered over me.

"Thou art so perfect."

I laughed, tangling my arms around him. "My parents disagree."

"They cannot see, you are a free soul. One who cannot be commanded. One who cannot be manipulated. One who cannot be bought. Thou art precious."

My soft smile couldn't banish the sadness from my eyes. "I may not have a choice about Adam," I whispered.

Sam's body stiffened. His fingers dug deeper into my skin as he held me closer. "You do. Do not marry him. I beg you. I shall sacrifice anything to make thee mine. Forever."

I nestled closer to him. "We take what is given to us. We enjoy every moment." I grabbed his face with both hands. "We give thanks for what we share, knowing it shall not last forever. We follow our path with no regrets, Sam. Promise?" It sounded like a daily reminder for a love that couldn't last.

"Thou art the one choice regret cannot touch." And they shared a kiss. A passionate, desperate kiss. The tear falling down her cheek was the last thing I noticed before returning to Sam's bed.

I moved away from Sam like he'd burned me. I tugged on my hair as I sat up and curled my feet beneath me.

Breathe in. Breathe out.

"Oh my God, Sam. Tell me you didn't. Tell me all of this isn't because we fell in love and you did something stupid? Tell me you didn't go look for more? You promised," I said. "We'd take the time allowed to us and nothing else." I felt the vow as my own, feared for its severance as if we'd made it yesterday. "Tell me I've gone completely crazy." I couldn't carry that guilt.

His jaw tensed. "I never promised you that."

I gripped my knees close to my chest. "You knew. When you first saw me," I accused.

Sam shook his head gently. "No. I didn't *know*. Not like you think. A lot has happened in a millennium. I mean, you did intrigue me. But that memory—"

"Which is saying a lot. The guy likes no one," Nat chipped in from the hallway. "Seriously. He barely even tolerates me."

Sam stood and shut the bedroom door with his foot. "Like he said." The confirmation almost looked painful for him. "I didn't *know,* but I knew something was odd. Different."

Sam came back and sat beside me in my little ball. "Sort of like a far-fetched memory. I could almost reach it but not quite grasp it." His hand found mine, and I forgot how to breathe altogether. If Sam noticed, he gave no sign. "But the second I saw you at the campus, I recognized your essence. My essence. The part I gave you to preserve your soul. To protect you. The memories slashed me to ribbons. I hadn't forgotten the feeling of meeting you. The excitement. The interest. The pull. The desire." He took a moment. "I had forgotten one thing though. One thing I never hoped to recall."

"What?" I asked, my palm getting sweaty.

"The pain."

I couldn't fathom what he had gone through. Being cast to Hell. Losing Heaven, God, and his brethren.

"All because you broke a rule." To meet me. He'd started a chain of events that spiraled way beyond our control.

"I did."

Still, I failed to grasp why he'd done it.

"Our friendship grew everyday until..."

"Until what?" I pressed, heart racing like a trapped animal.

"Until it was no longer a friendship. Until you were all I wanted, Nyssa. Nothing else mattered. But being who you were, you didn't push for more. You were...content." He shook his head, recalling a memory. "I told you about the rules. That we weren't allowed to claim what we had. In response, you enjoyed each moment like it'd be our last. That was enough for you."

Sam's thumb traced patterns on the back of my hand. "It wasn't enough for me. You wanted me to be grateful for what we had, which was already more than should have been possible. I couldn't. I wanted more, Nyssa. We were on borrowed time, and it was never going to be enough. You own me in ways I never conceived possible." Sam twisted to face me. "I planned on giving up my divinity. Becoming mortal. To be with you."

My mouth parted, but I was at a loss for words.

"Fate had other plans. Actually, my brothers did. Some witnessed my behavior. They were envious that I'd fornicated with a human without consequence, and they sought punishment."

A trembling hand flew to my mouth. "So you *were* cast to Hell as punishment for wanting me."

He gave a sad laugh. "Wanting you? If only." He shook his head, his curls brushing his square jaw. "You owned me. It was so much more than want or desire or even love."

I stood, looking for a sweater to ease my uncontrollable shivering. "You lost Heaven because of me, Sam," I said while taking a hoodie from the hanger in the closet. This place was so neat.

"It's much more complicated than that. I never lost Heaven, Nyssa." I heard his footsteps move closer. "Where is heaven for you?" he asked against the nape of my neck.

I turned to face his midnight eyes.

"For me, it's in here." He pointed at my heart. "Or in here." His fingers tapped my head. "It was on that beach. Now, it's right here. Because my heaven is wherever you are. It always has been." He caressed my face, leaning closer. "For the first time in my eternal life, someone made me *feel*."

I brought my hand up to his jaw. "Did God really not find it in him to forgive you?" Forgive us?

He slowly shook his head. "It's not that easy. Either way, I never cared about losing my divinity or spending eternity in Hell. I can take all of that, but I could never endure the pain of losing you. Not again." Sam cupped my face in his hands, staring at me with the kind of determination that could make or break a steadfast will.

I covered his hands with mine.

"They'll try to get to you to hurt me," he said. "To destroy me."

A shiver of fear ran through my blood. "You mean demons?"

He nodded. "Yes. But who we must concern ourselves with is Lucifer, my most powerful brother. Bael works for him."

"Lucifer?" My voice quivered as my veins iced over.

He nodded. "He fell not long after me. Only he was out of control. His rage went beyond blaspheme and he set his sights on Heaven. I had to contain him. He pledged that one day, he'll be free. He'll take everything from me and achieve his goal."

Could Sam stop Lucifer if Bael set him free?

"But Lucifer and his followers aren't the ones I worry about," he continued.

Oh Lord. "Who could possibly be worse than Lucifer?"

"My heavenly brothers."

My breath caught in my chest. Could you suffer a heart attack at twenty? Dread consumed all my other concerns. "What are we supposed to do against angels?"

Gently holding my chin in his fingers, he leaned in so close his breath tickled my face. "I'll protect you, Nyssa. Always." His nose brushed mine. If I leaned an inch more, our lips would touch. "I can and I will burn the whole damn place down before I let anything happen to you," he vowed.

Chapter 30

I staggered across Sam's plush bedroom rug, a fist pressed against my seizing diaphragm as I tried to draw a breath through the shock. Lucifer, another fallen angel, and Sam's brother, might try to use me for payback.

Oh God, have mercy on my soul.

Space. I needed lots of it. Away from Sam. Away from my music. Away from my Shadows. Speaking of which. "My Shadows." The lump in my throat grew. "They were never really mine. Were they?"

A pitying look drew down Sam's face. "No, they're mine." That hurt. "But, I had no idea my hellhounds visited you."

"Hellhounds?"

"Yes. They probably…smelled the essence on you. I share a particular bond with them."

"Right." Then a neuron connected. "How do I exist in this time? Shouldn't my soul be…somewhere else? Like all sunshine or hellfire?"

His shoulders hunched, and his averted gaze spiked my stress levels.

"I gave you my essence to preserve your soul. As higher beings, we aren't beckoned to the Heavens as souls are. Same goes for Hell."

"Are you saying…" No, it couldn't be. "I'm Immortal?" I remembered growing up. "That's impossible. I haven't been nineteen for hundreds of years, Sam."

His angry eyes met mine. "Someone found a loophole. If I had to guess, I'd say it was a present from my brothers."

I had to sit. No, I had to leave. "Angels hate me?" I'd somehow drawn the ire of supposedly impartial entities of righteousness. Besides, who gets hated by angels? A terrifying thought.

Sam's phone beeped. His brows slanted together as he read the message. "Nathan found more about the contract."

I stormed out of the room.

"Nyssa, wait."

Yeah, right. God had answered my prayer for space with a distraction. Forget being an immortal muse or living bad luck charm or whatever. I had a friend to pull out of Hell and another demon to consort with.

Nathan waited on the living room couch, nose in his phone and feet propped up on the arm without a care in the world.

"You said you had news," I barked, startling him. "Share please."

He turned to me. "Well, good evening to you, too, Nyssa. Are you sure you're not a cat? Your steps are inhumanly light. Maybe you even have a few lives." Bad time for jokes.

"What news do you have?" I huffed, frazzled and over-stimulated. I couldn't even bring myself to think about what Sam did to me in the bedroom.

Nathan had no intention of giving me a break.

He grinned. "If I were you, Nyssa, I'd be very nice to me." He cocked his head. "Since I'm the only one who's got the answers you're dying to know."

A groan left my lips.

Demons. They played with my patience. All of them.

"Speak. Now," Sam ordered from behind me.

"Hell, you aren't any fun," Nathan complained. "I've spoken to everyone pertinent or even close to the loop. Isabelle's name isn't on the list of the damned. That's one thousand percent confirmed."

My brow furrowed. "What are you talking about? Check again. You've missed it. I saw the demon claim her." I folded my arms to my chest. My insides tangled at the memory.

Nathan stood, hands pressed to his chest as if wounded. "I am an expert in my art. I didn't miss it. Besides, this could be a good thing."

No, it wasn't. I felt it in my gut. "You missed it. Check again," I demanded, my voice cracking.

"Isabelle never sold her soul, Nyssa."

"Then what is she doing with a demon?" I snarled, advancing a step. "Did he break the deal?"

Was everything that simple? He'd found a better way to get at Sam and decided to let Isabelle go?

The sigh that escaped Sam made me turn. He had no smart remarks. No glimmer of amusement. He leaned on the doorframe, hands in his pockets. His midnight eyes looked baleful when they fixed on me.

I could almost taste his reluctance like it was mine.

My feet rooted deeper in the carpet, preparing for the impact. Then, it clicked.

"You've found her."

He passed a hand over his face. "I had hoped to be wrong. But if she's not on the list of the damned…"

"Why didn't you say anything?" And because I needed to be sure, "You found her though?"

"Your friend is gone, Nyssa. I'm sorry." Sam's cold tone stunned me.

I stumbled back from the punch his tongue just threw. Instead of a bruise, a lump swelled in the back of my throat.

"No. No, she's not." I sipped air, hair falling in my face as I shook my head. "She's not dead. You're lying. Is she in Hell? Can you get her?" The rules of the underworld remained blurry. Yet, I imagined if anyone could bend them at his discretion, it had to be the king.

Nathan's dry chuckle made me round on him. "You're cute, Nyssa."

I shot him my deadliest glare.

Sam cut off the impending cat fight. "Your friend isn't in Hell, Nyssa. But it doesn't matter where she is or why. There are boundaries even I have to respect, precious. I can't interfere if she hasn't made an improper deal."

"But you're the King."

"Yes. Which only means it's even harder for me. Rules are in place for a reason."

"You didn't care about rules once upon a time," I snapped.

Taking a sharp breath, his eyes flickered between shades of blue and crimson. "This is different. I'm the ruler. If I can't lead by example, then what's the purpose of my decrees?"

"The King of Hell grows a conscience the moment I need him?" I ground my teeth, hoping I looked as savage as the indignant creature growling in my chest.

"That's beside the point." Nathan chipped in.

"Even if Sam were to go to Hell to find Bael and even if that's actually where he's hiding—which I doubt—there's a high possibility the next time you see him, you'll be in your golden years or…gone." Nathan informed me. "As in dead."

"Time works differently down there." Sam conceded almost against his will. "But I will find Bael for you. I will make him tell us what he did to your friend."

That wasn't good enough. Not anymore. Now I needed to find Isabelle.

Sam stared behind me.

"Hell, you're serious?" Nathan complained. "And what if he kills me, and I get sent to the underworld?"

"Aren't you the best after me?" Sam asked.

"I want some assurances. In case."

Of course, no one bothered to fill me in on what the hell they were talking about. But if it meant tracking down my friend, then I'd keep my mouth shut in the name of not slowing things down.

"If you're cast to Hell, I'll send a soul to retrieve you," Sam told him.

Nathan pulled a stink face. "How thoughtful."

"Wait," I called after Nat. "Do you mind giving me a ride?" I kept my gaze away from Sam.

Nathan's eyes did the opposite. Of course, being the perfect little soldier, he waited for permission.

"I need time to process," I managed to squeak out.

Sam's body heat cloaked my back. "Why can't you process here?"

I shut my eyes for a few seconds, pushing down the guilt.

Why?

For plenty of reasons. Primarily, Sam turned my brain into baby puree and shot my hormones to hell.

I needed my brain.

"My family. I've explained it, Sam."

His arm wrapped around my waist, turning me to him.

"Liar," he whispered. "It's because of me, isn't it?" The pain in his voice mirrored the ache in my heart, but he didn't grant me the opportunity to deny it. "Will you come back, Nyssa?"

My chest constricted. "Do you still want me to?"

"I will always want you to, precious. Broken. Lost. No matter how."

The desire to leave vanished as fast as it had come.

"Take her home," Sam told Nathan over my head before meeting my eye again. "If you have any trouble, don't forget, just think of me really hard. All right?"

"Yes."

He kissed my forehead and vanished as if hell chased after him.

****

Nathan rolled right up to my mailbox, tires bumping the curb. I hopped out in a rush, worried about Micah peeking through the curtains. Nathan and I had barely exchanged a word on our way, but as I shut the car door, he called out my name.

I didn't turn, but neither did I leave as I heard the window roll down a crack.

"Don't shut him out. You're part of him, and he might not admit it, but he needs you." He paused. "He lost everything. Without guarantee. For a chance." That made it so much worse. He'd lost his family. He'd lost heaven. "Yet somehow, you've gained some of his losses. You carry his song, Nys. His music."

The revelation brought a swell of tears as I twisted to Nat. "The music is his?" I was never crazy.

He nodded.

I murmured a weak, "Thank you."

Despite the lifting of a burden I'd carried since childhood, I didn't feel any lighter as I walked up my driveway toward the pretentious, uninviting entrance of my house. Everything remained the same, only everything had changed.

The grieving, can't-catch-a-breath pain in my chest intensified with each mile put between Sam and I. Leaving his side might not have been the brightest idea.

Exhaustion seeped in my bones. A nap called my name, but I needed a shower first. I trudged to my room.

Unfortunately, resting was a luxury I couldn't afford yet.

On the edge of my bed, head down and hands pressed tightly together, sat my dear brother. I could've skipped the lecture, but I did feel bad. Micah must have been worried sick.

When he lifted his head, dark circles rimmed his icy eyes. His skin seemed a shade lighter, as if pulled taut over his bones, stretching it into transparency. I couldn't recall if I'd ever seen Micah look this tired.

"Are you okay?" I asked.

He stood so fast, I barely had time to acknowledge it. "You're kidding, right?"

"No? You look...awful."

His fingers mussed his golden hair. "You disappeared, Nys. I thought—" Micah took a deep breath. "I thought they got to you. But no, you went to

Maryssa. You did something...incredibly foolish."

My mouth opened but Micah wasn't done. "Now you've forced the hand of the group."

"Cult," I corrected under my breath.

His flared nostrils said he'd heard, but he just continued, "They know you're involved with Maryssa's mess and Gerard's death. I had told you to lay low. To do nothing!" He wrestled himself back under control, a vein ticking in his temple. "You've made everything worse."

"They were going to do nothing. I don't see how I made it worse for them."

Micah closed the distance between us. "I don't care about them, Nys. I mean you. You've made everything worse for you. They know. They all do." Dread awoke. "Father knows."

Crap.

"What does he know?"

"Everything."

"What's everything?" I mean, I'd done a fair share of forbidden things; maybe I could hope for a distinct gap in Father's knowledge and mine. Stealing from his shop—his baby—would probably be the most important indiscretion for Gavril. More so than me summoning the Devil or removing a secret veil while attempting to manipulate him. Maryssa would hardly tattle on herself, right? Maybe Gavriel didn't know anything about that bit.

Or the demons on my scent because of the veil mishap. And Sam's essence marked on me like a bad tattoo. No way he knew Sam and I had met in another life. That I caused his fall. God, just the thought made me blush. Everything about him left me flushed and panting, really. If I had any freedom or chance to relax, I'd—

I shook myself. Free time and getting my bodyguard brother off my back would continue to take a backseat to getting Isabelle back. Too bad none of my daring or ill-advised feats had brought me closer to her rescue.

"I mean every single thing." My brother's harsh voice was a bowling ball crashing down my memory lane.

"Can you be specific, Micah? I've had a rough few days." I walked past him, feigning nonchalance while my pulse spiked so hard I felt lightheaded, and opened my closet. I pushed away the jeans from the hangers. I needed comfort over style. I picked a pair of blue yoga pants from the shelves and a gray sweater. Selection in hand, I turned and bumped straight into Micah's chest.

He gripped my forearms with enough strength that I dropped my clothes.

"Drop the act, Nyssa. When I say everything, I mean he knows *exactly* how far you've jumped into the wrong side of our world. Every line you've crossed." The new diamond-hard edge in his voice flashed in his eyes, too. "And don't act dumb, like you don't know what we do about higher beings, or close to it. You're one of the smartest people I know. You know demons exist. I know you've seen how they're flocking here. You can't believe we're regular collectors. That we don't use the items we find."

No, I'd never believed that. But until now, I'd only had theories about what exactly Gavriel and the influential people he controlled did with the powerful items he owned.

I just hadn't gotten a chance to think about the implication of my new discoveries.

I'd been busy.

But now that Micah had brought it up, that opened a drawer of new interrogation. It also awoke another frustration.

"Perhaps if any of you bothered keeping me in the loop instead of pushing me aside, I wouldn't be so clueless." I yanked my arms away from him. Or I tried. Rather than budge, Micah's fingers sank deeper.

"Let go," I snarled.

He pulled me closer to his chest. "We did it to protect you."

A harsh chuckle pushed through my gritted teeth. "Sure. Like you said, I'm smart. Gavriel barely tolerates the sight of me. I'm surprised he didn't kick me out the day I turned eighteen. Probably for you. So please, Micah, save the whole 'did it to protect you' pretense for someone that'll believe you."

I jerked my arms again. "Let. Go." My flash of cold anger triggered a wave of hot energy radiating down my arms. Fear took over. Fear I'd hurt my brother.

As if sensing my turmoil, Micah's hands slipped from my arms.

"Gavriel—"

"Don't," I warned, "I can't take you defending him. Not today." I picked my clean clothes off the floor and walked to the bathroom.

"Nyssa Bear," Micah called from behind. I stopped but didn't turn. I heard his heavy sigh. "I'm sorry I kept you in the dark. I hate that you felt cast aside. I thought it was better this way." He paused, hesitating.

"Sometimes, I wish I had the same choice."

My hand on the handle, I spoke facing the door. "What does he really know?"

"Everything Maryssa knows."

My eyes closed for a second. Trust was very feeble in this world. Why did I feel surprised?

I twisted to Micah, our gazes clashing.

"You summoned him, Nys." His tone didn't hold anger. Only disappointment. I'd rather he yelled than look at me with those hurt puppy dog eyes.

I swallowed. Hard.

"You summoned the Devil." He shook his head with a mirthless laugh like the disbelief in my audacity hadn't fully worn off yet. "You've started down a path lined with dangers that go way beyond your control or comprehension." I blinked a couple of times, stunned by his calm demeanor. "It's our job to limit the damage he does. To send him back where he belongs. He never should've been allowed to roam around as he pleases to start with. He hadn't left Hell in centuries. He couldn't."

I think my heart stopped beating.

"What?" I whispered.

"Our purpose is much bigger. You knew that."

Yes. I knew they hid things from me. I'd guessed they used powerful artifacts to increase their wealth and maybe live it up at their weird revels. I didn't know they had a duty to ingrain themselves in another world or try to thwart demons.

Truth be told. I didn't even care about the extracurricular of my family. I cared more about the fact it involved Sam.

I crossed my arms. "You should care more about

demons wanting to live in a new world where rules don't exist." Bael was way more dangerous than Sam.

"No. We only care about the Devil and sending him back where he belongs."

"Makes you very stupid."

Micah's eyes became two gemstones. "What makes you say that, Nyssa? If I didn't know better, I'd say you're taking pity on him."

More like taking a liking to him. No one pitied Sam.

"You want to destroy someone in charge of keeping balance? Seems pretty stupid to me." I turned on my heels, but Micah snatched my wrist.

"You're smarter than this, Nys. Whether you like it or not, he must be sent back below," he said through his teeth. "That's where he deserves to stay."

Something snapped inside of me. Micah and Gavriel wanted to hurt Sam. Keep him from me.

No one would lay a hand on him if I had a say. I'd rather stand with Sam and take his beauty with all of Hell's ugly than allow any harm to come his way. I intended to yell as much in Micha's face.

Fate intervened. The next second, a thunderous boom shook the whole house and my bedroom window shattered into thousands of pieces.

Chapter 31

Micah lunged for me and threw me on the floor, using his body above me as a shield. My arms covered my head while shards rained around us.

I waited, my heart in my throat, until my brother jumped to his feet. Pushing back the fear, I lifted my head. Outside the decimated window, I saw no obvious source. No hurricane or tornado whipping the trees. Nothing to explain this disaster.

"Are you hurt?" my brother asked, giving me a hand up.

I took it, standing on shaking legs. "No. Are you?"

"I'm fine."

I glanced around. "What in the world was that?"

Micah scowled. "Bad news."

I blinked, and he appeared. The demon from the university who could pass for a CEO.

"That was me. Very bad news indeed. For you," the demon agreed. He cocked his head at me. "You're unusually good at hiding for a human." He beckoned me with two fingers. "Let's be on our way."

The only rational thought I had was to protect my brother. I'd do anything to prevent him from sharing Professor Gerard's swift, gruesome fate. The demon's onyx eyes switched to Micah and flashed a creepy smile.

My blood hummed under my skin with the urge to

defend Micah at all costs. I tried pushing Sam out of my head, although every fiber of my being screamed for him.

I couldn't.

I shouldn't.

Not after what Micah had shared. I wasn't ready to pick a side.

At least, not today.

If Micah discovered my deeper feelings for Sam, he'd have a fit. No one would ever be good enough in his eyes. Falling for the Devil would be a declaration of war. He'd never acknowledge that Sam was so much more than the title.

Our unwelcome guest made the mistake of a step in my direction, and my brother struck with viperous speed. Micah's fist hit the demon's stomach with enough strength to double him over with a cry of pain. His skin drained of color.

Micah backed away, allowing the demon to stagger onto the rug, where he fell to his knee, hands on his abdomen. A golden knife handle protruded from the CEO demon's fingers pressed white shirt. Micah had landed more than a punch.

The handle glowed as the demon's eyes switched from black to an ordinary green before he swooned backward. The weapon's light faded with his life. I heard a rattling breath before his body disintegrated into dark clouds and vanished. The weapon clattered to the ground.

"Oh, my God." My hand lifted to my mouth. "You killed him."

I thought I might be sick. Was this what my future held?

To hide from demons.

To never be safe again.

To endanger the ones I cared for.

"Why was he coming for you, Nyssa?" My brother rounded on me. "Is it because of the Devil? Is he trying to get you to go to him?"

A hysterical laugh escaped me. "No. He's not."

Micah's swift execution was a mercy compared to what Sam would have done, but I couldn't explain it to Micah.

Chilly shock turned my skin to marble as Micah picked up the knife like it was nothing more than a dropped cell phone. I took a step back as he approached, seeing a total stranger behind my brother's face. I've never met this unmerciful warrior.

The blade looked pearly white in Micah's palm as he put it back in its sheath and, against all odds, he handed it to me.

I glanced between the weapon and my brother.

"Take it," he urged, closing my fist around the weapon's hilt.

I pinched it gingerly with two fingers instead, holding it out. "No, thanks. I wouldn't know what to do with this." I'd probably end up hurting myself if anything.

"That isn't a regular blade, Nyssa. It kills higher beings."

Oh, good Lord. So, Micah really knew everything. Bile burbled in my empty stomach.

"You could protect yourself when I'm not around," he insisted.

At least, it was featherlight and easily carryable. It couldn't be longer than my whole hand. With shaky hands, I tucked his offering through my belt loop, uncertain how to react. I'd had enough revelation to last me a few lifetimes. Then again…this was my second one, right?

Micah's arms encircled my shoulders, holding me to his chest. "I'm sorry, Nyssa Bear," he whispered in my ear.

I returned the hug. "You have nothing to be sorry for."

It wasn't his fault.

Micah had been groomed into this life. Gavriel forced it on him. Micah didn't have a choice in excluding me. And I got it. I had the choice to share my truth with him, and I didn't.

"Is that what you do when you go on your trips?" I asked, pushing away.

My brother shrugged like such slaughter was nothing. "A part of it, yes." He passed a hand through his hair. "Listen, Nys, we need your help. I need your help. To destroy him." A shiver of dread ran through me. "The Devil." I didn't need the specification.

I picked up my clothes from the ground, tossing off the slivers of glass.

"I can't," I whispered. My eyes clashed with his cold ones. This time, anger simmered beneath the carefully controlled surface of his neutral expression, shoving his jawline forward.

"Not all evil is defined with a title," I said. "He's not what it seems li—"

"So, he's gotten to you," he barked, startling me as his hand flew to slide down his face, like he could smooth the fury lines. "Did he hypnotize you, use his tricks on you?"

I took a step away from him, my fists curling.

"He's not like that." He hadn't even tried.

God, I'd literally thrown myself at him, and he hadn't touched me. Even when I'd begged.

A muscle popped in Micah's jaw. "You're going to pick him over your family? Over me?" Micah breathed like a charging bull. "If you go with him, Nys, I won't be able to protect you. Not anymore. You'll have all the angels searching for you. To destroy you." He emphasized the last three words.

I couldn't help the shiver of fear that ran through my blood.

"Do not choose the Pit, Nyssa. There's nothing dark about you." Micah drew closer, upturned palms supplicating. "Don't do this to me. It's you and I against the world."

He tossed our mantra at me like a blade that cleaved my heart. How many tough spots had that lifeline dragged me out of? Only, I'd begun to realize its inaccuracy.

Micah had always known the whole truth. I could live with that, I supposed, but the mere thought of turning my back on Sam tore me up inside.

I retreated a step, shaking my head. A ball of guilt the size of a clementine stuck in my throat. I swallowed back tears.

"It was never you and I against the world."

Micah had chosen Gavriel over me time and time again.

And devil or not, Sam had put his life on the line to save mine. Not to use me. Not for a hidden purpose. He might be a devil, but he was the devil I trusted.

"You and Gavriel shoved me in a box and left me

to claw my way out by myself."

I turned on my heel to leave rather than break, but Micah snatched my arm, pulling me to him. "You have no idea what you're about to start. An unwinnable war. A war against the sky and the underworld. There's no going back from that. Samael's wrath knows no boundaries. He will hold a grudge until everyone pays. Heaven will emerge victorious, but the collateral damage will be…biblical. And it will all be because of you. The worst part is, you won't survive this, Nyssa."

Before I could yank my arm back or knee the jerk, my brother flew across the room and disappeared through the wall separating my room from my bathroom. A cloud of dust floated in the room.

My eyes lifted to meet Sam's deep blue ones.

I almost ran to make sure Micah was all right, but I didn't.

I couldn't.

Not when he'd made it crystal clear he'd stand across the battlefield from me in his prophesied unwinnable war.

"I thought you couldn't poof anywhere?"

The corner of his lip twitched in place of a smile. "I still have many more tricks, precious."

I heard Micah groan from somewhere near the toilet.

Crap.

He might have another weapon like the one he'd gifted me. A blade that could kill Sam. I refused to wait and find out.

"We gotta go. Fast." Sam must have sensed my urgency because the next second, I was in his arms, my face nestled against his chest until he opened a car door, lowered me in, and sat himself behind the wheel. With a scream of his tires, we hit the road, but my body still begged me to run faster.

"What happened, precious?" Sam crooned in a voice that might have calmed me if his body wasn't tensed like a guitar string.

I spilled my guts, told Sam everything without boundaries. I kept nothing inside. My family, Glory. My history. The cult and their intention toward Sam, according to my brother.

Sam listened attentively without interrupting. He didn't seem fazed by any of it.

Until I told him about the music. His skin lost a shade of gold.

"The music?" he echoed.

I fidgeted in the seat. "Yes?" Maybe I should have kept it quiet. Everyone needed a secret garden.

"The music of the sky?" Sam specified as if I knew.

I had no idea, just that Nathan claimed it used to be Sam's. I shrugged. "Not sure, but the sound had never changed until we met." I thought further. "Actually, until the box."

Sam kept quiet, lost in deep thought.

"Say something. Please."

Sam shook his head. "I used to hear it."

"The music?"

He absently nodded. "Yes. When I abided in Heaven. It's probably the thing I miss most of my old existence. My music."

I put my hand on his without any thought. Automatically, he intertwined our fingers together. "I wish I could help you hear it again. Make you happy."

Sam's lips stretched halfway. He lifted my hand to his mouth for a kiss.

"You bring me greater joy, precious."

"Why do I hear it, though? I'm not in Heaven, and I'm definitely not an angel."

"Because of my essence." He stopped the car. I hadn't realized he was driving us back to the beach, to the grotto he built.

Sam got out of the truck and came to open my door.

"Sam."

"Yes."

"Aren't you the least bit worried about my father? He knows about you. My brother told me a war will start. A war we stand no chance of winning."

"We?"

The heat rushed to my face. "Yes?" Not that I'd be much of an ally in a real battle.

In a breath, Sam stood right in front of. "As in, you will side with me. Even against your family's wishes?"

I put my hand in my pocket and gave a shrug. "Well, you broke God's rule and got chased out of Heaven for me. How are you surprised I'd pick you?"

Sam's smile was blinding as he grabbed my waist, pulling me to his chest. In the celestial glow of his radiant joy, my arguments melted like ice cream in the sun.

I shook it off, remembering a very important point. "They have weapons, Sam, to kill you."

That only made Sam laugh. "I highly doubt that, precious. Few things could harm me, let alone end me."

"I saw Micah kill a demon." I slipped my hand inside the pocket of my jacket and pulled the knife out of its sheath. "With this," I said, presenting it.

His expression blanked like I'd tossed a bomb and wiped it out.

He lowered my wrist. "Hell, Nyssa! How did you get this?"

The Devil had attention disorder issues.

"I've explained that my father is a collector. This is one of his objects. My brother gave it to me. Told me it'd kill higher beings. I saw him use it on that demon from the university. The one dressed in a suit." I chewed my inner cheek. "He died instantaneously."

Sam stared at the dagger. "I have no idea who your family is, Nyssa, but this weapon falling into mortal hands is next to impossible. There's a total of three daggers like this one in the world. All of them belong to Heaven. It's just impossible."

I rolled my eyes. "Clearly not, if I have it."

Sam stared at me. "And there's so much wrong with the implications of that."

I nodded, staring absently at the entrance of the seashell grotto. "We'll figure it out. Let's wait for Nathan to get back with news of Isabelle, and we'll keep a low profile till then."

That made Sam frown. "Low profile?"

"Yes?"

"I will not be hiding, precious. Never have and never will."

"But they could hurt you."

"They could try."

I took a step back. "People could get hurt."

"Yes, that tends to happen in war, precious." He finger-combed his hair. "I have spent my entire fallen existence fighting enemies. I won't stop today. I just wish to keep you away from it."

"I don't want my family to get hurt. Or the professors. They think they're doing the right thing."

"Do you really care for people that don't care about you?" he asked.

I opened my mouth and closed it. Sam's words awoke a pain I had kept hidden for a while. He was right. The professors hardly tolerated me, and the man I called father accepted me out of respect for my brother.

"How would you know how they feel about me?" I replied.

"Does it matter?"

It didn't, but his inexplicable knowledge bugged me.

"Micah cares about me," I snipped.

Something ugly flashed in Sam's eyes. His fist clenched at his side. "Yes. The boy who lives with you."

I couldn't recall anyone referring to Micah as a boy.

"My brother."

"He isn't your brother. He's a boy. A boy that wants you. That wants what's mine."

His words baffled me. I shook my head, the denial on my lips. I curbed my rasher response, realizing Sam didn't comprehend the bond Micah and I shared.

"That *boy* has been by my side since I could remember. He's always defended me when it mattered. He stands up for me—"

"Like my hellhounds?" Sam interrupted me.

I ignored his comment and glared. "Micah killed a demon for me. He is my family in every way that matters. I don't want him to get caught in the crossfire of this."

"You say this to me as if I care about other people. In case I've not made it clear, let me wipe any doubts away." He pushed a strand of hair back from my face. "I care for no one but you."

I let out a heavy sigh. "Stop. I know that under this armor you've built up with legends and rumors and denials, you do care. You are good. You fight for a crown you didn't want because you think it's important to keep Hell balanced."

He stepped away from me, reopening the wound in my heart. "Don't do this, Nyssa. Don't come to me thinking I'm someone I'm not. I've done bad things. Horrible things. Unspeakable things. Things I don't regret one bit." Sam shook his head. "Or at least, things I didn't regret. Because I knew I'd never get a happy ending, and truth be told, I was fine with it. Until you came back." His blue eyes traced me with a reverence that flushed my skin. "I'd give all I have to come close to being worthy of you, Nyssa. But desire doesn't make it so. I am all I'm rumored to be, precious, and even you can't change that."

I closed the distance he put between us. I popped onto my tippytoes to cup his face. "Listen to me. You are worthy, Sam. You went to Hell because of me."

His hands covered mine. "No, Nyssa, not because of you. Because I was selfish." His eyes lowered, his fingers tangling with mine against his cheeks. "Because I couldn't bear the thought of never seeing you again." His forehead rested on mine.

That didn't ease my guilt. Sam had kept seeing me, knowing there was a price to pay. His suffering. His burdens. He'd fallen because I hadn't been strong enough to let him go either.

I didn't even realize I was crying until Sam's warm thumbs wiped the tears. "Don't cry. I'm sorry."

"You have nothing to be sorry for." If anything, I was sorry. "You chose the unknown. You got chased from paradise. Literally. For me. You fought that battle on your own, and if that doesn't make you worthy of me. No one ever will be."

My phone vibrated somewhere in my purse. I made no moves for it. "If anything, I'm afraid I won't be worthy of the punishment you faced."

"Can't you see? You're already worth every second of it." His lips crashed to mine with a newfound desire I could've only pulled from dreams. I didn't plan on letting him slip through my fingers again. Consequences be damned. He was mine, and I'd always been his, even when I hadn't known it. My arms entwined at the back of his neck, one hand in his hair, pressing him as close to me as humanly possible.

"I'm not going anywhere," I told him between two breaths.

"You'd better mean it because I don't have the strength to let you go this time." And his mouth returned, tongue demanding access I gladly offered. His hands explored each curve of my frame.

From the fog of the world beyond Sam, I thought I heard a laugh but ignored it, too engrossed in the sensation of Sam's hands on my body, of his lips playing with mine.

The way Sam's body hardened to steel told me I should have paid attention.

"Hope I'm not interrupting. I came to retrieve a little package." The demon struck before I could draw back, and Sam's upper body arced away from me, his arms scrambling to reach between his shoulder blades. I gaped, too paralyzed to reach out as Sam staggered backward. How could anyone have overpowered the Devil so easily?

I jerked my gaze from Sam's agony and saw the golden blade Bael twirled in his fingers.

One of the three daggers that could kill Sam.

"No," I whispered, numb hands catching at Sam's waist in a weak attempt to hold him up. Sam fell to his knees, taking me with him. Lifting his shirt, my fingers searched for the wound. Peeking over his shoulder, I couldn't see any tears in the skin, but my hands slid through a thick, warm liquid that glistened like melted opal when I brought my hand to my eyes.

Crimson washed through Sam's irises as he drew in swift, ragged breaths. His features twisted against the torment. I caressed his face, fighting back tears.

"Hey. You'll be okay. I'm right here with you." My voice trembled. "Keep your eyes on me, okay?"

I was yanked away before he answered. I struggled against the iron grip. Without warning, my Shadows swarmed.

"Nah, boys," Bael mocked. "If you get close, I will gut like a hunted deer. You wouldn't want that, would you? Move back." They swirled around Sam instead. He'd collapsed forward, braced on his hands, arms shaking.

"Sam!"

"Don't worry. He'll be fine. In a few hours. Long enough for us to reach our destination."

"Not with that dagger, you bastard!" I shrieked, choking on my tears and struggling to pull free and hold

Sam one last time. "It'll kill him."

A nasty laugh vibrated my back. "He's the Devil. Unfortunately, it'll take more than this to kill him, but it must hurt like a bitch." I jabbed my elbow backward, driving toward his nose in one last shot at freedom, but he dug his claws into my skin like hot needles, wrestling me back in place. "Stop or I'll make you. You don't wanna try me."

Sam's burning eyes locked on the hand wrapped around my forearm.

"This won't keep me down long, Bael. You'd better run fast because there's nowhere I won't find you. Slither to the ends of the earth or the depths of Hell, it hardly matters. Lucifer won't be able to save you from my wrath, and you will live eternity wishing you'd made a different choice."

At the animalistic growl beneath Sam's rasping voice, Bael seemed to hesitate.

"If you leave now. Alone. I may forget you were ever here. That's as far as my mercy reaches."

Bael took a glimpse at me, uncertain.

"He'll kill me," he finally told Sam.

Sam's jaw flexed. "Perhaps, but I'll never give you that privilege. Choose wisely, Bael. This is your last chance to be on the winning side."

Bael must have expected Sam to offer him more.

After a few unbearable seconds, his eyes took on a new glitter. His smile sent a shiver of fear through my whole body.

"Do you know what my demonic power is, little girl?" he asked.

"Disturbance."

He dug his claws deeper, snarling as he drew

blood.

The hellhound Dale growled, stirring the other into wild agitation.

"Watch your mouth. I won't say it again. Do you understand?"

I nodded, gritting my teeth.

"Words. Do you understand?" he repeated.

"Do. Not. Touch. Her," Sam's voice boomed from the ground.

Bael ignored him and leaned closer to me, his repulsive breath hitting my jaw. "I can tell people's deepest, darkest secrets." He glanced at Sam. "Never him, though. His walls were always too strong." His smile grew bigger. "Not anymore. And guess what? He won't ever do anything to me. Not as long as I've got you. The Devil's one and only weakness. His downfall. The key to the underworld." He chuckled. "Now, sleep."

Bael's rough hands touched my forehead, opening a void in my mind, and Sam's scream chased me as I tumbled inside.

Chapter 32

The stank of humidity and sulfur assaulted my nose. My palms pressed into the cold ground as, with a groan, I pushed onto my elbows and opened my eyes. Hundreds of bins contained in metal shelves stood on unfinished walls.

I had to get out of this basement. ASAP.

I feared Bael's tactic might work. Sam might agree and hand over the crown to pure evil, plunging the entire world into chaos. All because Sam put me above everything and everyone else.

That alone was a very scary thought.

I glanced around as I rose to my feet on the cement floor. No windows.

"Finally. How did you sleep?" Bael asked from the corner.

I whirled to find him seated in a low-backed metal chair. The school-grade ones that left your butt numb after ten minutes. He'd kicked his feet up on a shelf, toying with a cell phone in his hands.

"I've had better."

He chuckled, getting up. "I imagine." For every step Bael advanced, I retreated, which only served to please him.

"Don't worry," he cooed. "I can't harm you. Not now anyway."

How comforting?

His head tilted, scanning me from top to bottom until I squirmed, his eyes like spiderwebs clinging to my skin.

"I'll give it to him—you are a pretty face." His face was now inches from mine, a strand of my hair tangled around one of his fingers. "Still, I don't see it?"

"See what?"

"To give up being God's right hand? To choose Hell over Heaven for a human. It's madness, even to me."

"Sam had no say in the matter. He was punished for nothing but wanting free will," I hissed.

Bael laughed. "No. He chose Hell."

I went rigid, almost forgetting his hand on me.

Chose? As in, Sam decided. As in, God didn't sentence him to ruling Hell?

His grin started small and curious but grew into a stretched image of sick revelry. "You didn't know," Bael purred.

No. I had no idea.

He laughed at my stony silence. Loud enough that his guffaws bounced back off the metal shelves, so a whole host of echoing Baels laughed with him.

"Why do you think so many now oppose his rule?" he asked me, but my tongue had glued to the roof of my mouth. "I followed Samael blindly. He knew how to punish souls. Not enough souls for my liking, but I was content. He's an artist at inflicting suffering." A giddy light cast a sheen over his onyx eyes. "Until Lucifer told me the truth. Samael met a human. He broke a rule, refusing to only watch."

That I knew.

"And then, well, he broke several more rules. I'm

sure you're aware since most of his indiscretions involve you." Bael wiggled his brows. "So, Samael's brothers sought punishment. God offered Samael a..." He tapped his lip with his finger. "What do you call it? Oh yes, a compromise. As punishment, Samael would have to stay in Heaven for one hundred years."

That...didn't seem bad.

"But guess what's the hot part for you." God, I knew didn't want to know just by the reek of excitement coming off Bael's latest stolen form. "God vowed to Samael that He'd give you a full and happy life. That once you died, your soul would enter the pearly gates. Shouldn't that have been enough? If his love was so pure, it should have been? No?"

I locked every joint, hardened every muscle, determined to keep the gale of emotions whipping around inside me hidden.

"I had no idea you and the King of Hell were so close," I casually responded.

That made him smile. "We're not. Lucifer is. Or used to be. He's one of the first fallen, along with Samael. One of the few who knows the truth. Samael wouldn't accept any punishment that involved parting with you." He flashed yellowed teeth. "See, Samael's selfishness runs so deep, he preferred that you suffer over letting your soul out of his reach. See, in one hundred years, your soul would have entered Heaven, where God's influence is strongest, where His rules that angels not interact with souls on Earth or in Heaven would be enforced with insurmountable power. Sam would never see you again."

I tried to stay composed, but a lump of marble formed in my throat.

"He sought the first real evil and made a bargain. That's how he became King of Hell. By preserving a soul. Your soul. The price to pay was taking a seat on the throne of the Underworld."

Oh God. My stomach turned and the basement spun with it. I clutched my head.

"Lucky the essence accepted you rather than kill you. Another risky move on his part." His last monologue didn't filter through the shock of the previous revelation.

"You're lying." I didn't want to believe him. I stumbled away like a drunk, needing distance from his lies.

"You know I'm not." He let out a beleaguered sigh as he followed me. "Truth be told, I would have preferred it to be a lie, too. Now he looks weak. We can't have a weak leader, especially not if he insists on all those rules forbidding us to do as we please."

Bael tried to touch my cheek. I turned my face away, pressing my body against a shelf.

"So, you'll just hand me over to Lucifer? A more fitting king," I spat, sarcasm coating my tongue.

He dropped his hand to his side. "I can't hand you over to anyone. I'll be dead either way. If I do, Samael will find me and use those admirable torture methods on me. I can't have that. And if I don't give you to Lucifer, he will end me."

"So, what are you going to do?" I wondered. "Let me go? I'm sure Sam would be willing to let it slide."

"Have you not heard what I said?" he snarled. "Lucifer will have my head for breakfast."

My hands felt along the shelf at my back. Finally, I located a cool handle and tested the unseen object's heft. *That'll work.* I screamed a silent prayer in my head, invoking Sam's name so loud there'd be no chance he'd miss it. Now all I had to do was wait.

I hoped.

"Then what? We wait it out down here?"

The wicked tilt of Bael's smile woke my dread. "No. I'll steal your essence, but instead of using it to free Lucifer, I'll keep it all for myself."

God no.

With that, I struck, hitting him with what turned out to be a cast iron pan right in the face. He fell back, and I bolted.

I didn't make it far. As soon as I neared the door, I ran up against an invisible electric fence. The barrier pulsed with heated energy that blew me backward with unexpected force. My back hit the cement with enough force to steal my breath and leave my spine in splintering agony. What in the world was that?

Bael's hand wrapped around my throat, yanking me up until my feet dangled in empty space. "I'll give it to you. You've got the hellfire." He spat in my face. "Too bad I can't keep you. I'll drain you of your essence, and once it's mine, I won't need you to make Samael bend." He flushed with pleasure. "I'll be as strong as he is."

I wiggled in his grip, clawing at his hand, but he didn't flinch. If anything, it made him smile bigger. Demons fed on fear, and I'd become one big meal for him.

He dropped me without warning, and my ankles buckled. I dropped to my hands and knees, coughing.

The bastard couldn't kill me yet. He needed Sam's essence. Speaking of which. Why wasn't it defending me like it had at Maryssa's shop? Why weren't my Shadows sensing my distress? Where was Sam?

"Do you want to know why I picked this specific spot?" Bael asked, strutting a slow circle around me.

Not particularly.

But Bael loved the sound of his own voice. "Because we cannot be found. Not by demons. Not by angels. Not even Samael himself." He knelt beside me, trying to peek through my hair so he could gloat better. "More importantly, the hellhounds won't find you."

My hope evaporated like boiling water. "What did you do?"

His grin grew. "See, I observed you, Nyssa. I'm very good at that. Masking my own essence so I'm invisible to my kind. When I saw you at the store, I couldn't search your heart. That has never happened, except with Samael. I knew you'd lead me to my goal."

"Maybe I got lucky," I said between two breaths.

"No. Luck doesn't exist in our world. Something told me I needed to watch you, and look how right I was?" Pride stretched his smile into ghoulish proportions. "The Hellhounds act like they're your pets. That alone, if I hadn't witnessed it with my own eyes, I would have never believed." He seemed to take a few seconds to linger in the memory. "Actually, my surprise then was matched only by the realization that Samael treated you as more than a simple distraction. He rarely ever cared for those either." Bael shook his head. "And then the cherry on the sundae, you surprised me again by killing one of *my* own demons. With one touch. And not some low-ranking worm either. Imagine my surprise. A human with powers is…unheard of. Then, as an answer to my prayers, your essence appeared, as if sprang straight out of the darkness of hell. When I first sensed it, so powerful, so strong, I thought it was Samael himself." God, how stupid was I to have opened that box? "But you happened to be a much better prize. The one he surrendered all for. The one he'd do anything for. The one thing he searched for, for centuries. I thought you were an item. I'll give it to him, pretty damn brilliant."

I was the treasure Sam had searched for?

"He'll find me," I warned with confidence. God, did I hope to be right. Because I had no doubts Sam was already turning the world upside down for me.

Bael seemed to consider my words. "He'll try," he concurred. "But it'll be way too late by the time he gets close to a promising solution. By then, Samael won't find more than your body."

Oh God.

This was it. How it ended. How I died. As a catalyst for the overturning of the Underworld. Because I wouldn't listen. Because instead of laying low, I'd continued my charge after Isabelle and unfindable answers.

Sam deserved better than this.

He deserved better than me.

I didn't know how, but I'd do everything in my power to avoid an end where Bael or any other evil being won.

The demon kept talking, jubilant as ever in his presumed victory.

"After our little encounter the other day"—when he'd killed Professor Gerard—"I had the brilliant idea of coming back to the place of my failure. Who would think to look in your usual haunts?" he beamed. "Of course, I had to make some renovations." He waved his hand at the floor in a sweeping gesture.

I spun a slow circle, taking in the enormous design painted wall to wall in dark red. I recognized some of the markings and the positioning of the lit candles from the demon trap I had made. But there was also a black circle made up of what I guessed were ashes. "I made an angel trap mixed with a devil's trap. Enough to contain one as strong as you. You can't use your essence's abilities here. It'll give me the chance to take it."

"And how do you plan to get out of a demon trap?"

"I am so glad you asked," he said, voice brimming with triumph.

The arresting click-clack of a woman's high heels echoed on the other side of the door. My heart accelerated with each step as the person drew nearer to the humid basement. Miraculously, at the far end of the room, the door creaked open.

The visitor tossed back a mass of lustrous ginger hair and put a manicured hand on hourglass hips. My best friend, looking better than ever.

And I knew I was screwed.

Chapter 33

Isabelle sauntered in like a fabulous runway model, curves like oil in leather high-waisted shorts and a matching low-cut crop top. Not a scratch on her, makeup flawless, and wearing her usual breezy smile.

"Isabelle," I whispered.

This couldn't be the girl who'd sold her soul for her mother, whom I'd battled to free from her bond to a demon.

"Hi, Nys." She twiddled her fingers at me.

Bael met her halfway, resting his hands on her ample hips with a familiarity that curdled my stomach contents.

"You've kept me waiting." He tugged her closer to his chest, sporting a lopsided grin like a smitten puppy. Isabelle flashed him the signature seductive smile she pulled whenever Micah wandered into the same room.

"I wanted to make an entrance."

Her doe eyes flicked down to my spot on the floor as I straightened up on my knees, my trachea still aching from the demon's grip.

"Entrance?" I rasped. "What are you talking about, Isabelle?" I swallowed with a grimace. "Don't you know how worried everyone's been? How worried I've been? I've tried—"

Isabelle interrupted me with a raised palm. "I know, I know. You've tried." She shook her head.

"You always try way too hard, Nys. This little hero game you've been playing all over town wasn't worth the effort, either." Her words cast me into a vivid nightmare, bottoming out my stomach in an endless tumble. "All you had to do was offer to take my place. But you managed to get demons in your corner. I don't even know why I'm surprised." She let out a derisive snort, despite still wearing a pitying smile. "You were always one to achieve the impossible."

My brother's words echoed in my head. *She's always been jealous of you, Nyssa Bear.*

Sam's question returned next. *Are you sure the bargain was selfless? They wouldn't be able to take her soul. Would she do the same if the tables were turned?*

There are rules, Nyssa, Nathan had said.

All of them were right. I had been wrong. So so wrong.

"Take your place?" I echoed, my heart clinging to hope, to the friendship that had driven me into demon dens.

She tucked her perfect red hair behind her ear, turning to Bael. "Can we get on with it?" Isabelle asked, rubbing her forearms like she was cold. "I'd like to return to my life now."

"How could you?" We'd called each other sisters.

Her head drooped on her neck when she turned to me, a glint of regret shining in her eyes. "Believe it or not, I am sorry, Nys. I wish there had been a different way. I thought I was okay with selling my soul...at first." Her hands tangled together. "But...cast into Hell?" She exhaled a sheepish laugh. "You know me. I wouldn't survive." She pouted like she was the victim. "And when Bael saw what you did at your house, he offered to give back my soul if I could get you to replace me." Isabelle sighed as she sashayed toward me, throwing up her hands like she did whenever I said I didn't want to go out. "But of course, you didn't because you're too smart for that, right?" For a moment, she looked like she might offer a helping hand as I stood on wobbly legs but crossed her arms instead. "We settled it by getting you here."

"Your soul never should've been on the line, Isabelle. When you bargain for righteous reasons, like saving your mother, demons can't make that a term. He's tricking you."

Isabelle's soft laugh had no echo, but it summoned a sheen of tears across her pupils. "I was selfish." Her stiff smile had no mirth, only grief. "I wanted it all, Nys." She hugged herself tighter. "I bargained for fame. To be noticed by all. To have it all." Her smile stretched almost painfully, but she shook her head, and I realized nothing would ever be enough for Isabelle. She was an eternally unsatisfied soul. "If I had known the outcome, I'd never have done it."

"There are rules. You ask for one thing and give one thing in return. Everything's not an option. He isn't your genie."

"Oh, but see," Bael interjected, "I serve Lucifer, not your lover and his rules."

Isabelle nodded. "So, when I learned he was special, I added my mom to my requests."

"Special. Suiting, isn't it? My pledge to Lucifer changed my allegiance and, eventually, my restrictions. With each demon I've turned to his side and convinced to pledge, he's grown more powerful. By the time Samael finds out that Lucifer's followers are no longer under his thumb, I'll be out of reach."

Not while I still had a beating heart.

"But your mom's sick again."

"That's your fault," Isabelle snipped. "Since you didn't offer to replace me in the deal, he took that away in the renegotiation. Nothing I can do about it now." She drew herself up in defiance, but I noted the melancholy dip in the corners of her lips. "For what it's worth"—Isabelle took my hand in hers in a matronly show of affection I was no longer convinced she felt—"I do love you, Nys. So much. You will always be my sister from another mother."

I shook my head. "If you loved me, you would have never put me in this position."

She pursed her mouth, dropping her hands, and let out a salty humph. "You don't realize what I'd give to have half of what you've got. A student. Natural genius. Always there with the right answer, without even trying. My own father, much as he can't stand that you've invaded his precious university program, respects you. He tosses his credit card at me, tells me to do whatever I want if I'll just get out of his way, but oh, he'll rant about your refusal to quit until he's blue in the face."

I scowled as she belittled my achievements—every scrap of success I'd clawed out for myself with relentless hours and a refusal to give up—to a lucky draw at the gene pool.

"And to top it off, you're stunning. You could roll out of bed and book a modeling shoot. You could have any guy. Yet, you waste it away. Not interested in anyone." I hadn't even realized my appearance had been such an issue for her. "Meanwhile, I take hours to look my best and can't even get Micah to notice me. I just got sick of trying to be perfect when I'll always be in your shadow. Never at your level."

Isabelle had more than most. More than me. Two parents. A bunch of friends. A good circle. A look few could achieve. Yet it was never enough.

"You weren't deserving of the blessings you got," she continued. "So yes, I hated you at times. But you were impossible to keep hating. I realized I'd always love you, but I just love me more." She reached for my face, but I smacked her hand away.

"Do. Not. Touch. Me."

Isabelle bit her lower lip. "Listen, all that baggage, that's not why we're standing here, Nys. Yes, I envied you, but you weren't part of my deal. I didn't drag you into this; he did." Her gaze dragged to Bael. "He wanted you, and when I snapped out of it and realized what it really meant to sell my soul, I panicked."

As if that made any of this okay. I pressed my lips together.

She turned on her heels and returned to Bael, speaking in low tones. I wasn't listening.

She's gone, Sam had told me. She was. The Isabelle I once knew, my best friend, was indeed long gone.

The betrayal struck me in the face so hard, it ripped tears of rage from my eyes and left my ears ringing. "Isabelle!"

She startled, whirling, but I was already on the move, wearing my anger like armor. "You missed the most important lesson about Heaven and Hell. Damnation isn't only for those who bargain their souls," I said, voice cold and indifferent. She frowned, uncertain. "When you die, your soul will be tested, and if it's tainted, you'll be dragged into the pit, deal or no deal, sweetie."

Perhaps Bael had screwed up his fancy trap because a surge of power coursed through my veins, energizing every fiber of my being. The energy wrapped around my skin at an alarming pace, fueled by rage and pain.

"The only regret I have is I won't be there to witness it."

Isabelle's eyes narrowed on me, her full lips flattening into a straight line. "I have time to earn redemption."

Bael threw back his head, laughing. Isabelle's head snapped to him. "What's funny?"

Bael shrugged. "You."

"How am I funny?"

He poorly stifled a snort. "Redemption is obtainable for those who made a mistake. Not souls as blackened by sin as yours. Pride is the deadliest of sins, and you're loaded with it, honey. Hell is where you belong."

I could almost see the wheels in Isabelle's head turning, calculating unexpected news. Did she truly believe Heaven would open its door for her after allying herself with demons?

Somehow, she did. The haughty tilt of her chin said as much. "Perhaps I'll use a page from your book and seduce the King of Hell myself."

She lit me up like hellfire, throwing oil on the fury I barely knew how to control.

"You stay away from him," I said through my teeth.

That made her smile. "Or what, Nys?"

Bael sidestepped out of my crosshairs. "You shouldn't tempt her."

"Or I'll send your soul to Hell today, Isabelle."

Isabelle marched right up in my face, her doll features deformed with cocky rage. "I'd love to see you try."

"You should listen to your demon boy toy, Isabelle. I'm sure you think a catfight is the *one thing* you're better at"—my smile curled higher when that blow landed, deepening the slant of her brows—"but a lot's changed while you've been gone." I scanned her, nose wrinkling in distaste. "Besides, Sam would never even look at a girl like you."

My head twisted to the side. I lifted my hand to the sting on my cheek, and Isabelle's satisfied sneer snapped my tenuous restraint like a twig.

Whatever Isabelle saw in my face made her back away a couple of feet. Blinded by my anger, I found no satisfaction in seeing her frightened.

Not yet.

I wanted to see her beg. Electricity twirled in the palm of my hand, agreeing with me. When I advanced, Isabelle lifted her hand again, only this time, I caught her wrist before it landed on target.

Isabelle let out an ear-piercing shriek. My grip didn't falter as I leaned closer, touching her jaw with the cheek she'd struck. "You are an embarrassment. For your family. For your friends. For humanity. You could have conquered the world if only you weren't lazy."

She screamed louder, falling to her knees. An orange light made a bracelet around her forearm where my palm squeezed.

"Stop, Nyssa! I'm sorry. I'm sorry!"

Her apology meant nothing. People were only as good as their word.

Without warning, I was gripped from behind and shoved face-first to the ground. I tasted blood in my mouth. Bael rammed a foot down my shoulder blade, and I let out a cry.

"How the hell did you do that?" Bael asked.

I gritted my teeth, keeping my mouth shut. His weight increased, squishing my front like dough.

He roughly turned me around, keeping me in a wrestler's hold.

"Tell me," he ordered through a deep frown. "Only Samael is strong enough to overpower a trap like this. Is it the essence?"

"I don't know," I cried out.

"You are much stronger than you should be." He licked his lips, excited. "That's wonderful news."

In my peripheral vision, I saw Isabelle rise on shaky knees, cradling her arm close to chest. A blackened handprint had been scorched into her flesh. And something clicked. Bael said I'd killed one of his demons. At first, I'd thought he meant the one Micah killed, but he meant the one that combusted in my kitchen when they came for Isabelle.

The tears streaking her cheeks didn't move me. The selfish woman standing there had nothing to do with the equally lonely little girl who'd slept over at my house and held my hand as we tried to navigate the cryptic world our fathers tried to exclude us from even as they caged us inside it.

"Get it over with," Isabelle told the demon through her teeth. "I want to get out of here."

Bael's head snapped to Isabelle. "You don't order me around. You are not the one in charge here. Do not make me have to remind you. Got it?"

She nodded like a cowed child.

"I can't use my powers inside the trap, but this should do just fine." Bael opened his palm above me and whispered something in a foreign language before he blew a black powder on me, and my limbs snapped to my sides, palms glued to the ground near my hips.

"I've only read how to do this, but from what I gathered, this will hurt like a bitch." He turned to Isabelle. "Start."

My gaze flicked to my former friend. "Start what?"

Isabelle couldn't meet my eyes. "She'll be fine after. Right?" she asked Bael in a small voice. I guessed a sliver of that girl who'd told scary stories under a sheet fort with a flashlight still remained, and she didn't want to harm me.

The demon smiled. "Well, given she'll awake in Heaven, I'd say she'll be better off than you, darling."

I gulped, and my voice pitched an octave as I repeated, "Start what?"

"The tricky part is your essence is powerful. It'll protect itself, making my job more difficult, unless…" He tilted his head. "Unless it's busy trying to keep you alive."

Oh crap.

"I didn't sign up for this." The quake in Isabelle's voice drew my gaze as she took a hesitant step back. "I never wanted her dead." Her eyes roved my face. "I just wanted more. He said that essence thing's not your soul. I didn't think…I thought he'd take whatever weird devil powers you've gotten, and we'd go back to our normal lives."

My heart softened. Sad and vapid as she'd become, she'd had no clue what this would cost me when she made her decisions. Isabelle never had learned to think through consequences, and in her privileged life, no price had ever been too high before.

"You start reading, or I'll gut you," Bael snapped, freezing Isabelle on the spot.

Given that choice, Isabelle picked herself, as always. She cringed a meaningless, silent apology, took a yellowed manuscript from her purse by the door, and read. It was old Latin.

Three words in, a pain like hundreds of needles pierced my skin, from my scalp to the soles of my feet. Bael splayed his fingers over my torso, and my back arched as he tried sucking out the energy rippling through my limbs. I convulsed as if he'd cranked up a defibrillator. My energy roared from the pit of my stomach, surging toward his fingertips.

I heard Isabelle gasping. Bael screamed at her to continue.

The hold he had on me suddenly broke. My shoulders lifted, no longer slammed against the floor, and the force leaching from me slammed back inside, singing to me as some of my strength returned, keeping me conscious.

"Impossible," I thought I heard Bael whisper.

That I hadn't died yet? Or that he didn't steal the essence?

Tasting blood from biting my own tongue, I accepted that Sam wasn't going to find me on time. I was too weak to have a fighting chance at killing a centuries-old demon. After one Latin verse and a nasty hug from Bael, I hurt all over and drifted on the edge of passing out. Yet, I got to my feet. My legs trembled, but I did it because I understood the stakes. Because I had one shot. I couldn't let Bael steal my essence.

I couldn't let everyone down.

Holding my breath, I slipped a hand inside my pocket.

There. Cold, reliable metal.

I thanked God.

I hated that I wouldn't have time to explain. To thank Sam for trying so hard to protect me. For choosing me over and over again.

My fingers encircled the hilt of the dagger as I unsheathed it. The object hummed against my palm, coming to life. A glow preceded the dagger out of my jacket. The heavenly light calmed my heartbeat.

Bael's head tilted. "How the hell did you find that?" he asked, almost impressed.

"I'm resourceful."

He gave a tight smile. "You'll never have the chance to touch me. Even the most powerful weapon becomes useless in unskilled hands. You're way out of your league, little girl." He still had enough brains to take a few steps away from me.

"You're right." I pointed the tip of the dagger at my stomach, willed my reluctant limbs to obey, and stabbed myself.

Bael's face slackened in pure astonishment as he screamed, "No!"

Chapter 34

I fell to my knees. I'd never been stabbed before, but this didn't match up with my imagination. The dagger hadn't cut me. No gash, no blood. Not even when I yanked it free, hoping to stop the internal agony.

No luck. I jerked and gasped, not burning like I'd imagined, but cold. As if my soul had clawed its way out and left a hollow void behind. My vision blurred, then spun like a carousel.

Distant sounds of chaos breached my cotton-stuffed eardrums. The world could've ended, and it wouldn't change anything. I was merely a host in a non-responsive body.

I wondered if Sam would be mad at me. God, how I wished I'd had time to be with him one last time. To tell him how I felt. How sorry I was that I'd let it come to this. I thought he must have felt much the same lifetimes ago when he'd had to disappear.

I wondered if Bael would be able to outrun him.

I wondered how Isabelle would pay for her sins. Perhaps the burden of her guilt would drive her uphill instead of a downward spiral. Maybe she'd manage the impossible and redeem her soul.

I truly hoped so. Because somewhere, underneath that self-injected darkness, was the Isabelle I loved.

I thought of my brother, regretting our last fight. I hoped he knew how much he meant to me and that I'd always love him, no matter what.

I wished my Shadows would come lie over me. They'd make everything better, one last time.

My fingers loosened, and the blade fell to the ground with a loud clatter. Despite the cold cement, a new warmth seeped into my bones, as if I were laying out on a beach. It was nice. Cozy. Familiar. I blinked, or I thought I did, and Sam's flawless face hovered above me.

"Precious. I've got you." He sounded angelic. My lips lifted like flower buds reaching for the sun.

The crimson ink swimming through Sam's midnight blue eyes reminded me of a painting. He was a piece of art. I now understood Alexandre Cabanel's need to put Sam's flawless face on paper. I wished I had.

His gaze flicked to something beside me and back as he whispered a low, "No."

"You're here," I said, barely above a whisper.

He held my body closer, and I drank in his addictive scent. "What have you done, precious?"

I briefly shut my eyes. "I didn't have a choice. I couldn't let him destroy everything. Hurt you." I swallowed with the effort of speaking, fluttering my heavy lids open to reach for his face. "You chose Hell."

His brows pulled together before the truth settled in. "No, precious. I chose you. I chose to have a chance to see you again. Even if it meant losing everything else."

The warmth he'd gifted me spread, giving my slow-pumping heart a giddy jolt.

"I loved you more than life itself, and that never changed. It never will." His eyes dropped to my wound and hardened along with his tone. "Why did you do this?"

"I had to."

He shook his head. "No! We could have left. I could have hidden you. I should have. I don't know why I listened to you."

"Shhh." My hand slipped, too weak to stay up, and flopped onto my chest. "It's okay. I'm okay. It doesn't hurt." My lips stretched. "It's warm. Nice." His big hands covered mine. "I wish…I do wish we'd had more time." The old me had loved Sam. The new me still did, but I hadn't gotten the chance to discover what that fully meant.

Sam shut his eyes and leaned down to kiss my cheek.

"Remember, Sam. No regrets."

He pulled back.

"Promise," I insisted. I'd never find peace knowing he'd spend eternity in grief.

"You will be fine, precious. Do you hear me?" He anchored me against him. "Or this whole world won't be."

When his eyes opened again, they'd gone completely crimson. They pledged punishment, revenge, and misery. Sam's wrath would devastate whoever dared wrong him. His raging breath made me bob against his chest. His hand squeezed mine, but then his head jerked upward in surprise.

"Brother."

Chapter 35

Brother? I tried to ask, but my tongue refused to work. The world seemed out of place. Different. Changed. In a way, I didn't mind.

The colors had bleached from my surroundings, yet everything seemed brighter. Clearer. As if I had lived with a veil on my eyes that finally lifted. My music remained, the uplifting notes hoisting me onto a cloud.

Sam had been wrong about one thing. God did answer prayers. He'd allowed me to reunite with Sam one more time. The underworld would not fall to Lucifer. Regardless of what anyone thought, Sam wasn't the greatest evil. And sometimes, in order to fight pure evil, you need to become evil.

I'd never seen it clearer than I did now.

I couldn't turn my head to follow Sam's stare, so I let it fall back and might have gasped, had I been able. On the ceiling, Bael was pinned by an invisible force, presumably the same power he'd used on me. His wide eyes screamed of agony, but only low moans could escape his sealed lips. He didn't shine like everything else. He existed in a cloud of darkness. Pure evil.

Then a shining visage blocked out the horrific sight. Micah. Deep frown lines carved channels between his ice-blue eyes.

Was I dead? Hallucinating?

"What have you done?" Micah snapped at Sam.

"Give her to me."

A terrifying growl, vibrating against my chest, answered Micah.

"You know who she is?" Sam asked, low and menacing. A promise to unleash vengeance.

I forced my lips to move. "He's…my brother." Rather than ease the tension, the revelation tightened Sam's arms around me.

"It was you; you're behind all this." It didn't sound like a question. "I should have taken a look at your face before I knocked you through that wall."

My next breath lightened the dead weight of my body.

The lights brightened.

My music swelled, drowning the sounds in the basement.

"You're the one who messed with the essence." Sam's angelic voice didn't cut through the music but harmonized with it. Even amid heavenly music and light, he stood out. I blinked and found myself back in his arms.

"If you care about her in the slightest, you'll heal her."

"You will leave her alone," Micah said.

Sam tensed beneath a ripple of transformation that called those crimson vines to the surface on his skin.

"You forget your place." The warning couldn't be clearer. "Heal. Her."

"I am not doing this for you," Micah said.

He could do nothing anyway. I'd stabbed myself with an immortal-killing blade.

Yet, Sam shifted me into Micah's arms.

"Here we go, Nyssa Bear," he soothed, voice

garbled with melancholy love as he petted my hair. "I'll make it better." He wiped the corner of my eye.

"It's okay," I forced out, using my last dusting of strength. "I'd choose this again, rather than stand against Sam." The hole left in my chest by Sam's absence wouldn't allow anything less. I couldn't explain it, but I *needed* Sam. "He's not what you think." I tried squeezing Micah's hand and barely managed to touch it. "He may be the Devil, but he's so much more than that. Sometimes, all one needs is a chance." Micah shut his eyes. "I'm sorry." And I was. Not for choosing Sam, but for being unable to have Micah, too.

Was I selfish to want to have them both in my life? Not that it mattered anymore.

His eyes snapped open with a newfound determination. "Don't be. We'll have time to figure it out."

The next second, he pushed both hands down on my chest. Hard. I gasped.

A new, foreign energy filled me, enveloping my body like a second skin before absorbing within.

Agony twisted my insides. My soul screamed under the invasion. I convulsed, jerking upright before collapsing back down.

"What have you done?" Sam sounded panicked.

"She's mortal!" Micah shouted back in matching distress. "It works differently. I've never done it before."

"Fuck."

It felt like molten acid coursing through my veins, a relentless stream of agony that consumed my senses. I had no control over the spasms nor the tears and cries until…it vanished.

My lungs inhaled much-needed air again, like a swimmer breaking the surface after a perilous dive.

The colors of the world snapped back into place. The ceiling, which must have once been white, sported yellow water-mark stains.

Loud sighs reverberated as Micah and Sam peeked at me, their foreheads nearly touching. I glanced between both of them, confused. "How? What happened?"

Sam hugged me to his chest.

"Can't breathe."

"Sorry," he said. "I thought you were gone." His red eyes switched to my brother. "Michael saved you."

I frowned. "Michael?"

My brother's lashes brushed his cheeks. "I'll always be Micah for you, Nyssa Bear."

My brain buffered while Sam laid me down gently and rose to shield me, matching Micha's height.

"You are nothing more than a fraud. An illusion. A lie. You got close to her to hurt me. Because sooner or later we were bound to be reunited again. And you knew I'd want her more than ever. You were there to make sure it never happened."

I struggled to my feet, sidestepping Sam and refusing to comprehend what was in front of my eyes. "You're wrong." He had to be. I couldn't handle any other option. "He's been in my life since I was four. We're family." There had to be a more reasonable explanation. One that didn't imply betrayal on the scale of Micah being an angel using me as bait. Right?

Sam fixed me with stern, cobalt eyes. "He deceived you, precious. You were a tool in the plans of heaven to get to me. And for that, he will pay. They all will."

A weak, "No," left me as Micah snarled, "She's not a tool." Yet all I could think was, *He's Sam's brother, not mine.*

Sam cocked his head, smirking at Micah before letting out a short, mischievous laugh. "A tool you grew attached to it seems, brother. But a tool nonetheless." He clucked his tongue. "After all this time. She's the reason you hate me so much, and yet, you fell just as hard. The only difference is, you'll never have the spine to turn your back on the sky like I did."

My human eyes hardly registered Micah's arm rearing back. His blurred fist connected with a sickening crack on Sam's jaw. His head snapped to the side, his body reeling from the impact. Sam's crimson eyes whipped back to Micah, his face twisting into a mask of pure rage.

The next breath, Sam kicked Micah, sending him flying into a metal shelf. With a groan of mangled metal, the shelf collapsed on top of him, but he shoved it off like it weighed nothing.

"You can't even try to deny it," Sam taunted with a cold laugh of derision. "Our shared blood still won't allow a lie between us, no matter how hard you try to act like I'm no longer one of you. Devil or not, we're still bonded."

Sam's muscles tensed to spring, but my fingers wrapped around his arm. "Sam, don't."

Micah poofed back in front of us. "Yes, Sam. Listen to her. You aren't ready for this fight."

"You, stop," I snarled, a fingernail jabbing at his chest. "You've done nothing but lie."

Sam stilled beneath my touch but continued his

verbal assault. "You decided to disobey, to abandon the Watch. I'll admit, I didn't believe it when I first heard."

Something snapped behind Micah's eyes. "It's all because of you!" he bellowed at Sam. "Ever since you made the first bargain. Ever since you led a number of our brothers astray, God has ignored us. Gabriel stepped up."

Sam laughed, the bouncing echo even colder. "Did he convince you that keeping her soul from mine would make God answer you?"

The answer was evident from the way Micah's jaw ground and his fists clenched.

"We used the Totem to follow her soul." Sam's fist clenched at his side as Micah kept talking. "Not to harm her, but to patiently drag you out. We never thought it'd take you this long. One day of roaming the earth per year for centuries, and you never even came close."

Sam's spine arched like a tightly wound guitar string. "That may be what Gabriel manipulated you to believe, but trust me, brother, it wasn't his only motivation. He wanted to keep her from me. Make me suffer. I bet he hoped to kill her in front of me if I ever found your hiding place. His anger and jealousy have few bounds."

"Shut up! Why could you taste freedom and get away with it? Why did God favor you?"

Sam gave another icy laugh. "Seems like Gavriel isn't the only jealous one."

"Wait…you're talking about Dad?"

"Dad?" Sam repeated, his gaze shifting to me.

I didn't get Micah's answer. Instead, a strong arm wrapped around my waist and jerked me backward into an unyielding chest.

For a moment, Sam and Micah stood stunned before Sam's eyes flashed with burning fury.

"Let. Her. Go."

"Thanks for fixing her up for me," Bael taunted Micah. "Oh, and distracting Master long enough for me to wriggle free of certain death."

"Not death," Sam corrected. "I'd never give you that courtesy."

"Well, your big glowy brother also broke the traps, so I figure I'll head out."

"You used the wrong ingredients. Don't remember much about angels, do you, Bael?" Micah advanced a step, and Bael's crushing grip tightened.

"You may be able to end me, angel, but not before I snap her neck. Even your little power won't be able to save her from that." Bael drew a more confident inhale. "Now kneel. Kneel before your new master." He paused. "You too, angel."

The bite of steel kissed my face, and I winced. A warm liquid trickled down my cheek.

Sam's right foot braced behind him, ready to spring forward.

"Don't you move, or it'll be her throat." Bael growled, "Kneel."

Sam and my brother obeyed.

Bael grabbed my jaw and brought it closer to his own. He licked the wound on my cheek like an animal. Repulsed, I struggled to break free.

"Holy Hell. You taste as fine as a perfectly aged wine, darling. It's in your blood." A chuckle escaped him. "How clever? I never needed the stupid ritual."

I won't take your blood, Sam had said. *You should never offer it to anyone. Ever. It's more precious than humans realize.*

"And you left her pure," Bael crowed in sing-song. "That's truly...shocking. And foolish."

Sam's knees tensed, but Bael's knife pressed to my throat.

"Come on, Master. You let your wall down. I saw what she meant. We both know you won't do anything." I heard the smile in his tone. "If only I had known I only needed her blood, it would have saved me some trouble."

Sam wore his rage like a second skin ready to shed.

The metal nicked my collarbone, and Sam went back to kneeling.

I wanted to glance down to see if it was a regular weapon or the demon-killer, but I decided against it. It wouldn't change anything. Not for me, anyway.

Micah studied Bael, oddly calm.

There was no way this story ended with Bael winning. Not with my heart beating against my chest. My hands curled into fists. Resolve fanned the new fire in my veins.

Surrendering to the overwhelming rage emotion that always seemed to summon the essence, I opened my palm. A burst of energy tingled and crackled along the lines of my handprint, contained...for now. Micah's gaze dropped to it, and he gave a nod. He really did know everything. I lifted my hand to Bael's arm wrapped around my neck.

The scent of burnt skin preceded a cry that faded from beside my ear as thick, protective arms lifted me off the ground.

I blinked, and I stood on the other side of the broken traps. My brother let me go, and in a flash, he cut open his palm, and let the pearly liquid splatter onto the circle's incomplete edge. The trap illuminated for one pulsing hum, the lock complete once more.

With Sam inside.

I raised a foot to step across and reach him, but Micah tugged me back. "Nyssa. Don't."

"Let go." I twisted toward him, baring my teeth. "You and I are not a team. We never were." He'd never made me his equal. I yanked my arm back, and a part of me shattered along with all his empty promises to stand with me against the world.

I turned to Sam and found him pinning Bael against his torso, his hands searing the demon's chest with blue flames.

Bael laughed. "Still a master of your art, I see. But can you feel how strong I got?" he gloated. "And I've only had a taste."

The flames in Sam's hand grew brighter. Bael's face twisted in pain. He threw his head back into Sam's face. "Playtime is over."

Sam didn't even flinch. "Playtime has only begun. I will cage you so deep in the underworld that humanity and demon kind alike will forget you ever existed."

Bael still wore his smile, but it lacked the arrogance of a few moments ago. His skin bubbled up into thick, red reptilian scales that appeared to repel Sam's flames. Bael took an indulgent breath, as if feasting off them instead. The smirk came back. He grabbed Sam's wrist, trying to break his grip and failing miserably.

"Drag me down, and she'll cease to exist by the time you return. I'd say it's worth it. To have you suffer in the pits of Hell right beside me. Either way, I win. If you let me go, I'll awake Lucifer with the taste I've had, and he'll kill her. You escort me yourself, and you'll never see her again."

The words slashed into me, opening wounds I had forgotten a very long time ago.

I stood on the beach where I had searched for seashells with Sam, gutted by grief more horrendous than when I'd first opened the box. A visceral pain that clawed deep and latched like hooks. My lungs seized, refusing air. My throat constricted too tight to swallow. I had been there when I thought Sam abandoned me.

I couldn't recall how it played out after, but I doubted I got any better. The agony I'd been feeling all this time, the hole in my chest the box had punched anew, was the reflection of how I'd felt then. Of how Sam felt.

Only I'd had no idea why Sam had abandoned me back then. If God had punished him or if his brothers had gotten to him. Or if Sam had done something incredibly reckless like bargaining with the first evil.

When my eyes shut, unable to tolerate the pain, I emerged back in the basement. But the pain was still alive, pulsing harder in my rib cage.

Bael was right.

Sam was trapped. The only way to prevent Bael from waking Lucifer and avoid a war was to put him in a cage in Hell. To do so, Sam had to join him for the ride.

"No." My weak plea earned me a wicked smile from Bael. Until Sam's blazing palm sent fresh shockwaves through the demon. And yet, Sam's face held no triumph. No pride bolstered his stance, even as he subdued Bael with tightening arms. He was broken, a crumbling, faded statue of a king.

"Everything I've done since I first saw you has been for you," he said, speaking as if only I existed in the room. "Because you mattered more. Because you were my heaven. Because I wanted to be worthy. Because I found my purpose the second I found you." My vision blurred as Sam's head swiveled to where Micah stood. "You keep her safe from them. All of them."

"I promise."

My ears buzzed.

"Now!" Sam ordered the moment Bael's eyes flashed a mix of black and red.

Micah grabbed my hand, took the dagger, and sliced through my palm. I hissed through my teeth as Micah chanted in the same language he'd used on Glory's vault door. A black hole the size of a fist appeared out of thin air. With shocks resembling lightning trying to get out of it.

A portal to Hell.

The portal Sam would disappear into, and I'd never see him again.

We hadn't been given enough time. Not in this life or the previous one. I wouldn't survive the heartache of loneliness.

Sam had stolen the choice from us both once before, and I'd be damned before I'd let him do it again.

The portal grew exponentially, and Sam wrangled Bael toward its edge, kicking his heels to force him forward before halting. "I'll live another thousand years in Hell to have a chance to see you again," he said, not looking back at me.

A part of me shattered.

"No!" I shouted.

Why did the stupidest decisions slow time? Was it so you could relive them again and again in painful detail?

Sam's grasp hadn't faltered one bit…until he heard me move. He twisted at his hips.

My feet flew over the trap, never stumbling, never hesitating.

Micah and Sam screamed my name in unison.

In fear, I presumed. My own fear gave me wings.

Sam once gave away heaven for a chance to see me again. If he thought he'd be the only one willing to sacrifice anything, he was gravely mistaken.

The portal reached for me, widening like a hungry mouth. Not much farther now.

My foolish actions had brought Sam here, and if he was going down, I wasn't about to let him go alone.

He pushed Bael to the ground, and a mist of darkness spewed from the portal and surrounded his prostrate form. Sam caught me in my run, his thick arms wrapped around my waist, lifting me up. I wrapped my arms around his neck and gripped his hips with my thighs.

"Nyssa." His hand cupped my face. "What have you done?" He kissed my lips in a flurry, even as he scowled.

The lump in the back of my throat melted. "You were going to leave me," I said between two kisses.

"To protect you."

"Who gave you the right to decide?" I murmured, my forehead resting on his. "You chose Hell instead of never seeing me again."

He froze, staring at me. "You know?"

"I do now." Not that I had doubted Bael's words. He'd enjoyed the truth too much. "Did you really think I wouldn't choose you, given the chance?"

"I had hoped you'd never have to."

He slowly put me on my feet as the flecks of dark mist covered us in a veil. I took Sam's face in my hands, refusing to lose sight of him in the shroud. "Can't you see it, Sam?" I wondered in a whisper. "A lifetime in Hell with you will be worth more than a thousand empty lives alone." He kissed me again. "I don't want to be protected if it means being apart. I'll take Hell with you because where is Heaven?"

"Heaven is where you are."

"It is." I kissed him hungrily.

A moment later, when Sam's ravenous mouth relinquished my lips, we stood in a place that could only be described as wonderful. My music got calmer, sweeter.

Sam's smile held trepidation, but those eyes, they sang a joyful melody that sweetened my music. "Welcome to Hell."

As my eyes roamed around the new landscape, flashes of blue fire blinded me. And then there was nothing but the feel of Sam's hands tightening around mine.

Glimpse of Sam's POV

I was damned. The second I had laid eyes on her, I knew it. My essence had awoken from the slumber it had been in. It hummed under my skin. It vibrated through my core.

Heavenly fucked may be more suiting.

It wasn't only because she was absolutely breath taken. I was surrounded by beautiful girls every day. It was…more. I felt drawn to her. The way she stood hesitantly at the entrance, biting her bottom lip. My feet had gone to her before I realized what was happening.

She stood out. She was pure. Innocent. Yet, all I could think of was tasting her lips. Very sinful given the circumstances. She smelled…like heaven did. I'd be damned all over again if she didn't taste like heaven. I wanted heaven. After being in hell for so long, who wouldn't?

I was damned. Was I selfish enough to drag her right along with me for the ride?

Hell yes, I was. After all, what would a taste change?

A word about the author…

Tanya Cimone hails from the vibrant city of Montreal, where French is her first language. She's the proud mother of two spirited young girls who fill her life with endless love and happiness. When not enjoying family activities with her partner, she is an avid reader, exploring genres from romance to fantasy to mystery. She also keeps time to weave her tales of magic.

Thank you for purchasing
this publication of The Wild Rose Press, Inc.

For questions or more information
contact us at
info@thewildrosepress.com.

The Wild Rose Press, Inc.
www.thewildrosepress.com

Milton Keynes UK
Ingram Content Group UK Ltd.
UKHW031004231024
450026UK00011B/606